MoonFlower

JD Slajchert

FOREWORD BY DR. KRIS M. MAHADEO

MoonFlower Charity Edition
Copyright © 2019 JD Slajchert

Published in the United States
Edited by Erika's Editing
Cover Design by Book Branders
Book design by Book Branders

Printed in the United States.

ISBN-13: 978-0-578-54040-5

To purchase bulk copies of MoonFlower at a discount for your school, team, organization, or to have JD speak at your school or next event, please contact him and his team at the email address below.

jd@jdwritesbooks.com

DEDICATION

To the countless families around the
world with loved ones fighting Sickle Cell Disease.

In Loving Memory of

Luc Matthew Bodden

May 12, 2006 – September 14, 2016

TABLE OF CONTENTS

FOREWARD
BY DR. KRIS M. MAHADEO

Unspoken words and unexpressed emotions in the patient-doctor relationship are common-place within the professional boundaries of modern medicine. Patients and their caregivers may seldom realize the impact that they have on the healthcare team. Herein, I share the doctor's perspective of treating Luc Bodden during his battle with Sickle Cell Disease. All opinions expressed are solely mine.

As Matt and Stacy Bodden presented with their six-year-old son Luc to the Pediatric Bone Marrow Transplant Unit at the Children's Hospital Los Angeles for his transplant admission, they immediately worked to orient him to his room and prepare him as best they could for the journey ahead. What they did not know, was that their preparations were immediately recognized and deeply admired by the staff. On day one of his admission, I could see from the hallways through the glass doors of Luc's transplant room, Matt Bodden reading with his son. Matt and Stacy had also already placed a plastic basketball hoop within Luc's range from his bed. As I walked with the unit charge nurse past his room, we agreed that we would invite this family to partner with us for patient education in the future. Luc's family later participated in a bone marrow transplant teaching video for patients and families; the decision to ask them to participate occurred on day one of their admission.

What also struck me on that day, was how prepared Matt and Stacy seemed to battle Luc's disease. It is typical for patients and caregivers to have butterflies as they begin the process of bone marrow transplant. If the Boddens had any, they did not show it. Matt, Stacy and Luc's older siblings were his clear pillars of strength and he looked up to them and admired them greatly. Matt and Stacy had long been strong advocates for their son, and they ensured he was able to access the best available therapies.

Sickle Cell Disease affects millions of people and is the most common cause of anemia worldwide. It is most common among people whose ancestors come from regions where malaria was once prevalent: Africa; Mediterranean countries such as Greece, Turkey, and Italy; the Arabian Peninsula; India; and Spanish-speaking regions in South America, Central America, and parts of the Caribbean. Sickle Cell Disease is the most common inherited blood disorder in the United States. Very few people may recognize that the study of Sickle Cell Disease in the 1940's first introduced the concept of a "molecular disease." Modern day molecular medicine began with an understanding that genes control not just the presence or absence of enzymes, but also the specific structure of protein molecules.

Genetic changes in Sickle Cell Disease, affect the structure of hemoglobin in red blood cells which alter them to a sickle shape. Sickled cells cause occlusion of blood vessels and have shorter life spans than healthy red blood cells. Newborn screening in developed countries has allowed for early diagnosis and access to treatment and supportive care. Symptoms of the disease may present as early as in infancy, with painful swelling of the hands and feet (dactylitis). Early diagnosis is essential to ensure that this complication is recognized and promptly treated. Fevers may be life-threatening and children with Sickle Cell Disease who develop fevers are instructed to contact their health-care team immediately for instructions. Patients may also experience recurrent severe painful episodes (vaso-occlusive crises) associated with blockage of their blood vessels by the sickled red blood cells. These episodes often require admission to the hospital resulting in many days of missed school or work. In fact, vaso-occlusive crises are the number one cause of emergency room visits and hospital admissions in the United States. The rapid turnover of the patient's red blood cells may also cause the appearance of yellow eyes which is known as jaundice. Sickle Cell Disease is a chronic condition associated with the progressive loss of function in multiple organs including the lungs, kidney, brain, liver and heart. The average life expectancy in the United States is 81 years for women and 76 years for men. For patients with Sickle Cell Disease, the average life-expectancy is alarmingly and unacceptably less. While new treatments are changing expectations, the estimated median life expectancy of women with Sickle Cell Disease is 48 years and men 42 years respectively.

Bone marrow transplantation from a matched relative or unrelated donor is the only curative treatment option at this time. Advancements in gene therapy also appear promising as another potential curative option. The first reported bone marrow transplant for Sickle Cell Disease occurred in 1984 in a child with Sickle Cell Disease who had also developed acute myeloid leukemia. She was ultimately cured of both and at last report was alive almost three decades later. During a bone marrow transplant, a patient receives high doses of chemotherapy with or without radiation to empty their marrow of the stem cells that produce their blood cells, including the sickled red blood cells. Once this preparative regimen is completed, the patient receives their transplant via a special IV line. The transplanted cells are collected from tissue matched relatives or unrelated donors, who are registered voluntarily on the National Marrow Donor Registry (NMDP). Of the nearly 15 million Americans registered with the NMDP, 9% are Latino, 6% are African-American and Asian and only 1% are American Indian or Alaska Native. About 85% of donors are Caucasian. When a patient needs a transplant, if you don't find a perfectly matched sibling, or someone from the family, we eventually go to the NMDP registry for an unrelated match. The best chances of ensuring all patients find the best possible match can be achieved by encouraging people of all ethnicities to volunteer on the registry; certain tissue types, are more common in certain ethnic groups.

Anyone between the ages of 18 and 60 and in good health can be an NMDP donor, if they meet basic eligibility guidelines. By completing the online form (https://bethe-match.org), you can order your registration kit, at no-cost to you. The typing kit comes with swabs and it's as simple as swabbing the inside of your cheek for cells and sending the sample back for analysis. The NMDP will tissue type the sample you provide and use the results to match you to patients in need. Marrow donation is very different from other organ donations. Unlike for example, a kidney donation, when you donate marrow, your body will regenerate its own stem cells. Marrow donation is therefore very safe. An NMDP associated doctor will also examine you before donation to ensure that you are healthy enough to donate. The NMDP website provides more information to understand the typing process and well as marrow donation.

Transplant cells are infused in much the same way that a simple blood transfusion is administered. I often explain that transplant is like planting a garden and that stem cells are like seeds. Once the transplant occurs, the stem cells travel to the marrow, where they are expected to "engraft" and later start making blood cells, including healthy non-sickle red blood cells from their donor. It may take several weeks after transplant for the new donor marrow to produce white blood cells (which fight infection), healthy red blood cells (which carry oxygen to the tissues of the body) and platelets (which prevent bleeding). Once this occurs, patients typically require medications for at least a year or longer to prevent rejection of the new marrow as well as to prevent the new donor cells from fighting with the patient's body (graft-versus-host-disease). The goal of a bone marrow transplant for patients with Sickle Cell Disease, is to cure the patient of this disease and hopefully allow them to live a normal lifespan, free of pain crises and with healthy organs. Patients are encouraged to talk with their doctors about whether a transplant is right for them. Bone marrow transplant is not a perfect science and complications may occur. Yet, for those who are cured, their joy never ceases to move me.

To say that Luc's journey through transplant was not easy, is an understatement. One day, when he had developed a serious complication associated with transplant and was transferred to the intensive care unit, I struggled to explain to his father why this was happening to his son. His parents had done everything right, advocated for their child, made sure he received the best available therapies and we had provided the best care we could. Despite this, he had developed a known potential complication. In trying to console Luc's family, they clearly noted my struggle in understanding Luc's misfortune. Matt leaned over and said to me, "Doc, we may not always understand God's plan, but we have to trust in his plan." It was not lost on me at that moment that his family was now consoling me. I didn't acknowledge that realization to his family in the moment and instead tried my best to help his family through the tough road ahead. Until now, Luc's family may have never understood the impact their strength and faith had on me. True partnerships between patients/caregivers and providers allow not only for optimal patient care but also allow for resiliency in medicine. Because of interactions with families like the Boddens, I have been able to continue to provide care for children with the highest acuity. In fact, subsequent to Luc's experience with that complication of bone marrow transplant, I joined a research consortia dedicated to reducing toxicities of transplant. Today, much of my research and leadership has centered around that very complication of bone marrow transplant which Luc experienced.

During Luc's long hospital admission, he had learned the times I went home after work by watching me walk to the parking garage from his hospital room window. His family had grown close to my hospital family of nurses and doctors and Luc soon learned bits of information about me that he would use to negotiate his discharge from the hospital. Luc was eventually discharged from the hospital and I ultimately left Los Angeles to return to the Children's Hospital at Montefiore, in New York City, where I had done my initial training in Pediatric Hematology and Oncology. Montefiore cares for a large, diverse group of patients with Sickle Cell Disease. It was there that mentors such as Drs. Catherine Driscoll and Deepa Manwani taught me that Sickle Cell Disease was not just simply a disease of mis-shaped red blood cells, but it was also a disease of the blood vessels which were increasingly damaged by occlusion over time. Later, during my bone marrow transplant fellowship at Duke Children's Hospital, I would be reminded of this fact when patients complained of pain many months after they had been "cured" of their disease. Bone marrow transplant rapidly cured the red blood cell deformations, but healing of the blood vessels after years of damage can often take as long as several months.

Just as I had returned to Montefiore, we hosted an annual Sickle Cell Awareness Day. Luc and his family agreed to join a patient panel by webcam. During that discussion, one panelist explained that even though his journey through transplant was challenging, he would do it again because he no longer had to deal with the ridicule he faced at school as a child because his eyes were yellow due to Sickle Cell Disease. He was also happy to no longer be living with chronic pain. Luc and his family spoke about their trust in me, their sadness that I had left Los Angeles and described their journey through transplant. I have been blessed to know many children and caregivers that we have since cured of this disease because of the patients Luc and his family inspired that day. I think of Luc's impact every time I receive pictures of their birthdays, graduations and matriculations. While Luc had a difficult transplant course, for many other patients, transplant (in particular when a full sibling tissue matched donor is available) offers lifesaving therapy.

I am so proud of the Bodden family's establishment of The LucStrong Foundation (http://lucstrong.org), but I am in no way surprised. I recall during Luc's admission inviting Stacy Bodden to a patient awareness event organized by a parent for another genetic disease. We discussed that advancements in treatment for that disease was only achieved because of the partnerships between caregivers, healthcare providers and community partners. I knew back then, that one day, the Bodden's would lead a similar movement in Sickle Cell Disease.

With each passing day, I understand a little more of Luc's legacy and the Bodden's journey. Early understanding of the molecular basis of Sickle Cell Disease founded areas of medicine that has today led to remarkable advancements, such as genetically modified therapies to cure blood cancers, which I now routinely use at MD Anderson Cancer Center in Houston. As foundations and partnerships such as The LucStrong Foundation raise awareness regarding the plight of Sickle Cell Disease, I know that together we will realize remarkable advancements in optimal curative strategies for this disease. The night that Luc died, I called Stacy Bodden from NYC. As we talked about Luc, I reminded her of a prior conversation that I had had with Matt. "We may not always understand God's plan, but we have to trust in his plan," Matt said. Luc's memory will lie not only in the memento he gave to me that sits on my desk, but in the legacy this foundation will establish in helping people afflicted with Sickle Cell Disease.

A Letter to Luc

To Luc,

It hasn't gotten much easier. Your brightness and promise of hope are missed every day. Although, out of all of your memorable trademark qualities, the thing that I miss most are your hands. If I close my eyes, I can still see them. I can see your hands gripping a leather ball. I can see your hands picking at a pepperoni pizza. I can see your hands clapping for me at one of my basketball games. I can see one of your hands gently holding one of mine and even though they were only about half the size, they could always lift me up through my darkest storms. They were the strongest hands I'd ever seen. The most powerful hands I've ever held.

Sometimes, I also even miss your snappy personality. I miss how much trash you used to talk. I miss watching you give your brother and sister a hard time. I miss watching you flirt with all of my girlfriends. I miss it all, the full package. I miss the good, the bad, the happy and the sad. I miss getting to fight together and I miss getting to cry together. I miss being right by your side. As I used to always promise you, one day, you were going to be the best man at my wedding—because when it came to you and me—we were inseparable.

In my 24 years of life I have never met anyone as unique and the hardest part is accepting I never will again. You were one of one. An angel with a limited amount of time in all of our lives, but also a profound and deep affect. You moved mountains. You showed us through your actions the look of true love and courage. You embodied them. Love is being given life threatening news at 10 years old and still being focused on the well-being of others. Courage is remaining positive for the sake of your family when there is little-to-no light left in your hospital room. But you also embodied hope. Hope is when our own hearts were shattered and broken, you never let your own spirit weaken. Your own fight. Hope is when in the darkest moments you remained brave enough to leave no stone unturned.

You taught me to practice all of these important things daily. Thank you for that. But probably what you don't know is before we met, I wasn't exactly the best person. I wasn't someone you should have been looking up to. I wasn't who you thought I was. I was the first person to say yes to things I shouldn't have. I was more concerned with my own personal well-being than the well-being of others. I wasn't one to remain courageous when there was no light left. I didn't leave every stone unturned. I was lucky, and I spent much of my youth complaining. I felt as though my own battles were tougher than anyone else's and I made excuses. I was selfish.

Then, you crashed into my life, but it didn't happen all at once. It wasn't some grand masterstroke or deep awakening. When I first met you, I didn't know what to expect. I felt like maybe I was doing one nice thing for a sick little kid, that's all. So, I did it, no matter how awkward or weird it may have been, I told myself I had to. And the day after we met, I thought that would probably be it for you and I. Life happens fast, and I felt like I might never see you again. I thought you might not want to ever see me again. Almost as though after we'd met you could tell I wasn't who you thought I was. Thank goodness I was wrong.

The more time I spent with you, I began to see you were so much more than just a sick little kid. You had a heart of gold and a personality big enough to fill up an entire room. You also totally had a mouth on you and were actually pretty funny. You sort of made me laugh a lot. The way you broke the ice between us is something that I still laugh about with your family to this day. Don't think I've forgotten that you used to think you were better than me at basketball. Although, because of the fact that you used to always make fun of me for having red hair, I thought I'd get you back by making you a girl in my book. Sorry, but that's what you get for talking all of that smack. I knew you could handle it.

You and I also started to find a ton of things we had in common. We both love pizza, basketball and writing books. Reading your book that you wrote after your time at CHLA brought me to tears. You were especially gifted in your way with words and the story you told represented all that you stood for. But it also made me laugh because what most people don't realize is that you beat me to it. Nice going kid, you wrote a book before me. You win, as usual. Congrats.

As our bond started to get stronger and our relationship deeper, I started to learn some valuable lessons from you. I started taking more pride in my relationships and I started to realize that my so called "problems" really weren't problems at all. You taught me how to appreciate even my worst days.

But then, we lost you, our angel. Even though none of us were ready, it was time for you to go. We had so many more things to do. We were only just getting started. I had so much more to learn. Once you left, I was all of a sudden even more lost than before we'd met. Everything hurt. Even playing basketball didn't feel as important without my #1 supporter anymore. I felt as though I needed to do more.

I started writing a book to keep you alive in my life. A way to tell our story. I had no idea if it was going to be any good, but I thought back to all of the things you had taught me. All of our times together began to give me strength and a confidence to make it happen. So, I wrote a page a day for a full year. As scary as it was, I gave up everything in order to tell our story, and I smiled the entire time doing it. It was my way to continue learning and laughing with you. Every second I held a pencil in my hand I knew I was making you proud.

What happened after MoonFlower was released was something I could have never imagined. People from all over the world started to hear your story. I got the chance to tell thousands of people all about you. And then something even more amazing happened after that. These people started to tell me their stories. I got to hear the stories of thousands of other angels just like you. Other little ones that brought hope into this world. You have now directly started a movement to promote good. People have heard your story and realize how lucky they are. Parents go home and hug their kids; friends and family reaffirm their love daily with one another. I have watched people laugh and cry as I walk them through all of our adventures and moments we shared. Sometimes it feels like you are still by my side.

People always come up to me and tell me how sorry they are. That everything must be so hard, and they are right. It is hard. But what they don't understand is that I am also so lucky to have known you. They don't understand you changed my life. They don't understand I get to see firsthand the thousands of lives you are changing every day. So, thank you. Thank you for changing all of our lives for the better. I get to now witness the same transformation that you inspired me to go through.

Although I may never hold your hands again, know that instead I can hear you guiding me. No matter where I am or who I am with, I know I am not alone. I hear you in my ear. Please keep giving me strength because we have more people to help. There are more Luc's out there and together we need to find them. Our journey together is far from over, in fact, it is just getting started.

I promise when I am old and grey, I will never forget you and your message. I will carry this fire for the remainder of my days. I will look after your family. I will do everything in my power to make sure that the entire world knows your story.

Missing you every day—rain or shine—my dearest friend. Keep watching over us. Don't stop teaching and I promise to always remember to smile more.

PROLOGUE

Emma Rey Finley might be the most sarcastic person I've ever met. Now, I don't know if that necessarily means she has the best sense of humor, but she certainly always thought she did. Her ability to make me laugh was one of my favorite things, but that was only one of Emma Rey Finley's many superpowers. She is drop-dead gorgeous yet, astonishingly enough, never seems to have the slightest clue about her show-stopping glow. Emm had the uncanny ability to bring out the best in absolutely everyone, and her smile itself could make her look distinguished and charismatic to a room full of intellectuals, as well as make her seem goofy and carefree to a crowd of college kids. But most of all, her smile made me feel alive. Whatever I was going through, seeing her smile made me fight that much harder, no matter the storm.

I met Emm during our freshman year of college…on our first day, to be exact. She was an outgoing city girl who was excited to finally be free of her parents and spread her wings. On the other hand, I was a too-tall, too-dorky athlete who didn't know anything other than school, basketball and co-parenting my sister, Lee. I probably seemed cocky to some—but in reality, I was just as scared as everybody else making the transition to college life.

My family lived in the area, but I chose to live in the freshman dorms so I could maintain the rigorous schedule of a Division I athlete and bond with my teammates. It also didn't hurt that I was getting a little distance from my anything-but-normal home life. Both of my adoptive parents were out of the equation by the time I was eleven, so Lee and I ended up being raised by my uncle. Since my scholarship included housing, and since my baby sister was finally stable, I'd decided to go all-in with the college experience.

A few hours after being dropped off at the dorms and saying goodbye to my uncle, I walked downstairs to refill my water bottle when—boom!—there she was. Through a large triangular window, I found myself staring at the girl of my dreams, who at the time was more preoccupied with soaking up the sun in her amazingly sexy, two-piece bathing suit. Right then, I knew college was the place for me.

Every single bone in my body told me to go up and talk to her, but my mind wouldn't let me. I quickly weighed the pros and cons of introducing myself, while fearing I wasn't ready to approach such a beautiful creature. Then, after what seemed like an hour but was probably more like forty-three seconds, I walked onto the patio and into the sweltering California heat to introduce myself to the most resplendently gorgeous girl I'd ever seen.

"Hey, my name is Tim Dexter...TD for short," I said to the newfound girl of my dreams, as she slowly sat up from her lounge chair and peeked out from the top of her tilted sunglasses. She grabbed her smartphone to turn down the Sheryl Crow that was blaring out of her wireless speaker while mouthing what looked like, "What?"—although I had no idea what she actually said. With a forced confidence, I repeated myself loudly just as she turned the music off completely, meaning that I basically screamed my name to the whole campus. Everyone turned and looked right at me. Then all the students around us, which mostly included her sunbathing friends, started laughing as well. My new soul mate laughed too, but somehow her giggle seemed a bit more playful than everyone else's, almost as if my humiliation made me cute or something.

In reply, she shouted back, mimicking both my words and my volume. "HEY, I'M EMMA REY FINLEY. EMMA FOR SHORT." Then we both shared a laugh. A laugh that was the first of many things we would end up doing together.

As I self-consciously stood over her, Emm asked if I wanted to join her. That was a no-brainer, so without the slightest bit of hesitation I said "Yes!" As I sat down beside her, I couldn't believe it. I hadn't thought it possible, but the closer I got, the more attractive Emm became.

We exchanged pleasantries, and I could tell right away she'd be easy to talk to. Emm had the softest smile, complimented by the tiny dimples that kissed each of her glowing cheeks. She didn't even make fun of me for sunbathing fully-clothed, which was necessary due to my extremely fair skin.

After awkwardly admiring her for probably a few moments too long, I asked the highly-original question: "So where are you from?"

"Why, the Big Apple, of course, can't you tell by my accent?" she replied slyly.

Playing along, I said, "Sure I can. It was one of the first things I noticed about you...other than your movie-star smile."

Emm giggled. "So, is that why you were staring at me through the window?"

"Uh...that wasn't me," I unconvincingly replied.

"Oh yeah? Then it must've been another six-foot-four ginger wearing pink shorts." Knowing that she had just absolutely owned me, Emm lay back into her chair and took a triumphant gulp of her iced tea.

"Damn, she's good," I'd thought to myself. And I was quickly realizing that I was in way over my head.

Not backing down just yet, I shot back with, "I'm actually six-six, and these are salmon shorts, not pink."

That's when I really got Emm's attention. Maybe she wasn't used to being challenged, or maybe she just liked me. Either way, she sat up and took off her sunglasses, revealing her beautiful brown eyes for the first time. "Okay, TD, salmon, whatever. So...where are you from?"

Emm and I talked until the sun began to set. We had an amazing time simply enjoying each other's company.

After she'd packed up her things and gone inside, I sprinted back upstairs. By the time I got to my room, I was almost in full song. That's when my roommate, teammate and unofficial lifelong-brother, Ken Zom, had stopped me and asked, "Where have you been? And what's up with you, bro?"

"I just met the hottest, coolest girl ever and I want the whole world to know!" I yelled. The pitch of my voice was way too high, but I didn't care.

Ken laughed hysterically. "Dude, you need to chill out! We literally just got here."

But I couldn't contain myself, she was just so freaking incredible. I also didn't care about the stupid smile I could feel snaking across my face as I quickly described my afternoon with Emm.

Ken, in all his wisdom, summed up our entire meeting with, "Oh yeah, bro, the really tan, Hawaiian-looking girl? She's really hot."

Feeling almost insulted, I responded by shouting, "Her name is Emma...EMMA REY FINLEY!" Anyone else might've thought I was actually angry, but Ken knew me better than that.

He quickly got the memo. "Okay man, no need to get all defensive. I got it now."

"Good," I exclaimed. "And she's meeting us for dinner in ten minutes so hurry up."

I'd been so anxious to get back downstairs to meet up with the tan, Hawaiian-looking girl that I basically dressed Ken myself and shoved him out the door.

Eventually we made our way downstairs and the three of us walked to dinner. Somehow Emm remained just as awe-inspiring the second time I saw her. I could hardly keep my tongue in my mouth as we made our way to the dining hall. My eyes were glued to Emm. No matter how hard I wanted to look away, I couldn't. And it seemed like her eyes were glued to me, too—though that may have been because of the now-deepening sunburn on my face I acquired while we'd been talking. As we walked, I took note of every detail, including her white romper and dark-tan lace-up sandals. I knew I'd always remember that outfit.

On our way to dinner, I quizzed myself aloud, making sure that I remembered everything Emm had told me. "Your favorite movie is Star Wars, your favorite color is yellow, and you hate sunflowers," I said as I sort of skipped ahead of her and Ken.

She flashed me a mischievously sly smile and instantly I knew she'd try to get the best of me once again. "Yes, that's right, but why is my favorite color yellow?"

Ken looked at me and smirked, thinking that I'd already blown it. But once again I didn't back down. "Because yellow is the color of the sun and everything revolves around the sun," I parroted.

In response, Emm blindsided me with her smile. I just about toppled over.

Ken, clearly bored by our banter, clapped his hands together and popped the idyllic bubble that had formed around me and Emm. "Bravo! Bravo!" he cried. "Now let's go eat."

Ken got the short end of the stick that evening, since Emm and I pretty much ignored him completely, though we didn't mean to. From the moment she and I had sat down for dinner, we picked up right where we'd left off. Emm continued telling me all about herself and I happily listened, intrigued by her life story. She was extremely well-versed and accomplished, but also humble. Spontaneous almost to a fault, Emm had never said no to a single adventure in her life, and she certainly had plenty of stories to prove it. Her adventurous spirit and sense of humor colored everything she said, and we laughed and joked so much that I almost forgot how beautiful she was.

Before the meal was over, I knew Emma Rey Finley was genuinely my new best friend, like we'd known each other for years. And poor Ken, who actually was my best friend and whom I had known for years, more or less got bumped-down a notch to "best guy friend." From then on, it was me and Emm in a bubble-world of our own design, a bubble-world so perfect it almost seemed like a dream. A real dream in the real world.

⌒∞⌒

That first quarter of college was a whirlwind of names, faces and new experiences, but Emm and I always made the effort to find each other. Classes, basketball and taking care of Lee kept me busy. But whenever more than a week or so went by without some quality time together, Emm would devise a mission for us. She'd send me a coded text message or slip a note into my shower caddy. These clues would always lead me to her and we'd set out on our next adventure, such as finding the best ice cream in town or discovering the best place to view the sunset. After we'd accomplished our mission, we would almost always end up in her dorm room watching her favorite romantic comedies and enjoying a glass or two of wine.

For some reason that still escapes me, Emm wanted to hang out with me just as much as I wanted to hang out with her, which was all the time. For the next three years, we were practically inseparable and everyone knew it. She hung out with all of my friends and I hung out with all of hers; we'd meet up for ten minutes in between classes whenever we could; she'd cheer for me at my games no matter how badly we were playing; and I'd help her with any boy trouble just like she'd help me with girls I was interested in. At times I had no idea what we were to each other—"friends" didn't really cut it. But in a weird way, that only made our unique bond stronger.

By the start of our sophomore year, Emm had practically become a part of my somewhat complicated family. Lee absolutely adored her. Emm gave my baby sister strength; no matter how awful Lee was feeling or where she was in her recovery, one visit from Emma Rey Finley would reenergize my sister and make her fight that much harder. In better times, Emm would spend the afternoon with Lee. My sister would call me up and declare that they had "girl stuff to do"—which often meant journaling together—and banish me from the house for the day. Even my Uncle Bill, who has a good heart but is quiet, terse, and as boring as a tree stump, turned into an actual human being whenever Emm was around. And to top it all off, although Emm gave me a hard time when it came to just about everything else, she never teased me about being the redheaded, twice-adopted kid—the funny/not funny taunt that she somehow intuited I was sick of hearing.

Hell, somewhere along the way, Emm and I even invented our own language. Like speaking in ciphers, but better.

"I'm so happy at you," Emm said to me one evening as she handed me our shared tub of coffee ice cream.

I laughed while scooping out a small portion of our delectable dessert. "I'm so happy at you? I don't get it, Emm."

We were sitting at the end of our local pier, one of our normal hangout spots. As usual, Emm had brought our moon blanket as well as a tub of ice cream with two tiny taster spoons. Also as usual, Emm had just cut me to shreds for trying to act smarter than I was—this time I'd insisted an unnamed patch of stars was, in fact, the Little Dipper—and she still had that satisfied look on her face she got whenever she knew she'd won.

After basking in her victory for a moment, Emm changed the subject. "I just don't understand why people say, 'I'm so mad at you,' all the time. Like, why can't we replace the word mad with the word happy, but still use the same phrase? I don't think I've ever heard anyone say, 'I'm so happy at you,' before."

Looking up at what was apparently not the Little Dipper, I answered, "I have no idea Emm. I can honestly say I've never even thought of that."

Emm, clearly pleased by her grammatically-groundbreaking discovery, replied, "Well, how about we make that our new thing? Since we aren't dating or anything, that can be our way of saying 'I love you,' to each other. Of course we can still say that, too, but this will be more special. More...us."

I scooted myself closer and wrapped our blanket around the two of us as we looked up at the moon. "I like it. It's almost like we're starting our own little 'happy' revolution."

"Exactly." She flashed her best show-stopping smile, and added, "We can include Lee, too. She'll love that."

After re-inventing the English language, we effortlessly went back to the stars and our ice cream. I had never been more pleased in my life to have someone as special as Emm sitting beside me. No matter what we were to each other, we were together.

In a time when a lack of commitment coming from kids our age was all too common, Emm and I had committed to each other fiercely, but in our own way. A nameless way. A way that reached into every corner of my life and helped me keep my head above water. It didn't matter whether Emm was out feeding the homeless or doing hot yoga, I was always ready to join. And she always wanted me around.

That was our first three years of college. Together. Happy at each other in our own little bubble. Then, in the middle of our junior year, Emm received some exciting news. News that— little did I know at the time—would ultimately bring our happy revolution to its knees.

PART I

THE MOON

Chapter 1

Just a Hop, Skip and a Jump

Normally, I never enjoy any form of travel, but I especially hate airports. I loathe being surrounded by tons of strangers, all of whom are exhausted and agitated and trying to get through the next five hours—or in my case, eighteen—with as little hassle as possible. Crowds, delays, screaming kids, impossible-to-understand announcements. Good times.

But, this was no normal day. On this day, I wanted nothing more than to be at a stinking, putrid airport, because my flight would be delivering me to my best friend. To Emma Rey Finley, whom I hadn't seen in months.

I happily hopped into the cab with a massive grin cemented to my face and greeted the driver with, "Good morning. To the airport, please."

"Yeah, sounds great, kid," the driver answered grudgingly in a half-awake haze. To be fair, it was 5:30 a.m., roughly. But who cared? I was about to embark on the greatest adventure of my life.

We drove along the coast and I rolled down my window so I could feel the refreshing ocean breeze. It was cool that morning, but I didn't care because it reminded me of all the chilly nights I'd spent on the pier with my best friend.

The ride to the airport was quick—no traffic, no delays. At the drop-off area, the driver grabbed my bag, slung it over his shoulder and plopped it down next to me in almost one fluid motion. I slapped $40 into his hand, grabbed my bag and put my headphones on. I brought up the "Emm Playlist," which was a compilation of three years' worth of our favorite songs.

As I rocked out to one of Emm's beloved tracks, I entered the sliding glass doors of the airport feeling like a celebrity. I was about to be a first-time international traveler, and as far as I was concerned I was traveling for the best reason possible.

Practically dancing my way through baggage check and security—the ninety-minute security line barely registered—I eventually arrived at my gate, where I took a seat in the waiting area. I had two legs to my trip; this first plane would bring me to Detroit, then my connecting flight would bring me to Emm. It was barely 8:00 a.m. and I had about forty-five minutes to kill so I called Ken. Since I'd gotten my own apartment off campus, I hadn't had a chance to talk to him outside of practice as often as I would've liked.

"Hey, Ken, I'm here and I'm so amped about this flight." I practically yelled into my phone.

He groggily replied, "I thought you hated airports? When my parents took us back East to see the Celtics in the finals, you were a whiny little bitch at LAX."

I chuckled. "Yeah. I mean, most of the time I can't stand these places, but this trip is different. What are you up to?"

"I just woke up, bro. Getting ready to head to the gym. When does your flight leave?"

Ken's athletic discipline was unparalleled. He worked out like an absolute animal every day and I respected the hell out of that. At one point in our lives, his arms became so massive he had to rub an oil pregnant woman use to reduce stretch marks on his biceps because they'd grown so muscular. I mean, the dude was stacked and he'd earned it. Ken also owned more sleeveless shirts than anyone I'd ever met—but hey, if I looked like him, maybe I would've invested in a few tank tops, too.

Ken was staying on campus all summer because he was in full-on, hardcore training mode. The team's required practices didn't start until later in the summer quarter—but to Ken, there was no such thing as an optional practice. As his co-captain, I probably should've been with him in the gym, but that would've meant missing out on spending time with Emma Rey Finley.

"At 8:45 a.m. we start boarding," I replied.

"Nice, man. Hey, I don't want to keep you from your great romantic adventure, so I'll see you in a week."

Ken was a good guy at heart—he really was—but he was also a world-class smartass. In three years, he never once got tired of teasing me about my friendship with Emm.

Slightly annoyed, I shot back, "It's ten days actually, you dumbass. And you might not hear from me while I'm there, so I love you, man. Don't do anything stupid while I'm gone."

With a bit more energy than when he'd initially answered the phone, Ken replied, "Ten days, whatever. Fly safe, bro. Love you too, and tell Emma I said hello!"

I hung up thinking how lucky I was to be in this crappy airport. I'd be able to deliver Ken's message in person soon.

A HOP

I boarded my flight to Detroit and my adrenaline and excitement turned off immediately, almost as if someone had flipped a light switch inside my body.

I fell asleep within the first five minutes of boarding, thanks mostly, I think, to my scented neck pillow I'd bought at the airport after checking my bags. I was lucky to have snagged a direct flight to Detroit, and even luckier that I don't remember a single moment in the air.

Out cold, I was jolted awake as our plane touched down in the Motor City. "Helloooo Detroit," the guy next to me said as we taxied along the runway. Maybe I wasn't the only one stoked about traveling today.

My connection was tight. I didn't have time to grab any food because I had to run to my next flight's gate. I don't think I got to stretch my legs for more than fifteen minutes, which was a bit of a problem. When you're six-foot-six, leg-stretching time is key; I should've thought of that and planned better.

"I'm sorry, sir, but your boarding pass isn't valid yet," the agent said calmly as I reached the front of the line at my gate.

My adrenaline surged. Utterly confused and probably visibly nervous, I asked, "What do you mean it's not valid?"

Puzzled by my reaction, the agent looked at me and explained, "We're not calling your row yet, sir. Please step to the side."

I calmed down a bit knowing I would eventually be allowed on the plane, but those five minutes felt longer than my entire trip to the Detroit. When I handed my pass back to the agent, she gave me the generic, "Thank you for choosing Delta—have a safe flight," that she probably said ten thousand times a day.

I looked right back at her, amused by her plastic smile and gave her the most genuinely happy response I could muster. Reading her name from the tag on her right shoulder, I replied, "No, thank *you*, Ramona," while also throwing her a wink.

Just then, an announcement came over the loudspeaker: "Final boarding call for Delta Flight #1543, with nonstop service to Leonardo da Vinci Airport, Rome."

And with that, I boarded my flight to The Eternal City, where I would spend the next ten days in the company of

Emma Rey Finley.

I was off to Italy. I'd never been to Europe before, so I was excited to explore this new continent with my adventuring partner, whom I now hadn't seen in over two months. Two months that had felt like two years.

Emm had been a world traveler since she was in middle school, which was another thing I loved about her. So naturally, as soon as she'd racked up enough credits in her Global Studies major, she applied to be one of 250 students who would receive an all-expenses-paid study-abroad scholarship in Rome. It was an elite program and her chances of being accepted were slim, even though she more than met the academic criteria. At least a thousand upperclassmen applied each year and, selfishly—although I hated to admit it—part of me hoped the long odds meant she wouldn't be leaving. We had never spent more than a month or so apart since we'd met: I wanted to keep it that way. Yet at the same time, I also had no doubt in my mind that Emm would be selected—not just for her grades, but because of her natural curiosity and ability to bring out the best in everyone she met. If the selection committee had even the slightest understanding of what made up a qualified candidate, they couldn't deny Emm this once-in-a-lifetime opportunity.

Sure enough, several weeks and several interviews later, I got a text from Emm that read, "I GOT IT!!! WOO WOO!!! Call me."

As usual, I heard Emm's voice in my head as I read her text. But for some reason, this particular text made me feel all warm inside. She was so dorky sometimes. I didn't call her back or even type out a response—I just ran to the convenience store, bought a bouquet of flowers and a Slim Jim, and jogged to her house.

Her door was ajar, so I didn't bother knocking. Letting myself in, I found Emm on the phone with her mom. I threw the flowers and Slim Jim onto the foot of her bed, picked her up, and gave her the biggest hug ever. I yelled into the phone, "We did it, Mama!" I didn't usually call Emm's mother

"Mama," but I was just so excited.

Once things calmed down, Emm and I went for a walk down one of our less-traveled paths. She was so psyched that she even let me have some of her Slim Jim, which was a first. We talked about all of the things she needed to do over the next six weeks before going abroad. And while I showed nothing but elation outwardly, inside I was absolutely terrified at the idea of facing six long months without my best friend.

"I'll write you every day, my love," I said, half-sarcastic, half-serious.

She laughed as she leaned her head against my chest. "I don't know what I'm going to do out there without you, TD."

Over the next month or so, I made it my mission to spend as much time with Emm as possible, more so than usual. No matter what I had going on with school or basketball, I made time for Emma Rey Finley. We made a bucket list of all the missions we wanted to accomplish before she left: We went on hikes, we tried new restaurants, we took Lee mini-golfing, we went swimming in the nearby hot spring and we even went so far as to toy with the idea of bungee jumping. We spent so much time together that we even got on each other's nerves a bit at times. When that happened, we'd take a day or two off, but we'd always come right back to each other like nothing had ever happened.

"Is someone sleepy over there?" I asked Emm after she finished her raspberry snow cone. We were just concluding a full day of flipping rides and furry animals at the local carnival. She was lying on her back on a grassy hill on the outskirts of the event, her arm folded over her eyes and blocking out the sunlight. We'd arrived early that afternoon and the sun was just beginning to set.

Emm didn't respond. I wasn't sure if she was actually asleep or not, so I asked again.

Groaning, she replied, "I have a headache, TD, and I'm hungry too, but not like carnival-food hungry. Like actual food hungry."

"Me too. Maybe we should stop on the way home and get

some real food?" I asked.

She hesitated a moment before answering. "I just want to get home. I'm having dinner with some of my other friends tonight. I need to spend some time with them before I leave— you've kinda been bogarting me."

A deep hurt prickled through me. "And so what? You're the one who's leaving!" I thought. A split second later, reason kicked in and, thankfully, took control of my mouth as I responded, "Okay, let's get our stuff together and get going."

My disappointment must have been evident. As I was packing up the prizes I'd won for us at various booths, Emm purposely caught my eye.

"But I *will* see you and Lee on Saturday morning for pancakes?"

"Of course, Emm, I'll be making my specialty," I answered, feeling my expression soften.

"Good." She gave me a peck on the cheek before we headed back to the car.

The weeks flew by and the quarter came to an end too quickly. As sort of a going-away gift, Ken and I threw Emm a Harry Potter-themed party, which was weird as hell for mid-March, but who cared? Emm and I loved Harry Potter and we'd read all the books in the series together. Unfortunately, the theme necessitated my going as Ron Weasley—I was the only true ginger in our group of friends—but when Emm saw me in my costume she laughed like a madwoman and that made it all worthwhile.

Spring break, which marked the end of the winter quarter, started a few days later. Emm would be leaving for a little time back home in New York, and then she'd be off to Rome. The study-abroad program would last through both the spring and summer quarters, so I didn't think I'd see her for a solid six months. Thankfully, I was wrong.

Feeling a bit indulgent, I ordered myself a glass of wine as the flight attendant pushed her cart up my row.

"Will that be all for you today, sir?" she asked as she handed me what I had hoped would be a strong enough adult beverage to knock me out. The more time I spent asleep in the air, the better.

"Maybe a bag of nuts, please," I replied.

The attendant handed me a bag of lightly salted peanuts the size of a tiny cell phone, but hey, I never said no to a free snack.

I reclined my chair just as the man next to me in the middle seat reached over to grab the drink he'd ordered. He immediately took a second glass and handed it to his wife, who was sitting in the seat beside the window.

Without looking directly at me, he said, "Pardon my reach, son, the red wine did sound like a fabulous idea. Isn't that right, sweetie?"

"Well, yes, there's never a bad time for a glass of wine, I've learned," she answered. The two of them smiled at each other.

The man turned fully toward me for the first time and asked, "So, are you from the city?" while pointing at my shirt.

"I'm not, but I'm going to see the girl who got it for me. She actually grew up there. She's studying abroad in Rome now, though."

"That's very sweet," the woman offered with a beatific smile on her face.

"I've always loved those 'I ♥ New York' T-shirts," the man added. "They're so iconic."

We got to chatting a bit. The couple was relocating from Montana to Rome because the husband had just gotten a job teaching creative writing at a university there. I told them I had recently taken up a new-found interest in writing because of how often I wrote to Emm.

Which was true. I wrote to Emm constantly while she was abroad. Kind of old school, but to me, letters meant more than a text or even a phone call; a letter could last a lifetime.

I had no shortage of material, either. I wrote to her when I was sad, I wrote to her when I was happy, I wrote to her when Ken did something dumb, I wrote to her when Lee was asking about her. From the exciting to the mundane, I always had something I was dying to tell Emm all about.

When I'd received my first reply from her, I was so excited you would've thought I'd opened up one of Willy Wonka's golden-ticket chocolate bars. I tore open the envelope and read the opening paragraph:

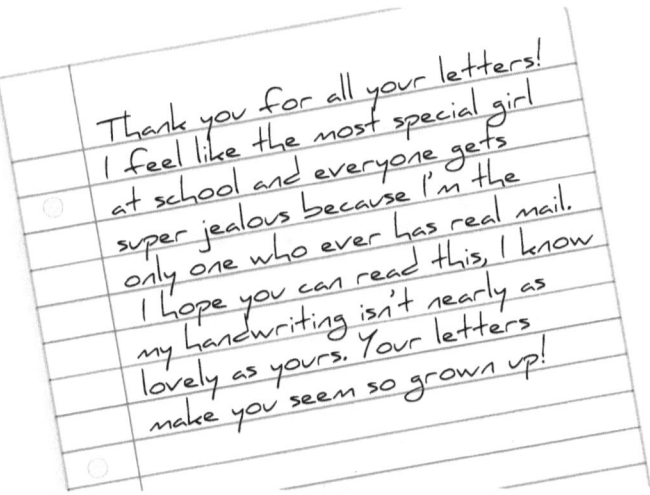

Thank you for all your letters! I feel like the most special girl at school and everyone gets super jealous because I'm the only one who ever has real mail. I hope you can read this, I know my handwriting isn't nearly as lovely as yours. Your letters make you seem so grown up!

Her letter went on for two pages, describing all she'd done in the past couple of weeks. Emm had the unique ability to make me laugh or even cry from over 6,000 miles away, with nothing more than a pen and paper. I considered it one of her superpowers. She also always concluded each letter with a heart that tightly wrapped around her full, three-part-name. It always made me miss her so much more.

I paused when I realized I'd been talking to this poor, captive couple, nonstop and uninterrupted, for at least five minutes.

"She sounds like a really special girl, son. You're lucky to have her," the man said. His wife gave a slight nod in agreement. He then politely asked me how long Emm and I had been dating.

I let out a bit of a chuckle before I answered. "We aren't dating actually. We're just great friends."

"Cheers, then, to friendship." The man and his wife both raised their glasses.

I raised mine as well: "To friendship."

Not long after, I fell asleep for the first time on my eleven-hour flight to Rome. I bet the couple was relieved to see me and my blabbering mouth nodding off.

After rolling in and out of an uncomfortable slumber (my neck pillow had somehow lost its magic), I put on my Emm Playlist once again and thought about our FaceTime call a few weeks earlier. That was when I asked her, almost completely out of the blue, "Hey, would it be crazy if I tried to come out there to see you, Emm?" Before she'd left, we'd never discussed the possibility of a visit, so it was a surprisingly new idea.

She jumped and gasped with excitement, "Please do! But I'm not sure when you'd have time to do that, with Lee and basketball and everything."

Emm's point had been more than valid. Except for a road trip here or there, I hadn't had a vacation of any sort since I was in high school. But my uncle had been encouraging me to plan a trip before the madness of my senior year began, and he'd assured me that he and Lee could manage without me for a week or two. Early in the summer quarter was the one time of year when I wasn't required to be on campus for basketball, either, so I'd known that I would have a bit of free time available on that front as well.

"I have some dates in mind, if a visit would really be okay?" I said, eager to hear how she would respond. I really wasn't sure if Emm intended her time in Rome to be hers and hers alone. I desperately hoped not.

"I'd love nothing more," she replied in the gentle, genuine voice that I'd come to know so well. "Whenever you can get here, I'll make the time."

That was all I needed.

Visiting Emm quickly grew from a fun idea to a realistic possibility. I scoured the web for flight information and costs. Fortunately, my passport was still valid—Mr. and Mrs. Zom had insisted Ken and I apply for passports as soon as we'd both turned eighteen. I had some money in the bank from when my mother had passed, so affording the trip wouldn't be a financial problem. But socially speaking? Socially, this trip would cost me more than dollars. No one in their right mind would believe that I would spend $1500 to go and see a "friend," and, honestly, I couldn't blame them. Most people our age wouldn't even visit a girlfriend or boyfriend who was studying abroad, let alone someone they weren't even sleeping with. But then again, most people didn't have a friend like Emma Rey Finley.

A SKIP

We touched down at 7 a.m. in Rome. In total, I had managed only maybe two hours of solid sleep on the flight, but for some reason I was now wide awake. I reached into the overhead bin and grabbed my backpack, pulled down on the strings to fasten it closely to my body, and headed for baggage claim.

After taking a few accidental detours, I finally made it to the cab stand. Just as I was about to take in my first deep breath of Italian air, I saw the couple who'd been sitting next to me on my flight.

"Enjoy Rome, son," the man said as he tipped his hat.

His wife waved and added with a wink, "And don't be afraid to explore everything that it has to offer!"

I was a bit confused by her comment, so I just sort of waved back and said, "Thank you! Enjoy your—". But before I could finish, they were gone.

I got into a cab as quickly as possible and handed the driver a wrinkled piece of scrap paper with an address scribbled on it. "*Via Giuseppe Parini 7, Trastevere, Roma*" was all it said. Half-expecting the driver to look at me as if I'd just handed him directions to Mars, I was worried he would have no idea of where I needed to go. But he looked back at me and in accented English simply said, "Okay."

Barely containing my almost uncontainable glee, I suddenly realized that I was only a car ride away from my best friend.

My phone's battery was critically-low, so I decided not to call Emm. Anyhow, a sneak attack would be best. I distracted myself as best I could by taking in the streets of Rome. I could hardly believe I had ten full days of freedom in front of me, ten full days with Emma Rey Finley.

We pulled up to a rustic-looking terracotta building about thirty minutes away from the airport. The driver had just given me his very best, "Thank you," in English when I heard a voice wafting through the air. Could that really be her? As I took a few steps closer, I realized my ears were in fact telling the truth: Emm was singing "All I Wanna Do" by her absolute favorite artist, Sheryl Crow. She seemed really into it, too, as if she'd forgotten for a moment that the world around her existed. Rather than interrupting her magnificent performance, I listened to my Sheryl Crow as she stretched her exquisite vocal cords. If my phone hadn't been so low on battery, I would've caught her song on video for posterity.

Once the song ended, I yelled up, "HEY, EMMA REY FINLEY…All I wanna do is have some fun!"

Completely unaware that I'd been there for the entirety of her performance, Emm ran to the window. "TD!" she cried, looking about as excited as I'd ever seen her.

She bolted downstairs and out the front door, tackling me in such an effusive hug that I actually fell over. But I was so happy I couldn't care less: Emm and I were reunited at last.

"I like your T-shirt," she said as she helped me take my bags up the staircase. Emm had two roommates who were both study-abroad students as well. Fortunately enough for me, one of them would be gone for the next two weeks, so I'd have my own bedroom. Which was a relief. I hadn't met a sofa yet that was made for a guy six-foot-six to sleep on.

"It was a hit on my flight," I said, beaming at her. "I told my seatmates all about how you gave it to me."

It was beyond good to see her. Emm looked even more amazing than I remembered, but her beauty was the least of what I'd missed. What I had longed for was our bubble-world: I could already feel it re-forming around us, even though we'd only been reunited for less than five minutes.

Once we put my stuff down, we went for a walk to get some breakfast before Emm's classes began for the day. We strolled around the neighborhood, passing dazzling fountains and alluring architecture. Italy was really something else, and I had a pretty cool tour guide to show me around.

"How was your flight?" Emm asked as we walked.

"Not too bad at all, surprisingly. How was your day?"

She laughed. "I just woke up, you dummy."

"That's right, my fault." I repeated it sheepishly several times. I was all jumbled up about the time difference.

"What classes do you have today?" I asked.

"Just Italian and Global Economics, but then I have a group project until 5:00 p.m.," she explained.

We walked to a newer-looking piazza where we chose a little trattoria with modern decor and flowing white table-cloths. Emm and I decided on a table outside; from where we sat we could see kids running around, as well as locals walking their dogs in the morning sunlight.

A waiter then approached us and said, "*Ciao.*" I realized this was the moment to take a step back and let Emm take the wheel. She responded in Italian and ordered for both of us. I was suddenly starving and hoped she'd ordered me something delicious.

Emm spoke English, Italian and Spanish, and she could read Portuguese, too. I thought maybe she even knew a little Mandarin, but I wasn't too clear on that point. With so many talents, and her enigmatic charm, I wouldn't have been at all surprised if Emm told me she was also a part-time ninja.

"*Ciao*' means 'hello.' I'll teach you as we go," Emm said, once she was done ordering. I smirked back at her; I was still in complete disbelief that I'd made it all the way to Rome in the first place. A language barrier seemed like a small thing, especially since I had my own personal interpreter.

We ate, laughed, and caught up as though we hadn't seen each other in eight years rather than eight weeks. Three minutes later, a whole hour had flown by and it was somehow already time for her to go to class. Which in a way was good, because with my stomach now full and the jetlag was starting to hit me. Hard.

"I'll see you back at the apartment around 5 p.m.?" I asked. It felt good to know I'd be seeing her again in just a few hours.

"Sounds perfect," Emm agreed, looking almost angelic as she slung her bag over her shoulder.

She gave me directions back to her apartment, then headed in the opposite direction to go to class. As for me, I was ready to hit the sheets and get some real sleep.

Nine hours later, Emm, returning from her day, opened the door.

"Chow! I hope you like pasta with cauliflower and spinach," I exclaimed as she stepped into the room.

"First of all, it's '*ciao*,'" she said while putting her bag down on the counter beside me. "But I must say, I've missed your cooking."

I don't want to give myself a ton of credit, but for a college kid, I could cook. I'd made dinner for Lee and me more times than I could count. My Uncle Bill was less than a culinary master. If it were up to him, we probably would've subsisted on cereal, cold cuts and takeout. Lee needed a much healthier diet than that, so I became the family cook, with the fortunate benefit of my cooking skills making me a hit with the ladies.

We sat down together to eat, and although the spaghetti wasn't my best work ever, it certainly got the job done. After we'd cleaned our plates, we freshened up and went off to Emm's favorite local spot for a nightcap.

"Drinks are on me tonight. I mean, it's the least I can do after you flew all the way out here to see me," Emm said as we walked into the bar.

"Hey, I came out here to check out Europe…It just so happens you're here, too," I taunted.

"Oh sure. Totally." Emm saw right through my bullshit, as usual.

She got the bartender's attention and ordered us each a drink, which turned into a few more drinks…and then a few more after that. Before I knew it, we were both completely drunk. Totally drunk—and having an amazing time. We danced—or, more accurately, we tried to dance, but Emm's one glaring flaw was that she had absolutely no rhythm. Embarrassingly so, because she'd never had any concept of how bad she truly was—I'd always been pretty sure that she believed she could go on tour with some major pop star and slay it. But, in that moment, I was simply happy to just be with her, no matter how terrible her dance moves were. I didn't even give a damn that we were making everyone else around us visibly uncomfortable.

When Emm finally said, "Let's go home, I'm exhausted," I couldn't disagree with her at all. We were much too drunk; it was time to call it a night.

As we walked (or maybe stumbled) back to her apartment, I thought I'd share my own rendition of her performance that morning. Using my empty beer bottle as a microphone, I started to impersonate her singing, belting out lyrics from earlier in my very best Emm voice.

"Oh, shut up!" she laughed as she punched me in the arm. Which didn't make me stop singing…at least not for another block or two.

As we approached her apartment, Emm stopped short, letting me walk forward a few steps while still talking to myself like an idiot. When I turned, she broke into a run and I knew she was going to try to ram me—with a hug that is—which was one of her typical "one too many" moves. But this time I was prepared. At the moment of impact, I grabbed her and swirled around. I sort of held her there for a moment, with her feet dangling six inches off the pavement, pleased with myself for having thwarted her ninja attack.

"I'm so happy at you, TD," she whispered into my ear.

I whispered back, "I'm so happy at you too, Emm."

I was about to put her down when she said, "Thank you so much for coming to see me. You have no idea how much it means to me."

After placing her down gently, she immediately wrapped her arms around me like a koala bear and again whispered into my ear, this time saying, "Just a hop, skip and…"

I laughed quietly and in a soft voice finished the line for her, "…a jump!"

With that, Emma Rey Finley, international traveler and dancing queen, passed out in my arms as I carried her the rest of the way home.

Chapter 2

My Buddy

I toppled out of bed the next morning as my alarm blared, nearly falling face-first into a mound of clothes that I had yet to put away. I laughed at myself, thankful that I hadn't face-planted into my own underwear. That's when it hit me— that too-familiar feeling of having had one too many. I wasn't hungover exactly, but I knew I'd been drinking.

I headed into the kitchen and helped myself to a large glass of water. Then I cracked a few eggs into a bowl, placed some bread in the toaster, and put the coffee on to brew. I tiptoed toward Emm's room, gingerly sliding my bare feet against the tile floor, to see if she'd woken up yet. No surprise, she was still out like a light.

A wave of euphoria hit me as I made it back to the kitchen: this would be my first home-cooked breakfast on my first full day in Rome. Last night, I'd placed Emm's phone in the cradle on the counter to recharge and took advantage of her music library. I selected one of her playlists, called *"Buongior-*

no." Adding bacon bits and fried onions, I started scrambling the eggs. I sliced up an avocado I'd uncovered after digging deep into the back of the fridge, and just as I was about to add cream and sugar to the coffee, Emm snuck up on me and finished, in Italian, the lyrics to the song that was playing.

She had the wildest, most out of control bedhead I'd ever seen, yet she somehow looked thrilled about it. Emm was wearing an oversized T-shirt that basically covered her entire body: "If you don't chew Big Red then F*ck You," it read, with Will Ferrell pointing straight outward—almost like an Uncle Sam recruitment poster from WWI. She was also wearing her glasses, which somehow tied together her "look" perfectly.

"Good morning, sunshine," I said to Emm as I bowed and presented my finished masterpiece—an average American breakfast—to her.

Curtsying in response, she replied, "Why, thank you, my liege. May I join you?"

"Verily, it would be my pleasure." I don't know why we did this 18th-century formality thing. It was pretty silly, I must admit—but every once in a while, we slipped effortlessly into this arcane patois.

Emm sat down and took a bite of her eggs, scratched her chin in mock contemplation, and said, "Delightful!"

We both giggled as I took a seat next to her. "I made enough for your roommate, too, for whenever she wakes up."

"You haven't even met her yet. You're always so thoughtful, TD," replied Emm.

We enjoyed our meal as the Italian sunshine streamed in through the window. It was Saturday, so Emm didn't have classes. We discussed the possibilities for the day.

"We could go to the beach and relax if you want," Emm suggested. "Did you bring your sunblock?" she chided.

Emm knew full well that I had sunblock with me at pretty much all times. While the sun's rays only gave her golden skin more of a beautiful bronze color, it wreaked absolute havoc on mine. With as little as ten minutes of direct sunlight, I would look like a boiled lobster.

"We could be in the Arctic Circle and I'd still have my SPF 100," I said, rolling my eyes a bit. "Geez, Emm, it was one time...*once*! I got a sunburn the day we met because I didn't think I'd be outside that long. I wasn't about to ask to use yours—I was wooing you, remember?"

"Wooing?" Emm just about doubled over in her chair as she laughed. "That was some grade-A wooing, TD, screaming out my name, EMMA RE—"

"—So you suggested the beach?" I said, cutting her short. "Let's do it."

Emm seemed determined to yell something, so at the top of her voice she screamed, *"Woo!* Let's DO IT!" She calmed herself down a bit, then added, "And don't let me forget that we have to be back by seven this evening. I have a surprise for you."

We put on our bathing suits, packed a cooler, and headed toward the train station which was just a few blocks from the apartment. The beach was only an hour or so away, but I'd be making the trip more or less alone. Emm was out the moment we sat down, despite the huge cup of coffee I'd poured for her at breakfast. Emm had the uncanny ability to fall asleep on any form of transportation; I considered it one of her many talents. Cars, trains, buses, planes—the instant we got moving, she was out cold.

With Emm in dreamland, I pulled out the book I was reading. I always liked having a piece of literature on me, especially when traveling. Reading kept me honest and in touch with a side of myself that I let very few people see. Being a Division I athlete, on top of caring for my little sister, meant that my life was high-pressure and high-stress—so in a way, reading was my escape. It kept me sane through the madness.

Emm and I were almost always reading the same book, as if we were our own two-person book club. We were currently reading *Me Before You* by Jojo Moyes. In the book, Louisa, a poor girl from a small town, is hired to care for Will. Will had been left paralyzed and deeply depressed after a motorcycle accident. Lou takes him on all kinds of adventures in an attempt to convince him that life is still worth living. I was loving the book because Lou and Will's relationship wasn't based on physical attraction; their love was all about enjoying each other's company, much like me and Emm. *Me Before You* scored bonus points, too, because it also gave me all sorts of great ideas for things to do with Emma Rey Finley.

Even though I was only at the halfway-point of the novel, Emm—who, according to her, was the brighter one of the two of us—only had a chapter or two left. We were competitive at everything, so she never let me hear the end of it when she was further along in one of our books. Now that I had a full hour to myself on this train, I hoped to close that distance significantly.

Eventually, we arrived in Santa Marinella, a small seaside town about sixty kilometers northwest of Rome. As our train pulled into the station, I softly nudged Emm to wake her up.

After she'd groggily sat up, I asked, "How was your nap, my dear?"

"We're here?" she said mid-yawn while stretching her arms. "That ride went by in the blink of an eye…almost, like, literally."

"Come on sleepyhead, let's get off this train." I dog-eared the page of my novel, grabbed our stuff, and helped a sleepy-wobbly Emm to her feet.

The station was only a few blocks from the beach itself. The sleepy beach town was relaxed and quaint and—on this particular day—very, very hot. The cool, salty sea-air breeze offered some relief from the heat, but I was eager for a dip in the waves to cool off.

Just as we stepped off the boardwalk and onto the beach, Emm turned around suddenly and looked at me like I was a total stranger. She met my eye, held my gaze, and teased, "Hey, do I know you?"

I smirked, not exactly sure what she was setting me up for. "Yeah, I'm your—" But before I could finish, she took off in a full-on sprint toward the shoreline.

Without hesitation I took off after her, the two of us running and laughing hysterically as the tide lapped our feet. After a minute or so, I caught up and tackled her, losing our balance and falling into the shallow water. We splashed around a bit, flinging water at each other, before Emm called out "uncle," pleading with me to stop. I proclaimed my victory before heading back onto the soft, dry sand to pick up the stuff we'd dropped. I don't know why Emm thought she could outrun me—since, at five-foot-six, her legs were literally only half as long as mine.

Emm may be fast, but on this day, I learned that I am a bit faster.

We picked a spot and spread out our beach blanket, which is when I realized Emm had brought a piece of our friendship all the way across the Atlantic. Touched, I thought I'd impress her with my 24-hour-old Italian language skills. "Chow, ill myo name e' TD."

She shook her head and grinned at my awful pronunciation. "No, it's more like, '*Ciao, il mio nome è* TD.' Now try again."

I took a deep breath before blurting out something that I hoped sounded more like, "Hello my name is TD," in Italian, but Emm's facial expression told me otherwise.

"You're getting better, though. It just takes practice, that's all," she offered, trying to keep my weakening Italian spirit alive.

It was a special day and the view from the beach was made all the more spectacular because we were enjoying it together. We watched the waves cresting against the shore while talking about everything and nothing, all at the same time.

"Did I ever tell you why Christmas is my favorite holiday?" I thought this was a weird topic for the middle of the summer, but every once in a while, Emm would blurt out a "fun fact" about herself without the slightest warning. These bits of trivia always came with a deeply philosophical bent. To Emm, there really was no such thing as a simple reason—she had her own take on everything, and I found every reason fascinating.

"Christmas is just about everyone's favorite holiday, Emm," I replied, looking forward to hearing her reasoning.

"Yeah, but I don't love it in the way everyone else loves Christmas. It's my favorite because it's the only day when everyone is happy and it's snowing," she explained.

"You like the snow?" I asked.

"It's not that I'm exactly crazy about the snow itself, especially in Manhattan, where fresh snow has about a fifteen-minute shelf-life. It's more about what it symbolizes to me…and how it reminds me of home. New York City at Christmas time, covered in a fresh, white blanket. In that sense, yeah, I guess I do like snow."

"Do you ever wish you went to school back home?" I asked. "The city has some amazing schools."

"Sometimes, but I don't think I'd appreciate being home as much if I'd never left." Emm wasn't one to get homesick, really, but she was a New York City girl at heart. Sometimes I had the feeling she was comparing the world itself to the Upper West Side.

"Are you keeping in touch with your family okay?" I asked. "The time difference must make it hard."

"We manage. My parents are my best friends, TD, you know that. I don't know what I'd do if I couldn't talk to them. We FaceTime in the mornings before class—I'm having breakfast while they're having dinner. The East Coast is only six hours behind Rome, so it's not as hard as keeping up with West Coast folks." Emm paused for a longish moment before asking gently, "What about your Dad? You haven't mentioned him in a long time."

"Not really much to say," I shrugged. "He's not really…I don't really…You know how it is, Emm."

"So…you still haven't spoken to him at all?" I could hear the hesitation in Emm's voice. She didn't want to push too far, but she also knew she was the only one on the planet allowed to ask me about the festering wound that was my father.

"Nope, no change there," I answered, feeling a bit vulnerable. "It's been over three years—not since Lee had her transplant."

"It's okay, TD. We don't—"

I cut her off. "No, it's fine, I should probably talk about this stuff sometimes, and if I have to talk about it, I want it to be with you."

Emm knew my history in a way that most people didn't. My father, to put it bluntly (if not kindly), was a junkie and a drunk. As far as I could remember, he'd started drinking when I was in first or second grade—years after the "wellness" home visits from the adoption agency had stopped. From then on, not a day went by without my seeing a beer or a glass of whiskey in his hand. He was a so-called "functional alcoholic," though. As long as he could toss back a few, he was fine. But, years later, when my mother died of a ruptured aneurysm not long after Lee was born, he lost all control. Prescription pills. Lost his job within three months. When he first threatened to beat me, I didn't take it seriously. I thought we could move past it. But the next time he raised his fist, I didn't wait another second. I couldn't. I just packed up my then eleven-month-old sister and showed up on the Zoms' doorstep unannounced. And the Zoms, God love them, worked it out with Child Services so we could stay with them until my Uncle Bill was appointed our legal guardian.

Emm smiled tenderly before asking, "Is he in touch with Lee at all?"

"Not that I know of—and not if I can help it. I'm planning a party for her in the spring. It'll be the four-year anniversary of her bone marrow transplant—and I'm not even going to invite him."

Emm put her hand on my shoulder and turned the subject to slightly happier things. "She's done so well, TD. Sickle cell anemia is a hell of a disease. She's fought hard."

"You've been a big part of that, Emm," I said sincerely. "She never knew our mother, and Uncle Bill's never been a major presence in her life. Your 'girl time' has been really good for her. It gives her something that I can't."

"I still can't believe how quickly she took to journaling," Emm replied brightly. "We've got a budding writer on our hands, I'm sure of it."

It was true. Emm had introduced Lee to journaling over two years ago, and ever since then my little sister wrote religiously every day, and would regularly "report" about her writings to Emm. Lee's journal was "super-secret and not for boys," but she'd opened up fully to Emm. If I were really lucky, Lee would sometimes share a song or story with me, but only in her own time and on her own schedule. That was fine by me, because writing was a better therapy than all the transfusions, immune-boosters, and antibiotics combined—and since Lee had been in-and-out of the hospital for most of her life, that was saying something.

"You've been really helpful, too, Emm, taking her to all those doctors' appointments when I couldn't be around. She hates going with Uncle Bill."

"It's never been a problem. You've always got too much on your plate and I'm happy to do it." Emm smiled a smile that was soft and sad and hopeful all at the same time. "I wish Lee was with us now. This beach is so beautiful."

I simply nodded my head. I was all talked-out and Emm knew it, so we just sat in silence for a moment as we gazed out over the waves.

Emm glanced down as her phone pinged. "It's my roommate. I should probably take this."

Grateful for the interruption, I replied, "Of course, go ahead. I'm going to hop in the water."

I took my sunglasses off and ran toward the surf. The sea was cool, but the day was so hot that the sharp contrast only seemed to pull me in deeper. The crisp water offered a much-needed renewal, especially after my long trip and our booze-filled night. I swam out a bit deeper, deep enough to where I couldn't stand, then completely submerged my head for the first time. It was an unbelievable sensation to finally be completely weightless. My whole body relaxed. Here I was, floating around in the Tyrrhenian Sea, with Emm soaking up the sun just a couple dozen yards away on shore.

A few minutes later, I saw Emm running toward the shoreline. Once she hit the water, the force of the waves practically slowed her progress to a crawl. I swam over to help her move past the breakers.

"Everything okay at the apartment?" I asked once we got close enough.

"All good. My roommate says thanks for breakfast."

We began to move deeper into the water, just up to the point where Emm could still stand comfortably. I sort of floated on my knees in an attempt to shield my torso from the sun.

"It was so funny trying to explain who you are to my roommates," she said, looking out over the ever-undulating sea.

"Oh yeah? How so?"

"When I told them I'd be having a friend coming to see me, no one thought you'd be a guy. Once they figured that out, of course, the next question was, 'Is he your boyfriend?' Just like always."

I felt myself blush. "I totally felt the same way back at school when I told everyone I was coming out here."

"Yep, same question, different continent," said Emm with a shrug. "Now I just try to mess with people when they ask me."

"Oh no, what did you tell them?" I asked, preparing for the worst.

Emm's face turned semi-serious. "At first, I just told them my buddy was coming to see me—I mean, the word *buddy* isn't gendered right?"

I burst into laughter instantly. "Your 'buddy?' Really, Emm?" I made air quotes around the word *buddy* to drive the point home.

She started to laugh with me. "Hey, why not? You're more than my friend, but we aren't dating so…you're my buddy."

Between peals of laughter, I managed, "I guess you're right." Then, when I'd finally caught my breath, "I'd be honored to be your buddy."

"I'm honored, too." Emm dipped her head under the water, then popped back up with her flawless smile. "Let's head in and find some food."

"Sounds good, *buddy*. I'm starving," I laughed before submerging my head, feeling weightless one last time.

We grabbed our things and headed into town. Small stores and quaint shops lined the streets. We enjoyed our stroll, doing a little window shopping, before hitting on a block that was nothing but restaurants. Emm and I poked around until we came across a cozy seafood hideaway.

"Table for two, please," I politely asked the hostess. She looked back at me as if I'd just asked to be seated even though I was completely naked.

"Geez, TD," Emm smirked. "Better let me do the talking. We'll starve to death otherwise." She nudged me in the ribs before turning to the hostess. "*Un tavolo per due, per favore.*" I turned about fifteen shades redder, and it wasn't from my already-blossoming sunburn.

The hostess said something brightly-animated and very Italian to Emm. "*Americano*" was the only word I caught.

Once we were seated, Emm asked, "I didn't know you were a fan of seafood?"

"I didn't know that I'd be going to Europe this summer either, but here I am. Trying all types of new things."

"Only you would come this far to see me, TD. Thank you for that."

"Of course, Emm...I would've gone to North Korea if that was what it took." I'd meant it as a joke, but as the words came out of my mouth, I realized they were true.

Saving me from any more potential embarrassment, Emm ordered for the both of us. We'd taken a table outside since the day's heat had finally started to wane.

Our food arrived, but I was a bit surprised to see what our waitress had delivered. She placed a plate of seafood pasta in front of me, while Emm was presented with a fresh piece of salmon that sat atop a bed of roasted vegetables.

"What's wrong?" The disappointment I'd been trying to hide was obviously written all over my face.

After a moment, Emm realized why I was upset. She sighed. "Gosh, I'm so sorry! It's been so long, and we're in a totally new environment...I forgot. Forgive me?" She flashed me a puppy-dog look. Puppy dog looks were another of Emm's superpowers.

"It's totally fine. But dessert is on you after this, that's for sure." I smiled, returning to my usual self.

In *Remember Me*, one of our favorite movies, the main character always ordered dessert first, almost like an appetizer. Emm and I thought that was just about the best thing ever, so we took this fabulous idea and made it our own: every dinner together started with dessert first. Well, every dinner except, apparently, this one.

As we lingered and finished up our wine, we watched as the sky turned from magnificently sunny into cloudy and gloomy. A few heavy drops of rain spat down, then the sky exploded, sending down a deluge.

"This is crazy," I half-shouted over the din of the rain. The awning above was already heavy with rainwater.

"We still have to get you your ice cream, though," came Emm's response. I thought she was joking, but her face said she was ingenuously serious.

"You're right. Let's go for it," I said. "As long as we grab it quick. We have to catch the next train if we're going to be back by 7 tonight. You said I'm getting a big surprise this evening and I don't want to miss it!"

The stand across the way advertised "*Gelato e Spumone*," so we paid our bill and I made a beeline across the street, trying not to get totally drenched in the process. But when I reached the stand, I realized Emm wasn't behind me. I looked back: there she was, singing and twirling in the rain, absolutely carefree and simply thrilled to be enjoying the day. Grinning, I gave her a minute to enjoy her revelry before reminding her that I needed her to order for us. I'd learned that lesson once already today.

We made it onto the train with about five minutes to spare. As we waited to get rolling, we attempted to dry off as best we could, while passing our ice cream back and forth between us. Apparently, Emm knew the Italian for "taster spoons," because she'd gotten us one little spoon each.

"Fun day?" she asked.

"Fun day, *buddy*," I replied with a huge smile spreading across my face. "But now I've got a question for you, something I've always wondered."

"Well, out with it," she replied impatiently, as if I'd been keeping some great big secret from her.

"Why do you always ask for a taster spoon?" I asked while struggling to get a decent-sized scoop onto my tiny piece of flatware.

"Because, TD, life is too short to waste it by taking it all in at once. I like to enjoy my life just like I like to enjoy my ice cream—in a savory fashion. My little taster spoon helps remind me to practice what I preach, because there's no hogging down my ice cream with a spoon this small. Both living life and eating ice cream one tiny scoop at a time."

"Wow. Poetic," I said sarcastically. But inwardly, these were the moments I loved most about our friendship. Only Emm could turn the simple act of eating ice cream into another of her philosophical bents. I turned and looked out the window, needing a moment to reflect on the brain-bomb she'd just dropped.

I gazed through the window for longer than I'd intended, mesmerized by the driving rain. It was so interesting to me that the day could turn from so beautiful outside one minute to so miserable the next.

After taking one more bite of our ice cream, I then turned back to my buddy to offer her the last of our frozen treat, but Emm was already out like a light. So, one tiny scoop at a time, I finished our dessert exactly as Emma Rey Finley would've wanted me to: In a *savory fashion*.

Chapter

The Girl in The Red Dress

eing the genius that I was, I hadn't been able to make heads or tails of the 24-hour format of European clocks. My phone was still on Pacific time so I could keep track of Lee's schedule, which probably only added to my confusion. Which is to say, I'd totally messed up the time in Santa Marinella—we'd caught the 5 p.m. train instead of the 6 p.m. train.

"You'll never be in danger of being mistaken for a Rhodes Scholar," Emm teased when I confessed my blunder as we were walking back to her apartment.

"Maybe, but at least I can stay conscious in a moving vehicle," I shot back. I'd meant it as a joke, but Emm didn't laugh.

Trying to lighten the tension, I devised what I thought was a brilliant scheme. "I was going to check in on Lee tomorrow, but let's FaceTime her now instead," I suggested glancing at my still-on-California-time phone. "It's 9 a.m. back home, she's probably up."

Emm unlocked the front door and started up the stairs. "Best idea you've had all day! I miss Lee so much—I'd love to talk to her."

We put our stuff down before I dialed my sister. Then I handed the phone to Emm. "Surprise her," I said. Her face lit up immediately.

"EMMA REY FINLEY!" Lee squealed with excitement. "What are you doing on TD's phone?" Lee wiped a drop of milk from her chin. I was glad to see she was eating a healthy breakfast, although I suspected she'd snuck an extra spoonful of sugar or two into her oatmeal.

"Hey, cutie!" Emm cried. "He's right here with me," she continued as I popped my head into the frame.

"Yeah, I was missing you, Little One," I said. "We've never had a whole ocean between us before." I paused as I realized that Lee looked like she was alone in the kitchen. "Where's Uncle Bill this morning?"

"In our garden," replied Lee. "I'm going outside to help him after breakfast. We have lots of new flowers to put in."

"Good. You're such a big help to him, sis." Gardening had always been my uncle's thing, but now that Lee was getting older, she was showing more and more interest in his hobby. Better still, gardening was something that he and Lee could almost always do together. Even when Lee was far from her best, helping Uncle Bill in his nursery was her one doctor-approved outdoor activity. "Garden time" was the one true connection they shared.

"How's your summer been?" asked Emm, changing the subject.

"Good, but I wish you were back home already, Emma. I have so much to tell you."

"Hey, and what am I, chopped liver?" I asked.

"I miss you lots, TD—I really do—but you've only been gone a couple of days when Emma's been gone for *months and months*." Lee emphasized the last few words so dramatically you'd think Emm had outright orphaned her.

"I know angel, but I promise I'll be back soon," Emm replied to my adorable sister.

Even from six thousand miles away, I could tell Lee wasn't having one of her best days. Her hair looked extremely thin and it seemed like it was starting to fall out in small patches—an all-too-common occurrence after her bone marrow transplant. Her eyes seemed torpid and gray.

"How've you been feeling since I left?" I asked.

"Good, I just really miss you guys. What have you been up too?" Lee answered quickly, dodging my question as if she were a seasoned adult who was adept at deflecting health-related questions.

Emm and I began telling my sister all about my trip so far. I'd only been in Italy for two days, yet Southern California seemed a lifetime away. Lee "oohed" and "ahhed" as she listened. She particularly enjoyed the part where we got caught in the rain earlier.

"Have you been writing in your journal, sweetie?" Emm asked.

"Of course! I'm writing a story right now. It should be done by the time you get back. And it's a good one too—probably my best ever!" Lee paused for a moment and I could tell she was cooking up something big. She placed the back of her palm on her forehead and heaved a dramatic sigh. "But I'm afraid I'm running out of inspiration. Day in day out, it's always the same," she continued, as if she were an artist suffering from the world's worst case of ennui. "The next time you guys go to Europe, can I come with you? It might help me find some more inspiration for my stories."

"We'll try, Little One, we'll try." After theatrics like that, I couldn't bring myself to say "no" outright; some things just wouldn't ever be possible for my little sister, international travel included. Which I hated—since I would've lassoed the moon and given it to her, if she'd asked.

Distracting Lee from the idea of world travel, Emm broke in, "I can't wait to read your story when I get home! What's it about?"

"You know I can't tell you that! It's like you always taught me—writers are supposed to write in silence."

Emm, clearly proud of her writing prodigy, asked, "And what else did I teach you about good writers?"

"Good writers make the expected come to life, but great writers bring life to the unexpected," Lee answered dutifully and with a gleam in her eye.

We chatted for a few more minutes. Lee promised to keep to her diet, get her full eight hours of sleep, ask Uncle Bill for help with her meds, and "all that annoying big brother stuff." Thankfully, Lee understood that all my "big brother stuff" was helping her to achieve her One Day, the day when she'd finally be strong and healthy. All my little sister wanted was to be a regular kid—how could I blame her for that?

"Okay Lee, I'll talk to you in a couple of days," I said, wrapping things up. Then Emm joined me and we said in unison, "We're so happy at you!" before clicking off the app.

The moment I hung up, I sighed heavily without realizing it.

"I know you worry TD," offered Emm, knowing immediately what was bothering me. "I've seen her looking better, but I think we really cheered her up."

"Yeah Emm, she was so happy to hear from you."

Emm jumped up from her chair, gave me a double thumbs-up and cried, "And now it's time for *me* to cheer *you* up. Go get ready. It's almost go time!" She topped it off with a shimmy and a half-twirl. A grin spread across my face: thanks to Emm's crazy, but nonetheless terrible, dance, I was suddenly eager for my surprise once again.

I jumped in the shower to get the saltwater off my skin, then headed into my borrowed bedroom to dig something out of my suitcase. While rummaging through my clothes for a moment, a question struck me.

"Hey, Emm!" I called from the doorway. "What should I wear for this surprise tonight?"

Emm poked her head out of the bathroom. With all seriousness she asked, "Did you bring your Batman costume by chance?"

I never knew what to expect from Emma Rey Finley—no adventure was ever completely off the table with her—and the look on my face must've reflected my two colliding thoughts: "Is she serious?" and "No, she can't be."

Emm let out a huge chortle. "I'm kidding stupid. Just wear something nice."

I tore back into my suitcase. What, exactly, did "something nice" mean? I still had no clue about where we were going. All I knew was that Rome would be our playground tonight. I thought maybe this might be a situation where it was better to overdress than underdress, so I pulled out my white button-down and black suit. I'd brought them along thinking I could mix and match the pieces in case "something nice" came up, but now I decided to wear them together. After all, "When in Rome…"

It was the only suit I owned, and I'd worn it to every formal event over the last two years. I'd had it custom-tailored over the winter—my arms had grown too long and my shoulders too broad—but now that the alterations were done, it fit even better than before. I couldn't lie, I looked damn good in it, but I also knew that no matter how well I cleaned up, I stood no chance of looking better than Emm.

Pulling my outfit together, I slipped on the all-gold Nixon watch my Uncle had given me for my high school graduation. Realizing I hadn't brought a tie, I undid the top two buttons of my shirt and called my look "Rome chic." Feeling confident and sharp, I stepped into the hallway and waited.

After a few minutes, I went into the living room and sat down for what must have been another fifteen minutes. Growing impatient, I got up and knocked on her door. "Emm, we're going to be late."

"I know, just one more minute...wait," she called through the door. So I sat down on the hallway floor, leaning on the wall opposite her room and did as I was told. I waited.

Time crawled. I mean, I did have an Emma Rey Finley surprise coming at me. My mind careened wildly as I considered the possibilities. With Emm leading the way, we could be headed to either a formal dinner, or an underground fight club. Both options seemed equally likely.

Just as I was about to get up and knock again, the door swung open. I shot up from the floor, utterly dumbstruck. Suddenly Emm was the gorgeous girl I'd met three years ago outside my dorm, except somehow now even more ravishing. My breath caught in my lungs as I took in her perfection.

Emm's scarlet dress hugged her taut, slim figure in all the right places. The fabric flowed over her, getting progressively less fitted as it cascaded downward. Three-inch tan heels completed her outfit.

Still without breath, the only thing I was able to drool out was, "Wow."

Emm blushed as if she hadn't been expecting to blow me away. Showing off her dress, she swirled around like a model, then blew me a kiss. I thought I was going to fall over when that air-smooch hit me, like in the old-fashioned cartoons.

"Come on let's go. You said it yourself, we're going to be late!" said Emm, grabbing my hand and pulling me toward the door.

Still unable to form coherent words, it was all I could do to keep my jaw from hanging open. But at least I finally knew where we were going tonight: the red dress had given it away.

Just like in *Me Before You*, we were headed to the symphony. Emm was in character as Louisa Clark, which made me a non-paraplegic Will Traynor. I knew Emm had never heard a live orchestra before, which made me all the more excited. Then I realized how much thought and effort Emm must've put into this evening and my stomach flipped in a weird sort of way.

I'd been to the orchestra a handful of times as a child. My mother had always wanted me to seriously pursue the violin, even though I didn't like it much—though I resisted my teachers and did just about everything I could *not* to learn. I had always liked going see these types of performances though, because I loved the unity and cohesiveness that went into a stellar ensemble. Much like a good basketball team, it took an unselfish mentality on the part of all the players to succeed and, in the end, it didn't matter who got the glory, as long as the performance evoked some sort of emotion out of the audience. What mattered was that the sum was always greater than its parts.

We walked outside, and I swear a cab pulled to the curb before Emm had even raised her hand to hail it. She looked so gorgeous she literally stopped traffic. I held the car door open for her and was very relieved when Emm gave the driver the address in Italian. Still flabbergasted, if I had had to speak just then—in any language—I don't know what would've fallen out of my mouth.

The venue was probably only three miles away, so the cab ride was short. As we rounded a corner, Emm pointed toward what looked like an old, converted church and said to the driver, "*Bene. Grazie signore.*"

Emm slid out of the car as the driver made change. He handed me back a few coins and in surprisingly perfect English said, "You're one lucky duck, kid." I held back a chuckle: I felt like the luckiest duck in the whole damn world.

Once inside, Emm's face lit up with telltale gluttonous delight as the woman in the lobby took our tickets and explained something in Italian. I'd never met anyone in my life who enjoyed free food more than Emma Rey Finley; I thought maybe there were appetizers inside for the patrons.

Emm turned to me and exclaimed, "She said there's free wine and pasta inside!" We didn't waste another second, stopping at the bar to grab our wine first, and I placed what I hoped was a reasonable gratuity into the tip bowl. We then found a small table that was just the right size for the two of us, and before I knew it, a waiter placed two heaping plates of steaming *spaghetti alla puttanesca* in front of us.

"This is exactly like the book, Emm. Except Louisa Clark couldn't hold a candle to you," I said after taking a sip of my velvety red wine. Something about its being free made the taste so much better.

Emm blushed. "I knew you'd love it."

"I hope these tickets weren't too expensive," I said, grinning back at her.

"You can just buy me dinner after this," she replied with a wink. I guess the free pasta wasn't enough to sate Emm's appetite for adventure.

"You've got yourself a deal." I extended my hand and we shook on it.

As if on cue, the same woman who welcomed us motioned it was time to take our seats. Then she turned to me and said something that, coupled with her odd gesticulations, looked like she was trying to explain that I couldn't bring my wine with me to our seats. I acknowledged her command, then chugged the rest of my wine on the spot. Emm burst out laughing although I didn't know why. Her laugh drew the audience's attention just as it was starting to get quiet for the beginning of the performance.

The woman then approached me and handed me my wallet. Confused, I looked back at Emm who explained, "She was trying to tell you that you left your wallet at the bar."

I turned just about as red as Emm's dress as I joined her in laughter. This only brought even more attention to us; no one else in the audience thought the misunderstanding was very funny.

Subduing our laughter to a quiet giggle, we took our seats as the conductor approached the stage. A moment later, the first bright notes of Vivaldi's *The Four Seasons* vibrated through the metallic gold cathedral.

We sat utterly transfixed as the musicians played, giving it their all. I loved watching each and every artist perform. Their focus and talent were obvious, even to someone like me who wasn't too familiar with classical concertos. The conductor, too, was a sight to see: commanding yet somehow gentle, he knew exactly when to slow his orchestra down and when to speed them back up. The resulting lulls and swells were so beautifully executed that they almost felt healing.

At one point, Emm was so moved she started crying a little. I couldn't blame her—she wasn't the only one in the audience who was emotional. I took her hand in mine and gave it a quick squeeze as I smiled at her. This smile felt different from all the other smiles I'd flashed at Emm, but I didn't quite know why.

Not wanting our night to end, we decided to walk home after the performance. Emm and I ended up taking the long way back—and by long way, I mean we walked and walked. We walked by the Spanish Steps and we walked by the luminously floodlit Colosseum, which appeared almost mirage-like from afar. Yet as much as I enjoyed seeing all of these historic sites, not a single one impressed me more than Emma Rey Finley in her scarlet dress. It was almost as if my lady in red, herself, was the famed monument I had traveled all this way to see.

Then, somewhere in the city of Rome, on a quiet little street, I said, "Thank you for tonight, Emm. It was amazing."

"It was my pleasure TD. But now it's your turn to return the favor." She pointed toward the corner, where a lit caffè glowed like a firefly during a Mississippi summer night.

"You and your cuisine," I laughed, "Come on, I owe you dinner, buddy."

Emm's eyes blossomed. "But this time, we'll order our dessert first, just like always."

Chapter 4

Secret Agents

*T*he following days blended together, flying by all too quickly. Soaring around Rome, we crossed site after site off our checklist. We visited everything from The Pantheon to Campo de' Fiori to Castel Sant'Angelo—all the while, lost in our own bubble-world. I was impressed by the way Emm rattled off facts and figures about every place we visited. She must've done a ton of research before I arrived. My mind was playing tricks on me, though, because every now and then, when Emm was just in the periphery of my vision, I'd see her in her red dress and smile for no reason.

I woke up to my phone vibrating beside me. I hated being jarred awake by that thing: no matter how many years had gone by since her transplant, my first thought always turned to Lee. But, thankfully, the buzz was just a text from Emm. "I'll be home from class in half an hour…be ready to go when I get back." As I pushed away my grogginess, I realized what Emm meant. We had just one full day left in Rome, which meant we only had one more site to visit: St. Peter's Basilica in Vatican City.

"Sounds good, buddy," I typed back, adding a yellow heart emoji at the end. With that, I peeled myself from the sheets and rolled out of bed.

We took the long route to the basilica so we could walk along the Tiber River for part of the way. "The locals call this 'The Blond,' because of the Tiber's yellowish color," Emm explained as we strolled along the promenade. "It's the third longest river in Italy, and I use it every day to navigate through the city," she continued. "If I ever get lost, I can pretty much follow it the other direction right home."

"Yeah, the river is sort of yellow, Emm, your favorite. No wonder you know so much about it."

"What can I say?" replied Emm. "I've learned so much about Rome since moving. But I'm really excited about taking you to St. Peter's. It's astonishing, TD. When I first arrived, my school set up a trip for study-abroad students as part of our orientation weekend. I can't wait for you to see it!"

Slightly disappointed to learn that today's adventure would be a return trip for Emm, I changed the subject. "Have you sent any of our pictures to Ken yet? I sent him a bunch yesterday afternoon, but he hasn't responded."

We really had been taking a lot of pictures, especially during our night at the orchestra. I knew I'd cherish these memories for the rest of my life, so like a selfie queen at prom, I'd been snapping away.

"No, not yet," answered Emm. "I've been really bad about sending pics in general. If I sent pictures to all my friends, the data charges would probably equal my grocery budget for the week."

I couldn't help but laugh, considering how much food Emma Rey Finley could pack away on any given day—although I did have the good sense not to say as much out loud.

"I shoot Ken a quick text now and again, though," she continued. "It usually takes him a day or two to respond, but eventually he always does."

"That's a pretty good turn-around time for Ken," I said. "You know he's a total jackass when it comes to things like that."

"No, he's just a jackass in general." Emm nudged me in the ribs and looked up at me with a grin.

With Ken being practically my brother, it meant a lot to me that he and Emm had such a strong relationship. There'd been many an afternoon with just the three of us hanging out on campus, and sometimes Ken would come with us to visit Lee, too. We were sort of like one little happy family. A sarcastic-as-all-hell family, but a happy family, nonetheless.

"Let's give him a call when we get home tonight," Emm suggested. "It would be good to catch up with him before we leave Rome." She paused and added sarcastically, "There's been a palpable absence of mocking in my life."

Tomorrow we'd be up at the crack of dawn and off to Florence to see Sal, another member of my somewhat-complicated family. I'd never understood how, exactly, Uncle Bill and Sal had met, but Sal was always around once Lee and I had moved in with my uncle. A part of me always saw my mother's personality in him though, which was great for Lee. When Sal was around it brought me back to some warm memories of my mother's sweetness. Thanks to Sal's influence, I'd always felt I had a little Italian in me. For a little while, I think Sal was even living with us as Uncle Bill made the too-sudden transition from "single guy" to "dad," although my memory was a little murky on that point.

I hadn't seen Sal in years—he'd moved back to Italy just before Lee's transplant—but he and I had kept in touch over the years. I had too little family as it was, so I didn't want to cross the Atlantic without our at least touching base. Fortunately, Florence was on the list of cities Emm wanted to visit, so we decided we'd do a week in Rome, one day in Florence, then two days in the south of France as sort of a crown to the whole trip.

"Sounds perfect, Emm," I replied wistfully. Why I sounded wistful I wasn't sure. I thought maybe I was getting homesick, but that couldn't be it. "Home," I thought, was wherever Emma Rey Finley was. So, in a sense, I had never felt closer to home in my whole life.

St. Peter's Basilica loomed above us. The dome was visible from pretty much anywhere in Rome—but now, as I stood in front of it, I realized just how truly massive the structure was. I felt short for the first time in my entire existence.

"It took well over a hundred years to build this, TD, and today St. Peter's is almost four hundred years old," tour-guide Emm began. "It's like 450-feet tall and over 700-feet long. Michelangelo, Fontana and a whole bunch of other famous Renaissance architects worked on it."

"Thank you, Wikipedia," I replied, only half listening. I was too transfixed by the Basilica's beauty to focus on facts.

"It's absolutely breathtaking, I know," she said as we approached what looked to be the line to get in.

"It's like you're looking right into the past...although at the same time, it looks beautifully preserved," I said as we tacked ourselves to the end of the long line of anxiously-waiting tourists.

Emm rattled off a few more facts about St. Peter's and the Catholic Church, but I couldn't tear my eyes from the building itself. At least not until I heard someone ahead of us say in English, "Is the wait really two and a half hours?"

Emm and I looked at each other with one thought between us: "TWO AND A HALF HOURS?"

"That wait is insane," I grumbled. "They've had four hundred years to figure out crowd control, what gives?"

"I don't know. The last time I was here, our group was brought right in. We didn't have to wait at all...and there's no way we're waiting today either." A gleam sparked in Emm's eye as she added the last few words.

"It's fine, Emm. We can just wait."

"Nope. This is your last day in Rome. I'm not letting you waste it in this line." The gleam in Emm's eye morphed into full-on mischievousness. "Come on, I've got a better idea. Follow me."

I didn't like the sound of this, but experience had taught me it was better not to resist. If Emm was determined to turn the day into a true adventure, I'd best just hop on for the ride. Hell, a part of me *wanted* to hop on for the ride. I mean, this was the same Emma Rey Finley who'd talked her parents into giving her a couple hundred dollars for a "science project" in the eleventh grade, only to then use it to buy a kickass Superman costume so she could wear it while skydiving. Her life was just one extravagant adventure.

"Okay, Emm, I'm right behind you," I said as I jumped out of line.

"Good, that's the idea. Follow me, but stay, like, ten feet behind."

Bewildered but complicit, I watched as Emm, stopping to snap a pic here or there, began meandering around the piazza like many of the other tourists. Yet, unlike the other tourists, she didn't stop to focus the camera or jump into the frame. I continued to sort of half-watch, half-follow her as I tried to figure out what my buddy's brilliant mind was up to.

A few minutes later, Emm disappeared around a corner and into an alley. I had no choice but to follow.

"What are we doing?" I whispered when I'd finally caught up to her.

"What does it look like? We're breaking in…*duh!* I'm almost sure there's a service entrance back here. I remember seeing some staff leave the building this way," she said, looking at me as if I was the crazy one. "Now be quiet."

Every single bone in my body was telling me to turn around and get back in line, but for some reason, I couldn't. Maybe it was because I was afraid of leaving Emm behind, or maybe it was because I trusted her way too much. But one thing was certain: I was having the time of my life. After all, when I'd woken up this morning, I hadn't known I would be an international criminal by lunch time.

We slid along the alley and came to a stop behind a half-wall that jutted out from the building. "Okay...I think we need to sneak over to that next alley," said Emm in a voice so quiet I could barely hear her. "But we'll be out in the open so we have to be quick—like secret agent quick. I'll go first."

"Okay. Got it," I whispered back.

I watched as Emma Rey Finley bolted across the cobblestones on her tip-toes, almost as if she were surrounded by land mines. She made it across the twenty-foot gap without incident and in a stunning fashion.

I drew a deep breath before I took off. Nervous as hell, I did my best to retrace her steps but I was unsure about this entire plan until I looked up and saw Emm's face. Never in my life had I seen anyone trying to contain so much joy, like she was having the most marvelous time ever. Almost as if she were finally living her childhood dream of breaking into the Vatican.

Reunited at last, we pushed through the next long alley, which brought us to a back entrance. Unfortunately, the door was under watch by two Swiss Guards.

"Great. This has been fun, but it's time to turn back now," I whispered, but this time Emm didn't say anything back. She just stared at the guards as if she was plotting something big.

In the next moment, Emm said something I'll never forget: "TD, I think our only option is a full kamikaze assault."

"What?" I asked, probably a bit too loudly. "What the hell does that mean?"

Obviously giddy about her "kamikaze assault," and clearly not concerned with my question, Emm instructed, "Wait a second or two after I go and then run like Forrest Gump...the coast should be clear for ya."

I nodded my head even though I hadn't the slightest clue what she meant or what she planned on doing. But I was in too deep now to back out and if Emm did get caught, there was no way I was leaving her to face Vatican law on her own.

In the blink of an eye, Emm was rushing the guards, yelling and screaming wildly as she raced past them. The two startled guards immediately left their post and gave chase.

Over her shoulder, she yelled, "Go, Go, GO!"

Panicking, I couldn't move for a split second. But then I ran, sprinting harder and faster than I ever had. Somehow, I slid right inside the doorway and found myself standing beside a group of tourists.

By some divine miracle Emm's plan had worked, so I did my best to blend into the crowd while catching my breath and keeping one eye on the door. Two or three minutes passed: where was Emm?

I waited for maybe another five minutes as I took in the beauty of the church and tried not to worry. Then suddenly, Emm strolled in from another entrance. Casually. Not even running or anything, like she *was* a goddamn superhero.

"See, no big thing," she said as she approached me. Flabbergasted, I didn't know what to say back—so, for once, I just kept my mouth shut. I don't think words could've captured my astonishment anyway.

We crashed a guided tour group and I began to relax as the beauty of the interior washed over me. St. Peter's was stunning; every inch seemed crammed with ornate paintings, beautiful statues, gorgeous frescos and brilliant colors. Every piece of art seemed perfectly placed and even more perfectly curated.

Once I thought the coast was clear, I said, "You've completely lost your mind."

"Please, I've done much worse," Emm laughed.

We continued following our adopted group and doing our best to blend in. We succeeded for a while but then Emm, looking past my shoulder, gasped, "Oh no, there they are!" I started to turn but she quickly grabbed me by my shoulders and held me in place. "Don't look now, TD! Have I taught you nothing?"

My eyes scanned the room for a hiding spot, but I couldn't find one. Emm was trying to play it cool, but I could tell she was starting to panic. She whirled around, surveying the room: there was really nowhere for us to hide.

"We're done for, Emm, unless you have an invisibility cloak so we can hide in plain sight."

"That's it!" cried Emm before quickly adding, "Sorry, TD." I thought she meant she was about to wave the white flag in surrender, but instead she hopped up and pulled me down toward her.

In the next instant, the brilliant colors of the Basilica faded to black and white. Our bubble-world shrunk in around us, closing off the whole of creation and forming a universe in which only she and I existed. Emm pressed her soft lips against mine as the heat of her body melted into me. Her lips tasted like cherries, like heaven and home and happiness incarnate. My mind raced and stood still at the same time: for three years, this is what I'd been longing for, although I'd never once realized it.

Emm pushed me away gently. In a soft but forgiving voice, she said, "TD...I think they're gone."

Embarrassed, I pulled away quickly as Emm slid her hand from the back of my neck. Completely lost in the moment, I'd held our kiss for maybe fifteen seconds—far longer, I now realized, than Emm had ever intended.

"Sorry, I...I just didn't want you to get thrown into the dungeon," I managed to sputter out. I could feel my cheeks turning crimson.

Laughing softly, Emm brought her finger to her mouth, then traced her lips. "Don't worry, *buddy*, you were the perfect distraction."

We decided hightailing it out of Vatican City was probably the best course of action, so we skipped St. Peter's Square altogether and hopped in a cab instead. Although our trip to the Basilica had been cut short, neither of us seemed to mind. The Trevi Fountain was the first item on our "auxiliary" bucket list, so Emm suggested we go there. I more or less would've followed her to the ends of the Earth at that point, so, of course, I agreed.

The Trevi Fountain was unlike anything I'd ever seen. All sorts of scenes were carved in marble, making the fountain itself look both alive yet trapped in time. I thought the fountain had to be at least a hundred-feet tall, but Emm said I'd overestimated by about fifteen-feet. Water poured serenely out of the statutes into the large pool below, almost like a cascading waterfall. Surely no fountain in the world could rival it, yet I found myself thinking it would be truly perfect if the statues of Health and Abundance were replaced with Emm's likeness.

We found a bench and took a seat so we could watch the piazza abuzz with activity; watching couples, friends and groups, Emm and I relaxed as they took the time to enjoy the amazing city that surrounded us all. Tourists threw coins into the fountain as they silently wished for their innermost dreams to come true.

I didn't feel like talking much, although Emm was still on a high from her kamikaze assault. "You should've seen the guards' faces as I rushed them. They didn't know what to make of me!" But after a few minutes, she, too, quieted down and we simply sat enjoying the afternoon. Together.

For all her antics, Emm knew how to stop and smell the roses, too. She appreciated all she had worked for, and I always respected her for that. While other people's lives were flying by, Emm took the time to soak it all in. We'd had tons of quiet moments together over the years, although—in this moment—I don't think we were sharing the same thought. My mind was still transfixed on her cherry-tasting lips.

"Let's take a picture," Emm finally said. "We didn't take any at the Vatican—not really. Not of the two of us." Emm pulled out her phone to take a selfie, but I stopped her.

"No, let's take a real pic this time," I suggested. "We have tons of selfies."

"But, who will—"

I cut her off as I added, "And I want to remember today," which was the God's-honest truth, even if Emm didn't know what, exactly, I wanted to remember.

I turned to a man who had sat down next to us. He looked like an American somehow, so I politely asked if he would take our picture.

"Of course," he replied as I handed him my phone. Emm and I posed in front of the fountain with our arms locked around each other. The man snapped three or four pictures.

"You two make a cute couple. Enjoy the rest of your honeymoon," he said, handing the phone back to me.

Emm giggled. "Thank you. But we're really just old friends."

The man looked directly at me, as if a light bulb had gone off in his head and said, "Well then, to friendship." With that, he tipped his hat and disappeared into the crowd.

"That was strange," said Emm quizzically. She raised her arm as if she had a glass of wine in her hand and toasted, "To friendship."

My own light bulb suddenly lit up: the man who'd taken our photo was my seatmate from the plane. But rather than trying to explain who he was to Emm I just responded, with "Strange, indeed." I wondered if that man knew something I didn't.

"He thought we were married, TD. Like *married*. With a big poofy white dress for me, and you in tux and tails. Like down the aisle and everything." Emm started laughing so hard I couldn't help but join her.

"Well, I suppose it's an easy mistake to make," I began, seeing the opportunity to test the waters. "We do everything together, Emm. Always have. And here we are just the two of us in Rome, which I guess is a kinda romantic city."

"Yeah, but *we're* not romantic, TD," Emm replied. "You've had your flings and I've had mine, and they've never once got in the way of *our* thing."

"But nothing serious, Emm, not for either of us. Whatever cool or fun thing I want to do, at the end of the day, I would always rather do it with you."

"And that's what makes us buddies!" Emm replied brightly. "When it comes down to it, I'd rather go on an adventure with you, too."

That's when I knew it was too soon to talk about the kiss. I backed off. We still had three days together and two more cities to see—I didn't want to blow it now.

Emm fished around in her pocket, pulled out a twenty-cent Euro and handed it to me. "Make a wish, TD. Legend says if you throw a coin into the Trevi Fountain, you'll return to Rome someday." That didn't sound all that bad to me, as long as I could return with Emm.

Taking the coin from her, I turned my back to the fountain and closed my eyes. I listened to the plop-splashes of other coins hitting the water as I dug deep into myself, searching for what I wanted most. As I stood there with Emm inches away from me, the only thing that my mind could focus on was our kiss. Our personal bubble-world. The gentle touch of her lips against mine. The warmth of Emma Rey Finley against my chest.

In that moment, I could've wished to play in the NBA; I could've wished for my mother back; I could've wished for a cure for sickle cell anemia; I could've wished for a blazing red Ferrari, or for world peace. Yet, Emma Rey Finley was all I wanted. She was my shooting star.

I flipped the coin over my shoulder and into the water behind me, wishing that Emm and I could run away together, leaving everyone else except Lee behind and forming our own real happy family. I opened my eyes to the sight of Emm delightedly clapping her hands together and smiling ear to ear. Then she looked into my eyes so intensely that I felt like she could read my mind, but I didn't care—I wanted her to know what I'd wished for.

Just as quickly, Emm's expression changed back to normal. "*Bene*, TD, *bene*. Now Rome is in your soul," she applauded, but she was wrong. To me, Emm *was* Rome; she'd been in my soul since the moment we met. And now, I thought, she was even more deeply a part of me.

I wasn't about to let myself blush again, so I began fumbling in my pocket as I said, "It's your turn, you need to make a wish too."

After searching through every pocket, I came up empty. "I'm sorry, Emm, but I don't have any change."

Emm took a small step closer to me. "It's okay," she began, then paused before continuing in one quick breath, "I don't need a coin...or a wish. You're already here."

Chapter 5

The Slow Train

We were up with the sun the next morning, scrambling around like crazy, preparing for our next two adventures. We would spend the day in Florence, then jump back on the train to Rome and catch a late flight to Marseille, France.

The night before, just after dinner, Emm had pulled out her roommate's tablet and researched train tickets online. We really shouldn't have left this to the last minute, but hey, secret agents aren't generally concerned with blasé details.

"Okay, I have some good news…and some bad news," said Emm, giving me her best puppy dog eyes and knowing I wouldn't be able to resist.

"I'm listening…" I said cautiously while crossing my arms and preparing for the worst.

"So, there are two options for tomorrow's train," she began. Emm had already taken her contacts out for the night so she was wearing her deep red tortoise shell glasses, which made her pleading eyes that much more irresistible. She also had her hair tied-up in a bun that sat smack on the top of her head, and her pajamas—shorts with a spaghetti-strap tank top—made her look especially cute. I caught myself admiring every inch of her as she finished what she was saying.

"Option one will only take us an hour and a half to get to Florence, but it will cost ninety Euros each. Option two will take us four hours to get there, but it's only twenty-five Euros each. Both trains arrive at 11:00 a.m."

Without saying anything aloud, I mouthed, *"Four hours!"* As soon as my vocal cords got over the shock, I said, "No way, Emm. That's a huge difference. A total-insanity difference."

"Listen, I took a bunch of shifts off from my work-study job for your visit. I'd rather put what money I *do* have where it counts, into *quality time*. With the money we save, we can have a ball in Florence!" Emm had said "quality time" like she was on the Hallmark Channel or something.

"Come on, you're not that broke," I countered. "It's not like you're in danger of eating cockroaches and salt after I leave."

"Eww!" she squealed, scrunching up her nose and trying to keep a straight face. "Come on, TD. Plus, we can just sleep on the train."

"Well maybe you can snooze away, but I'm six-six—not exactly travel size."

"But sixty-five Euros each is huge. Pretty pleeeease?" she pleaded. She looked so pitiful, so eager, that I was defenseless. Emm had always known how to work me, but now she was laying it on especially thick. Or maybe it just felt that way because I was thinking way more about holding her in my arms than about some stupid train.

"Okay…but you're making breakfast before we leave. I'm not starting a four-hour train ride on an empty stomach."

"Deal," Emm declared, holding her hand out so we could shake on it. Her perfectly soft, perfectly formed, perfectly petite hand.

We had to drop our luggage in a locker before we headed to Florence, as we wouldn't be returning to the apartment. Luckily for us, Rome's airport and train station were connected—we had our bags stashed in no time.

"Locker L-11, TD," reported Emm. "Try to remember, because I'm sure I'll forget. The passcode is my birthday."

"Emm, I keep telling you, put things like that in your notes app so you don't have to worry." Despite speaking three or four languages, and even though she had whizzed through both calculus and anatomy during our first year of college, Emm always had a hard time remembering anything with a letter-number combo. The previous year, I'd left my car for her in parking spot WC330: she'd walked the five miles back to campus.

Once we were on the <u>slow</u> train, Sleeping Beauty did her thing as soon we got moving, except this time she wasn't so beautiful as she slept. With her mouth open and her arms sprawled out, Emm looked like a limp zombie. A drooling, limp zombie. Yet somehow, she was still captivating. What in God's name was happening to me?

I couldn't help myself. I pulled out my phone and took about a hundred pictures of her. I even asked a stranger in my very best Italian—*Per favore, signore, una foto?*—to take a picture of the two of us. The man shook his head in disbelief, but he snapped the photo as I put my arm delicately around Emm. I didn't blame him for giving me a weird look—we must've seemed pretty ridiculous, especially for this early in the morning.

After the novelty of my photo shoot with zombie-Emm had worn off, I sat back and tried to get some sleep. Which was futile. As soon as I closed my eyes, I was thinking about our universe—our kiss: Would we just continue to act like it never happened? Was it my job as the guy to bring something like that up? What would I even say? Hell, what would *she* say?

More importantly, was I really in love with my best friend on Earth or was I simply swept up by Rome's charm? Having hidden a secret this big from myself for three years seemed impossible, but then again, I'd heard of stranger things.

I had hundreds of questions but zero answers. I wasn't even one hundred percent sure I wanted any answers. So far, nothing between us—despite my swirling insides—had really changed, and everything about this trip had been so amazing. We only had a few more days left—why would I want to mess things up? These ten days were a once-in-a-lifetime experience. Did I want to potentially sully these memories? Was it right or fair to either of us to threaten all we had when I had no real idea of what was going on with me?

No. I decided right then and there I would keep my mouth shut. No matter how much I wanted to be with Emm, the risk wasn't worth losing my buddy. Not now, maybe not ever.

I gave up on the whole sleeping thing and checked the time. It was just after 11 p.m. in California, so there was a good chance Ken hadn't gone to bed yet. We hadn't called him the previous night. I'd meant to, but the kiss—coupled with the whole slow-train debacle—had caused the idea to fly right out of my head. I knew Emm was looking forward to speaking with Ken, but she'd have to do that on her own time. Right now, I wanted to talk to my best guy friend. Alone.

I fished around in my backpack until I found my headphones so I wouldn't be that asshole on the train who was broadcasting his life to the entire car. I sent Ken a FaceTime request, doubting he would actually answer his phone. But, surprisingly, he picked up on the third ring.

Ken's always-positive, shining face popped up on my screen. "Hey man, how's the honeymoon?" he asked, which was Ken's idea of a friendly greeting.

"I haven't talked to you in a week, bro, and that's the first thing you ask? Like, even before 'hello'?"

"Alright, alright…So, what's up, my man!" he yelled. He sounded a bit slurry, like he'd been out partying.

"How ya doin', Ken? I miss you, man."

"I miss you too! Some of the guys on the team are starting to come back to campus, they were asking about you." He paused before asking, "Hey, where's Emma?"

"We're on the train to Florence right now…so, you know, she's catching some z's, as usual."

"Better not disturb her then. You know what she's like if you wake her up too suddenly."

Ken had a point. Two years ago, when the three of us were driving to Pismo Beach for the weekend, I'd stopped short at fifty miles an hour to avoid a coyote that had jumped out onto the road. Emm, in the backseat, woke up and screamed, "We're gonna die! I knew I shouldn't have let you drive!" as if we really were in a life-or-death situation. Then she was this weird combination of angry and scared until we reached our next rest stop.

"Yeah, good point," I conceded. "But I'm wide-awake and bored as hell and didn't get a chance to call you from Rome."

"Well you've got me now, so let loose. What's up?"

I recapped my trip. And then I told him about the kiss.

"YOU DID WHAT?!" Ken yelled. From the look on his face, I think I completely killed his buzz.

"Relax man, it was just to make sure the guards didn't see her—no big deal," I explained again, trying to downplay everything.

"NO BIG DEAL?!" he yelled even more loudly. "Come on, TD, I don't buy that for a second." And he wasn't wrong to think that, because I didn't believe it either.

"Yeah, bro. It was pretty crazy." I said, trying to laugh it off. But then I added more somberly, "At least I don't want it to be a big deal. I mean…I don't *think* I want it to be a big deal."

A part of me wanted to tell Ken about every confusing, crazy, yet somehow perfect feeling I'd had since Emm had pressed her lips against mine, but I was too scared. Almost as if the minute I admitted those feelings out loud, there'd be no going back.

"I knew this wasn't just a 'friends' trip. I knew it! She put the moo-ooh-ooves on you." Ken made a smoochy face and kissing noises, then added, "Congrats, bro."

This wasn't helping at all, yet talking with Ken was exactly what I needed. He was such a pain in the ass that way. A pain in the ass in a way that only a true brother could be.

"Enough of that from you," I said. "Time to rein it in, bro."

"Okay, okay, I'll cool it…but tell me one thing first." Ken's tone was serious now, he wasn't joking around anymore. "Did she kiss you before or after you gave her that kickass birthday present?"

One of the many things Emm and I had talked about before she left for Rome was her fear that her friends would move on or forget about her. I thought she was crazy, but six months *was* kind of a long time, especially in college-time. So, for her birthday—which was actually coming up next week—I bought a small notebook, tracked down some of her closest friends, and had each of them write Emm a note. Everyone had so much to say that the entire notebook filled up—all one hundred and fifty pages—essentially becoming a massive birthday card.

"Nah, I haven't given it to her yet. We've been running around since I got here. There hasn't been a good moment."

"Well, that's something you gotta consider, TD. Cuz that notebook would do it for just about any chick on the planet, ya know? If she 'accidently' kisses you again after you've given it to her, I think you'll know for sure where she stands."

For being a bit of a moron, Ken did have a point. I didn't reply, but instead sighed heavily.

Knowing when to stop, Ken changed the subject. "So, how's Lee? When was the last time you spoke to her?"

"I text her like five times a day, of course, but we haven't FaceTimed since Saturday. She keeps telling me she's fine—and Uncle Bill says she's doing pretty much okay—but she looked exhausted."

"Maybe I'll run by there tomorrow, check up on her," Ken began. "I could bring her some food, or maybe one of those strawberry-vanilla milkshakes she likes."

Ken was practically reading my mind. "Man, you really don't have to do that," I replied, although I didn't know why I'd bothered to lie. I really wanted someone to check up on my sister—and I didn't want just anyone checking in—I wanted Ken. Good or bad, I knew he'd give it to me straight. Plus, Lee was always glad to see him. Ken was pretty much always around my house when we were in high school, and anytime Lee had been in the hospital, Ken had always made it a point to go see her.

"Are you kidding? You're not the only one who misses her," he answered.

And that's why I considered Ken family. Again, I didn't say anything back, but he knew how grateful I was.

Ken changed the subject again. "Oh, I almost forgot to tell you," he said enthusiastically. "It does look like I'm gonna enlist full time after we graduate. I finally talked to my parents about it and they're stoked!" Excitement was written all over his face—he'd been thinking about joining up since we were kids.

Mr. Zom had been in the U.S. Army for almost twenty-five years, but he was just one in a long line of proudly-serving family members. The Zoms could trace their military lineage all the way back to 1850, when California first became a state. Most of Ken's uncles and great-uncles were in the services too, as was his aunt. It was almost a given that Ken would enlist at some point, but Mrs. Zom had insisted he go to college first. The athletic scholarship he'd received sealed the deal, but now that we were about to be seniors, the question of whether Ken wanted to go into the Army Reserves or enlist full time had been weighing on him.

"Congratulations, my man! I'm so happy for you," I said, trying to act surprised.

"Thanks, bro, now all I gotta do is convince you to join me," he joked.

"Yeah. Good luck with that." Ken knew full well I'd never leave Lee. In fact, this trip was the longest I'd ever gone without seeing her.

I started to hear female chatter in the background. Flirting was Ken's true calling in life, so I wasn't shocked when his next words were, "Listen, I have to run. Duty calls. But I'll see you when you get back! Enjoy Rome."

"Florence, stupid. We just left Rome."

"Whatever man, I'll text you after I catch up with Lee. Have fun and keep fighting the good fight." Ken signed off with a hard salute: I burst out laughing.

Our *slow train* had been stopping almost every ten minutes—at every damn station, no matter how small. Each halt had brought with it an abrupt jolt, so I always shot a glance at Emm to see if the jostling had woken her up. Every time, she was still sound asleep, which is why I'd been able to talk to Ken so freely. Although now, with another hour and a half left, and little hope of finding a comfortable sleeping position, I was deeply regretting this painfully slow arrangement. Not even my scented neck pillow was helping.

Still wide awake, I thought I'd try to knock back another chapter or two of *Me Before You*, but as I was reaching into my backpack, I felt Emm's birthday notebook and decided to give it one more look. Back home, whenever I found myself missing Emm or wanting a good laugh, I would pull out her birthday present and read a message or two.

The pages were filled with different color inks and different types of handwriting—hearts, exclamation marks, smiley faces, and even a few doodles accented the pages. After mine, Ken's entry was the first in the notebook:

Hey Emm,

I hope you're slaying it out there in Rome. But don't go too wild... think of poor Mrs. Finley, you know how your M ♡ M worries! And I'll look after TD while you're away——I'll take him on long, romantic walks for you, and I'll even bring him out for ice cream, too.

But FOR REAL, ~~Happy birthday~~ girl, you are such an amazing human and I don't know what I or my idiot best friend would do without ya.

I'm still waiting on my invitation to your wedding so when you get back hurry up and propose, to TD already because you and I both know that you're the one who wears the pants in this relationship.

Love Ya,
Ken Z

P.S. Don't tell Lee, but I call dibs on being your flower girl!

Emm was right, Ken was a jackass.

I read through the entries for another ten minutes or so until I finally started to feel my eyelids getting heavy. I shoved the notebook deep into my backpack and let sleep wash over me.

I woke up to Emm's voice. "*Mille grazie, signore.*" I rubbed my eyes and as they refocused, I saw that she was talking to one of the train's attendants; he was handing her phone back to her.

"See, TD, you said you'd never sleep on the train. But I got you this time. I'm not the only one who fell asleep… look!" Emm held her phone up as she spoke, which displayed an image of me off in dreamland—all cramped up with my knees practically touching my chin—but asleep nonetheless. I pretended to focus on the picture, but as Emm leaned toward me, the smell of her hair—something invigorating and fresh, cinnamon maybe—was too distracting.

Rather than bursting her bubble and explaining that I'd pulled the exact same stunt earlier, I sat up and said, "You're right. I just couldn't help it." I would save my pictures of zombie-Emm for another time.

"Come on, TD, we're finally here, so let's go!" Emm said with adventure lighting up her face. "I'm looking forward to meeting Sal, and we don't want to keep him waiting!"

Chapter 6

The Smiley Italian

"*Ciao caro TD! Benvenuto!*" Sal greeted us excitedly as he sprang up from his chair. The hole-in-the-wall restaurant he'd chosen for us was only a fifteen-minute walk from the train station; he'd texted us directions, and now we were about to have an early lunch. The idea of having lunch at 11:30 a.m. didn't bother me at all because I was now ravenous. Emm had fallen a bit short on her promise to make breakfast this morning. In my opinion, coffee, juice and some kind of Pop-Tarts-like, prepackaged pastry things really didn't constitute the most important meal of the day.

"Good to see you, Sal!" I replied warmly as I held my hand out to shake his. But instead, Sal grabbed my open palm and pulled me toward him, then kissed me on each cheek. It felt a bit over the top for a guy-to-guy greeting, but hey, Sal was family.

"And this is Emma…Emma Rey Finley. The friend I've been telling you about." Sal, without missing a beat, pulled

Emm in for the same warm greeting. I loved that.

"Sit, sit, both of you, sit! Make yourselves at home," Sal said in his heavy Italian accent, as he pulled Emm's chair out for her. He was acting more like we were in his dining room than in a restaurant, but that was okay by me. Judging from the smile on Emm's face, it was okay by her, too.

"You made time on your trip to visit an old man like me, yes? *Grazie*," he said as we were seated.

"Of course, Sal," Emm chimed in. "It was one of the first things TD mentioned when we started planning his trip." Emm was stretching the truth a little bit, but the fib was charitable. I shot a quick, sly smile of appreciation toward her.

"Yeah, it's been much too long," I said truthfully. I'd missed Sal's warmth and energy far more than I'd realized. "I haven't seen you since high school, but now I'm going to graduate college this year."

"*Bene*, TD, *bene*. Education is *importante…molto importante*," he said encouragingly. Then came a stream of words that I didn't understand at all, followed by Emm's laugh, which—if nothing else—was a language I was a bit more familiar with.

"*L'italiano di TD è terribile*," offered Emm. "He's pretty much lost after 'hello,' 'goodbye,' or 'Where's the restroom?'"

Sal's well-groomed handlebar mustache shook up and down as he laughed. "Okay, okay, I forgot. Only English for TD."

"Hey," I began defensively, feeling a bit embarrassed, "I speak Italian food! I've gotten good at that."

"Ah, yes, the food. I've ordered us some wine and a few starters," said Sal. "You're my guests today. Lunch is on me."

"That's very generous of you," I replied. Our waitress approached the table with a bottle of wine. As she poured, she and Sal started chatting in Italian, almost like old friends.

Emm took the opportunity to whisper, "I think I like him. He's so smiley."

"Smiley, Emm? What's that m—"

Just then Sal broke in. "Pardon the interruption. I've been coming here for years. The waitress and I are friends."

At the word *friends*, Emm picked up her newly poured glass of wine. "A toast to friends!" she said, then turned to me and added, "And to *kamikaze* friends!"

"To kamikaze friends!" I repeated as the three of us clinked glasses. Little did I know that this would be my last sober moment in the capital city of Tuscany.

"TD, what's 'kamikaze friends?' I don't know that expression," asked Sal, genuinely perplexed.

"Don't worry, Sal. It's something between me and Emm."

"Yeah, TD and I have been 'kamikaze friends' since yesterday," Emm explained. From there, the two of us told Sal about our harrowing adventure at the Vatican. I left out the part about Emm's cherry-tasting lips.

Sal looked at us with shock the whole time, obviously stunned by how much we'd enjoyed tempting fate. But nonetheless we made him laugh. Which made Emm and me laugh. Which made us all laugh that much harder, until the three of us were practically making a scene in the restaurant. I hadn't realized how much I'd missed laughing with Sal; he could bring happiness and vigor into just about any situation.

Just as we were catching our breath, our waitress showed up with a spread that looked more like a meal for a family of eight rather than "wine and a few starters." The huge platter of food included stuffed zucchini, squash, and roasted red peppers. The seafood pasta was bursting with clams and lobster. On the side, the fried calamari was surrounded by bread and cheese. Just in case we were still hungry after all that, there was a small margharita pizza, too. Thankfully, I could tell that Emm was at least as hungry as I was. And—as I'd just remembered—Sal, for being such a short, slight man, could pack away almost as much food as a man twice his size.

With the red wine beginning to relax us, we dove into the food, eating like it was our first meal in weeks. I thought about my coach—he'd kill me if he knew how far afield I'd gone from my off-season diet this past week. But who cared? This was Italy: the whole country was one delicious peninsula.

We chatted and laughed and joked throughout lunch. Sal was happy and healthy. When he'd moved back to Florence, he'd started his own business and had been pretty much working around the clock for the last four and a half years. His company had become successful so quickly that he was now in the process of selling it for an astounding profit. He'd soon be able to retire at only fifty-nine years old, although he planned to consult every now and again. This, according to Sal, was *la dolce vita*—the sweet life he'd been striving for.

With Sal being such a gracious host, I'd been completely oblivious to his ordering two more bottles of wine as we ate. It wasn't until he called the waitress over to order three shots of sambuca ("A *digestivo*, TD, to keep the stomach happy") that I realized Emm and I were both incredibly drunk. Almost frat-party-level drunk.

"Tomorrow I'll take you to see Brunelleschi's Dome atop our great cathedral," said Sal, eagerly, as he paid the bill. "It's the crown of our beautiful city!"

Emm and I looked at each other quizzically. I thought I had told him we were only going to be in town for one day, but maybe I hadn't explained it well. Texting wasn't always an ideal way to communicate, and this was especially true with Sal.

"Sal…" started Emm gently, "that's kind of you, but we're flying to Marseille late tonight. Didn't we tell you?"

"Yeah," I jumped in, "I only came to Florence to see you." Like Emm had done earlier, I was stretching the truth a bit—but not by much. And, if it was at all possible, I would've stayed with Sal for another week.

Sal's radiant smile dropped from his face for an instant, and even though I was unreasonably drunk, I could tell he was disappointed. But before I could offer anything further, Sal's face lit up again.

"Then you will be my guests for dinner too, yes? I'll bring my Maggie, and we'll feast twice in one day!" Sal made his invitation with so much zest and sincerity I couldn't stop myself from chuckling.

"Of course, Sal, we'd love to. Thank you," Emm accepted. She flashed him her very best smile. "We're broke college kids. We'll eat pretty much whatever you give us," she added with a wink. A wink that made Sal—and me—melt.

Emm and I had purposefully left our day in Florence unstructured. Our "plan" was to wander the city and let adventure find us, which was never a problem when Emma Rey Finley was involved. Florence had been the focal point of the Italian Renaissance—so if we couldn't find something fun to do here, we didn't deserve to call ourselves secret agents. Neither of us knew the city at all, and that added a touch of risk to our visit: we would have to navigate Florence successfully or we'd miss our train and connecting flight to France.

Making our way through this new city reenergized me. I loved our "unstructured" afternoon; many of my days back home were often scheduled down to the minute—making today's freedom (coupled with the wine in my system) seem that much more magical.

"I just love him," Emm said as we floated through Florence's historic streets. "I'm so glad we're meeting him for dinner. He's so smiley—I didn't want lunch to end."

"Emm, you didn't explain what 'smiley' meant in the restaurant."

"It's my new adjective, and Sal inspired it. He was so warm...so much gusto, such a perfect host. I don't think he stopped smiling once! And he welcomed us like family. I've never met anyone so sweet. So...*smiley*!"

It was true. Sal gave off such a warm and caring aura that he reminded me of my mother. He did more than just put me in a good mood—he gave me a sense of hope; a hope that maybe Lee and I would be okay without my parents. I had no idea what I wanted to do after I graduated, but I knew that Lee wanted to come live with me: and that I was going to do my damnedest to make that happen. How was I going to juggle both a new career and Lee's teenage years—which would be complicated by her sickle cell—without my mother? I didn't yet know, but Sal made me feel that he was someone I could turn to for advice and support. Someone who really was family. I mean, I knew I could count on Uncle Bill in terms of reliability, but he had about as much emotional intelligence as an ironclad door knob. In that sense, Uncle Bill and Sal were polar opposites; I had a feeling that in the coming years I'd need more than reliability to hold me up.

"Kamikaze friends, buddies, and the Smiley Italian," I said to Emm. "I haven't learned a ton of Italian on this trip, but "our" language is growing by leaps and bounds." I liked the way *our language* sounded as it came out of my mouth, as if it were somehow enchanted.

"Yeah, well it was inevitable that you'd learn *something*," replied Emm sarcastically, giving me a playful shove on the arm and breaking the spell that I'd cast in my head.

We meandered aimlessly through the cobbled streets of Firenze, tipsy as hell but loving the no-stress afternoon. It was also a good deal cooler in Florence than in Rome, although the sun still shone brightly above us.

Eventually we wandered onto a piazza in the newer part of the city. Like every other square I'd seen, this one was teeming with people and activity. But unlike the others, this one seemed to be sort of a performers market—mimes, jugglers, musicians, and dancers all had their talents on display. I particularly enjoyed the theatrics of a monkey named Charlie who, at his owner's command, danced a jig to Beyoncé's "Single Ladies."

"He looks like Ken trying to impress the ladies at a double-kegger," Emm quipped. Which made us both laugh so hard that we (thanks largely to the liquid portion of our lunch) made complete idiots of ourselves and stole poor Charlie's thunder. I threw a generous donation into his bucket to make up for our antics, before we slipped into the crowd as discreetly as possible.

"Look over there!" Emm cried. She pulled on my arm

like a kid trying to get her friend to join her on the swing set. Emm had zeroed in on an artist a couple of yards away who was drawing caricatures for a few Euros apiece. "Can we get one?" she pleaded.

Amused at her eagerness, I agreed immediately. "Of course, Emm. As long as he doesn't make you cuter than me, then sure!"

"We'll just have to see about that."

A few seconds later Emm and I were sitting in the hot seat. The artist stared deep into our souls as he worked, almost making me feel as if I was being interrogated for manslaughter or something.

The crowd behind the artist swelled as he transformed us into caricature form. We tried to sit still and control our giggling as he worked—but after watching Charlie, neither of us was in a mood to behave. But then again, when did Emma Rey Finley and I ever *really* behave?

A few moments later, Emm stood up and announced, "He says he's done drawing me, but you have to stay put for a few more minutes," which left me in the hot seat alone. That wouldn't have been a big deal normally, but Emm had been sitting on my knee as we posed: I'd been in my own little paradise.

Emm shuffled into the crowd, trying to sneak a peek at what the artist had finished so far. As soon as she saw the sketch, her hand shot up to her face. Seeing her reaction, I started to stand up, but the artist hit me with an absolutely lethal death-stare. I sat myself back down obediently—after a look like that, I didn't want to ever get on this guy's bad side. I spent the next few minutes wondering what Emm knew that I didn't.

"*Finito!*" The artist finally declared as he lifted his drawing and showed it to the crowd. I'd assumed the caricature would be a sweet sketch of Emm and me, but as the crowd broke into jeers, I knew something was very, very wrong.

Emm got her hands on the finished product, and I headed over to see what the big joke was. As expected, Emm looked exceptional in the sketch—her features were exaggerated, of course, but the artist had captured her cute, soft smile as well as her sinuous physique. But as for me? No mercy. I looked like an oblivious jock who lacked any sort of smooth game. I mean this guy made me cross-eyed and salivating for crying out loud. And, as if my image needed something even more ridiculous, the artist had drawn me with a massive hard-on. Embarrassed beyond belief, I couldn't help but look down to see if I had actually had one! The erection was fictional, thankfully...but I hastily adjusted my shorts, just to be safe.

"I would've paid a million dollars for this," Emm said, laughing. I nodded sheepishly as I rolled the sketch up into its protective cardboard cylinder. Thank God I hadn't been blushing like this when I was posing for this renegade, would-be Da Vinci—otherwise the guy might've given me devil horns as well.

In a strange and, perhaps, slightly perverted way, the artist had seen right through me—I had to give him some credit for that. He knew I was absolutely crazy about Emma Rey Finley. But was it that obvious? And if it was that obvious, why could everyone see it but her?

I wanted nothing more than to flee the piazza at that point, so I suggested we walk over to the Ponte Vecchio, which according to my GPS didn't seem far: much like the Tiber in Rome, the Arno River ran straight through Florence and we could follow it to the famous bridge. When I saw the blondish Arno, I realized how much I missed Rome, even though I'd only "lived there" for a week.

Like many medieval bridges, the Ponte Vecchio was/is both bridge and marketplace. Shops lined either side of the pedestrian-only walkway, and this particular afternoon, legions of mostly-tourists had flocked to this historic site. The throng of visitors rubbed up against us as we walked. I could barely manage to see the river below, but Emm, being a foot shorter, couldn't see the water through the wall of people.

We tried our best to battle forward, but I somehow managed to lose Emm in the crowd. As I was looking for her, I noticed a woman drop her bracelet. Trying to get the woman's attention, I called out, but she'd already been swallowed up by the crowd. I yelled out a second time before scooping up the turquoise bracelet, if only to prevent anyone from stepping on it.

The bracelet wasn't ostentatious or overly-expensive looking, but it was unique in its own special way. The almost-translucent turquoise stone was perfectly cut, yet somehow understated. Smaller, but no less-fine pieces of turquoise surrounded the main stone and were set at intervals into the chain's links. The lobster-claw clasp didn't seem broken at all and I wondered how this little treasure had slipped off the woman's wrist. I realized this treasure seemed almost as beautiful as Emm: Almost as perfectly crafted as my buddy.

I spotted Emm a few feet ahead of me and caught up to her. We made our way to a quieter and much less crowded spot on the bridge where we stopped to catch our breath.

"That was insanity!" Emm jumped up and tousled my hair. "Like Manhattan at rush hour, Italian-style!" I laughed, thinking that only a New Yorker could be homesick for crowds like that.

"What's that?" she asked as she pointed at the bracelet in my hand.

"I just found this on the ground back there. Nice, huh?"

"Wow," she exclaimed as she examined the bracelet. "That chain is silver, TD, not the plated stuff. And the stones are gorgeous, I love that color. Should we try to find out who it belongs to?"

"I saw who dropped it, but I couldn't catch her—and I don't know how I'd ever find her again." I stood up on my tiptoes and scanned the crowd once more. "Why don't you have it, Emm? Here, hold out your arm, I'll do up the clasp."

"Oh, no, TD…I can't accept that," replied Emm, looking uncharacteristically nervous.

"Come on, it'll look much better on you than on me," I joked.

I guess Emm couldn't argue with that logic because she took the bracelet slowly from my outstretched palm. Her eyes twinkled as she admired it. I'd always wanted the chance to spoil someone I cared about, but I'd never had a couple of hundred extra bucks laying around, either. But with the sheer joyance now blossoming through Emm's face, spoiling her was now something I wanted to do for the rest of my life.

I fastened the clasp—and the instant it was in place, Emm hugged me ferociously...and our bubble-world shrunk in around us once again, shutting out the crowd completely. For a split second, I thought I might get another kiss, but when I looked down and saw Emm's glow, her happiness was all I needed: if I could make her smile like that, then I must be doing something right.

"Every time I look at this, I'll remember how amazing this trip has been...I'm never going to take this off, Tim Dexter."

We hit up a couple more sites in Florence before it was time to meet Sal again for dinner. As we approached the restaurant—another hole-in-the-wall place—Sal appeared to be accompanied by a small horse.

"Do they allow ponies in the city? Is that, like, a Florentine thing?" I asked, completely perplexed. I was sincere, but Emm, who had at that moment been taking a swig of water, thought my question was so hilarious that she actually sputtered and choked a little.

"Glasses, TD. You might want to invest in a pair," she replied, wiping her chin.

I squinted as we drew closer. What I had thought was a horse was actually a Great Dane. The most massive Great Dane I'd ever seen. And with Sal being so short and slight, I didn't see why a small horse was an unreasonable initial assessment on my part.

"*Buona sera! Buona sera!*" cried Sal, before he greeted us each with a double kiss. "This is my Maggie," he said as he patted his dog vigorously. "We'll eat in the garden so she can join us, yes?"

I hoped I'd hid my shock, but in truth I was blown away. Sal had mentioned Maggie earlier, but from the way he'd talked about her, I'd sort of assumed she was his girlfriend. Thankfully, Emm had the situation well in hand, and as she scratched Maggie warmly behind her ears, a hello "yip" burst from Maggie's enormous mouth.

"*Eh*, that looks just like you, TD," Sal said as we started on our wine. "The artist did a very good job, except for the crossed eyes." Then he lowered his voice conspiratorially, "But he was *molto generoso* where it counts, yes?"

I turned the brightest red ever; I really could've done without his mentioning my cartoon erection. I adjusted my shorts again.

"I know, right?" Emm exclaimed, giggling. "Now I know why you've never had any trouble with the ladies."

Maggie barked, as if in agreement.

Feeling a bit teamed-up on, I quickly changed the subject. "Sal, were you able to do that favor for me?" I asked.

Almost as if on cue, a waitress popped up seemingly out of nowhere and set down a dessert platter, which contained a chocolate cannoli for each of us as well as a tiramisu and a vanilla panettone for the table. Even Maggie got a small scoop of mint sorbet.

Emm smirked at me in awe. I'd never quite seen that look on her face before and I didn't know what to say.

Fortunately, Sal—being the perfect host—had me covered. "In our culture, we sometimes do dessert first too," he said gently. Emm smiled at him with delighted appreciation.

Sal wasn't kidding about feasting twice in one day. Dinner was even more abundant than lunch, with almost as much wine. The time flew by as the Italian sun slowly disappeared, leaving behind a fiery canvas of oranges and reds above the horizon.

Sadly, Emm and I had a train and a plane to catch so we had to say goodbye to Sal and Maggie sooner than either of us would have liked. "I really hope to see you again soon, Sal. Come back to the U.S. and visit," I said earnestly. "California isn't the same without you."

"*Sì, Sì*, TD. Now that we are reunited, I promise to come as soon as I retire," Sal replied. "And now that I have a *bellissima amica* to visit," he continued, winking at Emm, "you won't be able to keep me away!"

"Yes, please. You are always welcome, anytime!" Emm said eagerly.

I pulled Sal in for a goodbye hug. As we embraced, he said genuinely, "*Ti voglio bene come un figlio*. Until we meet again."

Emm broke in, "*Addio*, Sal!" Which was good, because I was more broken-up about leaving Sal than I could've possibly expected. Why couldn't my own father have a little bit of "smiley Italian" in him?

Once we were outside, I asked Emm, "What does '*Ti voglio bene come un figlio*' mean?"

"It means 'I love you like a son.' Sal really does think of you as family. I can tell."

I was too touched to reply and had to stop myself from running back into the restaurant to tell Sal the exact same words.

"You know, TD," Emm continued, "We're…adults now. It's up to us to choose who we keep in our lives. It takes effort, but some people are more than worth it."

"It's 7:02!" Emm screamed as she realized what time it was. We were at least a fifteen-minute walk from the train station, and our train was leaving at 7:15. If we didn't make it back to Rome on time, we'd miss our flight, too. In other words, we were screwed.

"Can you flag down a cab?" Emm suggested. But as I

panned the street, I realized just how few cars were on the quiet Florentine road.

"That's a no-go, Emm." Then, in a complete panic, I blurted out, "Maybe we could ride Maggie?"

"Great idea, genius," Emm said flatly. "We'd better start running!"

We switched into high gear and sprinted madly, as if the Swiss Guard were gaining on us. How the hell Emm kept up with me I'll never quite know…even my coach had never pushed me to run this fast.

Just as we entered the station, I yelled, "Time, Emm?"

"7:12! Move, move, move!"

I scanned the terminal looking for our *slow train*. When Emm cried out, "Over there!" we raced toward the track. Just then, a wave of nausea and the very real possibility of vomiting up my cannoli hit me. I doubled over with a cramp just as the train blew its 'last-call' horn.

"Shit," I said loudly as the train, pulling away from the platform, blew its horn one more time. But my brain pushed through the pain as a thought coalesced. "The horn, Emm! Our train didn't have a horn! Keep looking!"

I scanned the terminal for the older, local-routes-only train and I spotted it on the next platform. Grabbing Emm's hand and practically dragging her behind me, I yelled, "Come on!"

Thirty seconds later, the slow train's attendant yelled out, "*Tutti a bordo!*"

With no manners whatsoever, and with Emm practically hyperventilating behind me, I pointed to the train and shouted at the attendant, "*Roma, sì?*"

The poor man looked at the two of us with a combination of shock and pity as he waved us in. We hadn't even made it off the gangway and into the main car before the train started moving.

The train was packed. Since we were the last passengers to board, we had to take what we could get for seats. Which meant we wound up wedged into the only two remaining adjacent seats, near the very back of the last car, practically sitting on top of each other. I could've used a little more legroom, but having Emm huddled up so closely was not an unappealing prospect.

We took a few minutes to catch our breath, doing nothing but panting and staring at each other with looks of, "Holy shit, we made it!" plastered on our faces.

I expected Emm, as usual, to nod off as soon as the train began its dull rumble, but I guess she was too wired. She fidgeted around for a few minutes, then held up her wrist and said, "Thank you again for my bracelet, Tim Dexter...it's perfect."

"You don't need to thank me. I'm the one who hit the jackpot—I wouldn't even be in Italy if it wasn't for you."

I looked down at Emm as she toyed with her turquoise bracelet. I don't know what kind of devilishness took a hold of me just then, but the words fell out of my mouth before I could stop them. "I do have one more surprise for you, Emm...*if* you want it."

"TD...what are y—" but before Emm could finish I grabbed my phone and held it up to her face.

"Zombie-Emm on the train to Florence!" I exclaimed. Emm bolted up and laughed as if she couldn't believe her eyes.

"Well...I guess great minds think alike," she said, still shocked.

"Yes they do, buddy," I replied, but I wondered if Emm's great mind would ever realize what I now knew in my soul: We were meant to be so much more than buddies. We were meant to be together.

Chapter 7

Soak Up the Moon

I jolted awake, unable to recognize where I was. For a split second, I thought I was back at Lee's bedside in the hospital—I'd spent many nights in that very position—but the sunlight streaming through the window immediately put me at ease. When I realized I was lying in a comfortable, over-stuffed recliner, my memory came flooding back: I was in the studio apartment we'd rented in Marseille.

As soon as I'd gotten my wits about me, I remembered the most important thing about our red-eye flight the night before: Emm, utterly exhausted, had fallen asleep and curled into a sweet yellow ball in my lap on the plane. With all the naps I'd watched Emma Rey Finley take over the years, she'd never once snuggled up to me like that. With her flipped-back hair showing off her flawless face, I wanted desperately to once again taste her cherry lips, but I resisted the urge. I sat there for a full hour cradling her gently, but I absolutely did not kiss her. I had the girl of my dreams lying across my lap and we were on our way to the south of France: that was enough, at least for now. I told myself there was no reason to push things.

We'd arrived at our apartment a little before 3 a.m., only to find there was just one bed. Emm had collapsed onto the mattress and was out cold within seconds, but since I didn't feel right crawling into bed beside her without asking first, I'd grabbed a blanket and made myself comfortable in the adjacent oversized recliner. I mean, Emm was still fully-clothed, and it probably would've been fine, but I still thought it best not to presume.

I stretched as I sat up and searched the room. I didn't see her, but I did hear the shower running so I knew Emm was close by. That's when the smell of bacon hit me. I padded into the kitchen area, where I found two covered plates. I whipped off the paper towel covering each and discovered a stack of pancakes on one plate and a pile of bacon on the other. God bless that girl…because I was in no mood to cook, but I was starving.

I poured myself a cup of coffee and took a seat at the narrow marble island, which separated the kitchen area from the sleeping area. I really wanted to dive into those pancakes, but the least I could do was wait until Emm was ready to eat. To keep myself occupied, I made us each a plate; as an artistic touch, I made a third plate as well, using some of the decorative plastic fruit that was sitting in a basket on the counter: apples for the eyes, a strawberry for the nose, two kiwis for ears and, of course, a bright yellow banana for the smile.

As Emm walked into the kitchen, I presented her with my happy masterpiece.

"Aww, for me? It's beautiful."

"It's to thank you for making breakfast, Emm. It's almost noon, I must've really needed that extra sleep."

"I thought I'd give Chef BoyarT the morning off," she replied. "Especially since I didn't make us a real breakfast yesterday."

I hadn't yet mentioned her breakfast fail, so I was surprisingly touched that she'd tried to make right on her promise.

Taking a sip of my very first cup of actually-French French roast, I felt compelled to say something about her thoughtfulness when I second-guessed my own bliss and wondered whether, perhaps, I was reading too much into pancakes and bacon.

"Hey, our fruit man reminds me of Sal!" Emm exclaimed. I looked down at my artistic creation but didn't see the resemblance. Emm continued, "Because he's so smiley, TD."

We'd scheduled ourselves another unstructured day because tomorrow was going to be very, very structured. One of the reasons we'd decided to come to Marseille was because Emm's housemate back at school had raved last year about her trip to Calanques National Park, which would be our only pre-planned outdoor adventure in Europe. Emm had gone into great detail about how amazingly beautiful the park sounded, so I hardly put up a fight. I didn't need to be sold on traveling with her to begin with, but her excitement made the tour sound all the more appealing. Our trip to Calanques National Park would be the last of our European adventures, because from there we'd practically be heading straight to the airport: Emm would fly back to Rome, while I'd be heading home.

As France's second-largest city, and with a history dating back to the ancient Greeks, Marseille always had a lot going on. The city was an important Mediterranean port, and the refreshing scent of saltwater permeated the air. Walking through the city was somewhat disorienting, though. I think my ears got used to hearing Italian—but now, just about everyone was speaking French and I was *not* understanding the language in a whole new way. I felt like I had time-traveled or something.

We wandered around for a while, just taking in the city, eventually stumbling onto the port itself which was lined with boutiques selling just about everything imaginable. We popped into a couple of shops here and there as we walked. But when Emm saw a retro clothing store—one of the few large shops at the port—she was immediately hooked. As I followed, the memory of Emm in her red dress appeared in my head: I tried to push it from my thoughts.

Knowing how Emm liked to shop (she needed her time) I decided to go check out a section of retro sports jerseys, to keep myself busy. I was surprised to find so much of America right here in France—Kobe Bryant, LeBron James, and Kevin Durant were all represented. Most of the uniforms were replicas, but they did have one of Larry Bird's game-worn jerseys. I was seriously considering busting out my for-emergencies-only credit card, but when I saw the price tag, my brain almost exploded. I had to walk away before the temptation overwhelmed me.

Emm was looking through the children's section when I found her. "What are you up to over here?" I asked, as she searched through the clothing rack in front of her.

"I think it would be nice to find something for Lee. You can bring it home to her," she said as she pulled out two small dresses.

"Emm, you're too sweet," I said, truly touched by her gesture. "Lee would love that."

"Good. Now help me find something she would like," Emm replied without lifting her eyes from the apparel she'd selected. "These stink. We can do better."

Not being very good at this sort of thing, I joined Emm and did my best to try to make myself appear useful. A few minutes later, Emm pulled out a purple silk dress that was accented with gold stitching along the hemline.

"I love it!" she squealed as she held it up against herself.

Not wanting to ruin her treasure hunt, but still wanting to be completely honest, I said, "That *is* cute, but...maybe you've forgotten how much Lee hates purple? She says it's for bunny rabbits and babies."

Emm scrunched up her nose in frustration, which smushed the light spray of tiny freckles on her nose together. "You're right. I don't know why I was thinking purple...Blue's always been her favorite."

"Yeah, and she goes crazy for anything baby blue, especially."

Without losing hope, we continued to look. Emm and I found a few "blue" options as we scoured the racks but discovered nothing nearly as nice as the purple and gold frock.

"Emm, come over here," I called out from the next aisle. I pulled out something baby blue that had caught the corner of my eye and held it up.

Emm, running over to me, stopped in her tracks. "That's IT!"

The dress was silk, just like the purple one, but it was the softest baby blue I'd ever seen. Instead of a gold-embroidered hem, this dress had small sunflowers encircling the bottom. For a finishing touch, the dress also came with a matching sunflower headband, which was awesome, since Lee loved both headbands and sunflowers. I knew Lee would jump up and down with delight when she saw it.

As we walked to the checkout I asked, "Didn't you say you hated sunflowers?"

Emm partially smiled, and I knew she was about to drop one of her deep thoughts on me. "I *really* hate sunflowers, TD. But sometimes, if you care enough about someone, then nothing else matters, other than making that person happy."

"Even if it means having to face the evil sunflowers of the world?" I laughed.

"Yes, Tim Dexter. Even when dealing with those horrible things that for some reason call themselves 'sunflowers.'"

"Let's see what's going on," Emm cried as we walked into the square. "Something's up!"

A distinct electricity surged through the air. A group of about sixty men were gathered by the plaza's main statue and were pulsating with energy—and probably with a good bit of liquor, too. More and more men were joining them as the group grew by the minute. Most were wearing matching sports jerseys, but others waved mini flags.

"It's a team of some kind, Emm, but I don't know that flag."

Just then, one of the men jumped up on the statue and shouted something in a language neither of us understood. In response, the crowd cheered wildly, "*Ísland! Ísland! Ísland!*"

I pulled out my phone and did a quick search. "Emm, this says Iceland is playing Hungary tomorrow in the Euro Cup."

"If I'd known Marseille was hosting the games, I'd have probably gotten us tickets!"

The crowd was still swelling and getting rowdier by the minute. Some men even set off homemade-looking fireworks, which colored the sky in blue and red sparks. The men had added a sort of slow clap to their cheer, and now the word *Ísland* was followed each time by a resounding, rhythmic thump.

I thought that maybe it was time to move back and distance ourselves from the riotous celebration. I was about to suggest as much when a firework exploded just over our heads. Wincing as it cracked, I covered my head with my arms. After what couldn't have been more than three seconds, I pulled my arms from my face: Emm was gone.

How could she have disappeared so quickly? I spun around, searching everywhere, but saw absolutely no sign of her. I started to panic, thinking she'd been swept away or trampled or something awful. I hadn't felt this stressed since I'd landed in Europe; the adrenaline rush hit me hard and the irrational part of my brain feared Emm had disappeared forever.

"Emm! *Emm!*" I yelled at the top of my lungs, but with the noise coming from the crowd, it was pointless—I doubt she could've heard me, even if she were standing right beside me.

Rather than standing there and screaming my lungs out, I thought I'd try a 21st century approach and called her phone. Dead end: Voicemail on the second ring.

I must've searched for another ten minutes, getting more and more worried as the seconds ticked by. The center of the plaza was now completely packed. I honestly didn't know how

I was going to find my buddy in this thick, inebriated, over-ly-enthusiastic swarm.

But out of the corner of my eye, I caught sight of a lone female form on the other side of the plaza, riding on the shoulders of one of the men. At first, I didn't pay her much attention—she was screaming and chanting along with the crowd—but when I looked more closely, I realized there was nothing even remotely Nordic about that girl at all. In fact, I knew that girl. It was none other than my "famed monument" that I had traveled all this way to see.

Even from that distance, Emm managed to make eye con-tact with me. She smiled right into my heart. All my anxieties from the past fifteen minutes evaporated.

When I finally caught up to her, and after she'd descended from her Icelandic perch, I chided, "A little warning would've been nice."

"Don't be such a weenie, TD!" She stuck her tongue out, mocking me a bit. "That was so much fun!"

"I know…I was watching from a safe distance. But you really did look like you were one with the group."

"They just did a really good job of including me and mak-ing me feel welcome is all." Her modesty was extremely cute. So cute that, for some reason, I nearly blushed.

Our unstructured day soon found us at *Les Petits Trains de Marseille,* which are sort of open-air trolleys made to look like old-fashioned locomotive trains. The train route we chose would take us to Marseille's Grand Cathedral—one of our "would like to see" spots—but when we'd discovered the ca-thedral was atop a massive hill, we decided our tired feet just couldn't manage the trek. As it turned out, this particular *pe-tit train* would solve that problem, and we hopped on without hesitation.

We found ourselves seated next to a couple of Emm's new Icelandic friends. Even though I couldn't understand a word they were saying (they both spoke French with Emm), I could see how she immediately put them at ease and wel-comed them as if they were old friends. Part of me resented the intrusion into our bubble-world, but the better part of me admired the way Emm's charm could bring out the best in just about anyone.

The cathedral, a Catholic basilica with roots in the 12th century, looked like something out of *The Lord of the Rings*. Being the solemn and respectful tourists we always were, we wound up having a dance-off right in the middle of the nave. I'd just declared myself the winner—obviously, considering Emm's dancing "skills"—when a stern and frowning security guard made us take ourselves and our dance moves outside.

"*Pas d'enfants dans l'église sans surveillance parentale!*" yelled the guard as he slammed the door behind him. This was followed by Emm laughing so hard that she literally doubled over. I didn't care about getting kicked out, but I didn't understand what was so hysterically funny.

"He said, 'Children aren't allowed in the church without parental supervision!'" Emm finally managed to translate, which made me double over as well. We laughed until our sides hurt and our eyes teared-up. Quite possibly the best laugh I'd had in years.

"We're always such an issue, everywhere we go," Emm said as we calmed down.

"Me, or *you*?" I retorted.

"*Us*, TD…I think it's *us, together*." My heart jumped into my throat: she'd said "us, together" like we were really a couple. I felt both unabashedly hopeful and totally doomed all at once. If I ever did reveal my feelings to Emm, I'd have to make damn sure I was well-prepared for the possibility of our perfect bubble-world bursting for good. A risk I wasn't sure I'd ever be willing to take.

I held Emm's birthday present in my trembling hands. I *had* to give it to her tonight—it would be my last chance. I knew Emm would love her gift, but I didn't know how she was going to react. Would she cry? Would she laugh? Would she tackle me in a bear hug? As excited as I was to give Emm her personal book into which I had put so much time and effort, I wasn't sure I was ready for an onslaught of emotion, especially given the chaos inside of me.

As I held the book in my petrified hands, I scanned through a few more entries. Most were upbeat, supportive, or outright silly, but Lee's entry stood out from all the rest:

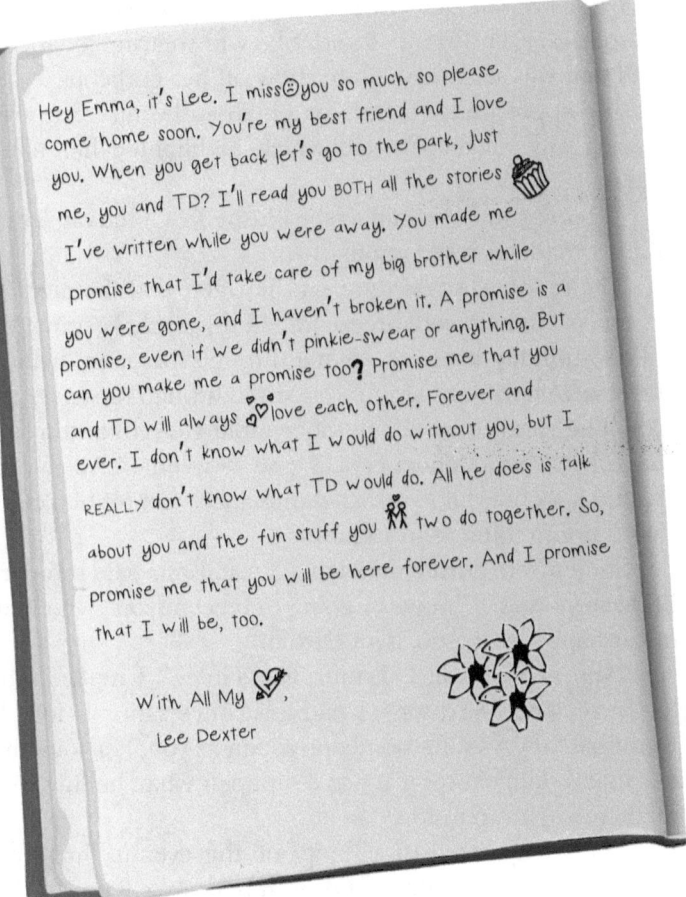

Hey Emma, it's Lee. I miss☺you so much so please come home soon. You're my best friend and I love you. When you get back let's go to the park, just me, you and TD? I'll read you BOTH all the stories 🧁 I've written while you were away. You made me promise that I'd take care of my big brother while you were gone, and I haven't broken it. A promise is a promise, even if we didn't pinkie-swear or anything. But can you make me a promise too❓ Promise me that you and TD will always 💗love each other. Forever and ever. I don't know what I would do without you, but I REALLY don't know what TD would do. All he does is talk about you and the fun stuff you 👫 two do together. So, promise me that you will be here forever. And I promise that I will be, too.

With All My 💗,
Lee Dexter

As I read the words my little sister had scribbled onto the page, I fought back my tears. For being so young, my baby sister really did have a way with words. She was also totally right: I don't know what either of us would ever do without Emm.

Regaining my composure, I wiped the tears from my eyes just as Emm emerged from the bathroom. Because this was our last night in Europe, we'd decided to pool together the rest of our travel funds and splurge on a fancy dinner. After having been out wandering the city all day, both of us needed a good shower and change of clothes before any swanky restaurant would welcome us.

I quickly slid her gift into my jacket pocket. "You look beautiful as ever, Emm," I said. She was wearing a light gray dress that was short enough to show off her gorgeous legs but was also appropriate enough for a high-end venue. She wasn't wearing any makeup at all, which highlighted her natural beauty.

"Thank you," she said as she blushed. "Come on, let's get going. I made us reservations."

The restaurant was right on the water and the night was extremely calm. A cool breeze joined us, gently keeping Marseille's humidity in check. Flying through the open, twilit sky above were dozens of seagulls, soaring through the air in great arcs. The candles on our outdoor table glowed, and a single blue tulip sat in a slender crystal vase between us. All of which created a wonderfully intimate ambiance—an ambiance that I tried not to think of as romantic.

Somewhere during the main course, Emm said something I'll never forget: "I'm never going to meet anyone who makes me as happy as you do, Tim Dexter."

"And neither will I, Emma Rey Finley," I replied, absolutely touched. We'd sort of had this conversation before, but Emm had always said "someone as fun as you," or something like that. I didn't know if it was a slipup or what, but her words made me light-up inside.

The Mediterranean serenity of the evening hugged us as we enjoyed our entrees. I'd promised myself not to drink too much, but the wine was delicious and complimented my scampi wonderfully.

Not wanting to sound too somber, but needing to get it out, I said, "You know Emm, I've been thinking about what you said in Florence, about our being adults and choosing who we keep in our lives."

"My mother taught me that," Emm replied. "And from what I can tell, it's the truest piece of advice she's ever given me. Like, take my roommates in Rome. If I don't make the time to stay actively connected to them, I may never talk to them again after I get home."

"That's just it, Emm. We only have one year of school left…and it's going to be a hectic one for both of us. We have to *make* the time, like we always have, but it's going to be harder. And after that, who knows? Things change, people change."

"That's true. But what's bothering you?"

"I want us to be forever," I began. "And I don't care how we define 'us'—maybe we'll get married and have two or three kids and a white picket fence, maybe we'll just be best friends. What matters is that we put the effort in. What matters is that we're best friends before anything else."

"You mean *buddies*, right? Not just friends," Emm said with her trademark impish grin creeping across her face.

"Emm…I'm serious," I said, sounding slightly upset.

Now as solemn as I was, Emm looked at me with her deep mahogany eyes. "TD, I'm not going anywhere. I promise. We'll always be there for each other." She reached out and gave my hand a quick squeeze

I didn't—couldn't—reply. Instead, I slid the tulip from its vase as I walked over to Emm's side of the table. Without a word, I pinned the perfect blossom to her chest—the velvety petals elegantly complemented the gray of her dress. As I secured the tulip in place, I could feel the familiar warmth of her skin through the fabric of her outfit.

Emm lowered her chin, savoring the tulip's faint, fresh aroma. She inhaled again, this time lifting her chin before exhaling. Before she repeated the motion for the third time, my eyes met hers: her lustrous eyes reflected every moment of our precious three years of friendship.

She didn't speak for a long moment. Finally, her expression changed back to her usual, sarcastic self. "I don't know about that white picket fence, though, TD. I'm a city gal—luxury condos are more my style."

"The penthouse, then…whatever," I said laughing. "We'll make it work."

It was pretty late by the time we finished our ridiculously pricey dinner, but neither of us was yet ready to call it a night. We walked along the quiet boardwalk with only the lapping of the waves to keep us company. In the night's soothing darkness, the marina now took on a whole new feeling, as if the sea went on forever and the possibilities for our future were endless. My eyes were trained on the night sky when I heard the softest little lullaby floating on the breeze.

> I see the moon, the moon sees me
> The moon sees somebody I want to see
> God bless the moon, and God bless me
> And God bless the somebody I want to see.

Although we were alone, I wasn't sure if it was Emm's voice or not. But I also didn't want to turn and look at her in fear that she would stop.

When the rhyme repeated a second time, I knew for a fact that it was Emm's angelic sound. I'd never heard her sing a lullaby before, and I'd never heard such tranquility in her singing. She was beautiful, open and vulnerable in a way I hadn't known she could be.

Emm snapped out of whatever state she was in as she realized I'd been listening. "I can't believe I just did that," she said, embarrassed. "My mom used to sing that to me when I was a little girl, but I have no idea why I just started singing it now."

"It's okay, Emm," I said, gently. "I understand. I thought it was really sweet."

"Oh, shut up. Now you're just making fun of me," she

said a bit defensively.

"No. Seriously, that was…I loved it." Struggling to describe how touched I was by her quiet singing, I couldn't quite capture it in words, and started singing the song back to her, hoping she'd understand. Her voice soon joined mine as we walked further down the boardwalk, whistling and humming quietly together in the night.

We found a nice bench under a streetlight to sit and watch the lights of the tugboats in the harbor. I put my arm around her and, much like she'd done on the plane, Emm softly leaned into my shoulder. I don't know what perfume she was wearing but it was intoxicating.

I'd just about convinced myself that this moment could never possibly end, when Emm catapulted up and almost dove headfirst into a stranger who was passing by. The poor man was as confused as I was until we both realized what Emm was after: Cuddles with his teacup pug. Smaller than the palm of my hand, the puppy couldn't have been more than a few months old.

"Excuse her, sir. She just really loves pugs," I said to the man as Emm, without a thought to her best dress, scampered around and played with the puppy.

The man gave me an icy stare. Maybe he hadn't understood me—I literally couldn't say two words in French—but he was clearly offended. He scooped up his pug and walked off in a huff.

"Did you see how small he was?" Emm yelled as she jumped up. "I want one!"

Trying to calm her down, I replied, "Well, maybe I'll get you one as a graduation gift." I said.

"And I'll bring it over every weekend for Lee to play with! She'll love me forever!"

"What would you name your teacup pug?" I asked, grinning.

"Crow. After Sheryl, of course," Emm replied, as if she'd been well-prepared for that exact question for years.

We sat back down on the bench. The sky suddenly began to glow as the wispy clouds occluding the moon parted. The moon had finally seen us. I took it as a sign that it was time to give Emm her birthday gift.

I reached into my jacket and handed her the notebook. "Happy birthday, Emm," I said with just a touch of coyness in my voice.

Puzzled, she took the notebook and flipped through the first few pages. I watched her expression as she slowly realized that the notebook itself was one giant birthday card. She lit up like a Christmas tree in Rockefeller Center, then her expression morphed into disbelief.

"TD!" she yelled. "This is amazing! How did you—?"

"Everyone wanted to let you know how much you're missed, Emm. Including me."

"This is the nicest thing anyone has ever done for me," she began. "I just...I don't know what to...I'm so happy at you, TD...Thank you!"

I pulled her in beside me and put my arm around her as she read the entries out loud. She looked back up at me with tears of joy in her eyes.

"Skip to Lee's entry," I suggested. "She had a few things to say."

"My little writer," said Emm wistfully, sniffling and wiping the tears from her eyes.

She flipped through the book and read Lee's note aloud, then read it once again silently to herself.

Through her joyous tears, Emm made good on Lee's request. Under the light of the moon, Emm vowed, "I promise to always love you."

The notebook had long since lost its newness to me, since I'd been holding onto it for almost a month now and had reread each entry several times already. But seeing how emotional Emm was truly touched me. Moved almost beyond words, I whispered, "Forever."

Wiping the small tears from her eyes, she echoed back to me, "Forever."

Snuggled under my arm, we watched the boats come and go for hours. Soaking up the moonlight. Just the two of us, together in the nocturnal glow. Together under our moon.

We got back to the apartment just before 4 a.m. Emm and I had to be up at 8 a.m. to meet our tour group at Calanques National Park, which only gave us a few hours to get some rest. I climbed into the recliner; Emm was in bed already, reading her gift by the light of her phone.

"Goodnight, Emm."

"Goodnight, TD."

Listening to Emm laugh and cry as she read, I lay in the still, dark room for a few more minutes. I felt a great sense of satisfaction as I began drifting off to sleep: I don't think she could've asked for a better gift.

That's when I heard Emm turn toward me and say, "Um...TD, would you...just sleep in bed with me tonight?" She must've sensed my hesitation because she quickly added, "Make a pillow-wall or something if you want, just come over here."

I slipped into bed beside her, placing two pillows between us. I'd never been in bed with her like that before and wasn't sure which lines, if any, we were redrawing. But Emm didn't seem to give another thought to our new sleeping arrangements; she was glued to her birthday present. I fell asleep to the sound of Emma Rey Finley laughing quietly to herself.

Hours later, just as our moon had finally fallen asleep and dawn's very first light was coloring the sky, I felt Emm rest her head against my chest and nestle herself under my arm. I don't know if she was awake or not, but what I do know was that it was the best four hours of sleep I'd ever gotten in my entire life.

Chapter 8

I ♥ Emma Rey Finley

I swear I didn't forget my sunblock on purpose, but as Emm slathered the lotion she'd borrowed from the visitors' center across my back, I was suddenly glad I'd forgotten my SPF 100. I had to fight to suppress goosebumps of excitement as Emm's hands gently slid across my skin.

Calanques National Park is a coastal reserve that stretches along Marseille's southern shore. The park itself is mostly ocean; the best way to enjoy it is by boat. Today we'd be kayaking to one of the park's more secluded spots and enjoying the stunning views of the coast's sharp, limestone cliffs along the way. I wasn't much of a seaman and I wasn't sure if Emm was, either, but we were about to find out.

At this point in our trip, and with our having gone to bed so late last night, Emm and I were totally exhausted, but we were committed to making the most of our last day together. Thus far, I had just been trying to keep up with her—and I felt like I'd been doing a pretty good job, I wasn't about to trip at the finish line.

A short, athletic-looking man wearing the national park's logo came up to us as Emm playfully smeared a blob of sunscreen across my nose. "Hello, I'll be leading our group today," he began in a thick French accent, "So I hope you guys are ready for some fun!" His enthusiasm clearly conveyed, "*I got more than four hours of sleep last night.*"

The tour guide's English was hardly fluent, which I hoped wouldn't be too much of a problem. But hey, he was the one who was bilingual, not me, so I probably shouldn't complain. I also had my buddy to translate, if things got really dicey.

He held out his hand. "My name is David," he said, but it came out more like "*Daveeed.*" Instantly, I knew Emm and I would be secretly laughing to ourselves about this all day.

"I'm Emma," said Emm as she shook his hand. "And this is TD."

A confused expression clouded David's face. "*Tee Dee?*"

"Umm...TD?" I repeated, not really seeing the misunderstanding.

"Tay-day," Emm interjected, approximating the French pronunciation.

"Ah! *Tee Dee* and *Eeeeema* Got it! *Allons!*" he enthused.

I was about to correct him for the third time when Emm cut me off by saying, "Yep. *Allons!*"

David introduced himself to the others in our group and instructed all of us to leave our belongings inside the visitor's center so they wouldn't get wet. We went to go pick out which kayak we wanted for the day, grabbed our life jackets and jumped into David's van so he could drive our party down the cliff to the beach. Of the two other couples riding to the beach with us, one was American, the other was Welsh. Emm had the good sense to have signed us up for the English-speaking tour, knowing full-well I wouldn't be able to handle both the high seas and a language barrier at the same time.

After putting on our life jackets and going through a safety check, we were in the water following our fearless leader to the promised land. Pulling out ahead of the pack, David gave us directions on how to navigate our kayaks, since all of us were basically first-timers. We would be, more-or-less, hugging the Mediterranean coast for most of the trip, but since our destination was so secluded, we would need to skirt a peninsula that jutted pretty far out to sea; we'd need to briefly leave the protection of the harbor to reach the other side.

Except for David's, all the kayaks were doubles. Emm had grabbed the front seat of ours and assumed the role of captain. I followed her every command. "Left. Right. Left. Right." she barked as we matched our paddle strokes. We were so synchronized that Emm and I cut through the water like an Ivy League rowing team.

With the sky and the water calm around us, we glided over the waves completely at peace. Her roommate back home had been right, the park was spectacular. After having been in cities for practically nine days straight, the vastness of the sea and the fresh, salty air were at once calming and invigorating.

Rowing in the sun *was* hot, though. Since we were surrounded by water, I thought there was no reason not to cool off. I purposely mis-rowed with my paddle, which splashed the cool seawater directly onto Emm's head.

"Sorry!" I shouted. By "sorry," what I actually meant was, "That was a warning shot." Thirty seconds later, I pulled the stunt again.

Emm turned around and yelled, "Quit it!" Having taken two direct hits, her hair was now dripping wet.

Barely able to suppress a smile, I replied, "Sorry, captain. Won't happen again!" I followed this up with a sort of salute—but this time a simple apology wasn't enough—as I kind of hoped it wouldn't be.

Emm began paddling backwards, splashing me with as much force as she could, which quickly progressed into an all-out splash war. Within minutes we were both soaking wet and laughing hysterically.

David finally noticed that we had fallen behind the pack and yelled something to us that I couldn't really hear. Not letting up in the slightest, Emm and I continued to splash each other when our kayak began to rock in the wake created by our battle. As Emm yelled at me to surrender, I saw David paddling toward us but didn't think anything of it. I wasn't about to let Emm claim victory in our duel, so I splashed her even harder which, as a result, made our kayak rock more and more violently.

Capsized.

I found myself completely underwater. Thankfully my bright-orange life jacket quickly brought me back to the surface. Catching my breath, I saw that Emm was floating right beside me and appeared to be alright. We laughed as we bobbed beside each other, treading water. But that's when we felt the wrath of "Daveeed".

"This is not a joke! I thought something was seriously wrong. You could have been hurt, or worse!" he lectured us as we floated below him. "Now get back in your kayak and row safely, or I'll take you back to shore."

Not fully understanding why David had flipped-out about our unscheduled dip in the Mediterranean, once he was gone and we were back in our boat I asked Emm, "Why did he just get so mad?"

"I have no idea. This all seems pretty simple and I don't know what could really go wrong. I can't see why he got so worked up about it."

After our minor delay, Emm and I quickly caught back up to the group. I continued to follow her commands as ship's captain.

David, still leading our pack, yelled, "Okay, we are headed out of the harbor. Remember what I taught you."

David had given us some brief instructions on special paddling techniques in case our kayaks got caught in strong currents or high winds. His accent had been a big issue and I'd understood maybe every other word out of his mouth. I wasn't worried about that, though—I mean, how hard could this really be? Plus, I had a pretty kick-ass and dangerous-ly-gorgeous captain to lead us, which had made it that much harder for me to pay attention in the first place.

Following the curves of the gleaming limestone cliffs, we turned into the bend that led out of the harbor. David was the first to make the turn, which he did effortlessly. Next, the American couple was up; although they didn't manage the smoothest turn, they had no real issues following David's lead.

The next couple attempted to exit the harbor when a strong current they clearly weren't expecting sucked them toward the open sea. Their frantic paddling only made things worse and before we knew it, they were too far out for David's shouts to reach them which, for someone as loud as him, was pretty damned far.

Emm gasped as we watched. Turning herself around in the kayak, she asked, "Should we do something?"

Not wanting to add to the problem, I replied, "I think we should just stay right here. We don't have any real training or anything."

"We should try to help them," she said flatly. The decision had clearly been made.

I didn't want to argue so I responded, "Well, you're the captain."

We pushed forward, heading for the treacherous turn. "Left. Right. Left. Right," Emm instructed. This time, I paid especially close attention to her every command.

David was getting closer to the stranded couple while Emm and I were on our way to hopefully assist. Once the two of us felt like we had made it safely past the danger point, we eased up on our paddling a bit.

Big mistake. The current caught us and whipped our kayak around before we could even react. In the next instant, we too were being swept out to sea.

"TD! What do we do?!"

"Just paddle, Emm. Keep us in synch." I didn't know if that was the right thing to do, but it seemed like the only logical move. I desperately wished that I'd paid more attention to David's pre-launch instructions instead of staring at Emm's vibrant, tan skin.

Emm continued to call out orders. No matter how hard we fought the current the best we could manage was keeping ourselves in one place, but we could only keep our sustained effort going for a few minutes. Finally, there was no point in continuing to fight the inevitable.

Fortunately—or maybe unfortunately—we floated toward a now-fuming Daveeed, who was towing the other couple to safety. He yelled something angry that sounded like complete gibberish before tossing us a rope. Emm caught the rope and fastened it to the front of our kayak, then tied the other end to the kayak of the couple in front of us.

"What did he say to us?" I asked Emm once I had the chance, but she just shrugged as if she had no clue.

The Welsh man who was being towed in front of us turned and said, "He called you 'stupid Americans,' mate."

Emm turned toward me with a serious expression…which suddenly morphed into her perfect smile. Now that we weren't in danger anymore, she was thrilled by the adventure. As for me, I would've dealt with these treacherous currents every day for the rest of my life if it meant I would be rewarded with that radiant smile of hers. Even if we were stupid Americans, at least we would be stupid Americans together.

The rest of the journey was a breeze. Once we got close enough to shore, we all unhooked from David and were finally back on our own. Emm once again led the charge as we glided over the water which, now that we were in the shallows, was suddenly crystal clear. We could see the sea floor below us: it was as if we were sliding over an expansive pane of glass. Blown away by the water's clarity, I couldn't stop myself from reaching down and dipping my hand into the swell to confirm that we were, in fact, still coasting along the farthest western reaches of France's fabled Côte d'Azur.

"This is incredible. I've never seen anything like it," I said, awestruck.

Clearly just as amazed as I was, Emm replied in a reverent hush. "Gosh, it almost looks fake."

As we rowed parallel to the coastline, small coves began to appear along the shore. Calm and completely uninhabited, each cove looked like a little slice of paradise. Slices of our very own little paradise.

Our testy tour guide circled back and signaled for the group to come together. "You guys are free to explore the park for the next forty-five minutes or so. We'll meet up again right here. If you wish, feel free to safely dock your kayaks on one of the beaches."

Not wasting another second, Emm directed us toward the most secluded of the coves. "Paddle faster!" she ordered. I did my best not to laugh at how eager she was.

A few minutes later, we turned into an inlet so narrow that a car would have barely made it through. The cliffs rose up along either side of us, making us feel as though we were exploring undiscovered territory. The inlet opened to reveal a small, sheltered beach that was one hundred feet long at best. The narrow strip of sandy seashore was only a few yards deep, at which point the landscape changed from beach to pristine forest. I'd never seen anywhere so serene, untouched and vibrant.

Completely awestruck, Emm and I sat floating in our kayak for a few minutes, taking in the cove's beauty. Eventually, the slow roll of the waves gently brought us to shore, securely docking us in the pink sand.

We stepped out of our kayak and onto our own private beach. Emm and I imagined we were the cove's first inhabitants as we found a boulder to sit down on. We sat in silence, watching the calm waves spill gently onto the shore of our personal sanctuary. There was no need for words; there was no way to describe this beauty. What use are words when the world is *exactly* as it's supposed to be?

After a few minutes, Emm, while staring out into the water said, "I know you have to leave tonight, TD, but…don't."

I let her words hang in the soft breeze before I responded. "You know I'd stay if I could, but I have to start training as soon as I get back. Plus, I have to get home to Lee. Uncle Bill told me she's had almost zero energy these last two days."

"I hate that. What's been going on, exactly?" Emm asked, genuinely concerned.

"Nothing too out of the ordinary, but it *is* time for me to get back to her. She needs me."

"I know she does…but I need you too."

Emm then grabbed my hand and turned, looking directly into my eyes. That's when she began to cry. The instant I saw the tears begin to well up in her eyes, I pulled her to me, grasping her tightly in my arms. But the tighter I held her, the more she cried.

"What's wrong, Emm?" I finally asked as I softly caressed her head.

She said nothing, continuing to weep in my arms.

What had happened? Why did she start crying all of a sudden? Was it something I'd said? And how was I supposed to fix it?

After a few minutes, Emm had cried herself out.

I carefully released her from my grasp and gently asked again, "What's wrong?"

Emm paused again before she finally began, "Nothing, I…I…" she hesitated, choosing her next words carefully. "I'm just going to miss you a lot, is all."

I knew she wasn't telling me the truth—at least not all of it. I could hear it in her tone, I could see it in her body language. And the craziest part was that she knew it, too, she knew I could tell she was lying.

My mind raced as I thought about what could possibly be so difficult for her to say to me. I couldn't help but think that maybe Emma Rey Finley was afraid to say to me the exact same thing I was afraid to say to her. I felt a surge of hopefulness; a new confidence that I had never felt before. Maybe Emm wanted to be with me as much as I wanted to be with her. Part of me didn't believe it, but it was the only explanation that made any sense.

Yet with Emm clearly so vulnerable, I didn't want to add any more stress to the moment, so I simply said, "It's okay.

We promised. Forever."

"Yes, we did. Absolutely," she replied, managing a slight smile.

We went back to enjoying what little remaining time we had left in the beauty of our paradise in silence. Then, as if the cove had sensed our stress, it sent a gentle breeze to cleanse our faces, carrying all of our doubts deep into the thicket behind us.

Suddenly Emm turned to me again, and with an urgency in her voice she asked, "Hey, can I ask you something?

"Of course. Anything," I answered seriously.

Flashing me her best puppy-dog eyes, as if she were about to make a huge request, she asked, "Can you be captain on the way back?"

She caught me so off guard that all I could do was laugh.

Just then, we heard David's five-minute-warning whistle pierce through the air. We stood up and slowly walked toward our kayak as we enjoyed the warm sand between our toes one last time. I took one more look around our beach, inhaled a deep breath and wondered if I'd ever find another place on Earth as perfect as our cove. But as I guided us out of the narrow inlet, I realized that the cove wasn't what I'd truly miss: The cove was merely our bubble-world incarnate.

We met David and our group at the designated spot. Paddling during our return trip seemed much easier, which I, of course, attributed to my being captain this time around.

"Left. Right. Left. Right," I hollered at Emm. I loved being in charge and wondered if this was a little bit like it would be when Ken and I are co-captains next season.

Paddling along, I did my best to enjoy the last of our time in this magnificent national park. As the sun climbed its arc toward high noon, the color of the water became brighter, almost fluorescent, as it gleamed. It made me think of Sal; the seawater itself reminded me of his gleaming smile.

The initially effortless ride suddenly became much more difficult. We were well past the current's strongest point, so I didn't really know what was going on. I didn't want to risk getting thrown out to sea again, so I paddled even harder while continuing my, "Left. Right. Left. Right," commands.

The extra exertion caused my brow to sweat heavily. When I stopped paddling for a moment to wipe a trickle of sweat from my eye, I realized that we were no longer moving at all. That meant that we weren't caught in any sort of current because we weren't being pulled out to sea. Puzzled, I turned toward Emm.

And then it all made sense. My former captain was behind me, asleep. In a kayak. I should have been shocked, but somehow, knowing Emm as I did, I wasn't.

Rather than waking my buddy, I secured her paddle to the boat and rowed us all the way to shore, with Emma Rey Finley slumped into herself and resting comfortably all the way.

"My flight is in six hours," I said as we climbed the stairs, returning to our rental apartment.

"Don't remind me," Emm uttered.

Getting out the door this morning had been chaos. We'd both overslept, and somewhere in the process of throwing ourselves together for the day, I'd completely overturned my suitcase. Just about every item of clothing I'd brought to Europe was now in a colorful heap on the floor. As I repacked, seeing each of the outfits I'd worn during the past ten days was almost as good as a highlight reel of our adventures.

I packed my new favorite article of clothing last. It was an ordinary white Kirkland T-shirt from Costco, but that had nothing to do with its now being my favorite shirt. The reason was because it was the shirt I had worn when we visited St. Peter's Basilica.

When Emm wasn't looking, I pressed the shirt against my face and inhaled deeply—I'd "accidentally" left it out of the laundry when we'd washed our clothes before leaving Rome. With my nose grazing the fabric, I was able to pick up the warmth of Emm that was locked inside. If I inhaled hard enough, I could almost taste her cherry lips against mine once again. Hell, I was *never* going to wash this T-shirt.

I set aside my I ♥ NY T-shirt that I'd worn on my way to Rome; I wanted to wear it on the way home too. It felt fitting to wear it as I traveled, as a reminder of where my heart always was.

"I'm all done!" announced Emm, throwing her arms up in victory as if we'd been having a packing race. Not that it would've been a fair fight. I had ten days' worth of clothing with me, while Emm had only packed a weekend tote.

"Me too," I replied. "I just have to grab Lee's dress. Where's that tissue paper we bought yesterday?"

Emm handed me the tissue paper from the counter. I grabbed the dress from the back of the bathroom door and smoothed it out. I didn't even know silk was supposed to be wrapped in tissue paper, but Emm had said it was a "must" when traveling with fine fabrics.

As I started wrapping the dress, I realized the headband was missing. "Shit!" I exclaimed. "Oh…Crap. Emm? Have you seen—"

"Looking for this?" she said slyly, pointing up. That's when I understood why I couldn't find the headband: it was around Emma Rey Finley's head.

I grinned. "Who would've thought that by the end of this trip I'd see you wearing anything with sunflowers on it?"

With love in her eyes, she almost looked like a sunflower herself. Emm absolutely beamed, emitting a wave of positive energy. As much as I wanted to get the headband back from her, it looked surprisingly natural on her.

"Hey, why don't you hold onto that?" I suggested, still smiling. "You can surprise Lee with part two of her outfit when you get home."

"That's a great idea! Two gifts in one. And Dexters just love surprises, don't they?" Emm winked at me as she said the last sentence.

"What's that supposed to mean?" I asked. Emm was obviously up to something.

"You'll find out soon enough, don't worry," she replied, enigmatically.

At any other moment, I would've pressed Emm for details. But right now, I had to hail us a cab while Emm called the apartment owner and wrapped up the last of the rental stuff. I had no idea how I was going to tell the driver (in French) that we needed to wait for Emm, but I figured I'd manage it, somehow.

The ride to the airport wasn't long, but something incredible did happen along the way. Something I hardly believed was possible: Emm didn't fall asleep.

We were oddly silent as we rode. We'd never had a real conversation together in a car, so I didn't feel any pressing need to break with tradition in that sense. Then I began to hear a familiar hum, followed by her soft angelic voice.

I see the moon, the moon sees me
The moon sees somebody I want to see
God bless the moon, and God bless me
And God bless the somebody I want to see.

Rather than chiming in this time, I closed my eyes and thought about how unforgettably wondrous the last ten days had been. I wished that I could wake up for just one more European morning and make Emm breakfast. I wished that she and I could sit beneath the moonlight and watch the tugboats of Marseille until 4 a.m., with her nestled against my shoulder. I wished that we could be secret agents outrunning the Swiss Guard one more time. I wished that I had one more day with Emma Rey Finley.

Then it hit me. Like a hurricane.

In the months that Emm had been gone, I'd never forgotten how hard it had been for me to say goodbye when she'd initially left for Europe. Since the moment I'd set foot in Rome, I'd been dreading the day this trip would end, but what I hadn't realized until this moment was that I would now have to say goodbye to her a second time. How had I never considered that? Goodbye. Again. Maybe that's what had brought Emm to tears at our cove.

Emm's flight to Rome was a good bit earlier than mine, so I walked with her toward the terminal. I slowed my pace, half convinced that if we never reached it, we would never have to say goodbye.

Emotion overtook me. I stopped short and began choking up before I managed to sputter out, "Emm...I hate doing this."

Emm looked back at me and I could see that she was holding it together better than I was. "This will be the last time. I'll never forget how spectacular this trip has been."

I looked down at her wrist and saw her turquoise bracelet glimmer. "Me neither." I paused before adding, "I just don't want this to end." If this trip had been a movie, I felt as though this was the moment where the credits would've started appearing on the screen.

Emm reached for my hand and grabbed it. Firmly. Strong enough to force me to meet my eyes with hers. "I don't ever want to be this far away from you again, TD." She jumped up, latched onto me like a kid on a jungle gym, and began sobbing softly in my arms. The chaos of the airport disappeared. With Emm in my embrace, everyone else around us vanished; we became the entire world. I never wanted to let go, never wanted to pop our bubble.

I could have kissed her right there, but I didn't. I was scared. Scared because life happens fast, and time apart from Emm was time I knew I could never get back. Scared because if I kissed her now, 6,000 miles would still separate us for the next eight weeks.

I stood there holding her until my too-tired arms gave out. As I gently put her down, Emm's face turned bright again. "I almost forgot...I have something for you!"

She reached into her carry-on tote and handed me a small paper bag.

"No way!" I cried as I opened it. "I'm never going to take this off!"

"I got it for you in Rome one morning after class," Emm explained, pleased with how happy I was. Seeing her happiness made my own parting-emotions calm down a bit.

The gift was a simple T-shirt, but it was also my favorite type: white background with "I ♥ Rome" printed on it. I immediately put it on over my "I ♥ NY" T-shirt. Through the fabric, I could just make out how each shirt's graphic hearts overlapped, as if my heart and Emm's were forever joined.

With both of her gifts now on my body, Emm sized me up. "Perfect fit!" Then she added with a soft smile, "Don't forget to keep writing me."

"Of course not, Emm," I said seriously then added, "Don't stop breaking into national treasures."

Emm laughed a sweet melodic laugh. A laugh more beautifully musical than the orchestra in Rome. I looked at her one more time. With a gentleman's bow, I said, "Until next time, Emma Rey Finley."

Emm curtsied in response. "And wherever next time may be, I shall see you there." She then danced up onto her tiptoes and softly kissed me on the cheek.

"I'm so happy at you."

"I'm so happy at *you*."

And then, just like that, she was gone.

Much in the same way as she had circled her lips after our kiss at St. Peter's Basilica, I reached up and traced the spot where Emm's lips had just touched my cheek.

I watched as Emm, still wearing the sunflower headband, melted into the crowd. Just as she disappeared, her turquoise bracelet caught the light and gleamed brilliantly, almost as if it were saying goodbye, too. We were both headed to our next adventures, only this time we wouldn't be together.

After making it through security and checking my bags, I finally arrived at my gate. My red-eye to Los Angeles wouldn't board until 9:00 p.m., which meant I had a good bit of time to kill. I missed Emm already.

I fidgeted in my seat for about an hour, doing nothing but people-watching and feeling somehow abandoned. I thought maybe FaceTiming Lee might help take my mind off of things. She knew I was coming home today, but she'd be glad to hear from me anyway.

I reached into the pocket of my backpack where I usually kept my phone. My phone was there, but my hand also rubbed across something foreign that I didn't recognize. I pulled the pocket fully open to find an envelope with my name on it.

Dear Tee Dee (Pronounced in a thick French accent),
Doomsday has finally come. I'm so sad to see you leave, but I've had the best, most exciting, most adventure-filled time with you. I don't think you'll ever fully understand how much your coming here means to me. Of all my friends, only you came to visit...and truthfully, you're the only one who I NEEDED to come.
Please tell Lee I miss her so much. Tell her, too, that I'll keep her promise. Lee says she doesn't know what you'd do without me, but I can say the exact same thing about you. You make me laugh every day, Tim Dexter, and you make me feel like I'm worth something special every single moment we're together. Thank you for that.
You know more about me than anyone else and I wouldn't want our relationship to be any other way, even if there is no real name for it. Thank you so much for the greatest birthday gift I've ever received—I'll never in a million years forget it. I'm already counting down the days until we are back home together.

Love Always, Your Buddy

Emma Rey Finley

I folded up the letter and held it closely against my new "I ♥ Rome" T-shirt. Only Emm could somehow make leaving her behind and being stuck in a dingy airport feel like a gift. Only Emm could've given me ten magical days where I could let loose and forget every stress in my life. Ten days in a dream. But then again, all that was just a part of her long list of superpowers. Emma Rey Finley: my international partner in crime, buddy and kayaking captain. But most importantly, my forever friend.

PART II

THE FLOWER

Chapter 9

My Little Sunflower

"How was school today?" I asked my precious Lee as I reached across the front seat and swung the car door open for her. Limp and sweaty, she basically fell into the passenger seat.

"It was good…just so *hot*," Lee answered as she stuck her tongue out. "That school needs a monster air conditioner. How am I supposed to *learn* if it's too hot to *think*?"

"Well, what about recess? Did Ms. Janice let you guys play kickball?"

"Yes! And it was my turn to be team captain today." Now that my car's AC was cooling her off, Lee was perking up.

"And people say that I'm the athletic one in the family. Nice job, Lee, that's my girl!"

"Sports are fun sometimes, but other times I'd just rather write my stories at recess," Lee replied. "Especially on days when the school is an oven."

"You hungry?" I asked. Today was a half-day for Lee, so

she hadn't eaten lunch yet. Neither had I.

"Starving! But I'll let you pick the restaurant since it's your birthday."

I'd returned from Europe almost two months ago and the summer was now over. Being on the quarter system, my school started later than most others, especially compared to local grammar schools. Lee's school year had started just after Labor Day, while my classes wouldn't start for another ten days.

Over the last two months, when I hadn't been working out or training, I'd spent almost every spare moment with Lee. She'd demanded, again and again, that I tell her about all my European adventures with Emm—Lee said I was "source material" for her new story. According to her, these "interviews" were essential to her writing process. I didn't argue with her at all; telling Lee about my exploits with Emm was almost as good as actually experiencing them. And I especially appreciated having someone listen to me talk about Emm—since she was basically all I thought about.

Right now, Lee wanted to hear about Emm's *Me Before You* inspired red dress. I had no problem recalling that evening—the moment Emm had emerged in her outfit was seared into my mind. I recounted all the details again as we drove to my favorite Greek restaurant.

"I knew it!" Lee laughed as we turned into the parking lot. "I knew we'd be coming here if I let you pick."

"Well...duh! Who doesn't like this place?" I replied with an easy smile.

Lee knew this was my favorite spot for Greek food, but she didn't know why. My mother, who was Greek on her mother's side, would make us delicious Greek dishes on special occasions: moussaka, stuffed grape leaves, pastitsio, spinach pie, fasolada soup. On my birthday, she always made my favorite dessert, baklava. This restaurant was the only place in Southern California that made a baklava like hers.

"What are you going to get, Lee?" I asked as I took her glasses gently from her face and began cleaning them.

"The kids' falafel with a chocolate milk," she announced,

looking up at me. "And you're going to get the gyro plate with a Greek salad, heavy on the feta," she added. "Then we'll have baklava for dessert."

I shrugged. Lee wasn't wrong. I had a go-to order at just about every restaurant. No matter the time of day or how hungry I was, my order was usually decided before I walked in the door. I was a creature of habit and I liked what I liked; Lee knew all my orders by heart, no matter where we went.

"Then go ahead and order for us, sis. You seem to have the situation well-in-hand." I said while handing her now-clean glasses back to her.

For someone so irresistibly adorable, Lee had a practical streak a mile long. She rattled off the order to our waiter in her best matter-of-fact tone.

"So, who else is coming to dinner with us tonight?" Lee asked.

"Well, we had that big blowout for me last year, so this year I'm keeping it small. It'll just be you, Uncle Bill, Ken and his parents."

"Sounds fun." Lee smiled back at me and then added, "I wish Emma was coming too...I haven't seen her in *so* long." Lee emphasized "so" as if Emm had been gone for years. The disappointment on her face was visible.

"I know you haven't," I said softly. "But she'll be home soon, don't worry," I added, trying to cheer her back up. "Just another week or so and Emm will be back."

Lee began to pout, sinking deeper into her chair to the point where she was almost completely under the table. Then she murmured, "But it's your birthday."

"I know, but we can celebrate again when Emm *does* get back. How's that sound?" I asked brightly.

Lee slowly sat back up in her chair, looking at me through her glasses. "Promise?" Her tone told me she was absolutely serious. I guess I'd be having two birthdays this year.

"I promise. We can all go to the park or something."

"Yes! Just like I wrote in Emma's birthday notebook! Let's go to the park where we can feed the ducks. That one's my favorite." Her smile was so wide that I could see all her teeth, including the empty spot where she'd finally lost her last baby tooth.

I laughed, thankful that I'd avoided one of Lee's all-out sulk sessions, which were a holdover from when she was younger, but still showed up every now and again. I had no idea what it was like to be a ten-year-old girl, but all the "parenting" blogs I'd read said this sort of thing wasn't unusual, so I didn't worry too much about it.

Our food arrived, and Lee dug in like she hadn't eaten in days. I was glad to see she had an appetite because she also had the start of a cough that I was a bit worried about. I wasn't going to mention her cough just yet, though. Lee would never let me "ruin" my birthday by worrying about her.

When Lee finally came up for air after spilling some hummus on her dark pink shirt, she asked, with a mouth half full of falafel, "TD, I know it's *your* birthday, but will you tell me the story of how I was born again?"

Lee didn't know the truth about her birth, and both Uncle Bill and I had sworn we would never tell her. My mother's mother had sickle cell anemia, meaning my mother (and Uncle Bill) were both sickle cell trait carriers. My father had no idea about his ancestry, but my mother made him get tested for sickle cell trait, too. Although my dad was pretty fair skinned with dark blond hair like Lee's, his genetic profile showed pan-European and African markers—and unfortunately, he was a carrier. This meant any children they had would have a 25% chance of being born with the disease. My parents still wanted a family, though, and that's why they adopted me.

Lee was a bit of a "surprise"—that's why there were eleven years between us—and although my mother would've hacked off her left foot before even thinking about terminating the pregnancy, I don't think she ever forgave herself for passing on the disease to Lee. In the few months my mother had lived after Lee's birth, she loved my baby sister with her entire being. I remembered that much distinctly. And so the story I told Lee was built on that love, and that love alone.

"Mom wasn't supposed to be able to have kids," I began. "She went to lots of doctors and they all said the same thing. Test after test."

"Doctors say a lot of stuff. You can't believe half of it," Lee interjected, this time after taking a smaller nibble of her lunch and using the corner of her napkin to clean her shirt. I suppressed a sigh. After dealing with doctors her entire life, Lee had a skepticism well beyond her years.

"That's exactly right. No matter what the doctors say, you can always fight. And that's what mom did. She fought for a family. That's why she adopted me when I was a baby. But she still wanted more kids and she never stopped fighting in her heart…and then one day, you came along! Our little miracle."

"I'm your little miracle?" Lee beamed.

"Of course you are. And that's why you're such a good fighter, like Mom." Besides Uncle Bill, the only person on Earth who could contradict my story would be my father, which was yet another reason why I didn't want him around.

"And miracles like me deserve milkshakes for the road, right?"

I laughed while shaking my head in disbelief. Lee had set me up. Again. Would I ever learn.

I got Lee her milkshake, strawberry-vanilla of course, then we headed back to the house. I had to stop at the administrative building on campus to take care of a few details before my party tonight.

As we pulled up to the curb, Lee asked, "Can I stay over at your apartment tonight? Tomorrow's Saturday, no school!"

"Not tonight, Little One," I responded. "I might go out with Ken after dinner for a little guy time."

Lee, clearly disappointed, rolled her eyes. "Ugh. Boys. All you do is watch sports…when you could be spending time with *me*," she said through pouting lips.

It was unusual for Lee to have one of her "little girl" fits twice in one afternoon, so I thought she was really hurt. "Alright, alright, I'll do guy time with Ken tomorrow. Pack an overnight bag so we don't have to come back after dinner. And don't forget your meds, okay?"

"Yay! I'll start packing right now," exclaimed Lee excitedly, as if we were going to Legoland for the week rather than having a simple sleepover at my place. If nothing else, Lee knew how to wrap me around her little finger.

"Now, since Uncle Bill is coming to the party right from work, I'll pick you up around 7:30—I'll text Ms. Wesley and let her know." We were fortunate that Uncle Bill's neighbor was usually available to sit with Lee when one of us couldn't be around. She had a granddaughter, a little younger than Lee, who visited often; it was nice when the two kids got to play together.

Lee gave me a hug, wrapping her tiny arms around me, before getting out of the car. Just as she closed the door she snuck in, "Happy Birthday again, big brother."

I took care of the stuff on campus before heading to my apartment to shower and change. I'd moved off campus at the start of my junior year—the dorms were too noisy and I wanted to live somewhere that was appropriate for Lee to visit. My apartment wasn't anything to show off, but it was quiet and private, which is all that I really needed. Plus, it had an alcove just large enough for a twin bed and a dresser, so I'd turned the nook into a space for Lee. She referred to it as her "escape corner" where she could write in secret. It reminded me of Harry Potter's cupboard under the stairs, but without the spiders and far more mystical.

My phone pinged as Ken's message popped onto the screen. "8 o'clock, right? Oh, and Happy Birthday, skinny."

Some best friend I had.

I typed back, "Yes. But I'm not skinny. Looking forward to seeing your parents." I hadn't seen the Zoms since just before I left for Italy, which was a bit sloppy on my part and I'd been feeling guilty about it. Where would Lee and I be if Mr. and Mrs. Zom hadn't stepped up when we'd needed them most?

Scrolling through the remainder of my texts, I saw that I'd received a message from my father. It simply read, "Happy Birthday, son. Call me if you can." Typical. In fact, I was surprised he'd remembered at all.

Of course I wasn't going to call him. Hell, I didn't even respond to his message. I wasn't going to re-open a line of communication that I'd worked so hard to destroy: life was better without him. He'd left me and Lee out to dry. I wasn't about to forget everything because of one stupid text message.

I needed to cheer myself up, so I logged onto Facebook, where I knew I'd find an onslaught of happy birthday wishes on my feed and thanked everyone by responding to each one individually. I looked carefully for a message from Emm but found nothing. Could she really have forgotten about me on my birthday? With the time difference, it was already *tomorrow* in Rome—why hadn't she called?

Lee, with her dusky blonde hair in pigtails, was the absolute picture of cuteness as she trotted down the porch steps. The baby blue, sunflower-kissed dress that Emm had bought for her in France practically floated around her as she skipped down the walkway and up to my car. I couldn't help but think how much Emm would have liked to see my little sunflower's stellar debut in her newly-imported clothes.

"You look adorable, Lee," I said as she opened the car door.

"Not adorable," Lee quickly corrected me, "Sophisticated. Like princess-level sophisticated."

"Ohh-oo-ohh, my mistake," I teased. Even though Lee's growth had been significantly stunted—another symptom of her illness—she *was* growing up and I was going to have to get used to her not being a little kid anymore.

Lee threw her bag into the back seat, then handed me a small, flat present. "Here, this is for you, but don't open it now. Now it's time to party!"

I knew better than to argue with the royalty now sitting beside me. We were running a few minutes behind anyhow, so we hightailed-it to the restaurant.

"Happy birthday, sweetie," Mrs. Zom said as she hugged me.

Mr. Zom greeted me with a firm handshake. "Good to see you, TD." I'd known this man practically all my life, but I'd never seen him hug anyone, including Mrs. Zom. In the few weeks when we'd lived with them, Mr. Zom would sometimes tickle Lee's baby chin or bounce her up and down on his knee, but I never saw a single hug. I'd always figured "no hugging" was a military thing.

"Thank you all so much for coming. It really does mean a lot," I announced to everyone.

"Anytime, my man," Ken said from the other end of the table.

My uncle slapped me on the back a bit too firmly. "It's good to celebrate these things," which was about as warm a greeting as he was capable of. In Uncle-Bill-talk, he'd just told me I'd grown up to be a fine young man.

This restaurant was famous for its chicken, bacon and ranch pizza which attracted customers from all over. We collectively decided this was going to be a pizza party and ordered three for the table, along with a host of side dishes that I really shouldn't have been eating in the pre-season. I insisted on Lee's eating something healthy too, though, so for starters we all got garden salads.

The conversation quickly turned to basketball as Ken and I described our hopes for the upcoming season.

"I think we'll be good enough to make it to the conference championship this year, Dad," said Ken.

"Yeah, we have a ton of solid players coming back from last year's team, and our size alone will help us a lot," I added.

"Ken tells me you two are co-captains this year," replied Mr. Zom. "I wasn't surprised to hear that in the slightest."

"We certainly weren't," agreed Ms. Zom in her ever-encouraging tone.

"You boys are both born leaders, especially you TD," continued Mr. Zom, who was now looking directly at me.

I added a bit of weight to my voice to drive home how seriously I took the responsibility. "Thank you, sir. We'll make sure the team brings its best every game."

Mr. Zom commanded a certain presence whenever he was around. He wasn't tall like Ken, but he was in exceptional shape and his torso, as far as I could tell, was made of pure steel. Everything about him exuded discipline and drive and although he'd always intimidated me, I respected him like mad.

Still looking directly at me he asked, "Have you thought about how you're going to use your leadership talents after you graduate?" I could feel the strength in Mr. Zom's voice as he posed his question.

"He's going to start a business," said Uncle Bill, replying for me. His six-word answer gave me just enough time to brace myself for what I knew was coming.

"Yes, sir, that's a possibility," I began, "but I don't have any idea what kind of business that may be."

Mr. Zom paused, letting my unsatisfyingly-vague response hang in the air. Then he said, "You know, you remind me a lot of myself when I was your age. Young and talented. Maybe I wasn't the smartest kid, but I was always the hardest-working, whether I was on the playing field or in the classroom. I took care of the people around me. Yet I still lacked a sense of direction."

"That's my brother to a tee," Lee interjected. "Except TD's so smart. You got that part wrong." I swelled with pride. Lee, who was as small as an eight-year-old, practically threw her response at Mr. Zom and his massive shoulders. She didn't get any points for politeness, but my little sister wasn't afraid of anyone. I turned and winked at Lee before jumping back in and smoothing things over: Mr. Zom didn't tolerate back talk.

"That's what I try to do, sir. I give everything my best. Especially to my family."

"What I'm suggesting, TD, is that you become a part of a new family. A military family. The U.S. Army will give you a sense of greater purpose. After my first tour in the Gulf War,

I knew I'd be a military man for life, like my father and his father. Not only do I serve my country every day, but I have the security of knowing that my family is provided for. And we're lucky here in California to have more military bases than any other state. After a few years of active duty, you may be able to find a permanent placement here, just like I did."

I didn't know what to say. Mr. Zom had always wanted what was best for me, but this was something I just wasn't sure we could agree on.

"And you can have that sense of greater purpose too, which is exactly what I told Ken," continued Mr. Zom. "Serving will change your life."

Trying to deflect as best I could, I replied, "It does sound like a life-changing experience, sir, but I need to think more about it."

It wasn't that the military was totally out of the question. I respected our service men and women, but I also had Lee to think of. Basic training alone would take me away from her for ten weeks or more; we'd never been separated for that long. And if I was injured on duty, I might not be able to care for her, or worse. I knew we had some amazing people in our lives—most of them (except for Emm) were seated at this very table—but at times I felt like I was all Lee really had.

"Dear, that's enough," said Mrs. Zom gently, saving me. "TD said he'd think about it…that's good for now."

Ken added, "Plus, nothing bad could happen to you man…'cause I got your back!"

Our entire table laughed at Ken's earnest, yet lighthearted, comment. Well, almost our entire table. Our entire table but Lee.

I was absolutely stuffed after finishing our dinner, but I had a pretty good feeling that a cake was on its way. I would've even put money on Lee's insisting that Uncle Bill arrange one.

As our servers cleared our table, I used the lull to make an announcement. "I'd like to invite you all to another party," I began. "The four-year anniversary of Lee's transplant is in a few months, and I'd love for all of you to celebrate this milestone with us! I'll be putting together the details and will email you as they come together."

Lee spoke up, rattling off her party plans so quickly she ran out of breath. "There's gonna be a clown and a bouncy house and an ice cream stand and an obstacle course!"

"A clown?" asked Uncle Bill to no one in particular. "We'll have to cancel that part." Like my mother, he was terrified of clowns. I'd forgotten about that.

I laughed at Lee. "I don't know about all that, sis," I said before I turned back to the table at large, "but it should be a fun day."

"We will be there, sweetheart. Count us in," Mrs. Zom said to Lee with a supportive smile. "We're all so proud of how brave you've been."

I saw the cake I had been expecting out of the corner of my eye. It warmed my heart to be around such a great group of truly caring people, and I didn't want to ruin the "surprise" they'd planned. So, trying to act like I hadn't seen the dessert, I turned toward Ken and asked him about the classes he'd be taking this quarter.

Before Ken could answer, Lee stood up on her chair and started singing me *Happy Birthday*. The rest of our table joined in, as well as a few of the other patrons. Heck, even Mr. Zom was singing, which made me wonder if something else was up. As the others finished the song, I sneakily ran my finger along the side of the cake and scooped up a dollop of frosting.

"Coffee-flavored?" I thought to myself. Coffee was Emm's favorite, but I thought maybe Lee had mixed things up; I'd told her a million times about Emm and I sharing coffee ice cream on our trip to Santa Marinella.

"Quick! Make a wish and blow out your candles!" Lee exclaimed.

"This looks like too many for me to handle. Think you can help me out?"

Lee bobbed her head up and down, giddy to participate. "I get to make a wish too," she said, climbing onto my lap.

"Ready, Lee? One…two…three!" I closed my eyes and

wished as we blew out the candles together. I wished for the only thing I was really missing: a birthday greeting from my buddy.

"What did you wish for, Little—"

"There she IS!" squealed Lee, cutting me off and practically causing my eardrum to hemorrhage in the process. I actually recoiled as she slid off my lap.

"About time," I heard Ken say. "Another ten minutes and the whole thing would've gone south."

I looked up. The best birthday present I ever could've asked for was standing right in front of me: Emma Rey Finley. It took me a moment to decide if I could trust my eyes, but in the next second, I jumped up, ran to Emm, gave her a bear hug lifted her up and twirled her around.

"I'm so happy at you on your birthday, Tim Dexter," laughed Emm.

"Emm, how did you—What did you—"

"Emma! Emma! You made it!" cried Lee as she wrapped her arms around Emm's hips and squeezed her tightly. "I thought you'd never show up. We were all so worried."

"I know, I'm so sorry, angel…My flight got delayed, and I didn't want to risk ruining TD's surprise by texting," explained Emm. "But it looks like I made it just in time for dessert!"

"But you're here now and that's what counts. Let's dig into that cake!" Lee cried.

Emm laughed while looking down at my little sister, "Haven't I always told you that dessert is the most important meal of the day?" Then she looked up quickly and flashed me one of her show-stopping winks.

"I was starting to think maybe you died in a terrible plane crash or something cool," Ken chimed in.

Mrs. Zom, visibly aggravated, bopped her son upside the head. "Watch your mouth, Ken." Lee shot me a look, and we both chuckled under our breath.

"Emma. Nice to see you," offered Uncle Bill. I was surprised he said even that much. Emm flashed him a smile and he practically shrunk into his chair.

Emm again looked down at Lee, who was still clinging to her waist. "I love your dress, pretty girl."

"Thank you! TD said you guys found it in France."

"Yes, we did," replied Emm. "But I still feel like something is missing from *votre ensemble*...so do you know what else your big brother and I found for you in France?"

Lee almost couldn't contain herself. "Tell me! Tell me!"

Emm reached into her purse and handed Lee part two of her flowery ensemble: the sunflower headband that matched her dress.

Lee, absolutely delighted, wasted no time putting on her gift. With her "look" finally completed, Lee twirled around like a fashion model. The headband sort of clashed with her pigtails, which made her presentation even cuter. "Thank you, Emma!" Lee finally managed. She wrapped her arms around Emm again.

Not wanting to be left out, I threw my arms around both of them. It felt good to finally have my two girls together again.

"Okay, cake time!" declared Emm, wiggling out of my embrace. Lee, who was sandwiched in between us shouted a muffled, "Yeah, I can't breathe in here!"

After we'd sat back down and portioned out the cake, I asked Emm, "So, what happened to your coming home next week, buddy?"

Ken jumped in before Emm could answer. "Aw, man, we've been playing you for *weeks*. Ever since you were in Italy. And you fell for it. Pshh...and Lee said you were smart?!"

Not giving Ken the attention he craved, I refocused on Emm. She replied, "When Ken reminded me that I was going to miss your birthday by just a few days, I *knew* I needed to come home early." Emm paused as she pulled a tiny taster spoon from her purse. "But really, it was Lee's idea for me to surprise you here tonight...and when she bribed me with coffee ice cream, how could I say no?"

"Dexters do whatever it takes to get the job done," recited Lee dutifully from my lap. I'd been telling her that since she was a toddler.

"Well, I must say you guys definitely surprised me…although I thought a coffee-flavored cake was a little weird."

No one had given me even the slightest hint that Emm would be here tonight. But now Lee's excessive pouting earlier all made sense. She'd thrown me off course brilliantly—and in the process, she'd wrangled an extra milkshake *and* a visit to the park out of me.

Before they said goodnight, the Zoms insisted on picking up the bill, so I didn't argue—it was nice not having to think about that stuff on my birthday. Uncle Bill announced that he too was calling it a night, and he even made it a point to say goodnight to Emm.

With the "adults" all gone, we ordered a round of beers—with a chocolate milk for Lee, of course—and sat around the table, laughing and joking and generally catching up. There was something about watching Lee, Ken and Emm giving each other a hard time that I thoroughly enjoyed. Our sarcastic-as-hell family, together again on my birthday.

"Yes! That's a great idea…and Ken can drive!" cried Lee, taking charge for no apparent reason.

Ken laughed. "Come on, you heard the young lady. I'm driving—so let's do it!"

Taking Lee bowling was one of our classic "family day" activities; the night was still young, so we'd decided a game or two at the alley was in order. Normally I wouldn't let Lee stay up so late, but it was my birthday. She'd barely coughed all night—I'd decided to let her have a little fun for once.

"Okay, so I'll type in everyone's name," Lee said as we laced-up our rental shoes.

"And I'll help you," Emm added.

Ken and I sat back, talking about how we hadn't bowled in ages. For us, "ages" meant "since spring," but that somehow seemed like a lifetime ago; I'd traveled across the Atlantic and back since.

Ken and I gazed up at the monitor simultaneously and looked for our names, which absolutely weren't there. "Sergeant Biceps, Birthday Boy, Sunflower Power, and Sleeping Beauty" Ken read aloud, laughing. "Sergeant Biceps has a nice ring to it…I can deal with that."

Lee and Emm were giggling at their little joke. It was so refreshing to see the joy Emm brought to Lee's face.

"We should make it teams," I hollered.

"We already did," said Lee. "It's boys versus girls."

"You are SO ON," Ken yelled in a sort of testosterone-fueled craze. He was so loud that half the bowling alley turned and looked at us. "You're going DOWN—I've got the luck of the Birthday Boy on my side."

I'd never been much of a bowler, but I figured a couple Division I athletes could handle two girls, one of whom was only ten. I was 100% wrong: Sergeant Biceps and Birthday Boy stood no chance. We got off to a terrible start and Lee—for being so young—held her own. Plus, Emma Rey Finley had an absolute cannon—strikes and spares left and right. Following a horrific gutter ball by Ken, the game quickly went from a losing battle to an abysmal defeat.

"Winners!" Lee shot up out of her seat as if she'd won the Heisman Trophy.

"Good game, Lee," said Ken. "Whatever you want in the arcade is on me." I was touched. Ken wasn't a sore loser, but he wasn't a particularly gracious one either. Even though Lee was only a kid, I knew he was keeping some smart-ass remark to himself. And it was extra-nice of him to treat Lee—the ten-year-old in a silk flower dress who'd just trounced him—to some games.

They disappeared into the bright, flashing lights of the arcade. Once they were gone, Emm turned to me and asked, "And what do I get for beating you, Birthday Boy?"

"You get a rematch. One-on-one, Sleeping Beauty. Let's see if you can beat me without my baby sister carrying you."

Initially, I thought I stood no chance against her dominance—Emm was still on fire. But as we approached the last few frames, she began to trail off and I quickly gained on her. Entering the final frame, Emma Rey Finley needed nine pins to win.

"Don't let it slip!" I heckled as she approached the lane. Emm took a deep breath and tossed her green bowling ball gracefully. I really thought I was done for. She hit the pins head-on, but only eight of them fell.

Soaking up my glory, I exclaimed, "I always knew I had it in me! Birthday luck or not."

"Happy birthday, TD," Emm replied tenderly as she sat down and began undoing her rented bowling shoes.

"I still can't believe you're here, Emm. I really thought I wasn't going to see you for at least another week—practically an eternity."

"At first, I wanted to tell you I was coming home early, but Lee insisted we keep it a secret." Emm scooted closer to me and rested her head on my shoulder. "I missed you so much. Rome was no fun without you."

I put my arm around her and we sat without speaking, listening to the arcade games ringing and bowling pins crashing around us.

In these quiet moments between us, I sometimes wished that I could've heard what Emm was thinking. But as she sunk even deeper into my shoulder, I knew she was thinking the exact same thing: If an ocean couldn't keep us apart, nothing could.

"Look! Look!" cried Lee, running up to us. She was holding a baby blue teddy bear that was almost half as big as she was.

"Very nice, little sis!" I said, popping up from my seat to greet her.

"Isn't it awesome? Ken won it for me!" Lee said, pointing at Ken.

"What can I say, I've got the touch!" Ken gave himself a thumbs-up as he spoke.

Emm got up on her tiptoes and sarcastically whispered

into my ear. "I don't care what you say…He's still a jackass." I did everything I could not to crack up.

We returned our rental shoes, then Ken drove us back to our cars. After he dropped us off, he peeled out of the parking lot shouting, "Happy birthday, bro!"

Lee ran up to Emm and gave her a hug goodnight. "Can we still go to the park soon?" she asked. "TD promised."

"I would love that, angel. Maybe this week?" Emm replied while looking at me for confirmation.

"I think I might be able to squeeze you two into my schedule," I teased. Lee still hadn't let go of Emm, so once again I wrapped my arms around the both of them. "Thank you for finally coming home, Emm. We missed you so much."

"It wasn't too bad," Emm replied. "Just a hop, skip and a…"

"Jump!" Lee yelled, cutting her off.

I got Lee home and tucked her into her alcove. She would've made Emm proud by falling asleep in the car, and she'd fallen asleep so soundly that I had to carry her upstairs. I went back to my car to grab Lee's overnight bag when I saw my birthday present still sitting on the front seat. I grabbed it and brought it back into the house.

Taking a seat at the foot of my bed, I carefully peeled back the wrapping paper after reading the tag that said, "From Lee and Emma." Inside was a framed picture of Lee, Emm and me, which we'd taken after one of my basketball games last year. The three of us, smiling. Our happy revolution captured perfectly.

Touched by how thoughtful the gift was, I held the picture, staring at it, until I fell asleep.

That night, my dreams were filled with visions of making Lee and Emm smile. Of making my girls' desserts sweeter. Of filling their lives with happiness.

Chapter 10

Game Day

"Do you think we're ready for Wednesday?" Ken asked as he drove. We'd just survived a particularly grueling practice and were both pretty spent—my knees felt like someone had said hello to them with a sledgehammer. Our team's home opener was coming up in a few days and Ken and I were beginning to have doubts about the strength of our roster.

"Honestly, no, I don't think we're ready as a team. But *I'm* ready and *you're* ready, so hopefully, that will be enough," I answered.

"Oh, it *will* be enough," Ken said firmly. "Leaders lead. That's what we do. If we're ready as captains—and with Coach riding our asses like this—the guys will follow." He shifted his tone, now sounding like a Klingon preparing for a galactic battle. "We will bask in the glory of victory!"

Ken always had an undying positivity about him, a positivity that helped keep me motivated. On occasion, he even referred to himself as a "vehicle for positivity." In that way, Ken and Sal were very much alike—two smiley people all around.

"Yeah, if you say so," I replied weakly. Utterly deflated, I didn't have the energy to say any more.

Ken let me sulk for a moment or two, then asked, "What's on your mind, bro?"

"Nothing, man, I'm just tired," I answered grumpily.

"Dude, you're so cranky when you're hungry." Ken reached into the cup-holder beside him and tossed me a Peanut Butter Snickers bar. "Eat," he demanded.

The last six weeks had taken forever to get through. Between classes starting back up and the pre-season, I'd barely found time to sleep, and I hadn't been spending nearly enough time with Lee. I'd known this first quarter of my senior year was going to be hell on Earth, but now the constant grind of my daily routine was really starting to wear me down, and—as much as I hated to admit it—I was prone to these lows in general. To top it all off, I still had no idea of what to do with my life after I graduated. Even when my body was resting, my mind was whirring with questions about my future. It left me with a weird, anxious, empty feeling that had only grown bigger as the weeks passed. And the worst part was that I couldn't quite put my finger on what, exactly, was missing.

"What's up with you and Emma?" Ken asked after I'd taken a bite of my Snickers. "Did you talk about that Vatican thing yet?"

"Bro, I've barely seen her, except for a few minutes in between classes when we can manage it. No time for deep discussions, ya know?" My tone was still grumpy, but I was already starting to feel better; the creamy nougat hitting my tongue felt like pure fuel.

"Fair enough. Emma's been busy just like we've been, plus I bet she's catching up with a ton of people," Ken reasoned.

Emm had a whole bunch more friends than I did. She was always more social to begin with, but being a student-athlete meant that I missed out on a lot of the normal college experience. And I was sure that Emm's being gorgeous, funny and the coolest person ever had a lot to do with her having a half-million friends, too.

I grunted in agreement as I took another bite of my peanut butter snack.

"But at least you'll see her Wednesday for the big game. She wouldn't dream of missing it, you know that."

Ken was right. Since our freshman year, Emm had never missed one of our home games, no matter what. If her study-abroad program hadn't been during our off-season, I had no doubt that she would've flown home every other week, just to see us play.

"True," I replied. "It's just that I hate not having my 'Emm time.'"

"What? I'm not romantic enough for you?" Ken joked.

"Shut up, you know what I mean," I shot back.

"We knew we'd have to make sacrifices this year," offered Ken. "You've been grinding in the gym like a PRO!"

I chuckled in spite of myself. Ken really did know how to cheer me up with his hyper-competitiveness. I didn't hit lows like this often, but when I did, Ken—like a true brother—hauled me back up to the surface every time. Hell, I'd been through worse. Much worse.

"Hey, I'm supposed to hear back from the Army soon," said Ken, changing the subject as we pulled up to my apartment. "By the end of the quarter, I'll know where I'll be for basic."

"Nice man, that's—"

"—And pretty soon you'll figure out what you're doing after graduation too. So, stop beating yourself up. And in the meantime, the team's going to be fine. Now go get some rest."

"The wisdom of Sergeant Biceps," I chortled. Then more seriously, I added, "Thanks man."

I dragged myself upstairs, plopped down on the sofa and let the cushions pull me in as if they'd never allow me to get back up again. I relaxed for maybe one whole minute before I realized it was almost Lee's bedtime. I hadn't checked in with her all day—no time—so I sent her a FaceTime request.

"Hey," answered Lee with a forced enthusiasm. My sister looked just as exhausted as I did. The circles under her eyes were deeper than I'd seen in a long, long time, which was especially worrying.

"What's wrong, baby girl?" I asked, trying to mask my concern.

"It's nothing, I just have a little cou—" Lee couldn't finish the sentence; she burst into a coughing fit that sounded as though it would never end.

"That's it. I'm coming over right now." Exhausted or not, I had a responsibility.

"No, you aren't, TD. Your season opener is on Wednesday and I'm not going to be the one who gets you sick."

"Lee, you can't keep these things from me," I said firmly. Lee had a much weaker immune system than most kids, a side effect of her bone marrow transplant. Anytime a bug was going around, she was more or less guaranteed to catch it—from the common cold, to a stomach virus, to the flu. Her weakened immune system also meant that her symptoms hit her hard; when she got sick, she got *really* sick. To complicate things even more, her doctors needed to limit antibiotic and steroid prescriptions—overuse would cause them to lose efficacy.

"I'm sorry I didn't tell you," Lee pleaded, "but I knew how you'd react. You need to stay focused."

"But you're *always* my focus," I replied as tenderly as I could. Lee managed to shoot me a sweet, but healthy-looking, smile before erupting into another coughing attack.

"You've been coughing for a while, but not like this. How long has it been this bad?" I asked.

Between labored breaths, Lee replied, "Only a few days. But Uncle Bill has been taking good care of me, I promise. And, yes,"—Lee rolled her eyes as if I were about to ask the stupidest question in the world—"I'm taking extra vitamins, resting, and drinking lots of hot fluids, too."

I suppressed a sigh. Lee knew her "getting sick" protocols

as well as I knew my pre-game rituals. I was glad she was taking care of herself, but none of this was fair.

"Now hold on for a minute," Lee continued, "I have something to show you." The screen went blank for a few seconds as she scurried into her room.

When she popped back into the frame, she was wearing her sunflower headband and holding her baby blue teddy bear. Grinning ear-to-ear, she said, "And I have these to make me feel better. See? I'll be just fine, no need to worry."

Cheering up a bit—Lee was such a little fighter—I asked, "Did you name your teddy bear yet?"

Lee giggled while holding her bear up to the screen. "I named him Moon, after the lullaby Emma sang to you in France. Sometimes before we go to bed, I sing it to him before we both fall asleep."

"Good. So go crawl into bed and sing Moon to sleep," I said. "I'll call you tomorrow to check in."

The next day was an uphill grind too. I woke up missing Emm something awful. As I cooked myself breakfast, our Roman mornings kept sneaking back into my thoughts—I couldn't even enjoy my extra-crispy bacon. As the day progressed it was difficult to focus on my classes because I was so worried about my little sister. Between texting Lee, Ms. Wesley, and Uncle Bill for updates, my phone was buzzing all day. I knew Lee needed me right now. Not being able to be there for her hurt me more than anything else. By the end of the day, even though I was mentally spent, I was itching to channel some of my angst on the court.

"You were a *beast* out there today, TD! Bring that energy to the game tomorrow and the season will be ours," Ken said after practice. "Everyone said so, even Coach."

We were the last two people in the locker room, as always. As captains, and as a show of support for the guys, Ken and I had decided we always wanted to be the last two players to leave after each practice. We also coordinated so that one of us was always the first to arrive as well.

"Yeah, well, sometimes it's easier to turn off my brain and

let my body take the lead. I probably should've been more focused on our game plan for tomorrow, though," I replied.

"Coach and I have you covered on that front, bro, don't worry about it. If your autopilot is gonna bring energy like that, go ahead and zone out."

"You're right, Ken, you're right," I said, feeling a little bit better.

Ken whipped a towel at me. "What else is new? I'm <u>always</u> right. I keep telling you, I'm pretty fantastic!" Ken shot me a smile that conveyed both "I'm a dope" and, "You know you love me."

I smiled for the first time all day. But when my phone buzzed and I glanced down—Uncle Bill's message read "no change"—my smile slid off my face with a heaviness that even Ken couldn't miss.

"Is something new happening with you, bro?" he asked.

I filled him in on Lee's situation. I found myself using platitudes like "nothing she hasn't been through before," "par for the course," and "just another bump in the road," as if I were trying to convince myself that they were true.

After I'd finished, Ken, appearing to be on Lee's side, said, "I hate to say it, but she's right. We do need you at 100%."

I sighed. I couldn't even feel good about my performance on the court—it was fueled by all the wrong reasons.

Sensing my disappointment, Ken added, "But that doesn't mean we can't still make her feel a little bit better. Let's get out of here. I've got a plan, my friend." Ken slammed his locker closed for emphasis.

I always drove us to campus on Tuesdays, so we headed to my car. "What are you thinking, man?" I asked.

"Don't ask questions, just follow my lead. You're gonna love this, and Lee will, too. Trust me. Now head on over to that supermarket by Lee's school."

I did as instructed, still not sure what Ken was planning. But I knew he only had Lee's best-interest at heart, so I followed and didn't argue.

Two bottles of orange Gatorade, a bouquet of tulips,

a bag of sour Skittles, and one book of mazes and riddles later, we were back in the car. Ken had grabbed a card too, and we'd even found a little basket to hold everything. I was touched. Random acts of kindness such as this always served as a reminder of why I considered him my "best guy friend". Especially when these "kindnesses" were aimed at my beloved little sister. That put him in the "emeritus friend" category.

"But how are we going to get this care package to Lee if she's on a self-imposed quarantine?" I asked. "Even *you* agreed I shouldn't see her."

Ken trumpeted out his rarely-used maniacal laugh, which was all the answer I needed. There was no point in pressing him—he'd never reveal his "master plan" until he was ready.

"Dude, now roll up to the curb stealth-like, but don't cut the engine," instructed Ken as we pulled onto Lee's street. "And don't close the car door behind me."

Before the car had even come to a full stop, Ken bolted out the door with Lee's care package tucked under his arm as if it were a top-secret briefcase. He ran up to the porch, dropped the basket, rang the doorbell twice and then sprinted back toward the car in one fluid motion. In all my years playing sports with Ken, it was the most perfectly-executed move I'd ever seen him accomplish.

"Move! NOW! That's an order, soldier!" he yelled as he practically army-rolled back into the passenger seat. Stunned, I floored the gas pedal; the squeal of my tires echoed through the quiet cul-de-sac as I peeled away.

"HELL yeah!" shouted Ken, riding his adrenaline surge. "Nothing like ding-dong-ditching the night before our last opening game. Mission accomplished!"

I felt a renewing smile spread across my face as I did my best to keep my car from flying off the dark road. Thanks to Sergeant Biceps, I was finally having some fun again.

Basketball had always been more than a game to me—it was my education. My athletic scholarship made attending a prestigious, four-year university possible. It was my community, one backed by the entire student body. And basketball was a way to make the people I cared about proud. In high school in particular, basketball had kept me out of trouble and had given me an outlet; I'd poured all my stresses and fears about Lee into my sport. But most importantly, the basketball court was the one place where everything made sense. There were no drunk fathers, no sick kids, no chaos or heartache. On the court, the hardest working team always won. Life isn't fair, but basketball always was.

It was game day. The season opener was a few minutes away and the locker room—even more than usual—was filled with a thunderous energy. My team could practically taste victory, and I knew it was up to me and Ken to deliver that win to them. Three months of pre-season training had led up to this point: the early mornings, late nights, and all our individual sacrifices were about to come to fruition on the court. The team around me was stretching, hydrating, and high-fiving as our coach psyched us up.

"Gabe, I'm counting on you to keep our communication solid on the floor tonight."

"Ami, don't be afraid to get in there and get physical. They can't handle you, big fella!"

"Use your speed, CT. Fly in there and get a goddamn rebound!"

Ever since high school, I had two quirky rituals that I performed before every game. I always wrote inspirational quotes on my ankle tape, and I always ran into the stands before each game to give Lee a kiss on the cheek. Except for the times when Lee was super-sick and couldn't be courtside, I'd done both religiously for the past eight years and I had no intention of stopping now. When I started playing in college, I added a third ritual: As we gathered for the pre-game huddle, I would look into the stands and Emma Rey Finley would flash me a winning smile for good luck.

Our home crowd, in blue and gold, exploded as we ran onto the court. I normally didn't get nervous before games anymore, but the opener was different—this game could set the tone for the season ahead. I swelled with pride as the crowd cheered: we wouldn't let them down. Ken was right. Even if the team wasn't exactly where I'd like us to be, it was up to us captains to lead.

As the team turned back to our bench for our pre-game huddle, I broke from the line and ran over to Lee who was sitting with Uncle Bill in her usual spot underneath our team's basket.

"I'm so glad you could make it, Little One," I said as I kissed her on the cheek.

Lee smiled for a split second before she turned serious. "Kick their ass, TD," she whispered in a hoarse voice.

I smiled and quickly nodded my head. It really was the least I could do for my little girl. Uncle Bill had told me her cough was a little better today, but I could see that Lee didn't have her normal energy. I'd have to work extra-hard to guarantee a win and cheer her up.

I ran back to join the rest of my team. Coach, as usual, was revving us up. "Alright, guys. We know what we gotta do—now get out there and play your hearts out. This game will be ours!"

In the huddle, I found it hard to focus. Emm wasn't in her usual spot. Hell, she wasn't in her second-usual spot, either. I frantically began scanning the stands for her, in vain. All my confidence disappeared instantly and my arms suddenly felt limp, like I'd just been drained of all my talent.

Sensing my anxiety, Ken got my attention and cocked his head in the opposite direction, but he said nothing as our coach continued reviewing our strategy. I looked up into the stands in the direction Ken had indicated, but I didn't see Emm there, either. What was happening?

A reflective flash caught my eye. I turned my gaze court-side, to the row of seats our school reserved for VIPs. The row was full of squirming-with-excitement Cub Scouts—and there was Emm. She and her roommate, Sarah, were handing out Mylar balloons.

Sensing my gaze from across the court, Emm turned and looked directly into my eyes, as if she'd been waiting for this very moment; as if she'd known how much I needed her right then. Once my eyes had found her, that empty void I'd had inside filled instantly. With Emm's show stopping smile now slowly spreading across her face, I could feel my strength returning to my limbs. Finally, I was ready.

"Nice game, stranger," Emm said as I walked out of the locker room after the game.

"Thanks. I wasn't at all sure I could do it until I found you in the VIP row," I replied, smiling back at her. "What was with the Cub Scouts?"

"Gosh, I'm so sorry. I should've told you I wouldn't be in my usual spot," she answered. "The kids won some sort of contest—one of them is Sarah's little cousin. When she asked me if I'd volunteer to welcome them, how could I pass up courtside seats? I'm surprised Ken didn't tell you. He popped over to do a photo op with the kids." Emm paused for a moment, got up on her tiptoes, then whispered, "I was trying to get your attention the whole time, though. I'm glad you found me."

We smiled at each other for a minute as we sort of enjoyed the silence that had settled in between us.

"Walk me to my car?" Emm asked, motioning toward the exit.

"Of course," I replied. "Lee's waiting for me outside, come say hello to her."

"Perfect! I didn't think I'd get to see her tonight since I was babysitting and everything."

It wasn't a long walk to the parking lot, but Emm and I *made* it long. We strolled the whole way, taking our time. This was the closest we'd come in weeks to hanging out, and I was afraid that once she'd gone home, the void inside would start tearing at me again.

Uncle Bill waved to us from the driver's seat as we approached, but Lee got so excited that she jumped out of the car.

"Emma Rey Fin—" she began, but Lee's excitement quickly morphed into a coughing fit.

"There, angel, what's this cough?" Gently petting Lee's head, Emm looked up at me with concern in her eyes

I filled Emm in on all the details as Lee squeezed herself around my buddy's hips.

"Don't listen to him, Emma, I'm fine," declared Lee. Then she looked up and addressed me. "Uncle Bill wouldn't have brought me if I wasn't okay. And you did SO GOOD tonight, big bro. That last shot you made…I didn't think it was going to go in, but then it fell off the rim and into the basket! Two points!"

"Only because you were there to cheer for me, Little One." I said tenderly.

"Lee, if I remember correctly," Emm began, "we owe you a trip to the park. So I'll make you a deal. If you stay in bed and get lots of rest and do everything your big brother tells you, we'll take you to feed the ducks this weekend. Saturday, after practice."

"Yes, yes, yes!" squealed Lee. This, unfortunately, was followed by a cough strong enough to dislodge her from Emm's hips.

"Sunday after practice," I broke in, correcting Emm. I didn't have anything in particular I needed to do this weekend except schoolwork, but Emm caught my meaning: Sunday meant Lee would rest one extra day.

"Sunday after practice. Deal?" said Lee soberly, holding out her little finger to Emm for a pinkie-swear.

"I swear!" laughed Emm, as she and my sister entered into the sacred and unbreakable pact of pinkie-swears.

"And you have to pinkie-swear, too, TD. No take-backsies!" demanded Lee.

"No take-backsies," I replied, holding out my pinkie which was probably four times longer than my little sister's. "But you have to hold up your end of the deal, too, remember."

We got Lee back into the car and Uncle Bill pulled away. Emm and I watched as his taillights cut through the cool night and out of the parking lot.

"Bribery," declared Emm. "Works every time."

Coincidently, Emm's car was parked only a few spots away, so I knew it was time to say goodnight. I wrapped my arms around her and held her there for a moment. It felt so good to hold her against my chest, where she belonged. I squeezed Emm just a little tighter before gently releasing her.

"You and Ken are going to be such amazing captains. Really great game tonight!"

"That's because we have really great fans," I replied modestly.

Emm unlocked her car and climbed in as I held the door for her. "I'll see you on Sunday," she said. "Remember, no take-backsies!"

Emm blew me a kiss as she pulled away. I felt better than I had in weeks. Happiness pulsed through me, yet I didn't know if it came from our having won our first game of the season or from making plans to hang out on Sunday with my forever friend. I'd bet on the latter. Given the choice, I'd always bet on Emma Rey Finley.

Chapter 11

Just the Three of Us

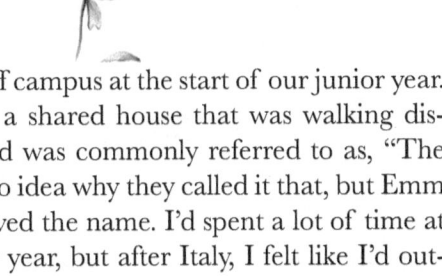

*E*mm had moved off campus at the start of our junior year. She now lived in a shared house that was walking distance from campus and was commonly referred to as, "The Nest." I honestly had no idea why they called it that, but Emm and her housemates loved the name. I'd spent a lot of time at The Nest in my junior year, but after Italy, I felt like I'd outgrown the place. Emm, knowing how focused I was on Lee and basketball, totally understood, but she thrived off of people; she wouldn't dream of living anywhere else.

Today, I wanted to pick Emm up quickly—without saying a hundred "hellos" to her roommates—so I merely honked as I pulled up to the curb even though I knew she absolutely hated that. To make up for it, I got out of the car when I saw Emm coming down the steps and held the passenger door open for her.

"And who said chivalry is dead?" she smirked as she took a seat.

"For you, Emm? I would've rolled out the red carpet if I had one."

"Is this your *Emm Playlist* I hear on the speaks?" she squealed when she heard one of her favorite tunes playing quietly in the car. "Turn it up!" Her turquoise bracelet caught the sunlight as she lunged forward toward the volume.

Laughing, I grabbed my phone and handed it to her. "Why don't *you* be the deejay today?" I asked. "But watch that USB connection, the cord's a little loose."

We pulled onto the highway and drove the few exits to pick up Lee. Emm and I sang and laughed the whole time, just like it should be. We skipped the classical pieces on the *Emm Playlist*, though. Today was a day for fun and freedom, not concertos.

When we picked up Lee, I let her and Emm take over the vocals and happily faded into the background of their concert. Their two voices, as they sang Sheryl Crow's "Soak Up the Sun," were too sweet—I just wanted to listen. My two girls sang back and forth, feeding off each other, almost as if they were a professional duet.

"I'm gonna soak up the sun,"

"I'm gonna tell everyone,"

"To lighten up."

Lee loved the duck pond, which always puzzled me, since she had been terrified of ducks as a little girl. A goose once nipped her finger while she was feeding it, which touched off Lee's duck-hating years. But now, as we pulled into the parking lot, my little sister cried with giddiness, "Park over there! In the shady spot!"

With all the things Lee *couldn't* do because of her illness, I was generally content to let her have her way when it came to minor things. I think controlling the little stuff helped her deal with the big stuff that none of us had any say in.

"Where do you want to sit, angel?" asked Emm brightly as we entered the park. "It's your day...it's up to you!"

Lee scanned the landscape, concentrating deeply, as if she were about to make the most important decision of her life. This wasn't a huge park, but it had a little of everything: Gentle hills, leafy trees, weatherworn wooden benches, a small hiking trail encircling the pond—and even a well-maintained flower garden.

"Up there!" Lee cried, pointing to the top of a small hill. "Shade for TD, with the pond right below."

Lee scrambled up to the hilltop, coughing just a little, with me and Emm doing our best to keep up. When we reached Lee's chosen spot, Emm gave me a quick wink as she spread a blanket across the grass. I didn't know what the wink was for until I looked down: She'd brought along our moon blanket. Our moon blanket, which had gone all the way to Rome and back.

"Such a pretty moon," said Lee as she plopped herself down. "Emma, did TD tell you I named my new teddy bear 'Moon'? I sing him your favorite lullaby sometimes."

Emm clearly wasn't expecting such heartfelt words; her eyes began to water. I couldn't blame her. Just hearing her mention Emm's favorite lullaby brought me back to our special night in France; all my emotions from that evening came flooding back.

Emm smiled, pushing back her tears. "When I was your age, my mom used to tell me that the seasons come and go, but when you're facing life's darkest moments, the moon will always be there. On nights when it seems like there's no light left in the world, just look up and find the moon."

"But—if you're lucky, like me—you can just roll over in bed and Moon will always be there," replied Lee earnestly. It both broke my heart and warmed my soul to hear Lee refer to herself as "lucky."

We began eating our healthy lunch under the bright sun. Rarely had I seen a November afternoon like this—I'd been worried that it would be too cool for Lee to be out for long, but the day was warm with a slow, refreshing breeze. For a Sunday, the park was pretty empty, too, which made it feel like it was just the three of us.

"I was so glad to see Ken's parents on your birthday,"

Emm said in between bites of her turkey sandwich. "I hadn't seen them in forever."

Lee, not hiding her sudden disgust, scoffed as she gave off a little grunt.

Concerned about her reaction but also slightly upset by her rudeness, I turned to my sister and asked, "What was that all about?"

"I don't like that Mr. Zom anymore," she replied with a firmness that told me she was really hurt.

"What's wrong? The Zoms have always been part of our extended family. It was very nice of them to come to the party…and to pay for our expensive meal."

Lee didn't respond. She just sat back and ate another handful of her Goldfish. She chewed her crackers slowly, then took a long and intentionally dramatic swig of her lemonade.

Attempting to console her, Emm slipped her arm around Lee. "I know he's a bit strict, but he loves you so much, pretty girl."

Lee relaxed a little. She looked up at me with pleading eyes and explained, "I just…I just don't want you to join the military. You're the only brother I've got!"

No wonder Lee was scared. I'd been the one and only constant in her life.

"Lee Rose Dexter, I would never do that to you…or even to Emm," I said. Hoping to lighten her mood, I forced my face into a big, dopey smile. "Could you even imagine me out there? I'm too tall!" Lee wasn't about to let me off that easy, though, which I sort of expected. "Then why didn't you just tell him that?" she asked bluntly.

Backtracking, I answered, "Because, Little One, Mr. Zom really thinks the military could be a good career for me. I didn't want to be rude."

Lee and Emm both responded at exactly the same moment and in exactly the same way: a death-stare so intense that I almost fell backward.

"Okay, okay…I got it you two. Army life is officially off the table, alright?"

Emm, still holding Lee, reassured her. "See? Your big brother would never do that to you. You have nothing to worry about." Lee, now feeling safe once again, lit up and finally hugged Emm back.

My sister then held her hand up to Emm's ear and whispered something. Something she obviously didn't want me to hear, but that I was just able to make out. "Thank you for being on my side, Emma. Boys are so dumb."

Clearly trying to remain serious, Emm let out a bark of a laugh in spite of herself. "Okay...Lee, let's all go feed the ducks. We've had our lunch, so let's go surprise them with theirs."

Lee jumped up with a spurt of renewed energy which caused her to cough a little, but not too much. "Yeah! I love surprises. I'll follow your lead!"

I thought it was a good idea to let my girls have some one-on-one time without any "dumb boys," so I said, "I'm going to finish my lunch first. Save me some bread to toss!"

Lee and Emm raced down the gentle slope of the hill. A flock of ducks surrounded them the moment Emm tossed her first piece of bread. Lee was having the time of her life as the ducks flapped their wings and competed for bits of food. As I sat back and enjoyed the remainder of my sandwich, I took a moment to appreciate how picture-perfect this afternoon was. Just me and my two favorite girls: Life exactly the way it should be.

Well, almost exactly.

Lee was expertly hiding the fact that she still wasn't feeling well. Three days of rest had done her some solid good, but she wasn't even close to 100% yet. She'd kept her end of the bargain, though, so there was no way I could deny my little sister her field trip, especially with Emm involved. Missing a promised "Emma Rey Finley Day" would've only made Lee sicker.

When I finished my sandwich, I snuck down the hill as quietly as I could, with a whole loaf of bread tucked under my arm. "These ducks do look hungry!" I cried, as I popped up behind Lee and threw a huge hunk of bread onto the bank.

"TD! That's way too much!" Lee said, giggling. Her giggle turned into a cough, which, somehow, she quickly suppressed.

When we were out of bread and the ducks lost interest in us, we decided to take a stroll in the flower garden. If nothing else, I thought it was a good opportunity to literally stop and smell the roses, just like Emm had always taught me.

"These are my favorites...they're almost baby blue, too" Lee said, pointing toward a patch of rare, lighter-blue tulips. "Hey TD, did you know that every flower has an everyday name and a scientific name?"

"I did, but where'd you learn that, sis?" I replied as I reached down and straightened her glasses for her.

"At recess! My friend is super into botany, just like I'm into writing. Sometimes we talk about our *life-passions* while the other kids are playing." Lee emphasized "*life-passions*" as if she and her friend had both had divine, if prepubescent, vocational callings.

Before I could reply, Lee continued, "Know what else I learned? Hundreds of years ago, tulips were sort of like money in the Netherlands. People traded them all the time. Everyone in the entire country...sometimes even up to ten times a day. It was called 'Tulip mania.'"

"Wow! I've never heard that before," Emm said, clearly proud of our little sunflower. I had to admit, I was also pretty impressed with my baby sister even though I was only half-listening.

"That's why tulips are cool!" Lee squealed. "The Dutch still have tulip festivals and everything...I want to go visit someday!"

"Okay, sis," I began. "We'll put all this tulip stuff at the top of your One Day list."

Lee immediately corrected me. "It's '*tulip mania*,' TD, not 'tulip stuff.' Weren't you paying attention?"

"Sorry, tulip mania. Got it." I replied, then kissed Lee on the top of her head.

Emm bent over and sniffed one of the tulips. "It's funny, though, I always pegged you as more of a roses girl, Lee."

"Roses are so *cliché*," Lee answered dramatically. "They're in every romance story ever. Tulips are much more original—and if you're not going to write something *original* why bother at all?"

"Well, you might be on to something there, angel," replied Emm encouragingly. "You have to include a spark of yourself in every story you write. And speaking of your stories, I have a surprise for you." Emm sat down on one of the garden's old wooden benches and pulled a square, cream-colored envelope out of her bag. "Come over here for a minute."

I had no idea what Emm was planning and even though I trusted her completely, my protective "big brother" radar went off in my head. Emma Rey Finley's world was huge; Lee's was painfully small. I hoped Emm hadn't bought tickets to some event that might overwhelm my little sister. Even when Lee was in the best of health, something as simple as an afternoon at an amusement park could wipe her out for days.

Lee clambered up onto Emm's lap with a speed that would've impressed even my coach. "Ohh…what is it, what is it?" she cried, barely able to contain herself.

I had to admit I was intrigued by the envelope, too. It looked like a gift card of some kind, but Lee's birthday wasn't until April.

"Go ahead and open it, angel. It's a little something I put together just for you," said Emm gently. At the word "open," Lee started attacking her gift with the excitement of Christmas morning in her soft blue eyes.

"Magazines for young writers?" asked Lee, reading from the paper inside. "I don't get it?" I could tell she was keeping her disappointment at bay and giving Emm the benefit of the doubt. Emm's gifts were never lackluster: Lee knew that.

"Not just magazines for young writers, angel, magazines that *publish* young writers. I made—"

"—I could get published?!" Lee burst out in absolute awe. "Like, not just in a school newsletter, but in a *real* magazine?" She practically leaped straight into the air from Emm's lap, then started bouncing on the balls of her feet. "NO WAY!

Really? TD, look!"

Lee's ebullience was unfortunately followed by her biggest coughing spasm of the day. I rubbed her back to soothe her as I took the paper and read it. "Emm, there's like twenty-five listings here. With contact info and everything. I can't believe you did… This is… is…"

"Awesome!" Lee finished for me but she'd once again quickly squelched her cough. I was glad she spoke up, because I didn't have any words in that moment.

With a quiet laugh, Emm replied to my little sister as if her words themselves were medicine. "Yes, angel, I think it's time to share your brilliance with the world. And that starts with sending your work out. Those are all magazines and websites that publish the under-thirteen-crowd only. It's a *très exclusif* group."

Lee was practically glowing. Yet, excited as she was, nothing could match the love now afire in my heart. In a single masterstroke, Emma Rey Finley had given my sister a new goal. Something real and achievable. Something Lee *could* do, rather than adding to the ever-growing list of things she'd never be able to do. I turned around and gazed at the duck pond. If I didn't look away for a moment, I was going to start crying in front of my baby sister, which was something that I had sworn I'd never do.

"So I can just send them my stories and they'll print them?" asked Lee.

"It's not quite that simple, angel," Emm replied. "These magazines get hundreds of submissions every month. The competition will be fierce. But if you pick your very, very best stories and we edit them together, then, yes, I'm sure we'll see your name in print someday soon."

"Yeah, Lee, it's like basketball," I broke in, trying to explain. "You have to keep shooting, no matter what. Even if you have missed your last ten shots in a row, you never give up. You always keep fighting."

Looking at the list again, Lee replied, "Dexters do whatever it takes to get the job done. And *my* job is to be a published author," which is exactly what I wanted to hear. Then she turned and climbed back onto Emm's lap, wrapping her small arms around her shoulders. "Thank you *so much*, Emma. I'll pick a story as soon as I get home!"

We ended our afternoon by stopping at the ice cream parlor. Emm wanted coffee-flavored, as usual, but we both knew that Lee would copy Emm's order. I subtly reminded Emm about the trace amounts of caffeine in her flavor of choice, so she quickly settled for rocky road instead.

"Thank you for everything, and for getting ice cream with me," Lee said from the backseat, with rocky road all over her face. "I just wish it was raining and we had a train to catch."

Emm and I both laughed. When my sister made these references to our trip, it was almost as if we were reliving Europe, but with Lee there with us. I had no problem with that. I wanted Lee to feel she'd been a part of our adventure. Hell, I wanted Lee to feel she would forever be a part of *all* our adventures.

I could tell from the way Lee was playing with her ice cream that her appetite was non-existent. This meant she was spent—Emm's surprise had sapped a lot of her energy and I could tell that Lee, even more than earlier, was running on her brave-face autopilot. I was suddenly glad we were dropping her off so she could get some rest; ten more minutes and she wouldn't be able to keep up the charade.

As we pulled up to the curb, Emm said, "Hey Lee, guess what?"

"What, what, what?" asked Lee with a clearly-forced excitement.

Emm clicked off her seatbelt and turned with a sort of hop to face the backseat. "Lee Rose Dexter...I'm so happy at you!"

"She was struggling today, TD, I could tell," Emm said as we sat on the pier in our usual spot. Neither of us had wanted to call it a day after we'd dropped her off. Since the sunset was now so early—daylight saving time had started over the weekend—Emm and I had decided to head to the pier to watch the sun evanesce. The sky was a canvas of oranges and reds and the brilliance of the colors dazzlingly reflected off the water. With the sky mirrored so clearly in the serene ocean, it was as if we were experiencing the sunset from two different angles at once.

I shifted my attention away from the spectacular sunset and turned to the even-more-dazzling beauty who was sitting beside me. "I'm calling Dr. Mallory tomorrow and moving up Lee's monthly appointment," I replied. "Season opener or not, I wanted to take her to see him last week, but Dr. Mallory was at some conference—I wasn't about to make Lee deal with someone new." I paused and took a deep breath. "At least today, she was wiped out for a good reason. That list, Emm...I can't remember the last time I saw my sister that excited."

"It was nothing. My work-study job this quarter is in the library—and it's a total bore," Emm replied. "I re-shelve like two books an hour. The rest of the time I just sit there. So really, it was something productive to do. I mean, libraries are for *research*, right?"

"It wasn't 'nothing'—it was *everything* to Lee...and to me, too." I spread the moon blanket around our shoulders as I put my arm around her. Emm didn't know it, but she'd made me fall even more deeply in love with her this afternoon—something I hadn't thought was possible. My heart itself felt that much bigger. I opened my mouth, hoping the right words would roll off my tongue, but they didn't.

Before I could summon the courage to try again, Emm asked, "You meant what you said? You're not going to join up, right? Every time I think about it, I get a sick feeling in my stomach." She looked picture-perfect sitting there with her feet hanging off the end of the pier.

I sighed contently, touched by Emm's concern. "Of

course I meant it. I'm not going anywhere, not with Lee needing me the way she does. And you and me, we promised forever, right? As long as the two of you are in my life, enlisting isn't an option." I tried to say something more, but my tongue betrayed me once again.

The sun at last slid completely below the horizon, leaving the twilit sky behind. "Yes, forever, TD. But...umm...I guess there's something I need to tell you," Emm's voice suddenly took on a weight and an uncertainty I'd never heard before, like she was about to tell me she was packing up and moving to the moon.

Fear shot through me, but I couldn't let it show. What in the world was wrong? "Emma Rey Finley," I began gently, "You can tell me anything—you know that."

"Well, I...I mean, I...It's like this," started Emm, with an uncharacteristic hesitation. "The first few weeks of the quarter...I wasn't just busy with school and work."

"I know, Emm, you had lots of friends to catch up with. It's okay. I'm just glad you made it to the opener last week," I replied, trying to take some of the pressure off her. I had no clue why Emm was so strangely nervous. I mean, wasn't this the same girl who'd gotten us kicked out of Marseille's grandest cathedral and then laughed about it until she literally fell over?

Emm didn't reply immediately. She gazed off into the distance until darkness settled over the pier, with the incandescent moonbeams enveloping us. Although my insides burned with tension, I waited as patiently as I could as the minutes crawled by. Emm needed to tell me something serious, and I knew I needed to give her the space to pull her words together.

Finally, Emm cleared her throat and pulled away from me as she wiggled out of our moon blanket. "I think I've met someone. We've been spending a lot of time together, and I...I...guess it's time for you to meet him."

My whole universe tore apart with her words. My heart, as if it were suddenly made of glass, cracked. A hairline fracture that started small—just a prick—then branched quickly into a thousand more increasingly-painful cracks—until it was held together by nothing but sheer force of will. Yet, whatever I felt for Emm, however close I'd come to telling her, I had to fight it back now. Like only a buddy could.

"That's amazing, Emm," I said, keeping my gaze focused on the sky above and grinding my teeth together from the shocking crush. I swallowed, then turned to her with a smile that I hoped didn't look forced. "I'm really happy for you."

Emm's face transformed into a huge smile of relief. "Wow. I'm...surprised to hear you say that," she started. "Wait, no. I...I don't know why I thought otherwise. That was really stupid of me," she added, backtracking and second-guessing herself.

I acted as if I were confused, for Emm's sake if not mine. "Why wouldn't I be happy for you?"

"I don't know...I just thought...I've been building this up in my head, I guess. I don't know why it was so hard for me to tell you. I got myself all wrapped up in knots with nerves."

"You? Nervous? Please. I don't even think that's possible," I teased.

We both laughed as the tension broke. Once the laughter had rolled over us, I said again, "Seriously, Emm, I'm happy for you."

Emm wrapped both her arms around me in an excited hug. But her hug no longer felt like home and happiness. It felt different, foreign, distant—as if every hug that had come before had been a dream. With Emm's touch, our bubble-world popped with a brutal finality.

"Thank you, Tim Dexter. You have no idea how much that means to me. And I've told Matt all about you. He wants to come to your next home game and meet you."

Emm rattled off a million facts about Matt, but I hardly heard any of them. Something about his being a transfer student. Something about Italian class. Something about family in San Francisco. Something about his parents traveling for work. None of it made sense—or maybe it made perfect sense. Maybe I'd had my chance with Emma Rey Finley in

Rome and missed it. Maybe I couldn't expect her to stay single for all four years of college. Maybe I was wrong to think she and I could be secret agents forever. Maybe this Matt guy was even more amazing than Emm was. Maybe he really did make her happy. And hell, what kind of asshole would I be if I couldn't be happy for my best friend?

Chapter 12

People Worth Fighting For

"You were very brave today," Dr. Mallory said to Lee as I lifted her back onto the exam table. Lee had a chest X-ray and some labs done earlier, and Dr. Mallory was just now finishing up her full exam. As I wrapped my hands around her hips, I could feel her bones between my fingers, which meant she'd lost some weight. I hadn't realized that.

Nowhere gave me the creeps more than doctors' offices. Lee and I had spent way too much time in exam rooms and hospitals. The years of familiarity had created an eerie, slightly nauseating, too-comfortable feeling. We'd practically grown up in this office but—through the years—we'd developed an exceptionally-close, personal relationship with Dr. Mallory, which made all the difference. He and his team were the only ones I trusted. He'd seen her through her bone marrow transplant four years ago, and afterwards, he'd also overseen Lee's mandatory year of isolation in the hospital, as her immune system regenerated. In the years since, he'd kept Lee in the very best possible health, all things considered. Plus, he did it all with a talent for working with children. His patients felt less like "patients" and more like kids who simply needed a little extra care.

"X-rays are easy, all you do is lay down and get a picture of your insides taken," replied Lee, who was still in her pediatric hospital gown. "Do you really like looking at people's guts all day?"

Dr. Mallory grinned warmly. "Yes, I do," he answered as he reached over and tickled her side. "All those ribs look like smiley faces to me." Lee started to laugh, but it turned into a cough.

No matter how awful Lee was feeling, Dr. Mallory managed to make her laugh at least once during every visit. Just one more reason why I trusted him. All the degrees on his wall meant less to me than his ability to keep Lee fighting—and smiling.

I handed Lee a cup of water from the water cooler as Dr. Mallory said, "Why don't you go ahead and get dressed. Your brother and I will step into the hallway and give you some privacy. You're not a little girl anymore!"

My stomach fell into my knees. Dr. Mallory only asked me into the hall when there was something he didn't want Lee to hear.

"Now, I don't want you to worry too much," he began as he shut the door behind us. The hallway was almost empty, making me feel even more uneasy about our conversation before it really began. "I'm almost positive this is something viral, a run-of-the-mill bug. Her chest X-ray is clear, so that's the good news."

I nodded my head, knowing full well that—in the hallway—good news was always followed by bad news. "Alright, so what can we do about that cough?" I asked. "It's gotten much worse since the last time we were here."

Dr. Mallory looked down at his clipboard while putting on his glasses. "We should get her labs back in the next few days, but for now, we'll get her started on some meds to help with the cough and reduce her discomfort," he answered. "But the cough itself isn't what concerns me. What concerns me is her inability to fight it off, her ongoing fatigue."

"But this is normal for her, isn't it?" I asked. "You've always said to expect this sort of thing as a side effect of the transplant." I knew Dr. Mallory could hear the genuine concern in my voice.

"Yes, that's true. Her immune system will unfortunately never be normal." He paused, giving me the chance to say something, but I couldn't. I wanted to hear his advice, digest it, then find the courage to properly relay whatever he said back to Lee. "The thing is," he finally continued, "Lee is going to have to scale things back. She can't be run down like this all the time—it leaves her vulnerable to a whole host of potential complications."

"Scale things back?" I parroted, hoping that Dr. Mallory would elucidate without my having to ask any more-specific questions.

"Lee needs more rest than she's currently getting, and less activity overall. No more trips to the park for a while. And... have you considered homeschooling at all?"

I sighed. "But she's already so far behind. She already needs to go to summer school every year. And what about her social development? How can she keep the one or two friends she has if she never gets to see them?"

Dr. Mallory looked back sympathetically. "I understand this is hard, but only a few years ago, Lee had a major procedure that, unfortunately, a number of patients don't even survive—we wouldn't have considered her a transplant candidate, had her case not been so severe. And with Lee, it was nothing short of a miracle that we found her a donor to begin with, since she doesn't have any biological siblings."

I slumped my shoulders and hung my head. I hated being reminded of this fact: Biologically-speaking, there would never be a goddamned thing I could do for my sister. I would've given every single cell of marrow in every single one of my bones if it meant Lee would live a normal life.

"Think about homeschooling, or even 'virtual' schooling. For long-term outcomes, it may be the best thing for her." Dr. Mallory continued to offer advice on shrinking Lee's already-too-small world. It pained me to hear his suggestions. We'd been fighting restrictions like these since the day Lee was released from the hospital. My utter frustration was palpable: This was the very reason Uncle Bill and I had always been so strict about Lee's diet, activities, bedtimes and regimen of daily medicines. All we wanted was for her to be a healthy, regular kid.

Even as we talked, I struggled with how I was going to tell my baby sister that her tiny angel wings were about to be clipped. Her energy, her fight, came from the people around her, from striving for her One Day. It came from bowling with Ken and hanging out in the park with Emm. It came from our lunches together, from just being with other kids her age in school. To me, Lee needed those quick escapes more than any pill or medication. How small could her world get before she stopped striving to be a part of it?

"We're supposed to have a four-year transplant anniversary party in a few months…Will she be able to participate in that?" I finally asked, pleading with Dr. Mallory. "She's just a kid, she needs some fun," I added.

"Hopefully. If her condition improves, I would say yes. But it is just too early to know for certain. I'm not saying she can't have a very-occasional day out if she's up to it. But for the foreseeable future, I'm recommending solid, ongoing rest."

I sighed again as I reached for the door. "Okay, we'd better get back in there before she starts to worry."

Just as I was about to turn the handle, Dr. Mallory put a reassuring hand on my shoulder. "It's just some lifestyle changes. She *is* going to be alright."

Lee gave me a half-smile that broke my heart, as Dr. Mallory and I stepped back into the room. "Geez, it took you long enough," she said, rolling her eyes dramatically. "How long do you think it takes to get dressed?"

Even though we were in the doctor's office, Lee's spirits

had been especially buoyant all day—she was still reveling in Emm's surprise gift (lasting positivity being another of Emm's superpowers). Even though Emm had broken my heart last night, I could still appreciate the brightness she brought to those around her—especially when it came to shining her light on my little sunflower.

Without saying anything, I walked up to Lee, leaned down and gave her a kiss on the forehead. She closed her eyes and gently touched my hand, as I pressed my lips to her surprisingly cool skin.

"Yeah...I don't know, man, this has been a shit coupla days all around," I said to Ken, unshelling yet another peanut that I probably wouldn't eat. I'd texted him after picking up Lee's prescriptions on the way back home. Once Uncle Bill had arrived, I gave him a quick run-down of my conversation with Dr. Mallory and escaped as soon as I could. My own well of unceasing positivity had run dry—which meant I needed to leave, STAT. No way was I going to let her see me this down. I'd done my very best by my baby sister, yet now—with this new, starkly amplified concern over Lee's health—I felt like a failure.

"Yeah, dude, that's like a double kick to the ball-sack. That's a lot to take in—especially inside of two days."

"Uncle Bill and I are going to let Lee come to the game tomorrow, but after that, we have to sit her down and tell her. I'm sure rest is good for her body, but it's her *spirit* I'm worried about. If her One Day doesn't feel achievable—like really achievable—I don't know how she'll react."

"Yeah, I get that, man. Makes total sense," Ken paused, taking a swig of his IPA. "Know what I'll do? I'll make it a point to visit her once a week. Like a 'Lee appointment.' Not just when I have the time. Every week, unless we're on the road. And maybe I'll bring my mom sometimes, too."

My stomach lurched in a strange way—equal parts appreciation and heaviness. Ken had offered something only a brother would. I didn't even have to ask.

"Thanks, bro," I replied slowly. "That'll give her something to look forward to."

"And it'll take some stress off you, too, man. Happy to do it. Guess I'd better brush up on my Mario Kart skills, though—there's no way I'm letting Lee beat me *all* the time. That girl throws a fierce turtle shell!"

I smiled for the first time since we'd entered the bar. "Yeah, put a Nintendo controller in her hand and she rules."

"I'll talk to your uncle and arrange something. I'm on it. Figuring out childcare is going to be a bitch for him—and if I can take over for a couple hours a week, I hope it'll help." Ken picked up his phone and typed a reminder into his calendar.

A waitress came by and asked if we wanted another round, which I definitely needed. We weren't supposed to have more than one drink per weeknight during the season, but I really didn't care.

"Now, what are we going to do about the Matt situation?" Ken asked, making air quotes around "Matt situation."

Ken screamed with shocked anger when I told him Emm was seeing someone seriously, as if Emm's choosing a guy who *wasn't* me was somehow an affront to him, too.

I didn't respond immediately, so Ken continued, "I still don't understand how you didn't freak out at all."

"I don't know how I managed it, either. I guess I…I…just tried to act like everything was normal. I mean, I *am* happy for her, I have—"

Ken interjected before I could finish. "Oh please. Maybe you can lie to *her*, but you can't get away with that with me. Hell, the two of you have been dancing around each other for over three years now." He leaned back in his chair looking smug as hell.

"Yeah, maybe, but it took me all of three years to figure it out. Three years *and* a trip to Europe."

Ken rolled his eyes. "You're not what they call a 'quick

study,' are you? You've been nuts about her since the day you two met. And nobody flies all the way to Rome for a 'friend.'"

"Dude, Emm makes me decent. Always has. She keeps me out of my own head," I replied. "It's confusing. *You* try risking a friendship like that."

"Plus, she's hot as hell," Ken most-unhelpfully added. Not that he didn't have a point. Emm's cherry-flavored lips suddenly felt like they were softly pressing against mine once again.

Pulling myself together, I paused before saying, "But I'm terrified of having that conversation."

"TD, your connection is strong. I don't see any possible way this doesn't work out for you, man." The smug smile from Ken's face disappeared before he continued. "Listen, I think both of you are just scared to make that leap, afraid that you might be the only one who falls in. So this new guy shows up and Emma latches onto him and—*boom!*—now both of you have an excuse not to talk about this 'thing' between you. It's our senior year, man. Have that talk now or you'll regret it. And have it soon, cuz this shit is killing you."

"But she just started seeing this guy. I can't just drop this on her, just as she's starting a new relationship. Emm seems to *really* like him. Matt must really be something…I've never seen her act like that before."

Ken turned even more serious. "Excuses. Bro, no one makes her happier than you do, and that's a fact. You and I both know it. And for all you know, Emma is even more into you than you're into her. Chicks can be crazy-hard to read. Especially the really hot ones."

"No, I'm just one of her million friends. Maybe I'm on the top of that list, but it's a list that goes on for miles. Me, I've got like four people in my life—outside of 'the team.'"

"Devil's advocate!" snapped Ken, now starting to get a bit mad. "We're talking about a *con-VER-SA-tion*—just like the one *we're* having. And ya know what? Maybe she says no. Maybe that's her truth. Fine. We'll deal with it. It's not the end of the world."

I paused for a minute, swishing the last of my second beer around in its brown-tinted bottle. Ken really was the only person who would give it to me straight; the only one who could smack me in the face with my own bullshit and make me grateful for it. My head started spinning, and it wasn't from the ale.

Whether he'd meant to or not, Ken had just posed a question I'd never even thought of before: Was Emma Rey Finley really my whole world? Or was that something I'd made up in my head? What about Lee? And Ken...and Uncle Bill... and Sal? Maybe I only had four or five people in my life, but they were damn good people. And last night on the pier, our bubble-world had burst far more easily than I ever thought it could.

Ken, returning to his usual meathead self, said, "What's really going on with you, Romeo? Are you just afraid of love or something?" He lifted his beer and threw back the last of his drink.

He'd had said it as a joke, so I didn't even bother responding. But as I stood up to pay our bill, I thought to myself that his question only missed the mark by a bit. I wasn't necessarily afraid of being in love: I was afraid of being the only one who *was*.

Ken slung his boulder of an arm around me as we walked out of the bar. "Listen, we need you in tip-top shape tomorrow. If this is gonna be Lee's last game for a while, we better damn well give her a win. Plus, Emma will be there too, so that'll also be sweet." He paused as we sidestepped a too-drunk patron, then added, "The way I see it, the only thing you can do is keep fighting. Fighting no matter what, just like you always tell Lee. And, dude, Emma and Lee are certainly people worth fighting for."

Chapter 13

Superstar

"Okay, we have twelve seconds left!" Coach shouted at us while pointing at his clipboard. It was so thunderous in the arena that we could barely hear him even though our team was gathered closely in a huddle. We were down two points and it was our ball, leaving us with the option of either going for the win or trying to tie the game.

Yet as I stood there with my team around me, the game was the last thing on my mind. My day had been tough. Although I'd tried to stay focused on my classes, Emm and the "Matt situation" were on my mind from the moment I'd woken up. Every time I tried to stop thinking about her, I couldn't. Emm—with Matt in tow—was supposed to be here at the game tonight. I hadn't seen her anywhere in the crowd, but I was also doing my best not to peek into the stands. I wasn't looking forward to meeting this guy at all, but—at the same time—without Emm to cheer me on, I felt "off" in a weird way. I'd botched a key possession earlier, and I had the sinking feeling that the score was *this close* because I hadn't been carrying my full weight.

The only thing that was driving me now, as I looked out from our huddle, was Lee. I knew she wasn't feeling at all well since she'd brought Moon with her to the game. Knowing this would be her last courtside appearance for at least a couple of months meant I needed a win. Not for myself, not for my team, not for the five-thousand fans in the stands—but for my sister.

"Hey, TD, care to join us? *Focus!*" barked our coach, as he noticed me staring at Lee. "Pay attention! This is your play!" I whipped my head back around and re-connected to the game. "Ken you're going to dribble toward TD as you bring the ball up the floor. Get it to him at the top of the key," Coach continued as he drew up the final play. "TD, give the ball up if you have to, but you should have the entire right side open to get to the rim."

"Got it, Coach," I replied. "I'm with you."

"Yeah. We're ON IT," Ken shouted with the full strength of his testosterone fueling his words.

"Okay. Bring it in," said Coach. "'Family' on three…One, two…"

"Family!" We all yelled before running back onto the floor. I shot Lee a quick smile right before I took the ball out.

Basketball once again became my escape. I'd never been one to shy away from the spotlight, but this was one of those moments I'd dreamt of since I was a kid. My hands were itching for the opportunity to put our team ahead. I felt the pressure of ten thousand eyes on me and wanted nothing more than to deliver the play they longed to see. And for Lee, I wanted nothing less than a win. Everything else finally, blissfully faded away.

Ken dribbled up the floor almost effortlessly—the defense couldn't slow him down—and delivered me the ball exactly where Coach had instructed. As I surveyed the court, it seemed as though the entire stadium jumped up out of their seats when I considered my move.

The whirlwind suddenly turned into slow motion. With defenders all around, and none of my teammates in a solid position to receive a pass, I saw no option other than to go for the win.

What had been a roaring crowd now became eerily quiet. Then all at once, they began counting down, "Five…four… three…" I took one dribble to the right before stutter-stepping and pulling up for a three-pointer, a move I had practiced a million times. I'd been perfecting it over the years—even in the quiet hours of the night, when I was the only one in the gym—but it was a shot I'd never attempted in live play, let alone in front of thousands of fans.

The defense was faked out by my hesitation, giving me the space to shoot. As I felt the Tuscan-leather ball snap away from my fingertips, I immediately knew it was going in.

Swish.

The buzzer sounded just as the ball splashed through the net. The whirlwind switched back on as the crowd exploded in a wild frenzy. I forgave myself for the earlier botched play as a swell of pride for my team swept over me. Before I knew it, fans were streaming onto the court as one synchronized, undulating wave of blue and gold.

In the next instant, I was hoisted up as the crowd chanted *"TD! TD!"* I threw my arms up in celebration as I was paraded around like a championship trophy. An amazing, elated, exhilarating feeling. A quality win on our home court. The kind of win I'd dreamed of for years. For Lee.

Eventually, the crowd set me down on my own two feet. I joined the team, where I was swarmed by reporters with microphones:

"What was going through your head in that last play?"

"How did you guys get yourselves back into the game?"

"Did you know you were going in for the win, or was the plan to tie things up?"

I answered their questions as well as I could over the crowd's cacophony. But as the media continued to barrage me with questions, my attention again drifted elsewhere. I surveyed the arena, grateful for every single fan who had given us the energy to win, but looking for one fan in particular. Where was Emm?

As the reporters turned their attention to our coach, Lee squirmed through the crowd. She ran up to me, Moon in hand, and yelled, "Nice shot!"

As I lifted Lee into the air and put her onto my shoulders, I noticed she was wearing her "Tim Dexter Fan Club" T-shirt. Uncle Bill had bought it for her during her year of isolation, when she had to watch my games from her hospital room. It was easily the most thoughtful and socially-cognizant thing my uncle had ever done.

"Love the shirt, sis," I said before delivering her a kiss on the forehead and setting her down. "How are you feeling?" Lees' glasses were all fogged up from her excitement; I removed them tenderly and cleaned them with my jersey.

"Much better now!" Lee took her glasses and placed them back on her face as she added, "But if you guys had lost, I don't know how I'd be feeling." She coughed a little, almost as if to emphasize her point.

"Uncle Bill is outside?" I asked. "Come on, I'll walk you out. I'll hit the showers afterward." I grabbed my gym bag from under the bench and slung it over my shoulder.

"Moon wants to give you a smooch!" cried Lee. I knew she was stalling for time, but I indulged her anyway; I bent down so I could receive a fuzzy, baby-blue kiss on the cheek.

I scanned the crowd for Emm one last time before we left the arena. Lee chattered rapidly as we made our way, hand in hand, down the long corridor. She was way too wound up and I hoped she'd be able to sleep when she got home. I loved how excited she was for me, but her health always came first.

Just as we took the last turn toward the exit, there she was: Emma Rey Finley. Standing beside some dude I didn't recognize.

"Nice game tonight, superstar," Emm said as she approached us. Lee immediately let go of my hand, broke into a trot, and wrapped herself around Emm.

"There you are, angel!" Emm giggled at Lee. "I was hoping for a great big Lee hug tonight."

Emm had a glow around her I'd never before seen. Not just her usual glow—which was luminous enough—but something new. A glow that was so bright, she'd stolen the spotlight from right out under me. Half of me couldn't have been happier about it; the other half was devastated.

"Well, thank you. I'm glad you made it," I replied tenuously. "I didn't see you in the stands."

"Yeah, you weren't sitting in the right place. I couldn't find you either," said Lee somewhat harshly. I probably should've scolded her, but my little sister had just blurted out exactly what was on my mind.

"We were sitting with Matt's friends," Emm replied. She paused for a moment before slipping her arm around Matt's shoulder and making introductions. "TD, this is Matt. Matt, this is TD."

I turned my attention away from Emm for the first time, and now focused only on Matt—so I could most likely (and totally unfairly) jump to conclusions about him. I really didn't want to give this guy the benefit of the doubt, but I couldn't let it show, either.

"TD, it's a pleasure. I've heard all about you. You really do sound like an amazing friend to Emma," Matt said as he shook my hand.

I suppose he was polite enough, but beyond that, I didn't see anything special about Matt at all. Average height. Average build. Average, if a little weird, haircut. Definitely overdressed. I mean, who wore Sperrys and a button-down, collared shirt to a college basketball game?

I forced my face into a smile as I replied, "Nice to meet you, too, Matt. Emm's told me all about you."

"And I'm Lee," my little sister interjected. "And Emma hasn't told me *anything* about you." Again, I probably should have scolded her, but I was doing my best not to laugh. Lee wasn't about to be sidelined, and she wasn't giving Matt an inch. I'd always admired Lee's brazenness. Whereas I struggled when meeting new people, Lee said what she needed to say.

"I love your bear," replied Matt, looking down and taking Moon's soft blue paw. He smiled a too-familiar, easy smile. A smile kind of like Emm's. Maybe that's what she saw in him.

Appearing to warm up to Matt a little bit, Lee squeaked, "This is Moon and he makes me feel better when I'm tired."

Matt got a point for his kindness to Lee. I had to admit that much as he turned back to me and said, "Great game tonight. That shot was pretty spectacular."

"Thank you," I replied modestly, "but really it was the team who set me up to score."

"We tried to get to you earlier," began Emm, "but the paparazzi beat us to ya. You're like a celebrity!"

Trying not to blush, I answered, "I just made one good shot, that's all."

"No, it was the BEST SHOT," exclaimed Lee at the top of her lungs. Her "Tim Dexter Fan Club" enthusiasm morphed into a cough; I rubbed her back as she caught her breath.

"So listen," Matt began, "Emma and I were thinking about going to the Getty Museum Saturday. There's a visiting exhibit on Louis XIV and his illuminated tapestries—it'll only be there for a couple of months. Would you two like to join us?"

"Yes! Yes! Please, TD?" Lee begged, tugging on the side of my jersey.

I did my best not to wince as I was reminded of the hard talk Uncle Bill and I needed to have with Lee. "That's very kind of you," I replied. "Let me talk to my uncle and get back to you tomorrow. Would that be okay?"

"Of course," answered Emm. "Just let us know." That "us" almost killed me.

We said our goodbyes and, after taking a few more steps toward the exit, I turned around to wave one last time, just like always. She didn't see me. Instead, I watched as Matt casually wrapped his arm around my buddy and pulled her in close as they walked away. As they matched each other's stride, they looked like they fit seamlessly in each other's arms.

Not able to watch any longer, I turned back toward the exit, doing my best to block out that image. To delete the scene from my memory.

A horn beeped outside. Through the tinted glass of the foyer, I could just make out Uncle Bill's car; he was probably wondering what was taking Lee so long. I gave her a kiss good-bye, made her promise to go to bed early and watched as she climbed into the backseat.

With Lee now on her way home and Emm off with Matt, I suddenly felt more alone than I ever had. I probably should've gone back to the locker room to celebrate with the guys, but I just couldn't do it. Instead, I walked back to my car and just sat in the driver's seat for a while without starting the engine. The quiet inside the car was painful, as was the noise in my head.

Although this was supposed to be my night, I didn't feel like any superstar. To everyone else in the arena, I probably looked like the biggest winner of them all, but in reality, I felt like I'd lost more than I could endure. In that moment, I would've traded in my jersey if it meant I could to go back in time to Marseille. To go back to our boardwalk. To our moon.

Under that moon, I should've told Emm, as the tugboats worked through the night, what was really in my heart. But that ship had sailed, and now Emma Rey Finley had found both heart and harbor with someone else. And I was either going to have to live with that, or I was going to have to live without her. A choice that was slowly creeping through my entire being like a cancer.

"No! It's not fair!" screamed Lee. "I won't do it! It's not FAIR!" She was so angry she threw Moon across the living room as she stomped her foot.

Since I didn't have classes on Thursdays, Uncle Bill had taken the morning off so we could talk to Lee together. The plan was to talk to Lee today, let her say goodbye to her friends at school tomorrow, then start her on her school's virtual learning program the following week. Lee didn't take it well.

"No, it's not fair. But that's what we're going to do," said Uncle Bill. His voice wasn't without sympathy, but sympathy wasn't his greatest strength to begin with. "No one is happy about it," he added grayly. In Uncle Bill-talk, he meant, "It's going to be hard for everyone, however your health comes first," but Lee was too upset now for translations.

I shot my uncle a look telling him to leave Lee with me. I knew he loved her, but the relief on his face was plain. He got up and practically scurried out the back door into the garden. Gardening calmed him down when he was anxious, and although I would never say as much, I was glad when I heard the backdoor swing shut. I needed to focus on Lee, on calming her anxiety and fear.

"I'm sorry Lee, but that's what Dr. Mallory said." I tried to put my arm around her, but she pushed me away. Hard.

"I don't care!" Lee shouted. "I do everything I'm supposed to. I eat all that rabbit food and I take all my stupid meds. But now you won't even let me go to *school*? I'm supposed to rot in this dumb house every day?" Angry tears began rolling down her cheeks, heavy and hot. I felt like crying, too, but this wasn't about me.

"I know it's hard, Little One, but—"

"—You <u>don't</u> know! You get to do fun stuff all the time! *You* get to go to college. *You* get to fly to Rome. *You* get to win basketball games!"

"Lee, you need rest. You've been sick for almost two months," I countered patiently, keeping my voice at least five notches below hers.

"But I told you already, TD, I'm feeling better. My new medicine is working!"

"Lee, those meds are helping with the *symptoms*, not the *cause*," I said gently, thinking that I sounded more like a parent than an older brother. "You know there's a difference between the two. We've talked about that before."

"What do *you* know?" shot Lee through her tears. "It's *my* body. I know how I feel! You just don't want me to come to the museum this weekend! Why do you get to hang out with Emma but not me?"

Lee shoved a pile of books off the coffee table, then fell to her knees and sobbed wildly. She simply couldn't take in all we'd just told her, and I didn't blame her one bit. Lee was all-too-familiar with restrictions in general, but this was a major setback and she knew it. A setback that I'd always feared might come. A setback that *we* always feared might come.

Watching my baby sister's reaction was utterly breaking my heart. Lee had fought endlessly for her One Day, but now I felt like *I* was the one holding her back, not her disease. And while I'd always done my best to include her in as many things as possible, the truth was my world was a lot bigger than hers—and not just because I was older.

I let her cry for a minute, then, as her sobbing started to ebb and I sensed she was ready to be comforted, I crawled up behind her. I put both my arms around her, cooing in her ear and rocking her, until she slowly started to accept her new, even-smaller reality.

It was times like these when I felt Emm's increasing absence the most. She was always so good with my sister and now—more than ever—Lee could've used Emm's magic touch. How could I possibly explain to my little angel that the road ahead would be harder and longer than she ever imagined?

Once Lee got control of herself, I offered, "I'd bring the whole museum to you if I could, Lee. But how about if I promise to bring you home something pretty? I'll have Emm pick it out for you and everything."

"Really?" Lee asked quietly, turning around and meeting my eyes. "That would be…okay, I guess."

I grabbed a box of tissues from the end table and gently dabbed Lee's puffy, damp face. Her glasses had fallen off in her rage; without them, her face looked even smaller than usual.

With Lee's anger now morphing into full-blown dismay, she raised her eyes to mine and softly murmured, "What about my transplant party?"

The truth was, I really didn't know where Lee's health would stand in four months' time, and I worried that she wouldn't be able to handle such a big event. But I wasn't going to take anything else away from her, at least not today.

"We'll make it happen, Lee, don't worry." I tilted her chin up with the tips of my fingers. "This will only be for a little while. We've just got to get you strong again."

"Promise?" she asked softly, almost begging. The simple word itself hurt me. The truth was, I didn't know what might happen next.

"Promise," I replied, doing my best not to cry. Doing my best not to let my own fear become visible.

"And what about my stories?" she asked, tearing-up again. "Can I still work on them? Can I still get published?"

"Of course," I answered earnestly. "You're going to be a writing superstar someday. We wouldn't stop you from writing, even if Dr. Mallory said so." Which was the absolute truth. Sickle cell disease could take many, many things away from my sister, but I would never allow that.

"Good, because I *am* going to be a published author," Lee blurted out, regaining some of her usual spark. "Stupid sickle cell or not."

"That's right, Little One. Plus, Ken promised to come and play Mario Kart with you every week, too," I said, trying to add a bit of brightness to my voice. "That'll be fun, right?"

"I beat him in bowling, I can beat him on the race track, easy," replied Lee with her usual confidence.

"And won't it be cool having a live-stream into your class-room?" I asked, latching on to every positive thought I could. "No more dress code—you'll be the only one who can go to school in her PJs."

"I guess that'll be nice. Ms. Janice is a real sourpuss about that. She always gives red marks for the dumbest things."

I took in a deep breath of relief. "See, Lee, there's a little bit of happiness in everything, if you look really hard for it. When you find it, grab it and never let go. Keep fighting for the little happinesses and the big ones will come."

"You never told me that before," Lee replied with a genuine curiosity in her tone. "Who told you that?"

"Sal. My friend in Italy—I told you about him. The smiliest man I have ever met."

"The one who used to live with us when I was too small to remember?"

"That's right. Finding the little happinesses are part of what Sal calls 'the sweet life.' It's like your One Day, but for grownups." I gently bopped Lee's small nose with my finger, which elicited a half-smile. A very welcomed half-smile.

"I'll have to include that line in my latest story," she said, while wiping the last tear from her cheek.

Lee picked herself up off the floor and started gathering the books she'd knocked over. As she grabbed her glasses and set them back on her face, she said, "And you know what? It's okay that I'm not going to the museum."

Surprised as hell, I asked, "Why's that? Art history isn't your thing?"

"Art history?" Lee asked, as if I'd just made up the strangest phrase in the world. "No, it's okay because I don't like that guy much. He'd be *too boring* to spend the *whole day* with."

Lee's train of thought was clearly going over my head. "What guy? Louis the XIV?"

"No, that Matt guy," she said firmly. "He seems like a total square...and he's not very smiley."

"Well, we don't really know him yet, and he's important to Emm," I answered in my best "we don't judge others" voice. But then I added, "You're right, though. He didn't seem very smiley to me, either."

"Well yeah—and that's not even the worst part!" cried Lee as she threw up her hands in exasperation. Clearly, she'd given a lot of thought to our brief introduction to the average guy with the weird haircut.

I couldn't help myself; considering how upset my sister had been only a few minutes ago, I took the bait and asked, "And what's the worst part?"

Lee turned and looked me straight in the eye. "The worst part is that he isn't you."

And that's when I knew Lee would keep fighting. Not just for herself, but for me, too. And if not for me, then for me and Emm, for the day when all three of us would truly be one little happy family.

Chapter 14

Third-Wheeling

My bedroom was a complete mess, which I was surprised about for some reason. I took a moment before leaving to meet Emm and Matt to throw all my clothes into the hamper and quickly make my bed. Just because I was turning into a confirmed bachelor these days didn't mean I should let basic stuff slide.

My phone pinged as I was finishing up. Ken had finally answered the text I'd sent the previous night. "Of course I can check on Lee today. But…what? You're hanging out with Emma's dude? Either you're a better man than I am, or you're really stupid, bro."

I couldn't help but take Ken's text more seriously than he'd intended. I was both looking forward to and dreading today's trip to the Getty Museum. I had serious reservations about spending the afternoon alone with Emm and Matt as a couple, and to be honest, the whole idea kind of made me sick, like, gas-station-sushi sick. Yet, somehow, I was still thrilled to be going on an adventure with Emm.

As I pulled on my "I ♥ Rome" T-shirt, my eyes fell on the framed picture of Lee, Emm and me. I walked over to the frame, grabbed it firmly and gazed at the picture for a moment. Every decision I made in my life was for those two people, for the two amazing girls who'd been captured perfectly in that moment in time. At the heart of it, they were my whole world: As long as I had this picture of the three of us together, I felt like I could overcome any obstacle.

Now a bit late, I ran out the door and jumped in my car. I'd be meeting Emm and Matt at The Nest, where we'd take Matt's car to the museum. I wasn't thrilled about that either; I usually drove when Emm and I were together, and the thought of riding in some new dude's car made me feel like I'd be third-wheeling.

The Getty Museum, although built fairly recently, is a world-class institution in Los Angeles. I hadn't been in a while—even though the drive from my place was relatively short, Los Angeles traffic often made the trip much longer, which meant that planning a visit required the whole day. The museum and its campus were well-worth it, though, and the museum was free to the public, except for parking. The building itself was a work of art. The architects constructed it right into a cliff overlooking the Hollywood Hills and much of greater LA. The grounds were equally spectacular, with gardens offering a tranquil oasis to complement the often-overwhelming museum experience. No matter how little a visitor may know about art, they could always stop for a minute and take in nature's glorious, universal beauty. A beauty that— thanks to Lee and Uncle Bill's garden—I'd grown to appreciate. I was especially happy about the Getty's gardens today; if I needed a break from the "Matt situation," stepping outside for a minute would look totally natural.

"You seem a little quiet today," Emm said, trying to regain my attention as I stared out the window. Traffic hadn't been bad, so we were almost at the museum. Thankfully, Emm had decided to sit in the backseat with me, which had made me instantly feel a little more comfortable, although my focus had been waxing and waning throughout the drive.

"Sorry…I just wish that Lee could've come with us, that's all," I replied, which was at least half the truth.

Before Emm could say anything, Matt caught my eye in the rearview mirror. "Emma's told me all about Lee's illness. I'm so sorry to hear it. Your sister sounds like an extremely brave girl, and I think she's very lucky to have you."

Genuinely appreciative, I replied, "Thank you. You're right—Lee's very brave, but I like to think that I'm the lucky one to have her…not the other way around."

"Well, I think that you're lucky to have each other," pronounced Emm. Then she reached over the seat and put her hand on Matt's shoulder. "How much longer, babe?"

At Emm's "babe," I almost threw up in my seat.

"Just a few more minutes," Matt said as he reached back with his free hand and squeezed Emm's fingertips. "I think I'm supposed to get off at the next exit."

As we pulled off the highway, Matt began hopping through the channels on the radio, clearly unable to find something he enjoyed. After a few more skips, Sheryl Crow came through the speakers. Just as he had with all the other songs, Matt listened for a few seconds before jumping to the next station. I shot Emm a quick glance and smirked, just as we pulled into the Getty's parking lot. This dude still had a lot to learn.

After we got out of the car, I offered a $20 bill to Matt. "Here, man," I began, "for gas and parking."

Matt shook his head as he put his hand on my shoulder, "Please, there's no need for that. I'm just happy you could come today—Emma talks about you all the time. And who wouldn't want to hang out with our school's superstar athlete?"

I thought Matt was trying a little too hard. I didn't know how to respond, but thankfully Emm saved me. "Pshh. He isn't that good," she teased. "He just made one lucky shot."

The three of us relaxed into a laugh as we headed toward the tram. The tram was another gem of the Getty; it would take us all the way to the top of the cliff and to the main campus. Almost as soon as we'd boarded, Emm pressed her face against the tram's glass wall, with Matt following suit and cuddling up beside her. I gave them a few inches of distance, but even I had to admit that the view—as we progressed upward—was breathtaking. We were high above the hustle and bustle of the City of Angels, and although the day was on the cool side, the sky above was bright and almost cloudless. The late-autumn sun seemed to be welcoming us as we ascended.

"I had no idea you could see Los Angeles National Cemetery from here," Matt said as he pointed into the distance.

"All those brave men and women," said Emm reverently.

"Thousands who served our country," replied Matt. Turning to me, he asked, "Emm tells me you've decided against a military career?"

"Yeah," I replied. "If things were different, I might've decided to join-up with our friend, Ken. But Lee needs me. I couldn't do that to her."

"Plus, you probably have NBA scouts all over you," added Matt.

"When I was young, pro-ball was all I thought about, but now I'm not sure how realistic that is," I answered. Which was true. I still had the "life after graduation" question hanging over me—and if the NBA was interested in signing me, I was pretty sure they would've reached out to my coach by now.

Matt hugged Emm even more closely as he answered, "Well, I never thought I'd be dating the prettiest girl in the world, but here I am."

Emm smiled as she looked back at him. They exchanged a knowing glance, then kissed. Not even trying to be discrete. No little peck either, a full-lipped kiss, right in front of me. Like it was the most normal thing in the world for Emm to be kissing someone other than me.

After their lips disconnected, Matt continued, "So, I guess what I'm trying to say is that anything is possible."

I turned my gaze into the distance, trying to focus on anything other than the glass box I now felt totally trapped inside of. In a way, I guess Matt was right. I never thought an average guy could be dating someone as singularly exquisite as Emma Rey Finley, so I guess anything truly *was* possible. If I was to get half as lucky as this guy, then I was going to be the next Michael Jordan. Although, in that moment, Michael Jordan was the last person I wanted to be. I only wanted to be with my shooting star.

The tapestries were breathtaking. Each woven with gilded threads, the tapestries literally glittered, seeming almost alive. Each and every one of them was hand-woven, and some stretched over thirty feet long. Stories of love, conquest, victory or sorrow were depicted in the masterpieces that adorned the walls. Classical gods and mythical beasts danced in each scene. Some tapestries had been commissioned by specific noble families, while others had been part of Louis XIV's permanent collection at Versailles.

"Woven gold for The Sun King," said Emm excitedly as she joined me in front of a tapestry depicting the Emperor Constantius appointing Constantine as his successor. It was my favorite piece in the collection so far. The sea crashed behind the two men as they negotiated with each other in the presence of the god, Poseidon, and an angel of the Lord.

I could tell, even from those few words that Emm's adventurous energy was building up inside of her. She'd behaved herself well thus far—she hadn't even mocked the docents as they shushed patrons—but knowing her history in museums, I was pretty sure Emm was about to burst. Smiling to myself, I wondered if we'd have the Swiss Guard on our tail any moment.

Almost as if she knew what I was thinking, Emm pulled out her phone and took a selfie with one of the tapestries. Flash photography was a big no-no in the museum, but she didn't even attempt to be discrete. She snapped away as I suppressed my laugh.

"Your turn. Go pose in front of that one," she instructed, pointing to a piece in the corner of the room. Which, of course, I did, no questions asked. I don't think I could've helped myself if I'd tried—Emm never failed to pull me out of my shell.

Emm had pointed to a tapestry that showed a flexing Zeus, so I jogged over and flexed my arms as well. It was fun to show off my biceps for once, which weren't bad at all. They didn't compare to Ken's, of course, so I was usually hesitant to show off my "guns" whenever he was around.

"Got it! Let's get another one. Go fast, TD!" The gleam in Emm's eye was pure mischievousness now: We were finally back on a mission. We hadn't been on one for months—not since Europe, and I sorely needed this to help take my mind off things after my tough conversation with Lee.

As I ran over to another tapestry, I tried to get Matt's attention. "Come on, man. Join me for this one," I called. Aghast at our behavior, Matt merely shook his head. Like any average guy would do.

"Don't be lame, come on," cried Emm. But Matt still wouldn't budge. He just stood there, shaking his head and frowning.

Picking up my pace, I made it to our next Kodak moment and struck a serious pose, Emm joyfully snapped away. By this time, we'd caused enough of a disturbance for security to take notice. Two guards were now heading toward us, grimacing all the while.

"See," Matt said, pointing out the guards. "I knew this was a bad idea."

All I could do was laugh as Emm tossed me her phone. "Just take one more of me and King Louis. *Hurry!*" She pointed to the exhibit's centerpiece, which was a statue of Louis XIV on his throne with his legs crossed and a too-serious, "I am your King" look on his face.

Emm faked-out the guards as she rushed over to the center of room. This was the exhibit's most crowded spot. Anyone else might've considered cutting through the crowds to be too risky, but not Emm. I sprinted after her, weaving in and out of innocent art-goers and generally causing a commotion.

"Quick!" Emm struggled to say in between labored, laugh-filled breaths. She then mimicked the Sun King's pose, although she didn't have an actual chair in which to sit. Balancing in an air throne—on one foot, so she could cross her legs just like the statue—she also copied Louis XIV's expression almost exactly.

I focused the camera as quickly as I could as Emm triumphantly cried, "*Liberté, Egalité, Fraternité*! This one's for Lee!" At that exact moment, two guards, lunging at Emm, suddenly appeared in the frame.

Snap.

The two guards surrounded Emm. A third guard approached me and started barking orders. A fourth was standing by the door with a mortified Matt in custody. The three of us were then escorted out of the exhibit before we received a lengthy lecture on proper museum decorum—Emm and I snickering all the while. We were then banished from the museum for the rest of the day, an all-too-common occurrence in our storied friendship.

"I can't believe that just happened," said Matt, clearly frustrated, as the museum door slammed behind us. "Why did you do that?"

"Awww, come on, babe," replied Emm. "There are too many rules in the world. I can't possibly follow *all* of them." She tried to put on a contrite face, but it turned into a mischievous grin. "What fun would that be?"

We'd been banned from the museum but not the grounds, so I walked a few yards over to a bench as Emm smoothed things over with Matt. Lee had been right: Matt was a total square. Anyone who wanted to hang out with Emma Rey Finley would have to loosen-up and be prepared to bend the rules every now and again. I'd learned that during our freshman year. To be fair, I really had to cut Matt some slack: I was usually a bit of a square, too, whenever Emm wasn't around. Whenever Emm wasn't pushing me to really *live*.

"Okay, TD, back to business," declared Emm as she and Matt walked over to me. "Did you get it or not?"

"Of course I did, buddy!" I held my hand up for a high five. "Come look."

Emm took a seat beside me and we began scrolling through her phone, looking for the illicit photos that led to our dismissal from yet another world-renowned institution. Matt clearly wasn't ready to laugh yet, so he sort of pretended to be overly-interested in the flowers and greenery of the grounds. Emm and I, laughing at our exploits, really didn't care—we were too preoccupied with our very own, newly-created art collection.

When we swiped through to the final picture, the two of us totally lost whatever little composure we had left. I had somehow managed to take a perfectly focused pic of Emm in her air-throne. But that wasn't even the best part: A few feet away from her were the two uniformed guards, almost in a blur, reaching toward her. As a bonus, there were even a few gasping patrons in the background.

"Now this is real art!" cried Emm. "*This* should be in the exhibit!"

"Only you, Emm, only you. The Sun King would've been proud," I managed to utter, regaining my breath. For an instant, I almost felt like we had our bubble-world back. Almost.

"Hey, Matt! Come on over here and look. *Pleeaasse,*" Emm beckoned to her totally-average boyfriend.

Matt wandered over to us and took the phone from Emm's hand. I could tell he still wanted to be upset, but he chuckled in spite of himself. "You two are something else," he said with a grin.

"Emm, send that pic over to me and I'll frame it for Lee,"

I said. I'd promised her something pretty from the museum, but since we were now banned, I'd have to make do with this. Even if I had all the money in the world, I knew there was nothing more that my little sister would adore than this photo of Emma Rey Finley.

"That's a great idea!" exclaimed Emm. "It'll make the picture that much more special for her."

Now that we had some unscheduled free time, we decided to hit up a little café on the other side of the garden. I was starving; missions with Emm always caused me to work up an appetite.

Once we'd received our orders, I scanned the gardens for a shady spot (owing to my complexion's inclination to turn instantly lobster-red, even in this diffused November sunshine) and took in the simple, natural beauty of the grounds—the statues, the lush greenery and the flowers were all landscaped to utter perfection. Nature's art in all its splendor was always, to me, much less-intimidating than the art itself in any museum.

"Over there," said Matt, pointing. "Decent shade, with a little seclusion."

I was about to agree, when Emm blurted out, "Not over there! Don't you see those horrible sunflowers?" She didn't wait for us to reply. She took off toward a bench that overlooked the cliff. "Let's go sit by the view instead," she called back to us.

Matt, absolutely befuddled, shot me a look that said both, "What just happened?" and "Can you help?" I struggled not to laugh; clearly his "fun facts" about Emm were lacking, and I was now beginning to feel as if this guy was the actual third wheel, not me.

"I don't know, man," I began, "she just really hates sunflowers. Like, it's almost a phobia."

"A flower phobia?" Matt asked as we began walking to Emm's safe, sunflower-free zone "I've never heard of anything like that."

"No, Matt, not a flower phobia, a *sunflower* phobia," I continued to explain. "She's cool with all other flowers, especially all other yellow flowers."

Still totally confused, Matt asked, "Well, what's wrong with the 'sun' part of sunflowers then?"

"I couldn't tell you, man," I said, shrugging. "She hates the damn things, always has. Don't ask me why, though. I've known her for years, but to me it's still the single-greatest mystery of Emma Rey Finley."

Emm had fallen asleep—of course—the moment we hit the road, which left Matt and me in a semi-awkward position. I don't know what our drive was like for him, but the forty-five minutes of small talk were absolute torture for me. He told me about his parents' real estate business—he'd be joining their West Coast branch after college—the reasons why he'd transferred schools, a few personal antidotes. To me, it sounded a lot like everyone else's life story. Average as hell.

For the life of me I couldn't grasp what Emm saw in this dude, though I really did try. After our afternoon together, which had been filled with far too many public displays of affection for my comfort, I could tell Emm and Matt had a certain chemistry, but *where* that chemistry came from was beyond me. Part of me had hoped hanging out with them today would prove that they weren't, in fact, very compatible, and that this relationship would soon fizzle-out. But from what I'd seen, I could tell Matt was here to stay—unless I garnered the courage to tell Emm how I truly felt.

When at long last we pulled up to The Nest, we woke up Sleeping Beauty before Emm and I climbed out of the car. Matt was working a late shift tonight, and I was glad to have a few minutes alone with Emm. I could've done without seeing their impassioned goodbye kiss, though.

Once Matt had driven off, Emm turned to me and asked eagerly, "So, what do you think of him?"

I honestly didn't have anything against Matt, in the general sense. He seemed like a decent-enough guy. He obviously cared for Emm, and as much as I hated to admit it, I could appreciate that. He made her happy, and I could appreciate that, too. But there was no way he loved Emm more than I did, no way he could make her laugh like I could. Why was it so hard for me to tell Emm how happy we could be if we were together?

I forced myself to reply, "He's a great guy, Emm." I kept a smile on my face as I said it, trying to act like I'd actually meant it.

"You don't have to do that," shot Emm, defensively.

"Do what?" I asked.

"Lie."

"What makes you think I'm lying?" I asked while trying to form my face into an innocent expression. Emm could call me on my bullshit like no one else, and she clearly knew something was up.

"Because anytime anyone says, 'He's a great guy,' it means he totally sucks. It's the most obvious cop-out in the world. Everybody knows that."

Feeling caught, I nervously replied, "I don't think that he totally sucks. I…I just think he's a regular dude, that's all."

Emm wasn't angry, but she sure was getting there. Her nostrils flared a little as she said, "And what's wrong with me dating a 'regular dude'?"

I quickly backed-off a bit. "Nothing at all, Emm, I just think you deserve the best."

"You just don't know him well-enough," she snapped, now actually mad. "He's sweet and genuine and he'd give me the whole world if I asked. He makes me feel special!"

I didn't think it was possible, but I felt my heart fracture even further. A quick, sharp pain. Emm had always told me *I* was the one who made her feel special, and if she'd ever asked me for the world, I would've given it to her and then some. What the hell was I supposed to do now?

I reached over and hesitantly touched Emm's shoulder,

then sort of pulled her in toward me. She was stiff for an instant, but then she relaxed as I put my other arm around her as well. "I'm glad, Emm, I really am," I said contritely. "If he's important to you, he's important to me, okay?"

"He *is* important to me, Tim."

"Then we'll make it work," I promised. "He'll be a part of our family, too."

Emm fell silent for a moment, then turned around in my arms. She looked up, meeting my eyes for the first time, and gave me a half smile that almost looked like a frown. "And you'll still be happy at me?" she whispered.

"I'm always happy at you, Emm. Forever."

As the words fell from my lips, I didn't know if they were true or not. They were obviously the words Emm needed to hear, but internally, I was boiling. Emma Rey Finley, with her boring, average guy. Almost too much to handle. I buried my chin into the top of her hair to hide the lone escaped tear now burning its way down my cheek.

Chapter 15

Chocolate Chip Banana Pancakes

For the first time since we'd met, I had no idea what Emma Rey Finley was reading. I tried to focus on the pages of my book as the streetlights flashed-by, but reading just wasn't as fun without my buddy to share the journey. Even when we were apart over breaks, knowing that Emm and I were reading the same story meant that I could always find a little piece of her inside of our book. A little piece of us on each page.

The Alchemist was a damn good novel, but my heart just wasn't in it at the moment. Which was a problem, because the team and I were on the bus back home after an away game at Arizona State—one of the strongest teams this season—and we had at least another two hours left on our ride.

I must've sighed audibly, because Ken, in the seat in front of me, turned around and asked, "What's with you, bro?"

"We played one hell of a game tonight, man," I replied, trying to avoid the question. But, of course, Sergeant Biceps wouldn't let me get away with that.

"Yeah, we did—and you sure do seem thrilled about it. What's with this funk?"

I looked up at Ken. He knew exactly why I was in a funk, but I loved him for asking anyway.

"I just can't get into this book," I evaded once again.

With that, Ken switched into his "vehicle of positivity" mode, climbed unceremoniously over his sleeping seatmate, and plopped himself into the empty seat beside me. "Come on. We killed it tonight! And we've won practically every game in the last three weeks! Who does that when they're on the road like this? Over Thanksgiving break and everything."

I shrugged, but Ken did have a point. The team had finally found its rhythm, which always happened a bit later in the season for us, and we'd won four of our last five away games. We really were on fire, and everyone in college basketball knew it.

"And, dude, at our last home game, you made the shot of your career! You should be on top of the world."

"I know, I know. It's just…"

"TD, you *always* do this. Unless someone comes charging at you with a banner that says, 'Welcome, Tim Dexter,' you think you're not really wanted—like some kind of adopted-kid syndrome."

I didn't reply. Even if he was the only one who was allowed to say as much, one of these days I was going to punch Ken in the teeth—since he was absolutely right. One-hundred percent right.

"Emm's been waving a banner at you for three and a half years," he continued. "Talk to her already."

I said nothing as our bus continued to cut through the night. Eventually, I muttered, "But she's happy with him. I saw it…they're in love. I can't ruin that for her."

When I was with Emma Rey Finley, time stood still. All of my problems seemed to fly far, far away, and I'd never realized until this quarter just how much she lifted me up. And now, with the, "Matt situation" I felt our distance—an eerie darkness—every waking moment. I yearned for another adventure with Emm, for my next afternoon with her, for the next moment when I'd really feel alive. As if my life were a movie, the times when we weren't together were on fast-forward—it was barely worth watching the miserable, anxiety-filled scenes in between. But when I finally got to an "Emm" scene, I would stop, take a deep breath, press play, soak in every second of our time together—and then fast-forward again. Ken was right. I had to tell her. I couldn't just keep fast-forwarding through my entire life.

"She may really love him, but what you two have *has* to be deeper than any new relationship," Ken reasoned. "She may just not understand how you feel."

"But what if I tell her and she…doesn't? If she turns me down? Then what?" I asked, holding my head in my hands. Emm's shooting me down was the one singular thought that had been plaguing my mind since Rome. It was the thought that kept me up at night; the thought that was running through my head on repeat.

Trying to answer this tough question as best he could, Ken said, "Then…well…I guess it'll be awkward for a couple weeks, but do you seriously think you guys wouldn't get past it? You've been friends forever."

"I honestly don't know. That line was pretty clear until this summer, I feel like once I put this out there, everything changes. For better or for worse."

"And anyway," continued Ken, ignoring my angst, "that's not gonna happen."

I smirked back at him, "Oh yeah? Then tell me what *is* going to happen?"

Pleased that he'd gotten a rise out of me, Ken's face morphed into a big shining grin. "Well, she's gonna collapse into your arms, of course, and then you'll live happily ever after!"

Just getting the "what if" question out of my mouth and into the real world had helped, and I chuckled a bit. I'd never figured out where Ken got his positivity from exactly, but he'd never once failed me.

"Okay, but seriously, how am I going to do this?" I asked.

"I mean, what am I going to say?"

"Man, do you have to have a plan for *everything*? It's not like you have to write her an entire book or something. Just speak from the heart, see what comes out."

I slumped my head again. "You know that's not how I work. I gotta have a game plan going into it. What if I say the wrong thing? Or worse, what if I start to say the right thing, then botch it? What if I…"

Ken cut me off. "Fine," he said, exasperated. "Fine, fine, fine. Tell you what. We've got some time to kill here, so let's do a lovey-dovey play-by-play. Map out some scenarios. 'Talking points,' at least. I've got a notepad in my backpack somewhere. We'll figure it out."

I crept up to the front door and slowly unlocked it, hoping that I didn't somehow look like a burglar—it was nearly three in the morning, after all. I hated not being able to spend holidays with Lee. The holidays for me always meant time on the road with the team—and I loved that—but it didn't stop me from missing my baby sister. So even though I was totally exhausted, I'd decided to make a quick stop before heading home. I hadn't seen Lee in over a week, and I still hadn't given her my promised gift from the Getty, so I decided to leave the framed picture of Emm on her air-throne as a surprise for Lee when she woke up.

Much to my liking, I found my baby sister sound asleep; she'd even closed her blackout curtains, which meant she was taking the "getting a good night's sleep" thing seriously. Her room was a bit messy, and I worried that I might wake her up as I made space on her nightstand for the frame. Lee stirred a bit, but then rolled over and actually started snoring. She must've been exhausted. I gently kissed her on the forehead before tiptoeing away.

I slept like a log that night, straight through the following afternoon. When I woke up and saw my alarm clock flashing 12:02 p.m. I decided right then and there to take the rest of the day off. It was a Saturday, in any case, and although I knew I would need to spend all day Sunday studying, I deserved a day to relax.

"TD!" cried Lee, as I popped my head into the living room a half-hour later. She scrambled up from in front of the TV and ran over to me, giving me a big hug.

"I've missed you so much!" I exclaimed, reaching down and hugging her right back. "I'm sorry I've been so busy lately."

"You played so great last night, I watched the whole game," Lee said, with her head buried in my stomach.

"You did? Well, how did I look on TV then?" I joked.

"Not too bad," she shrugged, playing along. "And thank you for my surprise this morning. It's awesome!"

"Emm had me take that picture just for you. We even got kicked out of the museum for it."

Lee's eyes widened. "You *did*? Just for taking a picture? I bet I can write a whole story about that."

"It's true. Scout's honor," I replied, laughing. Of course Lee wanted to write about my adventures with Emm. I suspected that most of her stories starred fictionalized versions of me and Emm in some way.

"Come watch cartoons with me," Lee said as she grabbed my hand and walked both of us toward the sofa.

I took a seat and wrapped my arm around my sister as she explained, in detail, the premise of *SpongeBob SquarePants,* as well as the plot of this particular episode. She kept her eyes glued to the TV the whole time. The detail she went into was astonishing, although it killed me to know she was stuck in the house, watching television all day.

As soon as I could get a word in edgewise, I asked, "How many episodes of this show have you seen, Little One?"

"About a hunnerd," Lee answered, mid-yawn.

"A hundred? Wow. I don't think I've seen a hundred episodes of anything, ever," I replied as I squeezed her quickly, to hide my concern: she shouldn't be this tired so early in the day.

Lee went back to explaining the current episode. As soon as there was another lull in her explanation, I asked what I really wanted to know. "How have you been feeling, Lee?"

"Good. Tired sometimes, that's all. Now, see that character with the tentacles? He's the…"

I didn't know why I'd even bothered to ask. Lee never told me the truth, and if I pressed her it would only upset her. I was surprised that she'd even admitted to being tired.

Uncle Bill appeared in the doorway to the kitchen. "Didn't know you were here."

"I thought I'd come and spend some time with Lee," I replied. "I can make her lunch if you want." With that, I turned to Lee and asked, "Are you hungry, sis?"

Her eyes left her cartoons. She shot a half-hearted smile up at me, which meant she wasn't really hungry but would probably eat if I cooked.

"Then I'd best get to work!" I jumped up from the sofa and headed into the kitchen. Uncle Bill quickly patted my back as I stepped through the kitchen door, which was his way of saying, "It's such a nice surprise to see you, I'm glad you're here."

"I think I'll make her my famous chocolate chip banana pancakes," I said as I took the flour out of the cabinet.

"Good idea," Uncle Bill agreed. "Maybe she'll actually eat those."

"What's that?" I asked, alarmed.

"Lack of appetite, some days. More so than usual," he replied.

"Are you—"

"—I don't know, TD," he continued, cutting me off—something so unusual I immediately shut up and listened. "Some days, she almost seems like a normal kid. Other days, she can barely get off the sofa. I've told Dr. Mallory."

"And he said…?" I asked, prompting my uncle to continue.

"Could be the new meds…the twice-weekly ones. Tired days seem to line up with those. Or it could indicate just how hard she was pushing herself when school started. Tough to say for sure."

"But it's okay as long as she's on rest?" I asked.

"Probably."

My uncle's "probably" punched me in the stomach. How was "probably" an answer to a question this big? Yet I could tell Uncle Bill didn't have any more information, so I left it at that. He'd just strung together a whole conversation; pushing him any further would likely cause him to clam up. And the one thing I couldn't have was Uncle Bill not sharing health updates with me, especially since the season was now in full-swing, and my absences would really start piling-up.

"I'll be around for a while if you have some errands to run," I said, letting my uncle off the hook. He immediately looked relieved.

"That's helpful," he replied. "I do have some things to do. I'll go tell Lee."

I normally only made Lee my chocolate chip banana pancakes on special occasions, but now that I knew she wasn't eating enough, I was extra-glad Uncle Bill had all the ingredients on hand. Chocolate chip banana pancakes were the one thing we'd always been able to get Lee to eat during her year of isolation following her transplant. If she ate them then, she'd eat them now.

Ten minutes later, Lee poked her head into the kitchen. "Smells like bananas," she cried. "Did you make my favorite, just for me?"

"I did, Little One. I thought we'd have breakfast for lunch today."

"I'll get the syrup!" Lee exclaimed. Thankfully, I'd have no trouble getting her to eat today.

As always, I cut Lee's pancakes into squares for her. Before I'd even finished pouring her maple syrup, Lee grabbed a bite-sized piece of pancake and popped it into her mouth.

"Lee! Manners?" I chastised as I handed her a fork. Being on rest didn't mean she was allowed to forget simple politeness.

"Okay, will you tell me the story now? Of how you got kicked-out?" asked Lee, her cheek somehow already sufficiently covered in crumbs and syrup.

I wiped her face as I began explaining all the trouble Emm and I had gotten into at the museum. I wouldn't have traded this afternoon with Lee for anything in the world, but remembering my day at the Getty only made me miss Emm even more—that omnipresent void inside of me seemed to growl that much more deeply.

If Emm had been sitting at the table with us right now, this lunch would've been absolutely perfect. Hell, there was a time when I would've texted her and asked her to come over, but now she was probably off with the guy with the weird haircut. Having an average day, talking about average things, and worst of all: probably even kissing his average lips.

I ended up spending most of the day lounging around the house with Lee. We watched cartoons and played board games for a couple of hours; her energy level waxed and waned throughout the afternoon. After a down period, when her energy picked-up again, I suggested we start planning her anniversary party. It was still three months away, but it was always better to plan ahead. And anyway, party-planning would make Lee's day a little bit happier, too.

"So we want to do it at the duck park right?" I asked as I pulled out a pen and paper from Lee's "homework nook" in the corner of the living room.

"Right!" she cried. "We can forget the clown, because Uncle Bill's too scared, but I want us to have a relay race," she said, smiling at me.

"You got it! It's your day, so we'll do whatever you want."

"And here's my guest list," she added, as she pulled a piece of white, lined paper from her desk. "Ms. Wesley said she's going away with her family that weekend, but I want everyone else to come."

I wasn't at all surprised that my aspiring little Hemingway had already handwritten her guest list. I grabbed the paper and read it aloud. "Tim Dexter. Uncle Bill. Emma Rey Finley. Ken Zom. Mr. and Mrs. Zom. Dr. Mallory. Moon. Sammy Woods and his parents."

"Yeah, that's everyone," declared Lee.

"Okay, but who's Sammy Woods? I haven't heard that name before."

Lee responded with a forced casualness in her tone. "Just a friend from school—he's in my class this year. Uncle Bill lets him come over and we just hang out."

"*He*?!" I responded, probably sounding a bit overly-dramatic. It's not that I wasn't glad Lee had a new friend. It's just that I thought we were still a few years away from *boyfriends*.

"What?" said Lee, clearly teasing me.

"You've got to be kidding me. First Emm gets a boyfriend and now you? I'm not sure if I can handle all this," I said, still shocked.

"He's not my boyfriend, he's my friend-friend. I told you about him. We always talk about our *life-passions* together," she replied, with an almost lyrical hint in her voice. "But he does say he likes me extra because my middle name is Rose."

I wasn't buying this "not boyfriend" stuff for a second, but I did remember Lee mentioning something about a friend who was into plants. "Well, I guess Sammy can come…but I need to talk to him first."

Clapping her hands together, Lee yelled, "Yes! And he can't wait to meet you either. He even comes over to watch your games sometimes. He's a big fan."

Just then, Uncle Bill, fumbling with a bunch of bags, opened the front door. "TD, help?"

Thankful for the distraction, I walked over and took the heavy bags from him. "Guess you really did have some shopping to do," I said.

"Groceries, yes," he replied. "Gardening stuff in the car, too. Bring that around back while I put these away?"

I lugged the bags into the kitchen before heading back into the living room. "Be right back little lady," I said to Lee as I jogged out the door.

I opened the trunk to find two, 25-pound bags of black mulch. I was supposed to be resting my body today, but I couldn't shy away from the challenge: I decided to take both bags in one trip, with one under each arm. Closing the trunk did prove to be a bit awkward, though.

I didn't have any problem bringing the bags into the back-yard, but as I got closer to the garden shed, a tag hanging from one of the flowers caught my eye. Then another. Then another. Tags everywhere. What was this?

I threw down the bags on the spot then bent down and squinted at the tag on the crimson flag plant. "*Schizostylis coccinea*," it read. "*Primula vulgaris*," was printed on the primrose tag. The lavender plant read, "*Lavandula stoechas*." The tag on the hollyhock said, "*Alcea rosea*." The sunflower by the shed read, "*Helianthus annuus,*" and Lee's beloved tulips were labeled "*Tulipa.*" The whole garden. Every single plant.

"Uncle Bill!" I called loudly. "Someone's been messing with your garden!"

A moment later Lee came outside, practically skipping across the lawn in her bare feet. "We did that! I forgot to tell you!" she cried excitedly as she came toward me, her small toes gripping the grass below.

"Wow, that's a lot of work for you and Uncle Bill. When did you do this?"

"Not me and Uncle Bill—although he helped, too," answered Lee, clearly proud of herself and with more energy than she'd had all day. "Me and Sammy. We do a few plants every time he visits. It's fun!"

"And where'd you learn all these fancy names?" I asked. "That's a lot of research."

"*Scientific* names," said Lee. "And I didn't even have to look them up. Sammy knows them all—he memorizes them. I told you, botany is his *life-passion*."

I looked across the garden again in utter disbelief. Clearly my little sister had found a true friend in Sammy, someone to help her fight. "Lee, you're one awesome kid, you know that?" I said, tousling her dusky blonde hair affectionately.

She looked up at me and smiled brightly. "I know. I'm your little miracle, remember?"

I swooped down and grabbed her in my arms. "You're the most amazing person I've ever known, sis. And you'll always be my little miracle."

Chapter 16

Action

*T*his isn't my normal Saturday night, but hey, I'm all for trying new things," Ken joked. His legs dangled off the end of the pier just like Emm's, except they were much less sexy.

I'd spent the last two weeks working on the talking points Ken had helped me with on our bus ride home. What had started off as an outline—bullet points and brainstormed notes—had somehow morphed into an entire monologue. There was just so much I needed to say, so much I needed to explain. I was afraid of leaving out a single detail, of not conveying just how much Emm truly meant to me. Of my tongue swelling up in my mouth. Of making an ass of myself. Of losing her forever. And so, Ken—truly taking one for the team—had agreed to stand in as Emm tonight so I could re-hearse pouring my heart out.

"Please," I said jokingly, "You know I'd trade you for her any day."

"You sure do know how to charm a guy," he replied, grinning. "Let's just hope you do better than that with Emma."

We both fell quiet for a moment as we looked out over the ocean. The water stretched into the night's darkness, yet the waves were placid. The Pacific, itself, seemed small in comparison to all I had to say.

"Before we start," said Ken, "I have to tell you that I found out where I'm going to be stationed after basic training. My dad pulled some strings to get me placed early."

"Where are they sending you, man?"

"After ten weeks of basic, they're shipping me off to Afghanistan," he replied.

From the gravitas in his voice, I didn't know whether I should be happy or upset, so I waited for him to continue. "I'm just happy I'm going somewhere I can actually make an impact," he explained.

"Exactly," I agreed as I slapped him on the back. "You'll be able to make a real difference over there."

Ken suddenly looked like he'd just come from a funeral, a totally unnatural state for him. He looked far into the distance and said, "It all just seems so real now, bro."

"You're going to do great, Ken. Your parents are proud of you, I'm sure. And so am I."

"Thank you, man, that means a lot. I'm just a little nervous going into it, I think. It'll be a whole new life," he replied. "You're right about my parents, though. I don't think I've ever seen my dad that proud of me, so that's something."

"Yeah, and I'm totally sure you won't shoot yourself in the foot or anything," I chided. "At least not on your first day."

Ken broke into a wild laugh before flexing his biceps and declaring, "I'VE SO GOT THIS!" Which made me laugh so hard I almost forgot the reason we were sitting on this pier tonight. Almost.

Eventually we settled down, although it took us a few minutes. "Now," began Ken, "let's get to the real reason we're out here on this Saturday night…when I could've been at a house party, buzzed and flirting with *the ladies*." Words of a man who always kept his priorities in order.

"Thank you again for doing this," I said sincerely.

"Anytime, brother. I'll shut up now. Go for it—I'm officially all ears," Then, right before he fake-zipped his mouth closed, Ken gave me one of his overly subtle cues. "And... ACTION!"

I thought about all the times Emm and I had sat in this exact same spot over the years. I psyched myself up, somehow managing to bite the inside of my cheek, recomposed myself and pulled my note cards from my pocket. Then I took a deep breath and forced myself to press 'play.' I concentrated on being fully-present while imagining that Emma Rey Finley was beside me.

"Can I tell you something?" I started, looking out into the ocean before us. From there, I continued to speak, the words tumbling out of my mouth in big, heavy swaths. But once I got warmed-up, my confession came to me much more naturally than I had anticipated. As I talked, my words turned on a movie reel in my mind: The day Emm and I met; the night during freshman year, when we watched *Remember Me* in her dorm room; the afternoon when I introduced Emm to Lee; our kiss in the basilica; our bubble cove in Calanques National Park. As I was reminded of the key moments in our storied friendship, I suddenly understood what Ken had been saying all along: Emm *had* to feel the same way about me. The more I thought back on each of these moments, the more I was convinced.

Having gained the confidence I needed, I flowed smoothly through the remainder of my surely-life-changing monologue. I fell silent once I'd finished. I'd gotten so intensely lost in my confession that I'd nearly forgotten Ken was beside me.

After a moment, Ken turned to me, his face awash with awe. "Dude, that's a lot. Like, *a lot*. Even I didn't know all that."

I looked over at him and met his eye. "Yeah, I know." Then, almost pleading, I asked, "So how was that? Did I do okay?"

Ken wrapped his finger around his chin. "I wouldn't change a thing," he answered. "So long as you're sure you want to say all of that. That's a...pretty tall pedestal you've put her on, ya know what I mean? I don't know if anyone could really be *that* perfect."

"Yeah, but you said to speak from the heart. If I'm going to go through this, I have to be honest. About all of it. I shouldn't leave anything out."

"No, you're right about that. I...I just wasn't expecting some of it. Emma really is *the one* for you, isn't she?"

"Yeah," I said definitively, smiling as I remembered the softness Emm's cherry-tasting lips.

"Then you gotta do what you gotta do. But Tim," Ken paused before he continued, "Once it's out there, you can't take it back."

The smile dropped from my face. "I know. Believe me, I know."

We looked out into the distance for a while, saying nothing. If I squinted, I could just make out a fishing boat sitting on the water, and wondered who would be out at midnight, casting lines into the moonlit ocean.

"So when are you going to do it?" Ken finally asked, breaking the silence.

"After our home game this Friday. Matt will probably be with her, but I'm going to ask Emm for some alone time afterward. I'm pretty sure she'll come as long as I give her a heads-up first."

"Well, whatever happens, man, I have your back," offered Ken. "But don't worry about it. You're her Prince Charming and everyone knows it—this Matt dude doesn't stand a chance."

"Let's hope Emm sees it that way, man."

"And tell you what. Once you two ride off into the sunset, I'll take Matt to my barber. I only met him for a minute, but God knows he needs some help in that department. So really, it's a win/win for everyone!"

I punched Ken in the arm as hard as I could before pulling him in for a hug. He really was a jackass. The most decent jackass on the planet.

As I released Ken from my embrace, my attention again drifted to the seemingly never-ending ocean before us. The secrets it kept. The possibilities it held. A world unto itself.

"You can do this. She loves you, too." For the next six days, I started each morning by saying this affirmation to myself in the bathroom mirror. Each afternoon, too, and sometimes in the evenings as well, Ken and I practiced my confession until I had it down cold—we rehearsed it so often that Ken himself probably could've repeated it word-for-word. By Friday, after breakfast, I felt ready. Or, as ready as I could be.

With my hands literally shaking, I picked up my phone and punched together a text. "Emm, can we go to the pier tonight? Just you and me?" I waited a whole minute for her to respond, with my phone in a vice-like grip, before my head started swirling with doubts: What if she had plans? Or, what if she didn't have plans before, but was now making plans just to avoid me? What if she didn't miss me at all? What if this whole thing was just one terrible, terrible idea?

In that moment, my phone became the most important thing I owned, my most prized possession. Why was it taking so long for her to respond? Three minutes passed; they felt like hours.

By the fourth minute, I simply couldn't take it anymore...I needed an out. I started typing again, "Never mind. We can get toge—" but before I could finish, Emm's reply popped onto the screen. "Yes, please! I could use some quality TD time. I really miss you."

I practically fainted with relief.

Going to classes that day was out of the question—I was too nervous. In four years, I'd never once skipped a whole day of school without a good reason—I decided I deserved it. I needed the rest anyway. I hadn't really slept all week and needed my energy for the game that night. We'd be playing one of the best teams in the country and nobody thought we stood a chance against them. Were it not for Sergeant Biceps and his always-positive, testosterone-filled drive, I might've felt the same way. Our team was on fire this season, but our opponents tonight could burn the place to the ground.

I spent the day watching TV, texting Ken for reinforcement and generally trying to distract myself. But there really was no distraction from Emma Rey Finley and my seemingly insurmountable task ahead. Several times, I caught myself rehearsing my monologue aloud, without even meaning to, because tonight wasn't going to change my entire life. Nope, not at all.

My confession was relentlessly on my mind, until about five minutes before tip-off, but it wasn't until I saw Emm in the stands—without Matt—that I knew tonight was actually going to happen. There was no backing-out now.

The one bright spot in my day was that Lee had a much-better-than-expected week, and Uncle Bill agreed to let her come to the game tonight as a special treat. So, as usual, I began the game by running over to Lee and giving her a pre-game kiss. I was surprised to see a boy about her age sitting next to her—but, of course, there wasn't any time to ask questions.

The game was a dogfight. We fought hard, but our opponents more than answered every punch we threw. Right from the jump ball, they clearly had an advantage and possessed a focus I'd never seen in all my years of basketball, yet we never once backed down.

We were trailing by eight points, with four minutes to go, when our coach called a timeout and ordered us into a huddle. "They want it more than us!" he yelled. "Maxwell, we need you to get in there and get physical, son."

"Yes, coach!" Maxwell replied before taking a swig of his water. The poor dude was a sweaty, exhausted mess. We all were.

As our coach continued to bark, our home crowd began chanting in unison. They were so loud that we could barely hear Coach's orders, but at the same time the crowd was giving us the energy we so desperately needed to tie this game up and bring it home.

Feeling a new sense of urgency, the five of us walked back onto the floor, ready for battle. We went after every loose ball, buckled down on defense and hit most of our outside shots. We fought harder than we ever had before. But in the end, it wasn't enough. The other team's talent was just too much, and though we managed to cut our deficit in half, we didn't have enough time to complete our comeback: We lost by only four points. Even though we suffered our first defeat at home this season, we left the floor with our heads held high.

Outside the locker room—after I'd had a quick blissfully hot shower—Lee came up to me and wrapped her comforting but too-thin arms around me. "I'm sorry, TD."

"It's okay. We played hard and that's what counts. Did you have fun watching at least?"

"I did! And I've really missed watching you play. But I didn't like that number fourteen on the other team—he was really rough with you," she said. Her pigtails swung freely as she frowned and shook her head.

Lee's concern cheered me up immediately. "Don't worry, I'm a big boy. I can take care of myself out there. He wasn't going to hurt me."

As the one and only card-carrying member of the Tim Dexter Fan Club, Lee always had more concern for me than for the game. In fact, even though she had been watching me play since she could walk, she didn't know much more about basketball than any other kid her age. Yet I needed that innocence sometimes; Lee helped remind me that, at the end of the day, this was all just a game. Plus, I loved watching her get all worked up when we lost, which I sort of thought of as a consolation prize.

"Who's your friend?" I asked, motioning toward the same kid who'd been sitting with her during the game. I thought this kid was a little too put-together for a ten-year-old boy—he had a flannel wrapped around his waist and he was wearing a brand-new pair of white Converse sneakers—and I got the sense that he was trying to impress my sister with all the pre-pubescent swank he could muster.

"This is my friend, Sammy. Sammy, this is my big brother, TD," Lee said, introducing us. That's when I noticed Lee was dressed up a bit too; she was even carrying a small pink purse.

"Nice to meet you, kid," I said flatly, putting my hand out to shake his.

Sammy meekly reached out his hand and shook mine. I could tell he was a serious kid, which did make me feel a little bit better about Lee's having a "friend" who was a boy.

Sammy didn't say anything back to me, so Lee spoke for him. "He is a really big fan of yours!"

I focused my gaze on Sammy and smirked. "Oh, is that so?"

"Yes, sir," replied Sammy, sounding a bit awestruck…and, hopefully, slightly intimidated.

Sammy was probably a sweet kid, but I resolved to keep a keen eye on him, just in case he turned out to be some juvenile delinquent heartbreaker. "Don't call me 'sir,' kid. My name is TD," I said sternly as I arched my shoulders and intentionally loomed over him.

Sammy nodded in response before timidly adding, "I've watched your games since I was little." With that, he retreated behind Lee, almost using her as a human shield.

Lee very conspicuously changed the subject. "Did Uncle Bill tell you he's letting me go to the movies tonight?"

"He didn't, but that sounds nice. Just be careful not to overdo it."

Lee rolled her eyes at me, dramatically. "I get *one* evening of freedom…you're supposed to say, 'I'm so happy at you,' and 'Have fun,' not hit me over the head with all that big brother stuff."

I smiled as I shook my head in bewilderment: Lee was apparently now scripting my words for me.

"And please tell Emma I'm so sorry I couldn't see her to-night," she continued. "Ask her to come visit me soon."

"Okay, Lee, I will. Have fun…and I'm so happy at you!"

Lee grabbed Sammy's hand as they scurried down the hallway, laughing about something. It was cute as all hell, but Lee and I needed to have a long talk about Sammy, and we needed to have it very, very soon. My little miracle was growing up.

Picking up my gym bag and slinging it over my shoulder, I caught sight of my other miracle. I saw the miracle who—with all of her sunshine—could fill the incessant void in my heart.

I saw *her*.

Chapter 17

Freakin' Flawless

*H*er eyes lit up when they met mine. Her warm energy surged through me, even though she was all the way at the end of the hall. I couldn't wait the full thirty-seconds it would've taken Emm to reach me; I broke into a run, grinning all the while, but stopped just short of swooping her up. I wanted to begin our evening on a more mature note—and, for starters—I wasn't even sure what "the rules" *were* anymore.

"That was a tough game tonight," Emm said, smiling sympathetically.

"I know. But I'm proud of our guys. We'll bounce back, I'm sure of it."

"You boys always do," she said as her smile widened. "I'd expect nothing less."

"It's been too long, Emm. I'm so glad you came tonight." In my mind, the distance that had cropped up between was already getting smaller; in reality, though, I couldn't tell if that was true. I was currently lost in the depths of her bottomless brown eyes and the sweetness of her nose that was kissed with teeny freckles. Even now with Emm being only inches away from me, I still wanted her closer. Close enough to be in my arms.

Emm bit down on her lower lip and raised her eyebrows slightly. I was afraid I'd made her feel guilty, so I immediately extended my arm to her, like a gentleman.

"Shall we?" I asked.

Emm put her hand into the crook of my elbow. "We shall," she said somberly. Then she changed her tone altogether and exclaimed, "Let's get out of here, huh?"

The pier was walking distance from the gym, so Emm and I decided to leave our cars in the parking lot and enjoy the unseasonably warm December night. We talked about the little stuff as we walked—almost like making small talk, but not quite. It was kind of hard to concentrate, though; all I could focus on was Emm's gentle, warm hand tucked into my elbow, and the softness of her body when she brushed against mine. It still wasn't our bubble-world, exactly, but it was nice. Really, wonderfully, nice.

It wasn't until I saw the pier that I remembered why, specifically, I'd asked Emm to join me tonight, at which point I turned back into a bundle of nerves. I swallowed hard. Audibly hard, apparently.

"What's wrong?"

"Nothing," I lied. "Just a muscle spasm. It happens to me sometimes after games."

Emm looked up at me like I'd just said the weirdest thing in the world, but she let it pass. "Come on, old man, let's go sit down."

When we reached our usual spot, Emm spread out her moon blanket. The night was so warm—almost like springtime—that I was surprised she'd brought it at all. I was touched she'd remembered.

The darkness stretching before us didn't seem real. The new moon was hiding away, and clouds blanketed the sky, blocking out the stars. It all seemed staged. Even still, I found the darkness comforting—maybe this wasn't real, maybe we were on a movie set, maybe the sky above was a projection, maybe we were just actors being fed lines. Maybe, after whatever came next, the director would yell out "cut" and we'd find ourselves back in Europe. Maybe this pier was really our pier in Marseille. Maybe we were still in our bubble-world, after all.

We sat chatting for a good long while. Emm caught me up on her classes, her parents, the latest happenings from The Nest, and—unfortunately—her trips back and forth to San Francisco with Matt. I could've done without the "Matt reports," but I feigned interest anyway to keep our conversation going smoothly. When, at last, she put her head on my shoulder, just as she used to, bliss ran through me—like peach tea at a summer picnic. In that moment, I forgot about the movie set, forgot about my confession…even forgot my opening lines. Always her most transfixing superpower: Emma Rey Finley could make me forget. Anxiety, fear, worry, chaos—Emm could make me forget it all.

At last Emm broke the silence and pulled her cinnamon-scented hair away from my shoulder. "I was surprised to see Lee at the game tonight," she said, snapping me out of my reverie. "I almost went over to say hi, but I saw her with that dressed-up little boy. Do we have a puppy-love situation?"

"Uncle Bill let Lee come tonight as a one-time thing," I explained. "And the boy with her, that was Sammy. She says they're just friends but…"

"That's so sweet!" exclaimed Emm as if she already adored Sammy. "They grow up so fast, don't they?" she teased.

I could've burst from the emotion inside of me, but I forced myself to remain calm. My confession came flooding back; what I had to say to Emm was nothing like puppy love, not even close. Tonight was about telling my best friend about all she'd meant to me—from our very first missions together to our inter-continental adventures. About how much we'd grown together. But the moment wasn't right. Not yet. I wanted to enjoy these last minutes of speaking to Emm solely as a friend. Because after tonight, one way or the other, things would forever be different.

"I'm keeping an eye on it," I replied. "But really, I think he just helps Lee with her writing, and she helps him with his botany stuff."

"Botany stuff? Like plants and all that?" Emm asked, smirking. "Well, that explains a few things." The sparkle in her eye told me she knew something I didn't.

"What?" I replied, puzzled.

"She seems very into flowers these days—she keeps writing them into her stories."

"Maybe this is more serious than I thought?"

Emm smiled at me sympathetically. "Relax, TD, they're just kids."

"She's not allowed to date until she's twenty—at least!" I must've sounded way more serious than I'd intended, because Emm started giggling. How a giggle could say both, "You're very sweet," and "You're totally ridiculous." I didn't know, but that was just yet another way Emm could cast her spell on me.

"She'll always be your little sister, so I guess overprotective brother is sorta your job for life," Emm managed to say as she caught her breath.

"That's the plan," I agreed.

"It does kill me to know she's cooped up in the house all day, though," Emm began softly, "I'm happy to hear she has someone her age to play with."

"Yeah, Sammy does help in that sense," I replied without enthusiasm.

"It's not the same, but one time when I was five or six-years-old, I got a bad bug and my parents made me stay home for almost two weeks. At first, I loved not going to school—my mom waited on me hand and foot and I felt like I was the queen of the castle."

"Queen of the castle?" I said, with a subtle laugh.

"Yes, TD, queen of the castle. But after a few days, I was begging my parents to let me go back to school so I could see my friends. By then, I felt more like a damsel in distress…like, in need of a knight in shining armor to rescue me."

A laugh crept out of me, even though I tried to suppress it. The idea of Emma Rey Finley needing rescuing was just too ridiculous.

"This kid could barely shake my hand when I met him," I said. "He couldn't rescue anyone, that's for sure."

Thankfully, Emm shot me her trademark smile before changing the subject. "Did Lee tell you we're just about ready to send out one of her stories? We've been emailing a lot, editing and stuff."

"I had no idea. That's awesome, Emm." Genuinely touched, I put my arm around her and gave her a quick squeeze. "Thank you, that means…"

"It's not a big deal. I just wish I had more free time these days so I could visit her."

I didn't know what to say. But just then, the opening lines from *The Fresh Prince of Bel-Air's* theme song blared from my pocket. Ken had obviously been screwing around with my ringtones again—that was a favorite prank of his—but why he'd mess with me tonight of all nights was beyond me.

"Wow, that sounded *really important*," Emm said sarcastically. "You'd better see what's up."

I reluctantly pulled the stupid phone from my pocket. I really didn't care who was trying to reach me: I wanted to tell Emm how I felt before the conversation turned to Matt again. I wanted to conquer my stage fright, get that first line out, start my monologue—and then confess everything. For better or for worse, it didn't even matter at this point; What mattered was telling her the truth.

"It's a text from Sal," I said, surprised. "He says it's official. He's sold his business after signing the papers yesterday. He'll be retiring at the end of the year. Look, he sent a pic, too." I handed Emm my phone.

And that's when I saw her bare wrist.

My heart instantaneously pulsed throughout my entire body. The absence of Emm's turquoise bracelet hit me like a guillotine slicing directly through my esophagus. All of my resolve, all of my urgency, all of my passion drained out of me, violently and instantly.

Emm said something as she looked at the picture, but I had no idea what. The void inside was suddenly more monstrous than it had ever been. I'd been fooling myself: Emma Rey Finley didn't love me and she never would.

Emm's voice came back into focus as my ears regained their ability to function. "…so maybe we can go visit him after graduation. I'd love to go back to Florence!"

"Yeah, maybe," I managed to utter, feeling defeated. There was no point now in confessing anything.

"That's a very serious face," Emm said, looking straight into my eyes. "I know you miss Rome, TD, and I miss it too, but it was just one moment in time. Our *happy* moment in time—I'll never forget it." I looked deep into Emm's fathomless gaze, but I couldn't speak. Almost like someone had stolen my voice.

"Come on, TD, let's make Florence our next mission— like a graduation present to ourselves! The three of us can go. Matt's never been to Italy, and there's plenty more national treasures for us to break into," Emm urged, trying to cheer me up. I appreciated that, but I also knew she had no idea of my true feelings. How could someone who used to know me so well be so oblivious to the chaos swirling inside of me?

"Maybe we can stop in the Netherlands, too!" Emm continued. "We can check out Lee's tulip-madness for ourselves… and bring her and her new friend back a few bulbs for her garden. I'm sure Lee and Sammy would love that."

I didn't know what to say next, so I just let the words fall out of my mouth. "Emm, I'd sweep you up and carry you to Europe any day. Just say the word."

"Careful now, I have a boyfriend," she joked, still trying to make me laugh. She paused and looked out at the ocean for a long moment, as if she was thinking something through. "But there's one thing I've always wanted to do that we don't have to tell Matt about…*if* you're not chicken." Emm's eyes glistened in the dark with her telltale mischievousness.

"And what's that?" I asked, relieved that we'd flowed back into familiar territory.

But Emm didn't reply. Instead, she jumped up and started getting undressed. Right in front of me.

"What are you doing?!" I gasped as I panned the area and made sure that no one else could see her.

Inch by inch, almost as if in slow motion, Emm's beautiful tan skin was revealed until not a single shred of clothing covered her. Only once she was completely naked did she finally say, "I've never been skinny-dipping! No way I'm graduating without crossing that off my bucket list."

I couldn't believe my eyes. I tried to speak, but my voice once again failed me.

"Are you gonna join me?" Emm asked her question so softly that if the breeze hadn't carried her message directly to my ears, I wouldn't have heard it.

Without waiting for an answer, Emm—in all her natural beauty and still in slow motion—glided off the pier and into the indigo deep, twenty-feet beneath us.

"Are you crazy?!" I yelled after she popped back up to the surface.

Her laughter echoed sweetly from the water, "Come on, Tim Dexter! It's now or never!"

My mind began throbbing: This was a bad idea—a really bad idea—which didn't stop me from peeling off my own clothes, tossing them into a pile beside hers, closing my eyes and leaping into the ocean after her. As blind as a fool.

The water was freezing, but I didn't care. This was our pier, this was our night, and I was once again on a secret agent adventure with Emma Rey Finley. Only this time, we were both *naked* secret agents.

"Dude, you can't tell me Emma stripped naked in front of you and not give me *details*. I need a full description!" cried Ken. "Come on, man, focus."

I was never one to "kiss and tell," and although I could certainly appreciate Ken's enthusiasm for Emm's beauty, I wasn't about to make an exception now. *Especially* not now. And hell, there hadn't even been any kissing.

As soon as I'd walked Emm back to her car, I texted Ken and asked him to meet me at my place. The night had been such a spectacular failure, and Ken was the only one who could get my head back on straight. Although it was after midnight, Sergeant Biceps came running to the rescue, pulling up in front of my apartment just moments after I did.

"Can't I even get a little hint?" he pleaded. Expecting an answer, Ken gave me a moment, then prompted again, "Well…out with it!"

In reply, I hit him with a piercing stare that told him to back off.

"Okay, fine," he said, retreating. "So let me get this straight, you were about to pour your heart out to her, but instead, Emm took off her clothes and jumped into the ocean?"

"Uh, yeah…and I did too. A complete birthday-suit-in-the-sea situation."

"Thanks for the visual, man, but you're not the one who I want to picture naked. I just want to pictu—"

I cut Ken him off with a swift punch to the shoulder. He grunted in pain and aggravation, but I could tell that I'd knocked him out of his hornball state, which was all I wanted to accomplish. Almost as an apology, I walked over to the fridge and grabbed us a couple of beers.

"So no confession? What happened in the middle?" Ken asked, as he opened his drink.

I explained the whole thing from start to finish, trying to make such an illogical scenario sound sensical. I'd planned the night so perfectly and felt so strong going in, but in the end it was a total failure. Even if Emm and I did end up on an adventure. An extravagant, naked adventure.

"Jesus, TD, who cares about a stupid bracelet?! Listen to yourself! You aborted the whole mission over a *bracelet*?" Ken looked a bit angry, but not angry at me. More like angry because things hadn't gone as planned.

"She always wears that bracelet. Ever since the day I fastened it around her wrist. I never thought I'd see her without it, new boyfriend or not," I explained.

"So, she forgot to put your bracelet on this morning and you decided...what? That she'd been faking a friendship with you for all these years? That she doesn't love you at all?"

"Something like that, yeah." Put that way, I did sound ridiculous—I had to give Ken points for that. "I mean, I don't know...I guess things were just going so well, and then—"

"—and then you freaked out," interjected Ken, now with sympathy in his voice. "Forgot your lines. Alright. It happens, man, not a big thing. You'll just have to try again." He reached across the sofa and grabbed my arm to reassure me.

"I guess it just wasn't the right time," I answered. "Not in the middle of the season, not with Matt dragging her back and forth to San Francisco every weekend. Not with Lee needing the extra attention."

"But TD, you *do* have to try again, you know that, right?" said Ken seriously. "You can't suppress those feelings forever. I won't let you—I'd be a shitty friend otherwise. No excuses."

I was about to object, but I took a long swig of my liquid courage instead. Ken was right. Emm was my happiness, the only part of my life that felt real. The only scenes in my movie worth watching. I couldn't keep walking around in this blur, fast-forwarding through my days. And I knew Ken wouldn't have put all that time and effort into rehearsing with me if he didn't think I had a real shot with Emm.

"Yeah, I have to try again," I said almost confidently, as if I hadn't just blown a perfectly-good opportunity an hour ago.

"Now that's what I like to hear!" cried Ken. "We just have to adjust the plan a bit. I mean, Emma's a lot better-looking than me. Maybe we didn't account for that in the nerves department? No wonder you got...distracted."

I couldn't help but start chuckling. "You're right. I definitely wasn't prepared for total nudity."

"A rogue factor in any operation," Ken joked back.

"It was definitely easier confessing to you than Emm," I countered. "You don't have her legs."

"Hey!" Ken cried, trying to sound affronted as he grabbed his thighs. "These legs are pure protein-packed muscle. Ask any chick on campus." I rolled my eyes as Ken started flexing his calves, showing off. As usual.

"And thanks so much for messing with my phone. Of all the things I *didn't* need to deal with tonight."

"Just keeping you out of your own head, bro. A little levity in case things got too heavy."

"Jackass," I replied, imitating Ken's grin and shooting him a stunned look.

After a second or two, Ken's face turned serious. "So… when do we start practicing again?"

"As soon as you're as pretty as Emm," I shot back. Then, I added seriously, "There *will* be a right time, I'm sure of it."

"Well, we have plenty of road trips over the next couple of weeks, so we can perfect your monologue on the bus. By the end of the season, that thing should be freakin' flawless!" Ken said enthusiastically.

Like Emma Rey Finley deserved anything less than *freakin' flawless*.

Chapter

Sneak Attack

The one good thing about flubbing-up my confession to Emm was that it gave my mind a break—which was helpful, because I needed time to focus on my finals for the quarter. We also didn't have a game that week, providing a much-needed respite. With this unexpected free-time, I spent an inordinate amount of time Christmas shopping. Lee had been an absolute trooper since going on rest and I wanted to spoil her for Christmas. I would be on the road for all of winter break, but that didn't mean I still couldn't make my sister's holiday special.

On Sunday morning, I arrived at my uncle's house much later than planned. I crept into the basement entrance, trying to sneak my pile of presents past Lee's watchful eye. I shouldn't have worried, though: Once the presents were stashed and I'd made my way upstairs, Uncle Bill told me Lee was still in bed. Since it was almost 11:00 a.m., I didn't think Lee could still be sleeping. I figured she was probably writing in her journal.

Just to be sure, I carefully cracked open her bedroom door and, much to my surprise, my sister was still fast asleep and cocooned in her favorite hot-pink *Frozen* blanket that she'd adored since she was seven-years-old. Sitting at the top of the headboard, positioned almost like a guard dog, was Moon, keeping a faithful watch over my baby sister as she peacefully slept. Normally, I would've been concerned to see Lee still asleep at this late-morning hour, but it just looked like a normal Sunday morning sleep-in. If she needed the rest, I wasn't about to interrupt.

I tiptoed away from the door and into the kitchen. Every year, the weekend before I hit the road for winter break, I cooked Lee her beloved chocolate chip banana pancakes—it was one of our special Christmas traditions. After I'd got the pancakes together, I found some fresh berries in the fridge, used them for garnish and topped both our plates with Lee's favorite maple syrup—Mrs. Butterworth's—before dicing up our fluffy treats. To add a touch of Christmas spirit, I topped each stack with a mini candy cane, just like I did every year.

I crept into Lee's room, carrying our meal on a large serving tray and squeaked the door shut behind me with my foot. Lee, facing away from me, didn't stir. I carefully placed the tray on her nightstand before slowly perching myself over her so that I could whisper in her ear.

"Sneak attack!" cried Lee, popping up and putting me into a playful chokehold.

Although she didn't have nearly enough strength to best me, I let her pull me down on top of her and yelled out, "Ahh! You got me! You got me!"

Laughing and giggling, we wrestled for a few minutes. Once I got tired of letting Lee have the upper hand I turned the tables and launched a full-scale tickle attack.

"Stop! Stop it!" she yelped in between uncontrollable giggles.

"If you want me to stop so bad, then why are you laughing?" I said, continuing to tickle her ribs.

"Be…cau…se…I…can'…t…hel…p…it!" she cried in-between breaths.

Finally, I released her from my perilous tickle spell. While still catching her breath, Lee looked up at me and asked, "You didn't know I was faking?"

"I had no idea!" I replied as I placed the serving tray between us. "Maybe you were pulled from your sleep-coma by the aroma of these?"

"TD! Those look so yummy!" Lee cried. "Does this mean you're heading out on the road tomorrow?" she asked as she reached for her glasses.

"Yep, tomorrow night, Little One. Which makes it time for our special meal. But do you want to know the best part?"

Eager to hear her surprise, Lee burst out "What! What!" I was especially glad to see how much energy she had this morning.

"Not only can we have them in bed this year, but we can eat with our hands today!"

Lee, overjoyed, clapped her hands together like a wind-up toy monkey banging its cymbals together. And with that, we scarfed our pancakes without using any table manners at all.

"Did you have fun with Ken this week?" I asked as Lee smacked her lips loudly.

"Yeah, and I have a new job, too."

Of all the things I imagined Lee saying in reply, a new career move was way, way down on my list. "Umm...okay?"

Lee smirked, clearly enjoying my confusion. "Ken didn't have time for his morning workout, so he bench-pressed me! And then I sat on his back for his push-ups, too—it felt like a little like having the hiccups."

I smiled. I loved Lee's enthusiasm, but at sixty-five pounds, she might've felt like a feather to Ken—he was easily benching two-twenty-five these days. Even still, I appreciated Ken's kindness; making Lee feel helpful always kept her spirits up.

"Awesome," I replied. "A new job for Sunflower Power and a new workout for Sergeant Biceps. A match made in heaven."

As we enjoyed our brunch, I examined my little sister

closely. Her skin was paler than usual, and her face was slight-ly bloated, which was a normal side-effect of her newest meds, although I still wasn't quite used to it. Despite the fact that her appetite had picked up a bit in the last few weeks, she was still thinner than I would've liked, and her hair looked stringy. I knew her previous cold had finished running its course a few weeks ago, but I was still concerned.

"TD, did you hear what I said?" Lee asked, breaking my concentration.

Lee hated my mini-examinations. To cover myself, I tipped my head, pretended to shake some water out of my ear and replied, "Hmm...? What...? Huh...? What was that?"

"I *saaaiiid*...Did you know that the tulip is the national symbol of the Netherlands?"

"Did you learn that from Sammy?" I asked.

"Yup. And next time he visits, he promised to bring me his book about tulip mania. All that flower-trading stuff, remem-ber?" Lee replied excitedly.

"You're so smart, you know that, right?" I said as Lee beamed up at me. "Hey that reminds me, you never told me about your movie with Sammy, what did you guys see?"

Lee shoved a handful of pancakes into her mouth but didn't finish chewing before answering, "It was so fun! We saw *Despicable Me*—it's a *super*-old movie but it was playing cuz the sequel just came out. And we had popcorn and M&M's and a big slushie, too."

Lee looked thrilled as she described her treats. I wasn't too pleased about all that junk food, but since she'd only had one night out in months, I kept my mouth shut.

"What's *Despicable Me*?" I asked. "I've never heard of it."

"Geez, what universe do you live in?" Lee replied, rolling her eyes. She then went on to describe, in detail, the animat-ed movie and its characters. From what I could tell, *Despicable Me*, featured the adventures of Gru, a super-villain who was plotting to steal the moon. Supporting him on his quest was an army of minions—short, yellow, pill-shaped, comically in-competent creatures, whose one true joy in life was blindly following orders.

"It sounds like a great movie," I said, once I could squeeze a word in.

"It was. The only part I didn't like was that there weren't any girl minions. I didn't think that was fair…and neither did Sammy."

"You have a point, sis. Girls are just as awesome as boys."

"Exactly. I used to tell that to the boys at school all the time," Lee said seriously before adding more lightly, "But…do you want to know what else Sammy said?"

"What? I hope he—?"

"—Never mind," she said quickly as she suppressed a giggle. "I shouldn't say." She covered her hand with her mouth as she snickered.

"Come on, Lee, no secrets." I crossed my arms and acted as if I was upset, but she didn't give in. Tittering all the while, Lee sat back and took the last bite of her pancakes, then wiped her hands clean with a wet-wipe that I'd brought in on her tray.

"Fine," I said as I took the towelette and began wiping my own hands. "I guess you just want another tickle attack, don't you?"

But Lee held firm. So, in one fluid motion, I stood up, swooped her out of bed, and hoisted her into the air by her armpits. She squirmed back and forth in my arms as I tickled her, with her giggling getting progressively louder.

"Tell me!" I cried as I spun her around her bedroom.

"Okay! Okay!" she managed to squeak out between giggles. "You win!"

I set Lee back on her bed and waited for her to catch her breath, eager to finally be let in on her secret.

"After the movie was over," she began, trying her best not to laugh, "Sammy and I decided that you are like…Gru."

"Like Gru? Am I an evil genius?"

"No! But he has the skinniest legs, like yours. And he towered over all the minions, too."

"I am completely offended!" I joked.

"Plus, I think you kinda scared Sammy a little when he met you. You can be a little intimidating at first."

"Good, that's what I was going for," I thought to myself. But I couldn't say as much to Lee, so instead I replied, "It's just because I'm tall, Little One. We don't judge people by their outsides."

"Yeah, like me for example. Just because I'm small doesn't mean I don't have big ideas!" Lee said her words with a laugh in her voice, yet at the same time I could tell she was absolutely serious.

"That's true. You have all sorts of big ideas, that's why you're going to be a famous author someday."

"Not someday, TD. Next year," Lee said, emphatically, as she reached over to her nightstand and picked up the picture of Emm at the Getty. "Emma said so. We're going to keep sending out my stories until I get published. It'll happen if I work hard enough."

"I like it," I began as I smiled down at my little sister, I was both filled with pride and astonished at her drive. "Lee Rose Dexter. Published Author."

Chapter 19

The Fast Train

*J*anuary and February rambled on. I didn't need a ton of credits to graduate, so my class load was light. I threw all my extra effort into basketball and leading my team. Ken and I had always dreamed about making it to the NCAA tournament, and this was our last chance: playing in March Madness had been our goal since the start of the season.

My life was fast-forwarding again, but this time in a good way. By the time winter quarter started, we were firmly in mid-season, which meant our games mattered more and more as the conference tournament approached. Ken and I were confident in our leadership skills and certain our team could achieve the high standard we'd set. January was somewhat rocky. We'd lost a game or two—and by the end of the month, we needed to win almost every remaining game to finish in first place. Which we did—by late February we were on a tear. We had a clear path to the conference finals and there was no way we were going to fall short at the finish line like last year.

Ken and I knew this was our final shot at fulfilling a dream we'd had since we were kids, so we pushed our team to its very limits.

Focusing on basketball had been just the escape I clearly needed. Except for peeking up and catching a glimpse of Emm in the stands at our games, I didn't see her at all during those weeks. Every time I got the urge to text or call her, I pushed the feeling deep, deep down, where the void inside of me continued to churn. Which meant that seeing Emm in the stands became the best part of the game, itself, even if seeing her with Matt did break my heart. Mentally, it was almost as though I'd convinced myself that the more success I had on the floor, the more likely it was for Emma Rey Finley to pick me. With that singular thought driving me, I played every game with a new intensity—as if my life depended on it—and the results showed.

Not having any contact with Emm also meant that I could quiet my mind. I'd firmly decided not to approach her with my confession until after the season was over, when I'd have the time to focus on her. But I did know that I'd see Emm at Lee's transplant party since she'd confirmed her invitation; every once in a while, no matter how hard I tried to drive it away, the thought of seeing Emm in the park, surrounded by happy flowers, would sneak back into my mind. As the season's end approached, a part of me was more excited about my little sister's party than she was.

Lee was doing better, too. Doctor Mallory had given her permission to go to school two days a week, and Uncle Bill and I had decided to let her come to my home games whenever she was up to it—having her back, courtside, only further fueled my performance. I still worried that she was pushing it, but I'd never seen a kid so happy to go back to school in my life. To Lee, the classroom meant freedom and made her feel as if she was back on track toward her One Day. On her resting days, Lee went to school virtually for a few hours, then spent most of her free time in the garden or writing. Sammy was around after school a bit more often than I would've liked, but the more I watched the two of them interact, the more I warmed-up to him.

After our most recent home game—an easy win—I walked up to Lee even before I ran back into the locker room. She'd been sitting in the stands alone the entire game, which was unusual, and I didn't want to leave her there by herself as the crowd exited the arena.

"Good job, big bro!" Lee jumped up from her chair and slapped me a high-five.

"Thanks, sweetie," I replied, "But why are you here alone? No Sammy today? No Uncle Bill?"

"No, Sammy had band practice tonight…just like you used to, remember?" Lee answered.

I smiled. I couldn't remember the last time I'd thought about my violin lessons, and I was surprised that Lee even remembered them. "Yep, I do. I was a band geek just like your boyfriend."

Lee, clearly not thinking my joke was very funny, crossed her arms. "He isn't a geek and he is definitely *not* my boyfriend."

"Good. There'll be time enough for boyfriends later. But for now, you have me."

"And right now, I need you to give me a ride home," declared Lee. "Uncle Bill texted you when he dropped me off, did you get it yet?"

"Lee's limo service to the rescue!" I said brightly, even though I was annoyed that Uncle Bill hadn't coordinated with me in advance. I didn't mind taking Lee home at all; it was more of a safety thing. "Come on, sis, you can wait for me in Coach's office while I get cleaned-up."

"Sounds good. Can Emma come too?"

I'd been careful not to let Lee in on the chasm that had widened between me and Emm in these last months. With Lee doing so well, that was the last thing she needed to hear. Hiding that distance was another reason why I'd warmed-up-to Sammy. Lee's new *life-passions* friend was an excellent distraction.

"I think she's already left with Matt, Little One," I said as I took hold of Lee's tiny fingers and we began walking hand in hand out of the gym. "They must've had something planned for tonight." There was a time when Emm would never have let Lee sit through the whole game by herself, but I didn't mention that part.

"She's always with *that guy*," Lee said, exasperated. "She helps me with my stories, but she never visits anymore."

"It's our senior year, Lee—lots of things change when you're a senior, and we're all very busy this quarter." Creating a diversion, I reached over and gently lifted Lee's glasses from her face as we walked. "You always fog up your glasses," I said as I cleaned them on my jersey.

"Eww, boy-sweat!" Lee exclaimed as she snatched her glasses back and began cleaning them on her own shirt. She did have a point: I was kind of a mess.

"What would you do without me?" I teased, as she finished cleaning her lenses.

"I can't help it if they get foggy. I always get so excited when I see you play." She smiled up at me, then added, "And you're my big brother—I don't have to worry about not having you. But could you imagine what you'd ever do without me? If I wasn't a little miracle and you were an only child? Your life would be so *boring!*"

I hadn't seen Lee this energetic in a while, so it was refreshing to witness. Her transplant party was tomorrow; I figured that was why she was in such good spirits. In the last two or three weeks, as I'd been pulling together the final details for the party, I'd grown more and more astonished and grateful. It had been four full years since my little miracle had been given her second chance.

I set Lee up in the office and showered as quickly as I could. I congratulated all my teammates and thanked them for yet another win. I also checked my phone, to make sure Lee wasn't up to any shenanigans—and the text from Uncle Bill was, in fact, there. "Not feeling great," it read. "Please bring Lee home."

Lee was dozing off as I walked back into the office, but when she saw me coming, she jumped up quickly. "Ready to go?" she asked enthusiastically.

"All set, but should we stop for ice cream on the way home? It's still early."

"Only if you're buying." Lee giggled a little as she gave me a strong hug that caught me off-guard. Once she'd wrapped herself around my legs, she sort of held me there for a second, then sighed contentedly, "I'm so happy at you, big brother."

We arrived at the ice cream parlor fifteen-minutes later. Lee, still full of energy, danced into a booth while I ordered for both of us. I got us each two scoops of good old-fashioned chocolate chip ice cream and—just to make Lee's day a bit brighter—I grabbed two tiny taster spoons as well. While I'd done my best to keep Emm from Lee's thoughts in the last weeks, I figured I could make an exception, since we'd be seeing her at the party tomorrow.

"Just like Emma!" Lee exclaimed as I handed her a taster spoon.

"That's right. But do you know why Emm always eats her dessert with a taster spoon?"

"Because she's a strong and independent-minded woman like me?" Lee asked.

I grinned, shaking my head at Lee's precociousness. She wasn't wrong. "I'll give you full credit for that one, sis, but there's another reason, too."

Lee didn't reply, but her eyes grew as wide as saucers. She rested her elbows on the table and cradled her chin in her hands as if I was about to reveal the secrets of the universe.

"Remember the day Emm and I got ice cream in Santa Marinella?" I asked.

"When it started pouring out of nowhere? When you lost Emma for a second but then turned around to find her dancing in the rain?"

"Yeah. But that was also the day I learned one of the greatest secrets of Emma Rey Finley," I said, doing everything I could to build the moment up and leave Lee on the edge of her seat.

Lee waited for me to keep going, but I paused just to watch her squirm with excitement. Finally, she burst out, "Tell me! Please!"

"Emm said taster spoons are sort of a philosophy. Eating one tiny scoop at a time is a way of reminding herself that life is too short to take it in all at once. Taster-spoons force her to eat her ice cream *in a savory fashion* and enjoy every bite."

Lee, fascinated, beamed with joy. "I love that," she replied with a captivating grin. Apparently, Emm's "savory fashion" method made quite an impact, because Lee softly repeated, "I really love that." Then she got up from her seat, scurried around to my side of the booth, and cuddled up under my arm—something she almost never did in public.

"What's up, Little One?" I asked.

"I'm enjoying life *in a savory fashion*," she replied from the crook of my arm. I snuggled her in closer, squeezing her tightly. She curled her hand into a little cup, softly ran it up my arm, and added in a whisper, "One scoop at a time."

One of these days, my baby sister was going to break my heart.

"Uncle Bill, are you okay?" I asked as Lee and I walked into the living room. He was on the sofa, stretched out and reading a magazine.

"Better now. Took my Tums. Had a nap." he replied.

Lee walked up to our uncle. "Do you want some water? Or juice?"

Uncle Bill smiled up at her warmly and took her hand, a rare show of obvious affection. "I'm okay, Lee. Really. A long week at work, that's all." He looked up at me before continuing. "TD will get you into bed. We all have a big day tomorrow."

"I confirmed everything yesterday with park services and

their caterers," I reported to my uncle. "We're good to go for tomorrow."

"And we're still having my relay race, right?" asked Lee, who suddenly looked very tired. "I already made teams and everything."

"Of course we are!" I replied. "But you need to get some rest for your big day. Let's get you into the bath and off to bed."

With Lee in the tub, I took the opportunity to go over the checklist for the party one more time. We wouldn't need to bring much with us. The duck park was providing food and decorations, but I wanted to make sure all Lee's personal stuff was ready for the morning, including the two small bottles of maple syrup that she insisted we use as relay batons. I threw in a tube of sunscreen for myself, too, just to be on the safe side. Now that we'd hit March, the sun's weak rays were starting to have a tinge of a springtime strength, and the last thing I needed was a sunburn slowing me down. The last game of our regular season was only a couple of days away.

I put together Lee's nightly cocktail of meds and made her a glass of chocolate milk to wash it down with. "Moon and I are ready!" Lee called.

I walked into Lee's bedroom just as she was pulling her curtains shut for the night. I closed the door behind me, set her meds down, then lifted Lee up and plopped her into bed. She felt a little warm as I lifted her, but I figured it was from the bath.

Lee began taking her pills one-by-one, drinking a gulp of chocolate milk in between each. "Can you tell me and Moon another story from your trip with Emma?" she asked.

"I've told you all of them at least five times already," I said as I took her empty glass from her. "You practically know everything better than I do."

"But please, TD. I like the way you tell 'em," she said with a yawn.

Giving in as always, I replied, "Of course, sis," as I tucked her under her covers. "What part of our trip do you want to hear about tonight?" I asked, carefully seating myself on the bed and began stroking her blonde hair.

"Umm…" she started, as her eyelids drooped, "Tell me about the fast train again." I was surprised Lee seemed so tired all of a sudden, since she'd been so animated all evening.

"I think you mean the slow train, Little One," I said, with a forgiving smile.

"Yes, sorry. I knew that," she whispered, pulling her blanket up to her chin to let me know that she was all tucked-in and ready for story time.

"Okay…so we were leaving for Florence in the morning to visit Sal…"

Lee's breathing deepened, and her head lolled to one side. Another minute or two and she'd be out like a light.

"…but Emm decided we should take the *slow train* to save our money for fun stuff. So, we had to wake up at the crack of dawn for the four-hour ride…"

I didn't even get to the next part of the story: Lee was already sound asleep.

I continued to sit by her side, watching her in the darkness. I thought about how far she'd come. How she defined my life. How she brightened my days, even as she struggled. How she was the single-greatest creation on the planet. How she was my world.

While I sat and watched her, I reached over to push back a lock of hair that had fallen across her eyes. As my hand gently grazed her skin, I realized Lee was hot. Too hot. I pressed my hand firmly against her forehead: She was burning up.

My pulse quickened, and I tried to avoid going into full panic-mode. I ran to the bathroom to grab the thermometer and decided to soak a washcloth in cool water for Lee's forehead. Not wanting to disturb her, I softly opened the door. But Lee was now awake, sitting at the edge of her bed with her feet hanging off the side.

Alarmed, I asked immediately, "What is it, Little One?"

Her eyes shone up at me in the darkness, but she didn't reply. "Lee, what's the matter?" I repeated as I carefully took another step toward her. I kept my eyes locked onto her face and searched for any clue as to what was going on.

Before I'd even made it across the room, Lee's whole body convulsed as she threw up all over the carpet. She managed a breath, then started retching again.

I sprinted across the room, grabbed the small trash basket next to her nightstand and threw my arm around her. Once she was done vomiting, Lee slumped weakly into my shoulder.

"TD...I feel so weird," she muttered as best she could.

"Probably just too much ice cream," I said, trying to hide my panic and keep her calm. I kept my arm around her, doing my best to hold her upright in case she vomited again. "Catch your breath and then we'll go get you cleaned up," I assured her.

"But, I..."

Right then, her body went rigid and began shaking. It started off slowly, but then became violent. A full-fledged seizure. I gripped Lee tightly, trying to calm her convulsing body.

"Uncle Bill! Get in here, quick!" I screamed. But he didn't answer—where *was* he!

"Uncle Bill!" I yelled even more loudly, as I flicked on the bedside light with my free hand.

And that's when I saw it: Lee's carpet was covered not just in vomit, but in blood.

Chapter 20

Little Ones

The door swung open as Uncle Bill entered the room. "TD, what's going—"

"Start the car! Lee…I don't know, but we need to get her to the hospital!"

But Uncle Bill didn't move. He stood in the doorway, aghast. Frozen in place as if the scene before him was too much to handle; as if all the strings that held him together inside had just broken.

"Uncle Bill…*NOW!*" I screamed, snapping him out of his shock. Only then did he scramble from the room. I heard him grab his keys from the hallway table.

I turned my full-attention back to Lee. "Stay with me," I said gently as her eyes rolled back into her head. "You're going to be okay, sis."

Lee's body went limp as the seizure passed, but her breathing remained choked and labored. Cooing to her reassuringly, I lifted her into my arms and began running toward the door, doing my best to keep her steady in my arms, completely frantic and beginning to lose my composure.

The next thing I knew, we were speeding down the highway, doing at least ninety-five miles an hour. It was almost midnight, so the road was fairly empty, but as Uncle Bill weaved in and out of the lanes, drivers honked at us angrily. Lee lay draped across my lap, gasping for air and hugging my elbow with her weak arms.

"Lee! Stay awake!" I cried as my little sister's eyelids began fluttering shut. "Come on, you have to stay awake!" She whimpered as she forced her eyes open, tears rolling down her face, yet the only thing I could do was soothe her. "Breathe, Lee, just breathe. All you have to do right now is breathe."

Lee tilted her head back, looked straight into my eye, and said in the merest, choked whisper, "TD...I don't want to die."

At Lee's terror-filled words, every muscle in my already hyper-tense body suddenly felt ready to shatter. For a split second, I couldn't respond. I couldn't even think. Couldn't absorb the terrifying possibility.

"You're not going to die, Little One," I said softly as I squeezed her tight, fighting back my own fear. "You're not going to die, I promise," I repeated, locking my gaze to hers. "Now breathe. In and out. Focus on my breaths," I placed my hand on Lee's sternum and began directing her breathing, even as she choked and sputtered. Why the hell couldn't she just breathe?

A moment or two passed, then Lee—either from a lack of oxygen or simply because she couldn't fight her body any longer—sunk into unconsciousness. My whole world, slipping right through my fingertips.

"Uncle Bill!" I yelled. "She's unconscious. What now?!"

"Keep her airways open, that's what they say to do," he replied. In a fit of frustration, he slammed the steering wheel with his fist. "Why doesn't this damn car go any faster!"

I rearranged Lee's limp body in my lap, cradling her head on my thigh and wiping her face and pajamas clean as best I could with some paper napkins. But it was too much. Trying to keep her awake, trying to keep fighting, trying to keep from crying. It was all too much.

I focused my gaze out the window as we sped by the Los Angeles National Cemetery. It seemed as though every one of the thousands of graves was staring at me as we drove past. I wanted to look away, but I couldn't. These endless rows of tombstones, illuminated by the cemetery's lights, were trying to tell me something. Their stares portended volumes without a single word.

Feeling more frightened than ever, I cradled Lee even more tightly and cried to her in between sobs, "Lee, stay with me!" But she probably couldn't hear me. No matter how much I cried or how loudly I yelled, my voice couldn't reach the dark place she'd gone to; a dark place where my sister was once again fighting for her life. My tears began to slowly roll off my cheeks and onto her limp body, but she probably couldn't feel those, either.

Twenty-minutes later, Uncle Bill pulled-up in front of the emergency room at UCLA Children's Hospital. Even before the car fully skidded to a stop, I swung the door open and leapt out with my baby sister in my arms.

"Someone, help!" I yelled as I burst through the emergency room's automatic doors. The ER buzzed around me as I called out again, desperately, "She needs help!"

"Lay her down on this, sir," a nurse said, appearing beside me with a gurney. The moment I put my sister down, another nurse began checking Lee's vitals and assessing her condition.

They asked me a bevy of questions, but I was more concerned about making sure they knew Lee's medical history. As I began rattling off Lee's list of medications, one of the nurses shouted, "We have a weak pulse…we need to administer oxygen."

The first nurse looked at me and explained, "Sir, we need to establish a reliable airway. We'll start monitoring her pulse and cerebral oximetries once we've started her on oxygen. Please head to the waiting room and we'll update you as soon as we can."

"But I need to be back there with her. My sister needs me. She's only ten!" I pleaded.

"I'm sorry, sir, but we don't have any time to waste," she said as her partner began wheeling Lee away. "We will come and—"

The second nurse looked back at us, even as he kept the gurney moving down the long hall. "Doris, *now!* Let's move!" he called.

Nurse Doris jogged after her partner. I watched as they disappeared behind a set of double doors. The hallway itself seemed as ominous as it was long, like the void inside of me, incarnate.

As the doors swung shut, all I wanted to do was rewind to only two hours ago and hold my little sunflower in my arms. To shield her from the darkness; to keep her from wilting under the depths of this nightmare.

I waited. Seconds felt like hours. Blind with concern, I was unable to sit still for more than a minute or two at a time. My T-shirt was speckled with blood and vomit, and Lee's tears had left a damp patch on my jeans—and I could feel my own tears joining hers after staining my red cheeks.

Uncle Bill had rushed into the ER moments after Lee had been taken back. He did his best to calm me down, but there was no point: I couldn't wrap my mind around what had happened. Lee and I were cuddling and laughing in the ice cream parlor barely an hour before she'd started seizing. A thousand possibilities flashed through my mind: food poisoning, a reaction to her meds, a rare disease. But none of them made any sense. How could everything go from being so beautiful one minute to so miserable the next? What could've possibly gone so wrong, so quickly?

"These damn forms," Uncle Bill muttered, disgusted. I reached over and took the clipboard from him, then gave his hand a quick but hopefully reassuring squeeze. "Put those down for the moment," I said. "Now's not the time for paperwork." Uncle Bill took a deep breath of relief, as if he'd been waiting for someone—anyone—to give him instructions.

"Was she even still alive?" I thought. But I stopped myself. I couldn't—wouldn't—allow my mind to consider that possibility, so I jumped up from my chair and started pacing again. "She's okay," I forced myself to think. "They've saved her before, they can save her again," I told myself, pushing the morbid thought far from my mind. I repeated the phrase in my head like a mantra, before eventually sitting back down. I buried my head in my arms, waiting. Waiting, and feeling totally useless.

"Is there a Mr. Dexter?" a voice finally called. I looked up to see a short woman in a lab coat walking toward us, emerging from the same hallway Lee disappeared into over an hour ago.

I shot up out of my seat. "Yes—how is she?"

The woman shook my hand as she introduced herself. "My name is Dr. Helmers. Lee's condition is critical, but thankfully. we've stabilized her for now."

"She's alive!" A thought of relief swept through me.

Dr. Helmers continued. "We've admitted her to the ICU. Would you mind coming with me?"

My uncle got up from his chair, intending to follow as well. "My niece," he said.

"I'm sorry," replied Dr. Helmers, "but only one family member can visit at a time when a patient's condition is this critical. Are you her guardian?"

"We're co-guardians," I replied. Which was legally true. We'd petitioned the court to grant me secondary guardianship the moment I turned eighteen.

My uncle and I exchanged a glance—and it was immediately understood that I'd be the one to see Lee first. I hugged him and told him to remain strong.

The hallway seemed endless, as I walked beside Dr. Helmers. "The good news is that all our tests so far have come back negative. Our CT scan shows full brain activity—Lee hasn't suffered any brain damage. Her heart-rate had slowed significantly, but we're regulating that now. I understand that she had a bone marrow transplant?"

I let out a breath that I hadn't even realized I was holding in. I repeated Lee's medical history to Dr. Helmers, including her full list of medications—medications, I now realized, that I knew by heart. "She's Dr. Mallory's patient," I concluded. "He should have all her records upstairs."

"I know Dr. Mallory very well," Dr. Helmers replied. "We'll contact him shortly. I'm sure he'll be here first thing in the morning."

The hallway went on and on. Fluorescent lights, nurses and orderlies, monitors and equipment, all blurred together. The smell of antiseptic invaded my nostrils.

Dr. Helmers guided me into the elevator and upstairs to the ICU. All I could focus on were the kids: I couldn't have looked away if I tried. Through the window of each plain room, I saw sick child after sick child—many still awake, with their eyes glistening back at me. Kids of all shapes and sizes, most of them with a parent or guardian dozing in a chair beside them. Dozens of frightened little ones awaiting life-changing news, much like Lee and I had received all of those years ago.

"This is her room," Dr. Helmers announced as a nurse passed us in the hall and flashed me a sympathetic smile. "Now, I have to tell you," she continued, "Lee is on a respirator. She's awake, but she won't be able to talk. We can't remove her breathing tube until we're sure she can maintain a steady supply of oxygen on her own."

"Thank you for everything, doctor," I replied, relieved to know that my sweet Lee was finally only a few feet away.

Dr. Helmers opened the door to Lee's room. "I'll give you a moment, then I'll send her nurse in. She needs more tests."

Tubes and IVs were connected to every part of Lee's small body. Monitors, beeping and buzzing, flickered with her vitals. She was half-propped-up in what looked like an unnatural and uncomfortable position. The breathing tube forced down Lee's throat looked more like it was attacking her than saving her.

"Hey, Little One," I said, trying to sound as upbeat and composed as possible.

Lee couldn't respond, but as I greeted her, the corner of her mouth showed the slightest hint of a smile.

"You were so brave," I said, as I pulled a chair up to her bed. I began stroking her hair, just as I'd done only a few hours ago. My little sister didn't deserve any of this, not after she'd fought so hard for so many years.

Lee reached over to the nightstand and weakly picked up a small notepad and red marker. Even with the IV running into her hand, she started scribbling. Only once she was done writing did Lee look up and train her tear-filled eyes on me. She looked absolutely terrified as she held up her note for me to read.

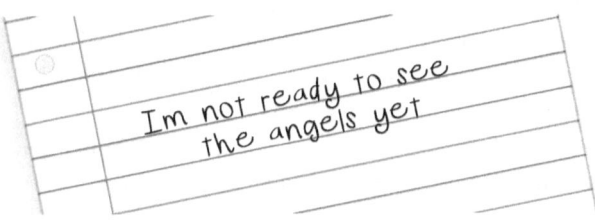

I tried my best to continue remaining composed, but that didn't last very long. An instant or two later, I felt my eyes begin to swell with tears. I leaned over, carefully enfolded Lee in my arms as best I could, then rested my head against her stomach. The two of us cried together in complete silence for the next fifteen minutes.

Even if Lee could've spoken, there really wasn't much to say. There were no words to describe this terror.

A soft knock came at the door. The nurse who'd smiled at me in the hallway popped into the room. "How are we doing in here?" she asked optimistically.

The look on my face must've told the nurse that her question, however well-intended, was far too complicated for me to answer.

"I'm Nurse Jen," she continued. Turning to my sister, she said, "Lee and I have already met, haven't we, sweetie?"

Lee nodded the slightest tilt of her head. I introduced myself, then explained that I was Lee's secondary guardian. Lee never once let go of my hand the entire time.

"Well, TD, Dr. Helmers has ordered more tests, but don't you worry—we'll be back in half-an-hour or so. But first," she turned back to Lee, "this doesn't look very comfortable. Can I adjust your bed? You tell me—up or down?"

Lee pointed to the ceiling, meaning she wanted to sit up. Nurse Jen adjusted the bed, with Lee's thumbs-up sign telling her when to stop, before she rearranged Lee's pillows as well.

I kissed Lee on the cheek and told her to be brave. Another nurse came into the room and began helping Nurse Jen rearrange Lee's IVs and tubes for transport.

"She's a fighter, this one. I can tell already," Nurse Jen said to me warmly. "We'll take good care of her," she added as she stroked Lee's forehead.

Once Lee was wheeled-away, I headed back downstairs to report to Uncle Bill. I'd been gone for a good half-hour at this point, and it really wasn't fair that he was still in the dark.

My uncle was still in the same seat in the waiting room. He didn't look like he'd been doing too well without me.

Uncle Bill relaxed his shoulders as I spoke, visibly relieved that Lee was alright for the moment. Then he said, "You look tired. I can stay with—"

"—Go ahead and go home," I said, cutting him off. "You're still sick. Lee and I will be fine here tonight."

I'd had this conversation with my uncle plenty of times during Lee's year of isolation in the hospital. For twelve months, we made sure Lee never spent even one single night

alone. I'd go to the hospital after I was done with class or practice, and Uncle Bill spent all of his weekends with her. Sometimes my uncle and I would have to trade a day or two and,
occasionally, Mrs. Zom would cover for one of us, but someone was always there. We knew how important our support
was for Lee: she needed to be able to face each morning with
the drive to take on whatever challenge the day would bring.
This time around would be no different.

"Okay," my uncle began, as he got up to leave, "I'll bring
clean clothes and a toothbrush in the morning. You look like
hell."

"Don't worry about me," I replied. "We've been here before. We'll work it all out."

Uncle Bill looked at me with the most disturbing mix of
fear, concern and empathy I'd ever seen. "But tell Lee…"
he paused, struggling to get the sentiment out, "that I…that
we're going to…" He took a deep breath, then managed as
he exhaled, "Tell Lee…tell her that her flowers will be fine,"
which was about as close as Uncle Bill could come to an outright declaration of love.

After saying goodbye, I headed back upstairs and waited
for Lee to return. It was now after 2 a.m. and the ICU had
taken on an eerie, almost disturbing, calm. I sat myself back
down in Lee's empty room as my head began spinning once
again: What the hell could I have done to prevent this? What
had I missed? I couldn't think of a single symptom or sign, but
I was sure that something must've slipped by me. It was my job
to protect Lee, but now…

Moments later, Nurse Jen, Dr. Helmers and a few nurses
wheeled Lee back into the room. They rolled her bed into
position before swiftly making themselves busy with her tubes
and monitors. Room 188, so unnervingly empty only moments before, was now suddenly cramped and crowded.

Dr. Helmers stood over me with her clipboard. "Everything so far has come back negative, which rules out a host of
more serious issues. With that said, we still don't know what,
exactly, caused this. I'm confident we'll able to find what we're

looking for in her blood work, though. It should come back from the lab tomorrow afternoon."

I simply nodded, since Dr. Helmers looked as if she had more to say. "The good news is that she's achieved a steady flow of oxygen," she continued. "We can go ahead and take Lee off the respirator."

"That sounds great. Thank you, doctor," I replied, trying to remain optimistic for Lee's sake. Dr. Helmers briefly spoke to her team before she explained to me the procedure for removing the breathing tube. Then, turning to Lee, she said gently, "We need you to stay very still and breathe only through your nose. Can you do that for us?"

Lee nodded slightly as she reached for my hand. I clutched her outstretched palm with both of mine, hoping my touch would give her strength.

A moment later, the team began the procedure. Lee winced in pain and her grip got tighter and tighter as the seemingly endless tube was removed. At first her eyes remained open, but then they snapped shut as if she wanted to scream but couldn't.

"You're doing so well," Nurse Jen encouraged. "Count to ten and we'll be done!"

A strong cough. A deep gasp.

"How are you feeling, Lee?" Dr. Helmers immediately asked.

Lee hadn't opened her eyes until Dr. Helmers had spoken. In a raspy voice, Lee replied, "Not so good. That thing tasted terrible."

Everyone in the room let out a laugh of relief, including myself. Lee was clearly back with us. Physically, she'd taken a hit, but her spunky, fighting spirit remained strong. Which was all I needed to know, for now.

The doctors and nurses cleared out of the room after one more check of Lee's vitals. "Can I get you anything, sis?" I asked.

"No...you've done enough for tonight," she replied, trying to joke with me a bit. "But could you maybe finish your story about the slow train?" she asked in a heartbreaking-ly-adorable rasp.

I almost couldn't believe what I'd just heard. "Seriously?! After all of this...*that's* what you want?"

"Yes, please," she said while tucking herself under the covers of her now-properly-adjusted hospital bed. That breathing tube really had been an evil-looking thing.

I laughed before I began the story again. When I got to the part about zombie Emm, I reached into my pocket to show Lee the picture on my phone, but she was already sound asleep.

Sound asleep and breathing on her own. Both good signs, but I winced at how painfully-tiny my baby sister's world had become tonight.

Chapter 21

Sorpresa!

Being in a hospital was bad enough, but trying to sleep in one was an entirely different struggle. After the many nights I'd spent with Lee during her year of isolation, I should've been a hospital-sleeping pro, but that just wasn't the case. I had tried to create a makeshift bed out of the two chairs in Lee's room, but at six-six, I simply didn't fit. There really was no such thing as a comfortable anything in a hospital, and my having grown a few inches since the last time I'd done this wasn't helping matters at all.

I gave up on sleep and decided to head to the water fountain in the hallway to get a drink and wash the bad taste out of my mouth. As I leaned down, I heard a soft voice ask, "Are you feeling okay?" I looked up and saw Nurse Jen, now in her regular street clothes. I was so tired and so stressed, it took me a second to recognize her.

"I'm fine, thanks, I just can't sleep," I said, trying to appear more alert.

"I could never sleep in hospitals, either. No matter how exhausted I was, I just couldn't," Nurse Jen replied.

I heard her words, but my exhausted brain couldn't make much of them. I wasn't trying to be rude, but my head just wasn't properly functioning. I must've made a weird face in response, because Nurse Jen clarified, "Sorry, that was probably confusing. I spent lots of nights here before I became a nurse." Her tone lost some of its brightness as she added, "My son had cancer when he was younger."

Seeing her positivity shift, I said sympathetically, "I'm sorry to hear that."

"Thank you. He's actually two years cancer-free, thank God, but his time here is the reason I became a nurse—so I guess everything happens for a reason," she explained, once again finding her positive energy.

"Look at that!" I said, genuinely happy for her. I knew exactly how she felt: any good that came from strife was that much more precious.

"I actually only became certified just a few months ago, but it's the most rewarding thing I've ever done," she replied, warmly smiling.

Nurse Jen's endearing aura instantly made me feel welcomed and at ease. One of her true talents was listening—something that I knew from experience didn't always happen in hospitals. I already felt I'd found a kindred spirit in her. She was already breaking down defenses that I put up whenever I felt like I had my back up against the wall.

"Now that he's cancer-free, I usually only work afternoons and evenings," Nurse Jen continued, "so I can see my son off to school in the morning and be home to tuck him in at night."

"Well, then, what happened tonight?" I asked, feeling as if I was snitching on her to my kindergarten teacher. I really did need some sleep.

She smiled. "I switched shifts, since I can't come in tomorrow. I'm taking my son to a party, which means we'll get the *whole* day together." She said "whole" as if she hadn't spent a full day with him in quite some time. "I'm heading home to catch a few hours of shuteye."

We talked for a few more minutes before she handed me a blanket from the linen cart. "Here, this should help. If I learned anything from my nights here, it's that you should try to get some rest—especially on your first night." She chuckled quietly before saying, "Goodnight, TD."

I cracked a smile, "Thank you for all your help tonight, Nurse Jen. Enjoy your party tomorrow."

Back in Lee's room, I paced back and forth, watching her sleep and still overwhelmed with concern. Lee didn't stir at all, though her monitors beeped at a monotonous—yet reassuring—pace. I never thought I'd be glad to hear those damned machines again.

I decided to crawl back into my makeshift cot and try sleeping once more. I wiggled around for a bit, but Nurse Jen had been right: The blanket really did help. As soon as I'd found a reasonably-comfortable position, I felt myself drifting off.

After what seemed like only a few minutes, I was jolted awake when several doctors and nurses entered the room.

"Sorry to wake you, Mr. Dexter" said Dr. Helmers. "We're taking Lee for another test, but we should be back shortly—if we're lucky, we won't even wake her up in the process. In the meantime, can I have one of our nurses get you anything?"

Still half-asleep, I replied automatically, "I'm okay, doctor. Thank you."

"Now, I also spoke to Dr. Mallory. He'll be here within the hour. I'll brief him fully before I head home."

"Thank you for reaching out to him," I said, as the fog in my head began to lift.

"Of course. It's always best to have a patient's primary specialist on hand. Now, this test should be quick—just a scan," she said as the staff began wheeling Lee out of the room. "Then we'll see if she has an appetite this morning."

I waved to my still-sleeping sister as her bed disappeared out the door. Once I was alone, the horrors of the night before came cascading back in a mortifying torrent. It was as if the moment Lee left the room, all the life inside of it left with her. What little remaining "happy" was gone.

A gut-wrenching rumble of *déja vu* overwhelmed me. How could we be back here again?

Thinking I should send a message to my uncle, I pulled out my phone, only to find it completely dead. I knew from experience that the nurse's station would probably have a charger I could plug into for a little while, so I headed down the hall.

"No problem, honey," The desk nurse said as she took my phone. "It happens all the time. Now, why don't you go downstairs and get yourself some breakfast."

I had zero appetite, but getting some fuel into my body—plus a cup of coffee—sounded like a reasonable plan. "Thank you. I'll be right back."

As much as I hated airports, hospital cafeterias were a thousand times worse. A whole roomful of people—none of whom wanted to be there—forcing down lukewarm, bland food under harsh fluorescent lighting. Other than a group of interns on their coffee break, everyone else was eating alone, each wearing their struggle on their face, probably just like I was. Still wearing the same blood-speckled clothes from the night before, I did my best to stomach a yogurt and some toast as quickly as I could. Who knows if the coffee was actually terrible or not, but to me it was the worst roast I'd ever had.

Back upstairs at the nurse's station, my phone exploded, as I was bombarded with texts and voicemails the moment it powered back on.

"Where are you?"

"What's going on?"

"Is everything okay?"

And that's when I realized: Lee's transplant party was today.

I had so many messages I didn't even know where to begin. It was already 10:47 a.m.—we'd invited everyone for a 10:00 a.m. start time.

After scrolling through a few more texts, I decided the

smartest thing to do was to call Ken. He deserved to know what was going on.

The phone didn't even finish its first ring before Ken answered. "Dude, where the hell are you guys?" He couldn't hide the concern in his voice.

"Ken, I'm so sorry I didn't call earlier—Lee's...she's in the hospital," I explained as calmly as I could.

I heard Ken gasp.

"She's okay for now," I added quickly. "We're still in the ICU, though."

I could almost feel Ken switching into crisis-management mode as he hesitated before asking, "Okay, TD. What exactly happened? What are we looking at here?"

I explained everything almost in one single breath, surprised at how familiar this type of conversation had become over the years.

Only once I was done, Ken cautiously asked, "Well, I'm here with everyone at the duck park. What should we do? Wait...never mind. You've got enough to worry about. I'll take care of things here. You just focus on our girl."

"And there's our brave little lady," Dr. Mallory said as he entered Room 188. "Lee, Dr. Helmers told me you had a rough time of it last night."

"Yeah, but I'm fine now. I'll be ready to go home tomorrow, I bet," Lee bravely replied with her voice still being a bit hoarse. I shook my head in disbelief. Only my baby sister, still in a hospital bed and connected to more IVs than I cared to count, would describe herself as "fine."

"Dr. Mallory. It's good to see you," I said as I stood up and held out my hand for a handshake. He ignored it and hugged me instead.

Compassion first. This is why he was Lee's doctor.

"Well, TD, we got Lee's blood work back and now we

know what's going on," Dr. Mallory said. "Would you mind stepping into the hallway for a moment?"

I winced at the idea of yet another hallway conversation, but I knew I had no choice. I had to be brave for Lee. We stepped out of the room. Dr. Mallory carefully closed the door behind us.

"The results came back with a positive match for E. coli," he began. "Now there are many different strains of E. coli and most are harmless, but Lee's weakened immune system complicates matters."

"E. coli?" I asked. "That causes seizures?"

"In Lee's case, yes. With her, we have a much more serious situation than usual on our hands." Dr. Mallory paused. "The good news is that E. coli is bacterial, so we can fight it with antibiotics. But before we begin any course of treatment, we need to pinpoint the exact strain of E. coli she's contracted."

I let out a long sigh as I ran my fingers through my hair. I had about a thousand questions already, but I wanted to hear the rest of what Dr. Mallory had to say first. As Lee's caretakers, it would be up to me and Uncle Bill to stay fully up-to-date on Lee's condition, medications and treatments. I knew all too well that hospital staff were as fallible as anyone else, despite their best intentions. Staying on top the details could prevent accidents before they happened. I wished that I could take on an even-greater responsibility, but knowing every detail of Lee's condition was the best way I could ensure that my little girl would be safe.

"It's not as dire as it sounds," Dr. Mallory reassured me. "But you do need to know that the epicenter of the infection is in her chest. She's having a hard time breathing because of a buildup of fluid in her lungs."

"Okay, so how do we clear that fluid?" I asked. "And how do we keep it from coming back?"

"The respirator she was on last night helped, as will the various inhalants that we'll be administering daily. It's important to keep her lungs clear. If not, long-term damage is possible." Dr. Mallory explained. "But, TD, that's not going to happen. You got her here immediately. Early intervention is quite possibly our best defense in any emergency." He smiled a sad smile. "You did well, son. Absolutely the right thing."

I appreciated Dr. Mallory's compassion and encouragement, but Lee came first. "Okay, but how did she contract the infection?" I asked.

"It's hard to know, but it almost certainly came from something she ate."

"There's nothing I can point to," I said slowly, trying to think if she'd eaten anything unusual. "As far as I know, Lee's been on the same diet as always. Healthy everything, supplemented with dairy-based treats for calories."

"It wouldn't have to do with her diet. It would have more to do with one infected food. E. coli can be present in anything raw or undercooked, from hamburger meat to lettuce."

"Could that be what's up with my uncle?" I asked as my mind made the connection. "He wasn't feeling well yesterday. Stomachache. Fever, maybe."

"It's hard to say without proper tests, but yes, in an adult with a normal immune system, those can be symptoms of many E. coli strains," said Dr. Mallory. "If he's been ill, I should talk to him immediately. Where's your uncle today? I expected him to be with you this morning."

"He just texted. He's on his way." I caught Dr. Mallory's eye and held his gaze. "Lee's party…it's a whole mess."

Dr. Mallory put his hand on my shoulder. "Yes, terrible timing. We were all looking forward to that. I'm so sorry."

"I don't think Lee's put it together yet," I said. "Don't mention it. Please?" I asked, practically begging.

"Of course not. We need to keep her spirits up."

"Thank you," I replied, knowing I could trust Dr. Mallory not to slip. "So what's the next step?"

"We'll need a day or two to pinpoint the strain of E. coli. For now, we'll keep her comfortable. We'll stay focused on keeping her lungs clear until we can put together an aggressive antibiotics regimen. I want her to stay here in the ICU, though, until we can get treatment started and make sure she responds."

"And how long will treatment take? Any idea of how long she'll be hospitalized?"

"There are too many factors in play to know exactly how long it will be, but I'd guess anywhere from two weeks to two months…depending on how her body reacts to the antibiotics."

I shook my head and slumped my shoulders. Two months. I couldn't possibly tell my little sunflower that she'd be stuck inside this hospital for up to two months. Stuck inside, when she deserved to be sprouting in the sun. How could I tell my sister all that, on the very day we should've been celebrating her health?

I sighed, fighting back fresh tears. "Thank you, doctor. Let's just get Lee through today. I'll fill her in on the rest tomorrow."

"Certainly. As I've come to learn, sometimes the best thing to do is simply get through things like this one day at a time."

Although he didn't mean to, Dr. Mallory had just broken my heart. For as long as I could remember, today was always supposed to be the beginning of my little miracle's One Day.

Lee fell back to sleep after going through another round of treatments on the respirator. Thankfully that evil breathing tube was no longer necessary. An oxygen-type mask could now deliver the medication into her lungs, although Lee found the mask a bit scary. Even though she did look ill, her spirits lifted when I'd explained to her what had happened and how we were going to fix it. My little miracle was being so brave, which was helping me keep it together—although I still hadn't mustered enough courage to tell her she might be here for two whole months.

Once Lee fell asleep, I found myself doing something that I rarely did: I prayed. Except for my mother's funeral, I could only remember going to church maybe once or twice in my entire life, but I was beginning to feel so helpless that I thought it was, indeed, time to ask for some Divine assistance. So, for the first time since Lee's transplant, I asked God to once again help my little sister, and to give me the strength to support her through this difficult time.

Just as I was about ready to wrap up my silent request, a knock came. "Excuse me, Mr. Dexter," began one of Lee's nurses as she cracked open the door. "There's a large group of people in the waiting room asking for you."

I walked down the ominous hallway and into the ICU's waiting room. Before I'd even made it fully through the door, I was tackled in a hug by someone—I couldn't figure out who'd grabbed me. But from the strength of the grip alone, I knew it could only be one of two people: Hercules himself, or Sergeant Biceps.

"We're all so sorry, bro," Ken said, releasing me from his powerful grasp.

"Yes, TD," added Mrs. Zom. "We'll all be here for you for as long as you need."

I panned the waiting room. Almost everyone who'd been invited to Lee's party was now here: Ken, Mrs. Zom, Mr. Zom, Uncle Bill, Moon and…Sal?! I did a double-take before rushing over to Sal, enfolding him in a warm embrace, followed by a kiss on each cheek. I felt his handlebar mustache brush against my face, which was a little bit strange but also surprisingly comforting.

"*Ciao caro!*" Sal exclaimed once he let me go. "*Sorpresa!*"

I was so stunned to see him that I couldn't reply in any language. My mouth hung open against my will. Sal…here… in this hospital. All the way from Florence. To support Lee. To support us. *The* smiley Italian, here in America.

Ken, as usual, ruined the moment. "Man, TD, you look like absolute shit."

"Ken, language!" came Mrs. Zom's sharp rebuke.

"Any new developments to report?" asked Mr. Zom in his practical, military voice. A genuine concern undercut his tone,

255

though—he couldn't hide that.

"No, sir, not since I talked with Ken earlier. Lee's sleeping now," I answered.

My uncle tossed me a backpack. "Clean clothes. Supplies. Go get washed up, you'll feel better."

With the people I cared about surrounding me, it seemed as though things were already looking up. All my loved ones, right here with me.

Well, not quite all my loved ones: Where was Emma Rey Finley?

"Thanks," I replied. "I guess I really do need some freshening-up." Everyone laughed as I ran to the restroom. I washed-up and changed as quickly as I could, then walked back to the waiting room to spend some quality time with my *family*. My big, complicated, smiley family.

"Okay, so you'll tell us everything now?" asked Sal. "Ken gave us the basics, but that's all we know." The instant his accent touched my ears it made me smile.

I recounted everything as best I could, starting from when I'd put Lee to bed last night. I went through every detail I could remember, right up until the moment when my phone exploded with messages and I realized what day it was.

Silence washed over the room for a minute, once I'd finished. The terror was too familiar. Everyone needed a moment to process the information, and I really couldn't blame them. I was still processing it myself.

Mrs. Zom broke the silence. "It does sound like everything's going to be alright, though, with time and care." She almost sounded as if she believed it, too.

"I know, I just…I just wish Lee could've at least had today," I replied. "She's already been through so much, and she's been looking forward to this party for months." I sighed heavily. "It's just not fair."

But no one responded this time, as if everyone could feel every ounce of my pain, and I could see the fear in their eyes. We'd been in this position before. The pain we were all now sharing wasn't foreign. In fact, it was disturbingly normal.

Ken forced his voice into his vehicle-of-positivity tone. "Well, that's why we brought the party to her!" he cried, as he pulled a stack of party hats out of his backpack.

After placing a paper hat on his own head, Ken passed the stack of party hats around to Sal, who happily put one on his own head. Everyone else passed on the offer, so Ken placed one on Moon's head instead. "If I'd known Lee would get so attached to this teddy bear, I would've won it for her years ago," he said, smirking. "Though I have to admit, her fuzzy blue friend was an awesome prize for a bowling-alley arcade."

I laughed freely for the first time in what felt like months. "Honestly, man, I don't know what Lee would've done without Moon when she was on bed rest." How could I ever forget the generosity of Sergeant Biceps?

"Yeah, I'm pretty special," replied Ken with an especially-goofy grin, which earned him another look of disapproval from his mom. He ignored her and asked, "Do you think Lee's awake yet? I'd like to bring Moon to her."

"Let's go check," I replied. I turned to the group. "I'll be back in a few minutes."

Ken and I started down the long hallway. "I can't tell you how much I appreciate your coming," I began. "But did you tell Emm what's going on? Lee will want to see her, too."

Ken dropped his shoulders and sighed as if he'd been expecting this very question, "Emma wasn't there this morning, and I have no idea why. You haven't spoken to her either?"

"No, I haven't...I was barely able to get in touch with you," I replied, sounding more annoyed than I'd intended. I figured Emm had been running late this morning—nothing unusual for her—but if that was the case, why hadn't she called?

Ken shook his head. "Do you want me to call her for you?"

I thought for a second. "No, it's okay. The news should come from me. Thank you, though."

"You guys still haven't spoken since...that night?"

"Nope. She RSVP'd to the party back in January, but nothing since."

"That's...interesting," Ken replied, sounding as though he didn't get it, either.

"I know. It was part of my plan, but I'd never thought she'd stop reaching out to me completely," I said, feeling defeated. "I thought for sure we'd be seeing her this morning."

Shooting me a guilty stare, Ken said firmly, "If I don't call her, then you *have* to. For Lee's sake if nothing else."

"I promise. I will," I replied as we finally reached Lee's room. I peeked into her window—and she was awake. Knowing how much Lee enjoyed having some private time with her visitors, I added, "In fact, I'll give you two some one-on-one time. And I'll go take care of that right now...before I think of a reason not to."

"Good," he replied.

Ken trained his eyes on Room 188, looking at the doorway as if it were the entrance to Hades itself. "I can't believe we're here again," he sighed, almost seeming to wilt right before my eyes. But before letting his sadness grow, he almost instantly pulled himself together. Ken slapped on a smile and puffed up his chest before marching into my little sister's room with Moon tucked under his arm.

God bless Ken Zom. A saint in disguise. A broad-shouldered, overly-muscular soldier from up above. Storming into battle armed with nothing but a baby blue teddy bear and love—the only ammunition a hero like him needed.

Chapter 22

Just Another Piece of Jewelry

The phone rang a third, fourth and then a fifth time before I heard Emm click onto the line. "TD!" she said in an excited and hopeful tone.

I couldn't deny it. No matter how disappointed I was at her no-show, it was always nice to hear Emm's voice. With just one word, all my feelings came rushing back. The skeptical sadness inside me had suddenly been tamed.

"Emm! Hey," I said as brightly and casually as I could, despite my churning insides.

"It is so nice to hear your voice! I've really missed you."

Before I responded, I told myself to remain firm, to not let her charm win me over just yet. "So…where were you today?"

"Oh yes, Lee's celebration! Craziest thing. Matt's parents finally came into town and asked us to stay the weekend here in San Francisco. And that worked out perfectly, because my professor invited me to a conference in Monterey next week— I'm actually giving a paper on Thursday."

"But Emm…" I began, trying to get a word in. Trying to tell her about last night.

"We left right after the game last night. Leaving early was a bit spontaneous, but I really wanted to meet Matt's parents while they're here. We decided to just go ahead and do it. I'm so sorry, TD, I should've let you know, but it just slipped my mind."

I had nothing to say in reply, so I just let my silence do the talking. What killed me more than anything else was how casual she was—like she didn't know that today was supposed to have been the biggest day in Lee's young life. I mean, maybe I could accept the fact that she'd blown *me* off—but Lee?

After a moment of dead air, Emm asked, "Well, how was it?"

I didn't want to make Emm feel completely guilty—not with Lee being so sick—but I also needed to tell her what was going on, for my sister's sake. Even though part of me told me that I shouldn't. Part of me wanted to simply hang up.

"The party actually didn't happen," I said somberly into the phone.

I could hear a voice in the background. Emm pulled the phone away from her mouth and laughed, playfully telling someone to stop.

"I can call back another time if you're busy," I said flatly, starting to get mad.

"No, it's fine, sorry about that. Did you say the party never happened?"

"That's what I said," I answered curtly.

"What? Why not?" Emm's tone now grew more serious.

"Late last night, Lee…It's kind of hard to explain, but she got really sick and we had to rush her to the hospital. That's where I am now."

I heard Emm gasp. "Oh my God! TD, I…I had no idea. I'm *so* sorry."

"She's alright for now, that's the most important thing. Stable, but still in the ICU."

I could almost see Emm's mouth gaping open as she

searched for her next words, knowing that there really wasn't much she could say. "If I had known... Jesus, TD, you know I would've been there, right?" she asked.

"I know, Emm." I paused, suddenly missing her even more, before repeating, "I know."

"Okay, tell me everything," she said, almost pleading.

I began walking her through the horror that had been my last fourteen hours. Not leaving out any details, no matter how horrible they were, and accepting the fact that she deserved to know. Even if things had seismically changed between us.

"And then almost everyone who was invited to the celebration came to the hospital this morning," I concluded. "They're in the waiting room now."

Emm choked back a sob as she realized how much her presence was truly missed. "I bet Lee's so upset that I'm not there."

"I haven't told her yet, but I'm sure she will be. It's just Ken in the room with her right now. But you know how much Lee adores you, Emm. You know how much you keep her fighting," I said, being honest with her.

She was quiet for a moment before she said, softly, "Please tell Lee that I'm so happy at her. Will you do that for me... please?"

"I'm sure I can handle that, Emm," I answered, fighting to keep my tone casual.

"Gosh. That poor girl. I'm packing my things right now and telling Matt that we're leaving. It shouldn't take us more than seven or eight hours to get there, if we leave right away."

I felt my heart rebuild as Emm sang those simple words. All the disappointment, all the frustration, all the pain I'd been harboring—vanished. This was the Emma Rey Finley that I loved and adored. Yet for some reason, my next words didn't match my feelings at all. What came out was something false, something feeble and flimsy. Something that I instantly regretted.

"Please, Emm, you don't have to do that. Just come see her when you get back." I didn't mean a word of it, of course—I wanted nothing more in that instant than for Emm to be here. And the craziest part was that she knew it, too. She knew I was lying.

"If you're sure, TD. I really wouldn't mind. I can miss the first day or two of the conference, and I'm sure Matt's parents will understand." But she said it just a bit too quickly. Perfunctory, almost. Like it was rehearsed. She was lying, too, even more obviously than I was.

When had we become so good at hiding our truths from each other?

The truth was I needed my rock. I needed the Emm I'd known for the first three years of college. I needed the girl who could make all of the chaos evaporate with a smile. Dealing with this situation was hard enough, but the Emm that I needed could take it all away. She was the superhero who Lee and I needed to rescue us from this nightmare.

Yet at the same time, I knew we weren't in that place anymore. We weren't us. And if I was really being truthful with myself, as long as Lee was stable, there was no real reason for Emm to rush home. I wanted her to *want* to come—to *need* to come—but I knew in her heart...she didn't.

"We'll be fine, Emm," I replied after a moment. "But I promise to call if anything changes." The conflict brewing inside threatened to overpower me as I spoke.

"And, TD...I mean...I'm not too far away, honestly. Remember that."

"It's okay, Emm. I know." Then I brought my voice down to almost a whisper, fighting off my tears. "Well, I need to go and check on our girl. Enjoy the rest of your trip. Lee and I can't wait to see you when you get back." The words themselves burned in me as they erupted up through my throat and vomited out of my mouth.

"Okay," she began. Her words were so flat, so cold, that I could almost feel Emm's sad smile on the other end of the phone. "We'll talk soon, I promise."

I pressed my forehead against the cool window of the alcove as hot tears slipped from my eyes. No matter what had changed between us, I'd always assumed that Emm would be around for Lee. But, obviously, I'd been wrong. And, truthfully, I wasn't sure if anything in this world made sense anymore.

In the waiting room, I said goodbye to the Zoms who promised to be back in few days. Uncle Bill had joined Ken in Lee's room—they were all watching a movie—which left Sal and me together.

"There's one thing I've learned in my life, TD," Sal said, with an uncharacteristic seriousness in his voice. I looked up at him, quizzically. Sal was never one for lectures, and I really wasn't in the mood to listen to one, either.

"It's a simple truth," he continued. "A full stomach is a happy stomach. Come, I'll buy you lunch, *sì*? Then everything will seem a little better," he said, as he placed his arm around me. "I think I saw a pasta place a few blocks away."

It was past lunchtime, but thinking back on our time in Florence, lunch seemed like a pleasant escape. I also needed some air, so I took Sal up on his offer. "*Grazie*, Sal. That sounds really good."

As soon as we'd stepped outside and escaped the hospital's miasma, I was ravenous. I practically began salivating on the sidewalk as I thought back to the platters of food Sal had ordered for us in Italy.

The restaurant was only three blocks away, and far from being a typical, casual California dining spot, it was surprisingly authentic. Sal started chatting with our waiter in Italian the moment we were seated. I looked at him and smiled as Sal's new friend disappeared into the kitchen. Having already been down this road before, I knew Sal had probably just ordered enough food to feed a small army, along with enough wine to drown a sailor.

"I won't be having any red wine today, Sal, but some starters sound nice," I said, truly appreciative of his generosity, but thinking it probably best to steer clear of alcohol right now.

Sal paused for a moment, stroking his mustache. Then, enthusiastically, he exclaimed, "Ah, well, then it's a good thing I ordered white."

I couldn't help but laugh. Sal was two steps ahead of me, as always. "Okay, okay, maybe just one glass," I replied, smirking.

"So, I played a little trick on you, eh? I bet you weren't expecting an old man like me to turn up out of the blue."

"I had no idea that you were coming to the States," I answered. "You didn't tell me!"

"But I *did* tell you. I promised to come as soon as I retired—and a man's word is his dignity. So now I'm here." Sal shrugged as if he'd gotten out of bed this morning and simply hopped on a transatlantic flight.

"But how? My uncle didn't say anything."

"When he told me about Lee's party, I thought I would surprise you at the celebration. But things turned out differently, *sfortunatamente*. Your uncle was supposed to pick me up at the airport this morning, but…"

"I know," I sighed. "Everything's upside-down right now. I don't even know…"

"It's okay, TD, I understand. And I want you to know… you and your uncle don't have to do this alone. I'll stay as long as you need me."

The knot inside of me unclenched as Sal's genuine warmth cascaded through me. I didn't doubt that he meant what he'd said: Sal really was family.

"*Grazie, caro* Sal," I replied in my best Italian, trying to restrain my emotion. "That means the world to me. Really."

"Of course, of course," responded Sal, gesticulating warmly. "But look—now we eat!" he cried, as not one but two waiters brought our food—two heaping plates of pasta, a large pizza, and a side of fried zucchini. "And don't worry, I was only kidding about the wine," Sal added, grinning from ear-to-ear.

I attacked my food, practically eating a whole slice of pepperoni pizza in one monster bite. Sal watched me in awe as I
crudely devoured it, but he didn't say a thing about my lack
of table manners.

Once I was mostly finished chewing, Sal's serious tone
caught me by surprise, "So how is she, your...kamikaze
friend?"

I stopped chewing instantly. "She's okay, thanks. I just talked to her. She's away for the week." I hoped the disappointment in my voice was disguised by the pizza in my mouth.

"Your muscular friend said she was supposed to be at the
celebration today?" From Sal's tone, it was obvious he suspected something was wrong between me and Emm. In fact,
I doubted he would've brought it up otherwise. He'd seen me
and Emm at our best, in the closest moments of our relationship.

Without even really thinking twice about it, I started telling Sal the long story of my friendship-turned-non-romance
with Emma Rey Finley. I didn't hold back anything and Sal,
God love him, became my shrink for the remainder of our
lunch.

"And I don't really know what to do now, because when
I had my opportunity to tell her, I blew it," I finally finished
after a solid five minutes of talking.

Sal then gave me a deep look, as if he were weighing his
words carefully. "She does care a lot about you, this much is
true. I saw it for myself...you two, it was like you were on your
honeymoon. But let me ask you this: If Emma loves you so
much, how could she have possibly let someone else into her
life?"

I looked up from my plate of pasta but didn't reply. I'd
been searching for the answer to that question for months: I
still didn't have one. I also wasn't sure if I wanted to find one,
either.

"Because you would've turned down any other girl—even
if she had all the beauty and brains in the world," he continued. "You would've said, 'No, thank you,' because of your

love for Emma. Friends or otherwise, you'd never take the chance of losing her by being with someone else."

My mouth hung open for a moment at Sal's wisdom. "I could deny that right now, but it wouldn't be true," I finally responded, conceding. "There's no one else for me. She's my shooting star."

"But you see, TD, Emma *did* take that chance. I'm not saying she doesn't love you, because she obviously does. But in *amore*, there must only be truth. And the truth is she doesn't love you enough to not take the chance of losing you. The truth is that she doesn't love you as much as you love her."

As I continued to listen, I thought that maybe it wasn't such a bad thing that Emm's missing bracelet had thwarted my confession. Maybe Sal was right. Maybe to her that turquoise bracelet was just another piece of jewelry. Maybe to her I was just another guy that she knew. Emm loved me, sure, but not like I loved her.

With his unmistakable, honest candor, Sal told me what Ken had been afraid to say. Sal called it as he saw it, not sugar-coating anything in the slightest.

My glass heart cracked once more. As a slicing pain shot through me, I realized nothing about Sal seemed smiley in this moment. As if this hard truth had finally cracked his heart too.

As we approached Room 188, I heard the sweetest sound on Earth: Lee's giggle. My gloom immediately departed.

"What's going on in here?" I chided as Sal and I entered the room. Ken was lounging in bed with Lee, just like he used to, during her year of isolation, making her laugh with his antics.

"Oh, look who it is, Lee. It's Gru himself!" cried Ken. The two of them busted-up laughing.

Looking at me as if he'd missed something obvious, Sal seemed a bit confused. I put him at ease. "Don't worry, it's an inside joke. Gru's my new nickname."

"Ah. Okay then, Gru," began Sal in his smiliest voice, "How about if you introduce me to *la bella bambina*? I'm not sure she remembers me."

Ken sat up as I made the introduction. "Lee, this is your Uncle Sal. He flew all the way from Florence to be here today."

Sal knelt-down at the edge of my sister's hospital bed, took her hand, then gracefully and softly kissed it. "You've gotten so much bigger since the last time I saw you. You aren't a little girl anymore—now you're a beautiful young woman!"

Lee's cheeks turned scarlet. I could tell she was thrilled about finally meeting the man I'd told her so much about. Lee hadn't seen Sal since kindergarten, so as far as she was concerned, this was their first real meeting.

"Gosh, you *are* smiley." She almost glowed with delight, appearing as though she hadn't quite believed my descriptions.

Sal, confused again, turned to me as he stood up. I did my best to explain "smiley" to him. Without missing a beat, he replied to Lee, "Thank you, missy. I'll be your smiley uncle, any time you need," as he bowed, theatrically.

"I like your hat," Lee said, pointing to Sal's head and giggling a little.

I hadn't realized it, but Sal was still wearing the party hat Ken had given him earlier. We'd been in the restaurant like that, which—now that I thought of it—explained the stares we'd received.

Sal, gracious as ever, returned the compliment. "I like your bear, especially since he has the same hat as me. A very fuzzy young man!"

Lee, as if she'd impolitely excluded a guest from the conversation, responded, "Sorry. Sal, this is Moon. Moon, this is Sal."

"*Ciao*, Moon." Sal stretched out his hand and shook Moon's baby blue paw.

Lee gently covered Moon's ears, then whispered, "I'm not sure if Moon understands Italian, but maybe we can teach him...together."

Ken chuckled. "Yeah, I'm pretty sure his tag says, 'Made in China.' Try Mandarin next time, Sal."

We all started laughing.

Doctor Mallory knocked on the door and stepped into the room. "Gentlemen, sorry to disturb you," he began, "but I need to check on the little lady."

Ken popped up from the bed. "Then we'll give you some privacy." Turning to Sal, he continued, "TD's uncle asked me to give you a ride back to his place. He's still not feeling too great."

Lee and I quickly said our goodbyes, with Sal promising to come visit again tomorrow. I walked them to the elevator bank.

When I returned to the room, Dr. Mallory was in mid-exam. "And how does this feel?" he asked as he held a stethoscope to Lee's chest.

"Good," she replied.

"And this?" he asked, moving the stethoscope to her back.

"Not as good, but not too bad," she said. "But it would feel better if your hands weren't so cold."

Dr. Mallory laughed. "My apologies," he said. "I just finished eating a big bowl of ice cream. Should I have a nurse bring you some, too?"

"Yes, please!" Dr. Mallory looked happy to see Lee's energy levels so high.

"Got it," he said, pretending to write a prescription on his pad. "One large bowl of prescription ice cream after dinner." Turning to me, he said, "Her lungs sound much better, TD. With any luck, we'll have our lab tests back on Monday and we'll start her on the antibiotics."

"I've never heard of 'prescription ice cream' before," said Lee, once Dr. Mallory had left the room. "I must really be getting better."

"Of course you are, Little One. Now tell me for real, how

are you feeling?" Lee did seem a good bit better. The bloating in her face had subsided, but the bags under her eyes told a different story.

"I'm okay," she replied. "It's just—" She turned her face toward the wall, as if she was afraid to tell me something.

"What is it, Lee?" I asked soothingly, hiding my suspicion.

"I'm…just so sad about the party. I don't know why I had to get sick now."

"I know, Little One, I know," I said, feeling a bit guilty at my relief. "But your health comes first. We'll reschedule your party when you're feeling better."

Lee took off her glasses and cleaned them with a tissue before asking, "At the duck park?"

"Yes, of course at the duck park," I replied. "But wasn't it nice of everyone to come by today?"

Lee took a deep breath, then said in a pout, "But it wasn't everyone." She turned her gaze away from me again. With a strength that made it sound as if there was a period after each word, she demanded, "Where was Emma?"

The question I'd been dreading all day.

I couldn't possibly tell her that Emm hadn't shown up. That she had chosen her boyfriend over us. That I, myself, had told her to stay in San Francisco. So I did the only thing a big brother could do in this situation: I lied.

"Emm wasn't feeling well," I explained. "And since she knew you were sick, she didn't want risk making you any sicker."

"She's sick? Is she in the hospital too?" Lee asked, her voice strained with concern.

"It's just a bad cold, don't worry," I said, stroking Lee's back. "She promised to come see you as soon as she's feeling better."

Lee finally looked back at me. I could see a heaviness in her pale blue eyes. "Promise?"

"Promise," I offered quickly, hoping that Lee wouldn't catch any hint of doubt in my tone.

"Well, tell her to feel better, 'cause I miss her a lot. Really a lot," Lee said as she hugged Moon tightly.

"She told me to tell you she's happy at you." I hated lying to Lee, but at least that part was true.

"Good," Lee said, laying back on her pillows. "Now, can you tell me about Daveeed? And the kayaking?"

I was relieved to see Lee switching gears more easily than I'd expected. "Sure, bossy pants, but only if you promise to get some rest after."

I told Lee the story once again, doing my best not to rush through the details. But by the time I got to the part where Emm had fallen asleep in the kayak, Lee, too, had drifted off to dreamland. Without her prescription ice cream, but with a sweet scoop of a smile on her face.

Chapter 23

Everything Happens for a Reason

On Monday, I woke up to the familiar, soothing sound of Lee's unmistakable morning yawn. This didn't stop my body however, from jolting awake; something I'd always done in hospitals. Some nightmares, no matter how badly I tried to forget, would never leave me.

"Good morning, sunshine," Nurse Jen said as she handed me a much-needed cup of coffee. I was touched by her thoughtfulness: I wasn't even her patient.

I sat up quickly, getting my bearings. The morning sunlight streamed through the window, illuminating the bouquet of tulips that Uncle Bill had brought the day before.

"Thank you," I replied. "Wow, I was totally out, huh?"

Lee giggled. "You were snoring and everything. *Really bad.*"

"Oh, be nice to your brother!" Nurse Jen teased. "It's okay, you needed the rest, TD," she continued, turning back to Lee. "And how are you feeling today, sweetie?"

"Really good. I'm just starv-ING!" Lee replied, emphasizing the "-ing" on "starving." I was so glad to see she had an appetite this morning. She'd progressed so much since Friday night that I hoped Dr. Mallory might change his mind and move her out of the ICU soon.

"I'll get you some breakfast as soon as I check your vitals and stats, okay missy?" asked Nurse Jen brightly.

"Deal. Thank you, ma'am," Lee answered, as Nurse Jen reviewed my sister's monitors and checked her IV. I made silly faces at Lee as Nurse Jen worked to try and brighten my little sunflower's morning.

"All done!" Nurse Jen declared after a moment. "Everything looks good. You're doing so well, Lee." She turned to me and continued "Let's go get your sister some breakfast, because she's…"

"Starv-ING" Nurse Jen and Lee said in unison, almost harmonically.

"She has tons of energy this morning," Nurse Jen commented as we began walking down the hall to the front desk.

"And so do you," I joked before taking a cautious sip of my fresh, still-scalding, coffee. Then I asked, "Hey, how was your party this weekend?"

"It didn't turn out quite as we'd hoped," she answered. "We were running a bit late when we got word the party was canceled. But my son and I still spent the full day together. A movie and lunch, just the two of us." She was obviously so grateful to have had some one-on-one time with her son that she wasn't at all fazed by having had to adjust her plans for the day.

"What movie did you guys see?" I asked.

"The second *Despicable Me* movie. He saw the original a few weeks ago, so I got to take him to the sequel. There's a big promotion at the theaters, since the third one is coming out this summer."

"Funny you say that… Lee wants me to take her to see the sequel as soon as we get her out of here."

We reached the desk where Nurse Jen handed me a photocopy of the day's menu. "Here's what's on offer today. Lee doesn't have any restrictions, so pick what you think she'd like best. Then, if you'd like, you can come down to the cafeteria with me. It's time for my coffee break."

"I'd love to. It'll give me the chance to return the favor," I answered, holding up my own cup of joe.

In the cafeteria, I ordered myself a heaping, if insipid, breakfast, along with coffee and a bagel for Nurse Jen. I had the feeling Nurse Jen could talk to just about anyone, but as our conversation went on, I felt as though we'd known each other for far longer than a few days—and it was nice to have company in this damned cafeteria for once. She told me more about her son, specifically about the ups and downs of his cancer treatments.

"Was he treated here?" I asked. "There're so many good hospitals in the area."

"Yes, but this one's the best. Everyone was so kind and supportive here—not just to my son, but to my husband and me, too. For a few years there, it seemed like we were in and out of this hospital almost on a weekly basis. I got to know the oncology staff so well…that's how I first got the name, 'Nurse Jen.' Managing my son's care, knowing his meds, helping the nursing staff with the little stuff. All that was my way of managing the stress, I guess."

"That makes a lot of sense, actually," I replied sympathetically. "There's nothing worse than the waiting, the not knowing. That useless feeling."

A darkness passed over Nurse Jen's eyes. "That's it exactly." But just as quickly, her eyes lit up again. "But it sparked my interest in medicine. Once my son was cancer-free, I just couldn't go back to my old accounting firm—the work just didn't have any meaning anymore. So I went back to school to become an *actual* nurse, and now here I am!"

"That's amazing. To be honest, this place gives me the creeps—I would've run for the hills if I were you. What drew you back?" I asked, trying to further stoke Nurse Jen's fire of excitement.

She smiled a smile at me that said, "I'm so glad you asked," before she answered, "I've always had a soft spot for kids, I guess, and nursing them back to health is honestly the most satisfying feeling in the world to me. Through the good and the bad, I really love my job. I really love what I do."

"That's so beautiful," I said admiringly, truly blown away. I was so happy for her I could've burst right there. A healthy son and a vocational calling.

Practically glowing, Nurse Jen replied, "So, like I always say, 'Everything happens for a reason.'"

"Hey, don't you have school today?" Lee asked suddenly, looking up from her journal as if she'd just remembered that I was in college.

"I do, but I emailed my professors and my coach…they gave me the day off to be with you."

"But don't you have a big game coming up? You have to win to stay on track for the finals!"

I couldn't help but smile. How Lee retained any awareness of my schedule in the middle of all this madness touched me. "That's not until Friday, don't worry," I replied. "But yes, if we win our next three games, we'll advance to the NCAA Tournament. I do have to go back to campus tomorrow, though, so tonight will be our last night together for a bit. Uncle Bill or Sal will come stay with you instead."

"That's okay, I guess," Lee answered. "If you miss practice, you won't win. And if you miss school, you won't graduate."

I couldn't argue with her reasoning, but I hated the thought of leaving Lee's side. The truth was, her seizure had planted a new terror in me. No one else had seen what I had that night. If something like that ever happened again, I needed to be with her. Even if all I could do was hold onto her little palm, I needed to be around to protect her. To keep the darkness away. To remind her of her own strength.

"It's true, we all have responsibilities," I replied. "But I promise you, someone will be here with you every night."

"Someone like Emma?" Lee asked earnestly. The look in her eyes, both excited and sad, made me ache. Made me remember better times.

"She's still not feeling well," I lied. "She's going to her doctor tomorrow, so maybe he can give her some medicine to make her feel better."

"I hope so," said Lee. "It's *so boring* in this place. Emma makes everything more...exciting." I didn't miss the dash of hope in her voice.

I smiled a sad smile. That's how I felt, too. Or how I used to feel. I really wasn't sure anymore.

"How funny is Sal?" I asked, purposely and quickly changing the subject.

"He's so nice, but Moon and I can't understand what he's saying sometimes because of his accent."

"All you have to do is listen a little more carefully, Little One. Lots of people have accents. And Sal flew all the way out here just to see you!"

Obviously pleased by how much she meant to Sal, my little sister replied, "Yeah, that was *super nice* of him. Kind of like how you flew all the way out there to see Emma?"

I had to stop myself from flinching: Sal had traveled all the way from Europe for Lee, while Emm couldn't be bothered to drive home.

"Yes, just like that," I replied. But before Lee could respond, I quickly changed the subject again—anything to steer the conversation away from Emm. "What are you writing about today, sis?"

"You know I can't tell you that. But I promise you'll see it someday."

Just then, Dr. Mallory caught my eye from the hallway. He held one finger over his mouth, "*Shh*," as he motioned to me with his other hand. I gulped—another hallway conversation. A hallway conversation he didn't want Lee to hear.

"Well, if you're *so* bored," I began, thinking up an excuse to leave the room, "I'll go down to the gift shop and get you a book of puzzles. We can do a few of them together."

Lee lifted Moon to her ear as if her stuffed bear was whispering to her. "That sounds good, but Moon wants to help, too."

I forced myself to laugh as I stepped into the hallway, terrified of what Dr. Mallory needed to tell me: What if there was something they'd missed? What if this wasn't an infection at all, but something much worse? Which ring of Hell would Lee have to leap through next?

"TD, how are you this afternoon?"

"I'm fine, thanks" I answered, practically trembling with fear as I shook Dr. Mallory's hand, which was off-putting in itself. I couldn't remember the last time Dr. Mallory and I had exchanged a handshake. "How's our girl?"

"Well, the good news is that we've pinpointed the exact strain of E. coli, which means we can begin treating it." Dr. Mallory stopped short, as if he had much more to say but didn't want to say it. His hopeful words didn't match his face, either; I'd never seen Dr. Mallory look quite so down before.

"What's the bad news then?" I prompted. If I had to hear whatever came next, I wanted it to be quick.

"I don't want you to worry unnecessarily," he began after taking a deep breath, "but the strain Lee has is a very rare type. We can still treat it, but it's going to be a bit of an uphill battle. And not a terribly comfortable one, I'm afraid."

I swallowed hard. "What does that mean? She's doing so much better already."

"That's true, but unfortunately almost everything we've done so far had been a Band-Aid. We've cleared her lungs, which is important, but mostly she's been feeling better because we've had her on pain meds and mild stimulants to make her comfortable. But most of those medications are counter-indicative to the antibiotics we now need to start her on. Basically, before Lee gets better," He stopped and took a long breath before finishing, "she is going to get much worse."

"It hardly seems fair," I said, utterly deflated. I didn't mean to whine, but I really couldn't help it. "How uncomfortable will she be?"

"We'll do our best to manage her discomfort with those medicines that remain available to us, of course, but the antibiotics supersede comfort. There's simply no way around that."

My only possible response would've been to grunt in pained frustration, but I managed to hold it in. I knew Dr. Mallory was right, but a part of me didn't understand why modern medicine couldn't make a sick child comfortable while she healed. No matter the reasons.

"I know, TD, I know. Believe me, if there was a better option…" Dr. Mallory put his hand on my shoulder. "But we really need to get her started right away. The longer the infection goes unchecked, the harder it'll be to treat."

"Okay," I said, full of anguish. "Okay. If that's what we need to do. But…I promised her a book of puzzles from the gift shop. Can I give it to her first? Would that be okay?"

"Certainly. My team is prepping now, but they won't be ready to start for another half-hour or so—Dr. Foley and Dr. Ojalvo will be heading the team. I need to get back upstairs to my practice for the afternoon, but go ahead. Make her smile. That's always the best medicine."

Even if Lee had come back from worse, even if she'd always been a fighter, it pained me to think that a smile was the only thing I could offer her now.

"But I don't need to be on oxygen!" Lee sobbed loudly as she kicked her feet against her bed. Dr. Mallory's team was finishing up their second round of treatments, which now included another stint with the oxygen mask. Earlier that afternoon, my poor sister had already had two new IVs inserted, as well as a direct antibiotic injection administered straight to her chest.

And now that her pain meds had been discontinued, it was clear that she was really starting to feel all that hurt. She still had plenty of energy for the time being, though; angry, frightened, pain-fueled energy.

"I'm not wearing that mask!" Lee screamed. "Can't you people just let me breathe like a normal person?" It killed me to see Lee like this, but there was little I could do except coo to her, trying in vain to calm her down. In that moment, I wished desperately that I had asked Emm to come home. She'd be able to charm Lee and quiet her fear.

"You wear it if you want!" Lee threw the mask at an intern who was clearly too shocked to respond as the mask hit him square in the chest.

I didn't know what to do—I nearly fell out of the room and into the hall. I ran my hands through my hair and paced around the corridor, doing my best to keep it together.

"TD? What's wrong?" I turned to see Nurse Jen in her street clothes once again, just like the night we met.

"Nothing," I lied, "Go home and see your boy, we'll be okay."

"TD, please." She reached up and put both her hands on my shoulders. "I'm here."

But I couldn't even respond. I was happy that she'd come by to say goodnight, despite being off the clock, but also distressed by her giving up time with her family. Especially now, with Lee being so upset.

"What's going on in here?" Nurse Jen asked as we entered the room.

"Lee is…she's…I think she's just *had it* with being poked and prodded," I answered as my sister continued to sob. "She's been through a lot today. And she's hurting, too, from the change in her pain meds."

"She's refusing her treatment, Nurse Jen," said Dr. Foley. "We'll have to sedate her. I'm going to get an attendant to write the order now."

"Let me talk to her first," Nurse Jen replied with her calm, healing aura practically radiating around her and happily spilling into our room. She smoothed her hand across Lee's tear-streaked face and asked, "What's worrying you, sweetie?"

"That mask," spat Lee. "I hate it. It makes me feel too closed in. Like I'm never going to get out of this room!"

"Okay, sweetie, I understand. That *is* a big mask for your little face." She picked up Lee's chart and looked it over. "Dr. Foley, this is just oxygen, right?"

"Yes, her pulse-ox is lower than we'd like."

"But not dangerously?" asked Nurse Jen, puzzling through the problem.

"More of a precaution. But we're not taking any chances with her."

"Of course we're not. But we need another solution here," Nurse Jen answered firmly. "And I don't see any reason why we can't employ a nasal cannula instead."

Dr. Foley responded with a stunned stare, as if Nurse Jen had just said the most obviously simple thing in all of medicine.

"Lee, can you be calm and patient for a moment and I'll be right back?" Nurse Jen asked, stroking Lee's face again.

"I guess so," she sniffled.

Nurse Jen jogged out of the room as I moved over to the bed and took Lee's hand, which was the one thing I knew I *could* do. I didn't know what a "cannula" was, but I really didn't care. As long as it made my Little One feel better.

Not a half-minute later, Nurse Jen flew back into the room. She handed one end of a long, clear plastic tube to Dr. Ojalvo, then showed the other three-branched-end to Lee.

"Okay, so I'll make you a deal, sweetie. No mask for now, but you have to wear this instead. See, these two loops go over your ears, just like your glasses. And these two little prongs, they just sit right inside the tip of your nostrils. They tickle a bit, but they don't hurt."

"That's much smaller," said Lee, looking at the tubing curiously. "That might be alright."

"I can't promise you won't have to wear that mask again, but for tonight this will do just fine. Okay?"

"Okay." A look of relief washed over Lee's scared face.

"Thank you, everyone, but I think I can handle it from here," Nurse Jen announced to the room at large. The team filed out one by one, each looking more relieved than the last.

Nurse Jen gently fastened the cannula in place. "I can't thank you enough," I said as my own distress dissipated.

"And I'll tell you what," Nurse Jen said to Lee. "I'll sit right here until the clock reaches 6, just so you can get used to it." And she meant it. With a warm smile on her face, Nurse Jen sat herself down on the edge of the bed and took my sister's hand. Looking as though there was nowhere else in the world she'd rather be.

"You don't have to do that...You've been so kind already."

"It's not a problem. I don't have to be home for a little while yet. Come over here and chat with us for a bit."

I did as I was instructed and walked over to the far side of the bed. Sitting down, I held Lee's other hand as she and Nurse Jen began talking. They started off discussing *Despicable Me* before Lee somehow steered the conversation to her favorite color.

Lee's contention was that the ocean should be more of a baby blue than a sea blue. As she outlined her clearly-well-thought-out reasoning, Lee grew more and more absorbed in her argument, as well as sleepier and sleepier. Her fit of frustration had worn her out, and she fell asleep well before the hand on the clock completed its climb to 6 p.m.

Nurse Jen and I tiptoed out of the room. I thanked her profusely as we said goodbye for the evening. I really didn't have words enough to thank her for coming to the rescue.

"You don't need to thank me, TD. It's my job...and I love my job. You know that," she said, stepping into the elevator.

I smiled to myself as the elevator door closed and Nurse Jen was whisked off for her family time. I texted my uncle with an update before heading back to Room 188.

"Tim?" came Lee's soft voice as I crept into the darkness of her room.

"What's wrong?" I said, forcing myself not to panic. Forcing myself not to fly downstairs after Nurse Jen.

"Since it's your last night…would you sleep in the bed with me tonight?"

I'd cuddled Lee to sleep so many times during her year of isolation, but I figured she'd grown out of the need. I hadn't wanted to ask about it for fear of embarrassing her. But if Lee wanted to put a hold on "growing up" for tonight, that was fine by me. Truthfully, having the comfort of her beside me might chase away my own nightmares and the terror that sleeping in this awful place brought back. Or maybe I'd wake up, only to realize that the past few days had all been a bad dream.

Without saying a word, I kicked off my shoes before carefully crawling into bed beside my baby sister. Within moments, my little sunflower had gently fallen back asleep in my arms.

As my own eyes grew heavy at the feeling of Lee's chest gently rising and falling against my ribs, I thought about how grateful I was to have Nurse Jen caring for my sister. For what she'd done today. Maybe Emma Rey Finley wasn't the only superhero who could charm Lee. Maybe that too, had just been a dream.

Chapter 24

Official Legal Document

I crept out of Lee's room early the next morning in the pre-dawn darkness—before Nurse Jen started her shift, before the red-orange sun had fully risen. It had been a rough night and I'd hardly slept. Lee had awoken several times, clearly uncomfortable, yet there wasn't much more I could do other than massage her back or get her a glass of ice water. Each time, a nurse told me that all this was to be expected, that it was a normal part of her treatment. Each time, I'd wanted to run through a brick wall: The word "normal" was starting to sound less and less like something I ever wanted to hear again.

My only consolation was that Uncle Bill and Sal had promised that one of them would be there every day and every night. Especially with Nurse Jen rounding out Lee's support team, I knew my little sister was in good hands. But why she couldn't be in *my* hands was another question altogether. I'd never been any good at leaving Lee's side during her year of isolation, but this was different. Back then, she'd been recovering from a lifesaving procedure. Every moment had been tinged with a tiny drop of optimism. This time around, I didn't know what to think. This time, the fear Lee and I were sharing was a new darkness.

I spent the next three days trying to focus on school and practice. Just being in class was hard—I was far-less-engaged than usual. But I needed to hold on to my solid GPA for graduation—and "tuning out" at this point wasn't an option. Practice, on the other hand, was easier. More comfortable. My coach, knowing me well, took me aside before my first practice of the week and ordered me to focus on getting all my consternation-fueled sloppiness out during the two practices remaining before Friday's game. Being somewhere where I could funnel my frustration, confusion, anger and hurt helped. As much as Lee needed me, so did my team. They were still counting on me to pull my full-weight and lead us to the NCAA tournament. With all the unanswered questions in my life, the one thing I did know was that I'd be ready for Friday's game.

Uncle Bill or Sal texted me with updates throughout the day, but I still made it a point to drive out to the hospital each evening. Even if I could only get a few minutes before Lee fell asleep for the night, I needed her to know I was there, needed to remind her how brave she was, how strong of a fighter she was. Which was especially important because, just as Doctor Mallory had predicted, Lee seemed worse with each passing day. Yet no matter how awful she was feeling, my little sister always managed to squeak out the same painful question: "Where is Emma Rey Finley?"

It broke my heart every time I heard Lee struggle to utter those five words. "She's coming soon," or "In just a day or two," I would answer. Then, hoping to placate my sister for just one more visit, I'd add, "Emm says she's so happy at you."

The truth was, Lee had no idea how much it weakened my already feeble spirit to hear her ask that complex question. Because to my sister, it was the simplest question in the world. All Lee wanted was to see Emma Rey Finley. And although I hated to admit it, that's all I wanted, too.

My Thursday classes ended in the early afternoon—and since I didn't need to meet up with my team for our late-night bus ride to UC San Diego until 8 p.m., I decided I'd stop at Uncle Bill's and make Lee her beloved chocolate chip banana pancakes. I desperately wanted to see her smile before we headed out for our big game. Just as I was leaving the house, I remembered to grab one of the small "relay baton" bottles of maple syrup from the fridge.

Forty-minutes later, I peeked into Lee's room, with her still-warm pancakes in hand, hoping to surprise her. But rather than finding Lee in her bed, I found Sal sitting on the bed's edge, with one leg crossed over the other, stroking his mustache pensively and reading a sheet of white lined paper.

"*Sorpresa!*" I cried as I jumped forward into the room.

Sal gave a restrained chuckle. "Your *Italiano* is getting much better, TD." He folded the paper in half and placed it on the nightstand as I walked over and greeted him with a kiss on each cheek, just like always.

"So, where's our girl?" I asked as I sat down beside him. But I could already tell that something about Sal's energy seemed off. Subdued, even.

Sal sighed heavily. Sensing my distress, he said quickly, "Lee's fine, but she's having a tough day…I thought to call you, but I knew you were leaving tonight. No need to worry you unnecessarily." He placed his hand on my shoulder as if he was attempting to soften a blow. Which was good, because I felt like I was going to puke.

"Well, then, where is she?" I blurted out. I practically yelled the words at Sal, but he didn't flinch. He didn't even remove his hand from my shoulder.

"Dr. Mallory ordered an X-ray. Her lungs. There might be a *minuscolo* amount of fluid building back up."

"When did that happen?" I asked, alarmed. As far as I knew, Lee's lungs had been clear for a couple of days at least.

"Not to worry, not to worry," Sal assured me. "Her breathing turned just a bit heavy early this morning. Could be nothing." Sal pushed back his sleeve as he glanced down at his watch. "She should be back any minute."

I ran my hand through my hair, trying to absorb this new information. Even the thought of a possible complication was too much, especially since I was leaving in just a few hours.

Filled with nervous energy, I started pacing, but Sal got up and stopped me. "TD, that's nothing to worry about," he began, taking the sheet of paper from the nightstand, "but *this* is what's troubling me—I found it a few minutes ago. Under her pillow."

Sal's features turned dark, as if he were somehow defeated; as if the rain cloud that had been looming over my family—the cloud only Sal's smiley timism could escape—had finally found him; had finally forced its darkness upon Sal.

"*This*, you need to know right now," Sal continued. "This, I cannot keep from you, *caro* TD. You must be strong." He unfolded the paper and handed it to me.

Lee Rose Dexter's Official Will

In the unlikely event that I don't get my One Day, I would like for these very important things to happen, So please give this official legal document to my older brother, Tim Dexter.

1. I want you (my awesome big brother), to have all my super-secret journals, So I can tell you stories, for once.

2. I want you and your teammates to win your conference and play in the NCAA Tournament, I've watched so many of your games and you deserve it, As the leader of the Tim Dexter Fan Club, no one knows how much you deserve it more than me.

3. I want Sammy Woods to look after Moon and raise him as if he was one of his own, Because I know Sammy will make an amazing dad.

4. Although this is the last thing on my list, it is the most important of them all, I once made Emma promise me to love you forever, no matter what, Now, I am asking you to promise me the same thing, Never lose her, TD, because if I know one thing, it's that she never wants to lose you,

Forever Your Little Miracle,

Lee Rose Dexter

My knees buckled. Scrambling forward, Sal caught me and lowered me gingerly to the blue-tiled floor. I stayed there trembling, slumped on my knees, with my bare skin resting against the cold linoleum beneath me, staring blankly at Lee's will. The dark cloud hovering above us had finally exploded into an effusive downpour. The evidence, if I needed any, was my own tears, as they rained uncontrollably from my eyes and spattered all over my little miracle's official legal document.

By some blessing, Lee wasn't wheeled back into Room 188 until a solid fifteen-minutes had passed, giving Sal just enough time to bring me back from my shock. Which he did. With a patience and a tenderness as intense as my own mother's. He reached inside himself and found his smiley once again, reassuring and comforting me with each word. It gave me the strength to paste on my bravest face ever. If Lee was *this* scared, I couldn't add to it—no matter the battle inside me.

Lee looked horrible as she was transferred from her wheelchair to her bed. Her thinning hair was brittle, as if stroking it would cause it to break off in my hands. Her bloated face, her sickly pallor and the deep bags under her eyes all told me she was feeling worse than she had all week. She gripped Moon tightly as the nurses settled her back into bed. While she remained distracted, I reached down, grabbed her will and quickly tucked it into my pocket. I couldn't keep my eyes from welling-up, though, and a few tears drizzled down my face.

Lee didn't say a word to me. In fact, she wouldn't even meet my eye. This worried me all the more: she wasn't even trying to hide how awful she felt. She almost looked angry as she turned her back to me and stared firmly at a spot on the wall.

Sensing that Lee and I needed to be left alone, Sal retreated into the hallway as inconspicuously as possible. Once he'd left the room, I said, "I brought you a surprise, Little One," hoping to elicit a response—any response—from her. "Chocolate chip banana pancakes. And we can eat them with our hands, I promise."

Lee finally looked me in the eye, fully turning herself toward me. That's when I saw the tears in her own blue eyes as she replied, feebly but coldly, "You also promised me that Emma would come see me, but she never did…She *never did*."

Her words gutted me. As if I'd been chewing on glass, the pain I'd been gnawing on was too intense for my jaw to even function—for my mouth to even form the simplest of words—let alone a response. I felt sick to my stomach again: I'd been lying to Lee all week and she knew it. In trying to protect her, I'd only added to my poor sister's misery.

Then Lee cried, "I don't want you or Sal. I want Emma! Where is she?!" as she burst into violent sobs, slamming her tiny fists against the mattress. "It's not fair. None of this is fair!"

My mouth opened and closed…yet no words came out. It took all the strength I had to keep from pounding the mattress alongside her. She was right: None of this was fair. Not one single moment of it. I pushed the thought of Lee's will deep into the ever-growing void inside me.

I let Lee cry for a moment—until I sensed she was ready to be comforted. She flinched slightly as I hoisted her onto my lap, but she didn't push me away either. "I want Emma!" she repeated. As I held her close in my arms, I told her over and over how much I loved her and how brave she was.

As her fit slowly began to weaken, I heard her mumble, "Is that too much to ask?" But I didn't know what to say: I simply sat with her and wept.

We cried together for what seemed like hours. I wished in that moment that I could take her pain from her. Why couldn't I be the one in that hospital bed? Hadn't my baby sister already been through enough?

"I'm sorry, Little One," I finally said as Lee's eyes started to dry and she pulled away from my embrace at last. "I'm so sorry. Stay strong for me." I began tucking her under her blankets, and I managed to slip her will back under her pillow in the process. "You know I have to go away tonight, but I promise to bring Emm this weekend. Even if I have to carry her here myself."

"Okay," Lee managed as she pouted under her covers. Under the covers that were doing a terrible job of blanketing her fear.

As I looked down at my trembling sister, I knew I needed my best friend. No matter where Emm was or whom she was with, none of it mattered anymore. What mattered was getting her here to keep Lee fighting. Boyfriend or not, I needed Emma Rey Finley back in my life—and so did my sister. And if that's what Lee required, I was going to do whatever it took to make damn sure it happened.

"I'm sorry I got so upset," Lee squeaked out, apologizing. A little more loudly, almost pleading, she added, "Don't be mad at me?" The weak, forced smile on her face conveyed far more than her words.

"*Mad* at you?" I began in an incredulous tone, "Lee Rose Dexter, I've never been happier at anyone in my entire life."

With all the remaining happy I had left, I reached for my sister and took her in my arms again. But it wasn't enough. My healing touch didn't have the magic she needed. Between labored breaths again, she started to cry.

My little miracle didn't need me. She needed a superhero.

I finished telling Ken about my afternoon with Lee, including everything about the will. I was glad to be on the bus, away from that damn hospital, away from school, away from the hell that had been my week. Six days that had felt like six months.

"I wouldn't worry about that paper too much, bro," said Ken. "She's scared—she has a right to be. And writing has been her thing for years now. Maybe it's good that she got all that out."

"Maybe," I replied slowly, considering Ken's comment. It didn't seem totally off base. The lined-paper looked as if it had been torn from her journal, and writing had been Lee's self-medication pretty much since she was old enough to string two sentences together. "She's so much older now," I continued, "but she's still just a kid. It's hard to wrap my head around how she's processing all this."

"I'm just confused about one thing," said Ken. "Didn't you tell her Emma is out of town?"

Feeling like a fool, I hung my head, embarrassed and angry at myself. "No...I...I just didn't see the point. I couldn't bring myself to tell her Emm blew off the party. And now... now Lee's hurting even more. She has her heart set on seeing Emm—it's the only thing she really wants," I answered.

Ken looked as upset as I was initially, as if he were questioning my tactics. But then his facial expression shifted, revealing that he, in fact, understood. "Yeah, I guess you really didn't have a choice there," Ken replied. "But I still can't believe Emma did that, honestly. I mean, she has a *responsibility* to Lee, ya know?"

That was it. That was exactly the problem. Lee was only a small part of Emm's great big world, while Emm was the brightest star in Lee's painfully small universe. A universe Emm had *chosen* to be a part of. A universe that wasn't dependent on *our* friendship, but rather on her relationship with Lee. Ken had finally said out loud what I'd been grappling with for days. Emm was aware that she brought out the best in others—including me—but Lee was much too young to understand any of that.

"I'm going to call Emm on the bus ride home tomorrow and tell her to get to the hospital this weekend. Her conference should be over by the afternoon, anyhow." I took a breath as I realized I was starting to get mad again. "There's no reason why she can't drive back Saturday morning, even if it means sacrificing a night with that square of hers. It's for Lee's well-being."

Ken looked me straight in the eye. "Agreed." He reached over the seat and clapped his hand on my shoulder.

I hung my head again. "I just wish I wasn't looking forward to seeing her, too," I muttered, betraying myself. I had every right to be mad, but at the heart of it, I still wanted my buddy. If she still existed.

"You're hopeless," chided Ken, chucking me lightly on the shoulder. "But I understand, it's complicated. Sometimes we just need who we need."

I could feel the heaviness in my own eyes as I looked up from my lap.

"Plus, I bet that full-frontal thing didn't make matters any easier. And speaking of skinning dippi—"

"—I'm still not giving you details, you perv." I laughed in spite of myself. Only Ken Zom.

The next night, we took the court with a swagger I rarely saw from our team. With a string of wins behind us and with every single play and scheme practiced to perfection, we were firing on all cylinders. By the second quarter, we were kicking our opponent's ass. Not just because we were the more disciplined team, but because we were having fun while doing it.

My coach had been right. Getting my angst out in practices allowed me to feel free in competition. With everything going on in my life, I was pleasantly surprised at how easily the game came to me, and clearly my teammates were following suit. We pummeled UC San Diego, achieving one of our biggest victories of the season. By the time the final buzzer sounded, I felt like I was back in the driver's seat of my own life.

After a brief celebration in the locker room, we piled back onto the bus. Boisterous and elated at being one game closer to March Madness, the entire team joked and laughed for the next thirty minutes. With Sergeant Biceps in ultra-testosterone-mode spearheading the ruckus.

We were all in such a stellar mood that I was the only one who noticed the change in the weather. A soft rain cascaded from the sky, lightly tapping the roof of our bus. The steady pitter-patter almost sounded like tiny footsteps overhead. A soothing sound that reminded me of all the times I had tip-toed into my baby sister's room.

Without warning, the gentle rain became a violent down-pour. In the next instant, our bus skidded to one side as we lost traction and hydroplaned. All twenty-five of us, including Coach, gasped in our seats as the driver grappled to regain control of the bus. We were damn lucky the highway was fair-ly empty, otherwise we could've been looking at a multi-car pileup.

With the team now shocked into a more subdued state, I decided it was time to call Emm. I started rummaging around in my backpack for my phone. I shouldn't have it off at all; I'd only powered down during the game to save the battery for our five-hour ride home.

My phone slowly regained its life as it powered back on. I waited patiently for it to reboot—I really needed to replace it soon—while I signaled to Ken that I was about to call Emm. Once it had fully turned on, the "new messages" icon practi-cally exploded across the screen: I had thirty missed calls.

A moment later my phone began buzzing out of control as each new text message loaded, one after the other. The first few texts, all from Sal, read with an increasing urgency. "Call me" then, "Call me as soon as you get this" then, "It's about Lee. You NEED to get to the hospital." My hands started to sweat, and my mouth instantly went dry.

I continued reading the stream of messages. My uncle's texts, a full dozen of them, all basically repeated Sal's.

Except, one didn't.

One message jumped out of my phone, stabbing me di-rectly in the heart. My breath caught in my lungs. My fingers turned limp as my hands began shaking violently. My phone crashed to the floor, seemingly in slow motion, as I complete-ly lost control. My body, almost of its own accord, whipped around in its seat. Everything went silent until I heard myself scream: "Why God?! WHY HER?!"

Chapter 25

Through the Good and the Bad

Pounding my fists blindly into the seat in front of me. Gasping for air. My face wet with tears. The stares of my teammates, dumbstruck and silent. The sound of my moans and sobs mixing with the hammering of raindrops above. The hissing wind as our bus sliced through the darkness.

Ken rushed to my side. I collapsed onto his shoulder, gripping him tightly. "Breathe, TD, breathe," he repeated over and over. "Shh…just tell me what's going on." But the more I tried to get the words out, the further I pushed them into my void. As if speaking them would make it real. Whatever babblings did come out were gasps of half-words, incoherent and almost deranged.

Forcing himself to remain calm and focused, Ken picked my phone up from between my feet. He scanned the messages until he, too, was stabbed in the heart. With me still buried in his shoulder, he held the phone up for a long moment, pushing his feelings deep down, yet at the same time also readying himself for action.

After lifting me gently from his arm, he marched forcefully toward the front of the bus. I heard my teammates, "What's going on?" and "Is TD alright?" and "What's happened?" as he passed by their seats, but Ken didn't answer any of them. He didn't say one word until he reached the front, next to the driver. By then he had the attention of our entire team, including myself.

Taking command, Ken announced, "We're rerouting to UCLA Children's Hospital. Now! TD's sister's life depends on it." He paused, carefully angling his neck to purposefully catch my eye. With more pain than I'd ever seen Ken endure, he forced his words out: "*Lee's had a stroke.*"

Ken squeezed his eyes shut as if he couldn't watch the team's reaction. He kept them tightly closed as he lowered himself into the empty seat in the front row. Pressing his temples with his hand and hanging his head sorrowfully.

As Ken emotionally dove into the empty seat, a collective gasp shot through the bus, but no one spoke. No one objected to Ken's order, not even our coach. Our bus driver had simply nodded his head as he pressed the accelerator.

Coach conferred with our trainer for a moment before he ordered, "Seatbelts, everyone. Ken, get back there and take care of TD. Ami, I want traffic updates every ten minutes." He panned the bus making sure he hadn't missed anything. "I'm calling the athletic office now."

Ken, now back in command mode, trudged back down the aisle and slipped into the seat in front of me. "We're *on this*, TD. We'll get you to her."

"Four hours," I muttered, still sobbing lightly. We were still almost four hours away from the hospital, from Lee. From her delicate little palm.

"As fast as humanly possible, bro," Ken said, trying to comfort me as he looked encouragingly into my eyes. "Now pull it together and get in touch with your uncle. He doesn't need to be worrying about you, too."

Ken was right. I had four hours to fall apart. Right now, I needed to follow his lead and shift into crisis mode. I opened my uncle's message again and typed my response: "I'm on my way. Tell her to stay strong and hold on just a little bit longer."

Almost before I'd finished texting, my uncle's reply popped onto my screen: "She's in surgery with Dr. Mallory. Sal's with me. The Zoms, too. Updates coming. Get home now."

My phone became my lifeline. My eyes remained glued to it in agony, yet I knew there was absolutely nothing I could do except wait. Sal sent messages of support every ten minutes or so, as if texting me was helping him keep it together.

Ken kept popping up from his seat, offering words of support and trying to keep me positive, but I couldn't think of anything other than being by Lee's side. But finally, after more minutes of blind panic than I could count, I realized that there was one thing I *could* do. The one thing I'd promised Lee. Now more than ever, I needed to call Emm. I needed her to come home. Tonight.

I prayed she would pick up. The phone rang once, twice, a third time before my call went to her voicemail; I quickly hung up before I gave myself the chance to leave a message. Anger rang through my skull. How could Emm possibly ignore my call at a time like this? After everything we'd been through. I almost threw my phone out the window, but I punched the back of the seat instead.

Ken sat up immediately. "What's up, bro? News?" But when he looked at my face, he somehow knew what had just transpired. "Call her again. She can't possibly know what's going on. And if she doesn't answer, try actually leaving a message this time."

Ken was right; I wasn't thinking straight. I redialed Emm's number, but this time my call went straight to her voicemail. I took a deep breath as I heard Emm's recorded voice prompting me to leave a message.

"Emm…it's…it's about Lee…" I began before my voice cracked. Through my sobs, I did my best to explain what was happening. Why I needed her. Why Lee needed her. But then

I paused, afraid to say the next words.

In that moment, I realized how serious the situation truly was. I forced myself to find the words. "It doesn't look good, Emm. Lee's...You may need...*We* may need to go and say goodbye."

Each passing hour was more torturous than the last. My shock and sadness morphed into anger and frustration, then flipped back again. Then again—back and forth as my head spun. An internal anarchy of colliding emotions.

I appreciated Sal's texts of support, but in a way they only made things worse: I wanted solid updates on Lee's condition. When my uncle did text with news, he had so little new information that it only discouraged me further. At the same time, I couldn't help but *jolt* every time my phone buzzed, afraid of what the next message might say. Afraid that it might be the one I'd been dreading ever since Lee came into my world. Afraid of the harsh reality that every single doctor had warned me of—the data, the facts, the stats. Afraid of the dark rain cloud that my family could never quite escape, no matter how many sunny days we had.

Yet through the agony of each vibration of my phone also came a tinge of hope, I was still waiting on Emm, still hanging onto the possibility of keeping my promise to Lee. Still hanging onto the thought that Emma Rey Finley could rescue us with her strongest superpower of them all: Her ability to make us forget.

But I was still trapped on this bus. This rolling prison, endlessly flying through the night. Every once in a while, one of my teammates would walk back to check on me, but I couldn't engage. All I could seem to manage was a "Thanks, man." I appreciated their concern, truly, but what was there to say?

A stroke at ten-years-old.

I jumped as my phone buzzed again. But instead of another text from Sal, this time my favorite photo of Emm popped onto my screen.

"Emm," I answered softly with a whisper. But she didn't reply. All I heard was the most agonizing sound imaginable:

Emma Rey Finley crying.

"Emm?" I repeated a second time, even more softly. I heard her breathing, struggling to get her words out.

"Just tell her to hang on. Tell her I'm coming."

"I will Emm, I promise. As soon as I get there," I answered as I began to cry with her.

"We're getting on the highway now," she explained. "I'm coming. I'll be there soon. Seven hours, maybe. Just tell her to—" But she couldn't finish the sentence, as her tears bubbled up once more.

With my phone plastered against my cheek, Emm and I spent the next hour crying. But at least now we were crying together.

The rain continued to pour. I stood up from my seat the second we pulled into the parking lot, ready to dash into the hospital's main entrance. Only a few more yards separated me from my little sunflower. Only a few more minutes before I could tell my sister that Emm and her healing light were on the way, knowing she was the only one who could keep Lee fighting.

Ken and I moved to the front of the bus, but as we walked by each row, my teammates—including Coach and our trainer—stood up as well. One by one, like an honor guard.

I practically flew off the bus the moment the doors opened, headed blindly toward the hospital's entrance. "TD, wait!" called a voice. I forced myself to turn.

Standing behind me in the empty parking lot of UCLA's Children's Hospital was my entire team. All twenty-five guys, in the pouring rain.

"We're with you. We're coming!" Coach cried. I felt a hint of a smile creep across my face.

"Seriously, I…" shouted over the storm, but my voice trailed off. I was too overwhelmed by their support to say anything more.

Ken jogged up to me and pressed his hand into my back, guiding me forward. "Let's move!"

We ran with the rainwater flying off our shoulders until we exploded through the front doors; only seconds later, the rest of the team piled in behind us. The security guard, shocked by our onslaught, jumped up and ordered us to halt by putting his hand out, almost like a human stop sign. "Friends or family?" he demanded.

"Family!" one of my teammates yelled from the back of our group. Which was the goddamned truth: These guys *were* my family—now more than ever.

The guard, easing up a bit, chuckled. "No way y'all are related."

Twenty-five pairs of eyes shot him a stone-cold stare in reply. He immediately realized we weren't playing around, so he straightened up and exuded as much authority as he could possibly muster. "Visiting hours are over. Immediate family only."

"Go, TD, go!" ordered Ken, not fighting the guard and not wanting to waste any more time.

I pulled my ID from my wallet and handed it to the guard as I turned to the team. "I love you guys. You're all my brothers, on and off the court." Breathing in deeply, I thought about how much more I wanted to say, how they held me up and kept me moving forward all these years. But they already knew that. So I said the only thing that was left for me to say. "Thank you."

"No thank *you*, TD," said Coach. "You've given this team your all. We all know you could've sat out tonight. We all know you would've rather been here, but you never let it show. You came out and you played hard."

"You've looked out for us all season," added Maxwell. "Now we're looking out for you."

"Yeah, man, that's what family is for, to be there through the good and the bad," said Ken, with a vehicle-of-positivity smirk. "So get going. Go make sure our girl is alright."

Without another word, I took off like a shot toward the elevators. As soon as I reached Room 188, I was greeted by four exhausted, utterly petrified faces. Even Mr. Zom was white as a ghost.

With tears in her eyes, Mrs. Zom came over and embraced me in a deep hug. I couldn't take in the words she whispered, but from the pain in her tone, I knew she was hurting right along with me.

"Where is she?" I asked, turning to Uncle Bill.

"Still in surgery," he replied plainly.

Without Lee, Room 188 felt joyless, stale. In place of her feisty energy, now there was only tension and fear, which were both palpable in the air; an air that stung my lungs with every breath.

"Okay, what happened? Walk me through it from the beginning."

"Just after six o'clock, she mentioned she had a headache," replied my uncle. "Then I…Then the nurse…I…"

Sal jumped in, knowing that more than three sentences was hard on my uncle even on the best of days. "He got a nurse right away," Sal began. "No fever, normal everything, nothing to worry about. We went back to watching TV, but *la bambina* said her head still hurt. A few minutes later, she started shaking. Eyes rolled back in her head and…"

"Another seizure, just like last week," said my uncle, spitting out the words. "Breathing tube again. But this time she wouldn't wake up."

"They did some tests, which indicated an injury to the brain," Sal jumped in again. "Then a minute later, Dr. Mallory said they were taking her for emergency surgery." Sal's eyes welled-up; he choked back his tears.

"They've been giving us reports as best they can, son," offered Mr. Zom, "but Lee's been in surgery for almost six hours now. We're not even sure yet if it was a stroke. It's still too soon to tell."

As focused as I was, all this was still a lot for me to process. "Six hours," I muttered to myself. All I could see in my head was Lee's little body, limp on the operating table, surrounded by a team of operating doctors. Monitors blinking all around. With the evil-looking breathing tube down her throat. How did she deserve this, when she'd done everything right? When she'd fought so hard? And why couldn't it be me on that table instead of her?

I took a seat at the end of the bed next to Mrs. Zom, who put her arm around me and guided me into her shoulder without saying a word. I couldn't help but remember the night all those years ago when I'd showed up on her doorstep with fear in my eyes and an eleven-month-old Lee in my arms. Mrs. Zom had done the exact same thing that night, promising me, again and again, that everything would be alright. Tonight, however, she knew better than to make such promises.

The Zoms left a little while later, leaving me, Sal, and Uncle Bill alone. Only once it was the three of us, I was able to finally relax just slightly. We were all dealing with the same horror, so we began yet another too-familiar hospital ritual: chatting about anything other than the storm surrounding us.

Eventually, Sal asked me, "How was the game tonight?"

"We won," I answered joylessly. "With two more wins, we'll get the NCAA Tournament."

Sal looked back at me, confused, "N-C-A-A?" he asked. I forgot the only sport that Sal ever followed was soccer.

"It's like the World Cup, but for college basketball," I explained.

Even with the dark cloud closing in on us, Sal's eyes lit up a little. "*Bene*, TD! You should be proud. When will you know if—"

Sal cut himself off as the door opened. Dr. Mallory entered the room, still wearing his surgical mask; a pair of lighted, magnifying goggles were pushed up past his forehead. He looked as if he'd finished operating only minutes ago. "Gentlemen…" he began. I didn't need more than that one word to hear the graveness in his tone.

The three of us simultaneously rose out of our seats, steeling ourselves for the worst. Dr. Mallory removed his surgical mask and goggles before saying another word. The longer the silence, the more anxious I grew. I'd only seen Dr. Mallory this serious on one other occasion, one that ended up being the toughest day of my life: The day he'd told us Lee needed a transplant to survive; that she needed a miracle.

Dr. Mallory straightened himself up, pushing his shoulders back as if he was willing himself to remain standing. "The surgery was, for the most part…successful," he announced.

The three of us breathed a sigh of relief. Sal took my hand and gave it a quick, excited squeeze.

"For the most part?" asked my uncle.

"Yes, as successful as it could've been given the circumstances. Lee suffered a hemorrhagic stroke in her brain's left hemisphere. Because we were able to get her into surgery so quickly, we were able to repair the point where the stroke occurred—but, unfortunately, that wasn't the full extent of the damage."

"What's a hemorrhagic stroke?" Sal asked, visibly clenching his teeth from the tension. "And what other damage is there?"

"This type of stroke occurs when an artery in the brain leaks or ruptures. In Lee's case, one of her arteries ruptured badly, which is extremely dangerous. Once we got that repaired, we hoped we'd be in the clear. But then we discovered blood on various other regions of her brain—hematomas that were probably present prior to the stroke. The neurosurgical team and I did our best to remove as much of the blood as we could, but we don't yet know the full extent of the damage."

The three of us looked at each other, doing our best to act as if we'd understood everything Dr. Mallory had explained, which of course we didn't. Especially not me. I was grateful Sal and my uncle were asking all of the questions because I could barely think.

"The next steps?" Uncle Bill asked. "When will we know more?"

"With these types of major neurosurgeries, it's vital that we allow the brain to properly heal." Dr. Mallory stopped, as if he didn't want to deliver his next words. "To facilitate that healing, we've placed Lee into a medically-induced coma."

My knees trembled. For the second time in as many days, Sal caught me and kept me from crashing into the floor, though I wished he hadn't. I wished he had let me collapse, let me fall so hard that the impact would've awoken me from this nightmare.

"I'd hoped to have better news for you, TD," Dr. Mallory continued after giving me a moment to recover. "But anytime we induce a coma, it's a last resort—especially in Lee's case. Despite the risks of full-sedation, we were left with no other options. It was our only chance at saving her."

The room began spinning. I didn't understand what I was hearing. The words *coma*, *risks* and *damage* rang in my ears and seemed to reverberate through the room.

"You said the surgery was successful!" Uncle Bill blurted out accusatorily. Or at least that's what I thought he said. His words were blurry, far away. I fought against fainting.

"From a medical standpoint, it was," Dr. Mallory answered gently. "We addressed the hemorrhage and complications. But I wouldn't be doing my job if I didn't fully inform you of the situation." Dr. Mallory ran his hand through his hair. "That said, Lee's always been a fighter. We're all hoping she'll pull through."

"Yeah...sorry. Understood," Uncle Bill replied, trying to pull himself together. Trying not to scream at this man who'd just seen Lee through a seven-and-a-half-hour emergency operation.

Doctor Mallory exhaled loudly as Sal spoke up. "But *dottore*," he began, "When will Lee wake up?"

"We'll be ending her sedative-intake tomorrow evening."

"That'll be enough time for her to heal?" asked my uncle.

"We hope so," answered Dr. Mallory. "If we wait much

longer than sixteen or eighteen hours, we're fearful that she may not wake up at all."

For the first time in my life, I heard my uncle scream. "What do you <u>mean</u>, SHE MAY NOT WAKE UP?!"

Sal lunged toward Uncle Bill and grabbed him, holding him tight, as my uncle broke into a storm of tears.

"Where is she?" I finally asked, speaking up for the first time.

No one said anything. But knowing that he would take us to her, the three of us fell in line behind Dr. Mallory as we followed him out of the room. All I wanted was my little miracle back in my arms. Right now. And I was never going to make the mistake of leaving her side ever again.

Chapter 26

Lee Strong

The room was cold. Bone-chillingly cold, as if we'd just opened the door to a walk-in freezer.

Lee was laying terrifyingly still in her new private room, a small space tucked into the corner of the surgical recovery ward. With the seemingly countless monitors crowding the room, there was barely enough space for the four of us to stand around her bed. The lights were intentionally dimmed as a grayness clouded the air.

She looked calm but far from peaceful. I didn't think it possible, but somehow my baby sister had even more monitors, tubes and IVs connected to her—far more, even, than the night she was admitted. The evil-looking breathing tube snaked down her throat as though it was choking her. A large gauze bandage oppressively wrapped around her head, covering most of her skull. From what little I could see of Lee's hairline, it looked as if her head had been shaved in at least one spot from the surgery. But the worst part was her stillness, as she lay on her back, perfectly posed by her nurses. Too perfectly. My little miracle was again battling for her life, yet this time she had no idea I was standing right beside her.

I fought back a wave of nausea that enveloped me as more tears slipped from my eyes and stuck to my cheek. Uncle Bill pressed his back against the wall, both heartbroken and horrified, almost as if he were afraid of touching Lee at all. Sal crossed himself several times in succession, muttering prayers.

After giving us a moment to take in Lee's comatose, post-operative state, Dr. Mallory spoke up. "Feel free to talk to her, gentlemen," he said. "She can probably hear you, even in this suppressed state. It may comfort her and make all of this seem a little more natural."

None of us spoke. There was too much to say. The words I wanted to speak, I couldn't. I was afraid I might burst into violent sobs. The words caught in my throat and lodged there, like a physical lump. I gagged.

Dr. Mallory broke the silence. "Tim, step outside with me for a moment." I nodded and followed him through the main portion of the ward, past the other recovering children. Recovering children at whom I desperately tried not to look, terrified of what their little faces might say. And terrified of what more Dr. Mallory could possibly have to tell me.

The door closed heavily behind us. "TD, if you'll allow me to…if I can just say…" But Dr. Mallory didn't finish as tears welled in his own eyes. Instead he pulled me in for a deep hug. As if he, too, couldn't find words. "I'm sorry, I wish I could've—"

"Not yet," I said, cutting him off and finding whatever strength I had left. "Not yet," I repeated. "She's always bounced back. This time will be no different." I spoke with so much conviction that I almost believed it.

A sad smile flitted across Dr. Mallory's face. "Now I finally know where she gets it from," he began as he pulled me in for another, even tighter, hug. "You're a very strong young man, Tim Dexter."

I returned to Lee's bedside. Uncle Bill and Sal stayed with

me for a good long while, with none of us saying much. But after an hour or so, when my uncle literally started falling asleep on his feet, I told them both to go home and get some rest for the night. They knew better than to ask me if I wanted to join them.

Once they left, my words finally came to me. I slid the room's only chair up to the bed and began. "Lee, I…I'm sorry I wasn't here earlier, Little One. We won our game, though, and then the whole team came straight here to see you. But a big, mean guard wouldn't let them come in." I stared at Lee's perfect little face, searching for any sign of a reaction. "And Ken was with them too. He told me to come take care of you." I started to cry again as the words poured out. I couldn't peel my eyes from Lee's face. A white film clung to her eyelashes, making her eyelids appear as if they'd been glued shut.

"I talked to Emm," I continued, "Emma Rey Finley. She's on her way now, actually in the car driving here. She said to hold on, just hold on—she'll be here soon."

Emm and Lee had a bond that was much deeper than even I could understand. At the promise of Emm's arrival, I half-expected Lee's eyes to flutter open like a butterfly. But of course, they didn't. Lee continued to lay still, unresponsive.

"It's my fault Emm didn't come sooner, Little One. I didn't tell her the truth. I didn't tell *you* the truth." At the thought of my deceit, my emotions overcame me. I gingerly took Lee's painfully cold hand in mine, being careful of her IVs, and begged for her forgiveness.

I didn't really want to talk about Emm—it was all too complicated—but I knew no one made Lee happier than she did. And no one, maybe not even me, wanted us to be together more than Lee. Nothing perked my sister up more than hearing about her own personal superhero.

"But you have to get better soon, Little One, so me, you and Emm can be happy at each other forever okay? We'll all find a way…to stay together. We'll figure it out," I continued, desperately hoping Emm would arrive soon; hoping-beyond-hope that her magic could see me through this dark, unfair storm.

But the more I spoke, the more disheartened I became. Lee showed no signs that she could hear me, not even the slightest stir. I prayed for a reaction—even a wiggle of her toe or a twitch of her eye—to prove that my baby sister could sense me beside her. Anything to prove she was still fighting. To prove she knew that she wasn't alone.

I turned to face the wall and let myself weep for a moment, trying to think of the good times. Of Christmas pancakes and duck park afternoons. Of the love in her eyes. Of the garden she planted and of her "super-secret and not-for-boys" journal. Of surprising her with milkshakes just to see her smile. Of morning tickle-wars and bedtime cuddles.

Then, suddenly, I knew what story Lee needed to hear. The story she would've begged for if she was awake. The same story she'd been requesting for months, but this time with nothing held back. Me and Emm's adventure in Europe. Our happy revolution abroad.

I began with the first moment I'd stepped off the plane, then recounted every single detail. All of it, including Emm's cherry-tasting lips. Including the night under the glow of our moon in Marseille, when Emm, after reading Lee's birthday greeting, had promised me *forever*.

As the memories came flooding back, I felt like maybe there was still a chance for us. Maybe Lee had been right. Maybe Emm never wanted to lose me. And before I knew it, my confession to Emm came rushing back. All the words I'd crafted and practiced. Maybe Lee needed to hear them as much as Emm. I focused again on my baby sister and gently asked, "Can I tell you something?"

I paused before I continued, imagining my little sister squealing, "Tell me, TD! Please tell me!"

Only after I'd heard her tiny voice in my head did my confession, reframed for Lee, come flowing out of me. All of it. "And at the Trevi Fountain, Emm told me to make a wish. I could've wished for anything in that moment, Lee, but the only thing I wanted was her. Emm and me together. With you.

Our happy little family. I wished for my One Day, the day when I would marry my forever friend. I wished that trip was a glimpse into the next twenty years. Thirty years. And we'd take you with us all over the world, Lee, until we were all old and gray."

I briefly paused, waiting for my little sister to respond with her adorable little giggle. But Lee remained painfully still and agonizingly lifeless. With only the sound of her monitors and ventilators as my reply.

"Old and gray, Little One, just like you'll be one day. Old and gray. You're not going to die here, Lee. You're not going to see the angels yet."

My tears slowly ran off my face and onto Lee's body. "Me, you and Emm," I said as I continued searching for any sign that Lee could hear me.

Not giving up, I once again recounted the story of me and Emm in Europe. Then, long into the night, I told the whole fairytale a third time, with Lee's hand in mine. Because now, in this nightmare, that's what those memories were: fairytales to shield Lee from the storm.

The following morning my eyes blinked awake to the image of Uncle Bill. I was still in the recovery room, but Lee wasn't. Her bed was gone, and so was the respirator. Half of the monitors had disappeared too. My heart soared.

"Not awake," reported Uncle Bill, "but they did wheel her back to her room. Orderlies…didn't want to disturb you."

"But that's good, right?" I asked. "That means something's changed?"

"Not exactly good. Stable enough to be out of post-op, that's all." Without another word, my uncle flung me a backpack. "Go clean up, then come see her. It's after eleven already."

Uncle Bill walked with me to the nearest bathroom. I washed up as best I could, thankful for the soap and the toothbrush kit. I threw on the fresh change of clothes Uncle Bill had packed, but I didn't pay attention the specific clothes he'd brought for me until I saw my shirt reflected in the mirror. A baby blue T-shirt, with *LeeStrong* across the front.

Confused, I walked out of the bathroom where Uncle Bill was still waiting for me. "Where'd this come from?" I asked.

"In the main lobby," he replied. "Go see for yourself." I wasn't sure, but I thought Uncle Bill almost smiled as he led me down the hall.

Walking out of the elevator, I saw a sea of baby blue. My whole team, including all of my coaches and trainers, had returned to the lobby and were all wearing identical *LeeStrong* T-shirts. With them were tons of people I didn't even recognize, all in baby blue. I was too stunned to do anything but gawk awkwardly.

Someone's voice cut through the ruckus. "That's him... That's Tim Dexter," Then another voice cried, "We love you, TD, and we're all Lee Strong!"

The next thing I knew, three reporters surrounded me, shoving microphones and cameras into my face.

"What's your sister's current condition?"

"Will you be playing in next week's championship game?"

"Is there anything you'd like to say on behalf of your sister?"

Through my shock, and as politely as I could, I told the reporters I wouldn't be answering any questions. Not that they let up. They continued hectoring me as I greeted each of my teammates and made my way through the lobby. One reporter even had the nerve to ask, "Have you contacted your father yet?" as if my deadbeat dad had any hand in raising Lee at all.

Ken and his parents soared to the rescue, pulling me away from the reporters. "Leave him alone!" Mrs. Zom yelled with such an unexpected ferocity that the press quickly backed off.

"Are you okay, sweetheart?" she asked as she smoothed my now-disheveled *LeeStrong* T-shirt.

"I'm okay. I'm just confus—" Ken grabbed my arm and pulled me even further away from the circus. His parents followed closely behind.

"Thank you for getting me out of there," I said, once the four of us had finally found some space. "Can you guys believe all of this?"

Ken laughed. "TD, you have no idea, my friend. This has been going on *all* morning." Ken went on to explain that a national news outlet had heard about our team's detour to the hospital, then aired a piece on the late news about Lee and me. After that, every local outlet had jumped on the story. "We're basically celebrities. We're even trending on social media right now," Ken concluded.

"The whole world knows about you and your sister, son," added Mr. Zom. "Everyone's watching. Everyone's here for you."

I panned the lobby again, overwhelmed by the outpouring of support. Our basketball community had always been a strong one, but this was more than I could have ever hoped for. I let myself take it all in before I finally asked Ken, "What's the deal with the shirts?"

"I'm glad you like 'em," answered Ken. "A group of fans came here early this morning with signs that said, 'Lee Strong,' so a couple of the boys and I went and had a few dozen shirts made. We thought that would be more than enough, but we've been running back and forth to the silk-screening place ever since. Come look!"

Ken walked me over to a window that overlooked the parking lot. Even more people were outside, forming yet another sea of *LeeStrong* baby blue. Signs and posters, some even with pictures of Lee, were everywhere.

"Ken, I love you so much, man," I said, pulling him in for a hug.

"I love you too, brother. Now get back in there and keep an eye on your sister for all of us. We'll all be here waiting for the good news."

As I walked back upstairs, I laughed at the thought of Lee seeing all these people here for her. Fighting beside her.

She was going to love it.

Chapter 27

A Sea of Baby Blue

We spent the afternoon in Room 188. Waiting. A waiting we'd all become far too accustomed to. Every once in a while, I'd think about going down to the circus in the lobby for a few minutes, but I couldn't bear to leave Lee's side. Never again. Periodically, Ken would come upstairs and sit with us for a bit, but in my absence, he really needed to keep the team—and everyone else, for that matter—updated. Leading the way and taking yet another hit for me.

The Zoms brought us a late lunch, then they, too, settled into Lee's frigidly-austere room and waited. We talked about Lee's favorite foods, her favorite cartoons, her favorite anything. At one point we took turns imagining the stories in Lee's super-secret journals, and we even managed a laugh here or there. A laugh that would always lapse into a moment of awkward, pensive silence.

I checked my phone almost constantly, waiting on a message from Emm. Waiting on *anything* from her. But my call log only showed entries from unknown numbers—the press downstairs, most likely—which I deleted without bothering to listen to. If Emm had left when she'd told me she did, she should've been here by this morning at the latest. I kept telling myself that she was on her way, that she and Matt had hit bad traffic, that the drive was too long and they'd needed to stop for the night. Again and again, I told Lee that Emm was close. At one point I thought I'd ask Ken to reach out, but I wouldn't allow myself. Emm was coming: there was no way she wouldn't be here for Lee. Not again, not now. Not after our conversation last night, not when I knew how much she loved my baby sister. Yet as the hours passed and our family's storm raged on, Emm's absence became more and more palpable. The whole world was in the lobby—the whole world except Emma Rey Finley.

Dr. Mallory checked in with us every hour, but it wasn't until late in the afternoon that he and his team arrived to discontinue Lee's sedation. He recommended we all stay in the room for the procedure, in the event that Lee woke up immediately; it would be less traumatic for her if she was welcomed by familiar faces.

There never seemed to be enough space in Room 188, but now the room grew even smaller as we all crowded along the far wall to give the medical team as much room as possible. To let them do their work and wake up the most important little girl on the planet.

Dr. Mallory and his team checked all Lee's monitors carefully before Dr. Ojalvo removed the IV from her right hand completely; a nurse removed two of the drip bags from the IV that was running into Lee's left hand. We locked arms and held our collective breath as Dr. Mallory and Dr. Foley removed the long, snaking breathing tube from Lee's little throat. With that completed, the entire team simultaneously took a step back.

Dr. Ojalvo was the first to speak. "Now, we wait. Don't be alarmed if it takes her some time to wake up."

"Yes," Dr. Mallory agreed. "Although it shouldn't be too

long before she's responsive."

None of us spoke. Instead, we shot each other excited glances, hoping to hear Lee's squeak of a voice at any moment.

Dr. Mallory added, "It might help if you speak to her. Recognizing familiar voices may help rouse her and could ease her transition." His tone of voice changed, shifting from medical doctor to the compassionate man who'd been looking after Lee all these years. "I hope you won't mind if I stay for a few minutes."

As Dr. Mallory's team left the room, Ken spurred himself into action. He walked up to Lee's bed, grabbed Moon and gently rubbed his fuzzy blueness against my sister's face. "Hey Lee, I'll win you every prize at the bowling alley if you'll wake up for us. Deal?" Ken offered. He waited a few seconds, but his only reply was silence. Not missing a beat, he continued, "Well, okay, missy, you sleep a little longer. But Moon told me he wants to keep you company, so I'm going to set him right here." He tucked Moon into the bed right beside her. "I love you, Lee."

Then each of us, in succession, tried bringing Lee back to us with our love. First Sal stepped up to her bed and told her about all the games of peek-a-boo he'd played with her as a baby. Uncle Bill promised that Lee could pick as many new plants as she wanted to add to their garden. Mr. and Mrs. Zom told her about the time when Ken, as a toddler, stripped completely naked in a hotel lobby, which if nothing else, offered us a much-needed moment of levity.

Eventually, my turn came.

"Lee," I began as I took her hand in mine. "I really miss you, and we're all ready for you to wake up now, so stop playing around, okay?" I paused as Ken let out a sad chuckle. "I love you so much, Little One. You're the reason I have the strength to get out of bed and fight every day. You're everything that's good and perfect in my world, and I don't know what I'd do without you."

The room grew silent as I continued to pour my heart out

to my little miracle. I must've spoken for another three or four minutes straight.

"So wake up, Little One. Wake up so you can see how much you mean to everyone in this room," I finally finished, convinced I'd see my sister's smile any second. But her face reflected nothing but an agonizing stillness.

"This is all perfectly normal," Dr. Mallory assured us after I'd fallen silent. "It could take up to a few hours. We need to be patient. I'll check in with you every few minutes."

With Dr. Mallory gone, we didn't know what to do with ourselves. We sat, transfixed, waiting. Waiting for the room to fill back up with Lee's presence. Waiting for the storm to let up.

Before I knew it, I again found myself praying. If God really did exist and he really was listening to me right now, then he certainly knew how cruel this truly was. He knew Lee's freedom had already been taken away once, but that her spirit never broke. God knew how much Lee appreciated her second chance, yet here she was fighting for her life once again. How much fight could God expect one little girl to have in her before she couldn't fight anymore?

I prayed for this storm to stop beating down on us. I prayed for a moment of clear sky, no matter how fleeting. I prayed for sunshine. I prayed for a lot of things—but most of all I prayed that if one of us had to suffer, it should be me. I challenged God to put me in that hospital bed in Lee's place. If someone had to die, let it be me instead.

Yet when I finally blinked my eyes open, I found myself as healthy as could be. Heart pumping, lungs clear, bones strong, and still standing three-feet away from my deteriorating baby sister. When I opened my eyes, God was nowhere to be found in Room 188.

"Well, screw you, God," I thought to myself, "we'll just do it without you."

We grew more anxious as the minutes passed. Dr. Mallory continued encouraging us to talk to Lee every time he checked in. So that's just what we did. Through tears, through the tension, through the occasional laughs. Sometimes we whispered, sometimes we even yelled. In English and Italian, we all said the same thing, over and over: "Wake up, Lee, wake up!" But all we received in reply was her stillness. A stillness that almost made me want to give up.

And then it came to me—there was one voice I knew she wanted to hear. One voice with magic strong enough to reach her. I jumped up from my chair.

"What is it?" Ken asked, surprised by my sudden excitement.

"I'll be right back, I need to make a quick phone call." Ken shot me a knowing grin as I bolted out into the hallway.

I returned to Lee's room only a minute or two later with a heavy frown on my face.

"What happened?" asked Ken. "Did you reach her?"

"Straight to voicemail. Twice," I answered as I hung my head. "She was supposed to be here. She said last night she was on her way."

"I'm sure there's a reasonable explanation," offered Ken. "Did you check your voicemail?"

"No messages from her number." I looked around the room: everyone looked just like me. Defeated. The room itself suddenly seemed colder.

"I don't get it, man. I'm so sorry. But I'm sure she's on her way. Stay strong." Even Ken's trademark positivity was beginning to falter.

But I didn't want to stay strong. I wanted this nightmare to be over. I wanted the storm to abate, for the dark cloud above to dissipate, for a ray of sunshine to finally arrive. Nothing—not one single thing on this Earth—was more important than my baby sister. I knew Lee was strong enough to do this without God, but without Emma Rey Finley? That was a storm too powerful for even my little miracle to weather.

I limped into dinnertime, mentally-speaking. By then, Mr. and Mrs. Zom had left to get a few hours of sleep, and Ken was back downstairs reigning over the madness. Uncle Bill, Sal and I took turns talking to Lee. I'd never been more grateful to have Sal around; he told Lee about the beauties of his beloved homeland long after my uncle and I were talked out.

I hated to admit it, but I was beginning to lose hope. Without Lee's voice, I felt alone. All I wanted to do was cry, and my uncle, too, started looking as if his strength were waning badly. And still no Emm—no matter how many times I called. I could've punched a wall I was so upset, punched anything at all. I wanted to punch God in the face for doing this to such an innocent little girl, only he was too much of a coward to show himself. I tilted my head upwards and silently demanded that he justify what he'd done. But I got nothing.

Livid to the boiling point, with angry tears burning in my eyes, I jumped up, intending to attack the next thing that moved. But just then, an unfamiliar knock came at the door. The three of us froze in place, staring at the door for a long moment. When the same knock came again, I let out a breath that I hadn't even known I was holding in.

I knew exactly who it was.

It had to be sunshine. It had to be a shooting star. It had to be a superhero. Maybe God had been listening.

I pulled the door open, hoping to see Emm's beautiful face, even if it was marred by tears. But that's not what I saw. It took a moment for my eyes to refocus and realize who was standing there.

"TD, I'm so sorry."

"Nurse Jen?" I blurted out, confused.

"We came the moment we heard," she replied, tears in her eyes. As Nurse Jen reached up and stroked my face, I realized she hadn't come alone. Standing timidly behind her, just to the right of the door, was a scared little boy wearing a pair of white Converse sneakers. A scared little boy I knew.

"Now, Sammy, be polite and say hello to Mr. Dexter," Nurse Jen instructed gently as she nudged him forward.

"But Mommy, he doesn't like to be called Mr. Dexter. He likes to be called TD."

"Hey, kid," I said, trying to put together a coherent thought. "What are you doing here?"

"I...I...brought this," Sammy replied as Sal and my uncle stepped forward and greeted Nurse Jen. "To keep her and Moon company." Nervously, Sammy held up the toy for me to see. In his hands was a plush *Despicable Me* minion.

I turned to my uncle, who looked as surprised as I was. "Sammy?" he said, reaching down for a handshake.

Exhausted and strained, I honestly wondered if I were starting to lose my mind. What the hell was happening? And why was Sammy's minion wearing a dress?

Sal, pulling together whatever little smiley he had left, warmly introduced himself to Sammy. He shot me a look that said, "I'll keep him busy for a moment," so I took the opportunity to pull Nurse Jen into the hall.

"How did you...? How are you here, and...?" I stuttered.

Nurse Jen smiled subtly as she cut me off. "Sammy's been telling me about his *life-passions* friend for months, but he always called her 'Lee Rose.' He told me about her bone marrow transplant, but I thought she was a cancer survivor, too. I thought that's why they'd bonded."

Still confused, my mouth gaped open. Nurse Jen took pity on me and connected the dots for me further. "Sammy spent a lot of time with Lee after school, but since I'm almost always working in the afternoons, I never had the chance to meet her."

Finally piecing everything together, I began, "And you would've met Lee last weekend at the anniversary party—"

"—but then...all this happened. And I never put it together until tonight."

"So what changed?" I asked, still in disbelief. "How'd you figure it out?"

Nurse Jen paused, looking into the room at Lee. "My husband and I were sitting down for dinner, and I called Sammy to the table. But he wouldn't come—which he almost never does because family dinners are the house rule when the three of us are together. When I walked into the living room to scold him, he was watching the news. He jumped up and cried, 'Mom, that's her, that's my Lee Rose!' At first, all I saw on the screen was the crowd, a sea of baby blue. Then Lee's picture flashed on the screen—and I realized I knew this little angel, too." Nurse Jen smiled sadly as she wiped a drizzling tear from her eye. "We hopped in the car and wasted no time getting over here. But with the crowd downstairs and visiting hours ending, the only reason we could get in was because of my ID badge."

I looked back into Lee's room, where Sammy was now staring at my sleeping sister. I pulled myself together as best I could and said, "Thank you."

Nurse Jen didn't reply in words. Instead, she wrapped her arms around me, providing me with the warm embrace I so desperately needed.

I began to fill Nurse Jen in on just how dire the situation had become. Her eyes grew wider and wider as I talked. Almost as if she had just realized what she'd actually walked into.

Just as she asked if she could review Lee's chart, I felt a tug at my *LeeStrong* T-shirt. "Sir, can I give this to her now?" asked Sammy, again holding up the minion. "I turned it into a girl minion, just for her," he added.

"Sammy was planning on surprising her with it at the celebration," Nurse Jen explained. "He kept explaining how much 'Lee Rose' would love a girl minion."

I looked down at Sammy's stuffed toy. Nurse Jen and Sammy hadn't just found a baby blue dress for the minion, but a baby blue dress that was kissed all over with sunflowers. It even had a ribbon with carefully hand-drawn sunflowers on its head, almost like a headband.

"Sure, Sammy," I answered, taking his hand and leading him back into the room. "Come on, we'll give it to Lee together." I asked Uncle Bill and Sal to give us a moment; they slipped out of the room without complaint.

Nurse Jen, Sammy and I quietly gathered around Lee's bedside. As Nurse Jen saw Lee's bandaged head up-close, she tried to stifle a sob, but it escaped anyway. Sammy stood for a moment, still holding my hand, his ten-year-old eyes wide with fear. He took a deep breath of courage, then reached up and nestled the girl minion beside Lee, placing it softly under her arm.

"You can talk to her if you want. I'll bet she'd like that," I said.

"I want...I just want...to sit with her for a while," Sammy muttered. "Will you lift me up?" Then he looked at Nurse Jen, "Mommy, is that okay?"

Nurse Jen nodded in approval, then I lifted Sammy and carefully placed him on the bed next Lee and her stillness. I took a big step back, giving him his space. Sammy sat there quietly with his hand on Lee's shoulder, looking far braver than I felt.

Nurse Jen began reviewing Lee's chart. The frown on her face grew deeper as I went over Lee's stats and meds with her. And that's when I heard it: Sammy's soft voice singing our song. In barely more than a hum, Sammy brought the moon into Room 188:

> *I see the moon, the moon sees me*
> *The moon sees somebody I want to see*
> *God bless the moon, and God bless me*
> *And God bless the somebody I want to see.*

But, Lee didn't stir.

Not even the magic of her beloved lullaby had reached her.

Sammy did his best to repeat the rhyme, but he couldn't. He choked up, snuggled himself even more deeply into his mother's arms, and began crying softly. Nurse Jen let her tears flow as well, powerless to stop them. The room filled with the sound of them, raining together in sorrow. I stood back and took in the scene, dying a little inside myself.

Nurse Jen lifted Sammy off the bed and held him in her arms as only a mother could. I perched my head over Lee's sweet face and carefully tucked an unshaved lock of hair behind her ear, as if I was going to whisper something. As if I was going to tell her how happy I was at her, or tell her again that it was time to wake up. Standing there, I almost expected Lee to launch one of her sneak attacks, as though she'd been faking all along, but nothing happened. I wanted to speak, but I didn't have any more words of encouragement; I couldn't say anything at all.

And that's when the full-truth gutted me: Lee didn't have an ounce of fight left in her.

The void inside me had won. I stood there, looking at my sister, for a long, long moment, shaking my head and tried to deny this awful truth. As soon as I found the last drop of my remaining fight, I reached across the bed and handed Moon to Sammy. "Here, kid. Lee told me she wanted you to have him."

Chapter 28

Friday Night Lights

At 1:43 a.m. on Sunday, March 12th, Lee Rose Dexter saw the angels. Her official cause of death was ruled as a traumatic hemorrhagic stroke, but I knew that wasn't it. The truth was that she had died of a broken heart.

Lee only had one wish in the end: To see Emma Rey Finley. One wish that I couldn't grant. One wish that I had derailed completely because I was the one who'd told Emm not to come home. And in those last hours, when it counted the most, Lee couldn't hold on long enough for Emm to rescue her from the storm. Without her superhero, and after so many years of fighting, Lee had given up. And it was all my fault. I'd lost the most important person in the whole world, and it was all my fault.

I didn't stay long at the hospital that night. I couldn't bear the thought of staring down at Lee's body, knowing that the little miracle inside was now gone. Knowing that I'd never clean her glasses on my shirt or make her chocolate chip banana pancakes ever again. Knowing that no matter how much I tickled her, she'd never wake up. Knowing that Emm, not Sammy, should've sung her that lullaby. Knowing that no amount of happy could bring my sister back.

As news spread around the ICU, there wasn't a single dry eye in sight, except for mine. Everyone's eyes rained down around me, but as much as I wanted to, I couldn't cry. I had run out of tears.

Against the advice of seemingly everyone, I went home to my apartment, alone. I didn't want to listen to people telling me how sorry they were or that they knew what I was going through. I didn't want to hear from anyone at all.

With Lee gone, the few die-hard fans outside quickly dispersed, but the media didn't. A security guard was kind enough to call me a cab and walk me out through a private entrance. My phone vibrated constantly in my pocket, but I didn't bother checking it.

I somehow managed to hold it together on the ride home, but once I was in my apartment, I let out every damn emotion I'd been keeping bottled up. More than anything else, I was furious. I became the storm, itself, giving-in to its darkness. Letting it take a hold of me completely. Rampaging through my kitchen, I broke the dirty plates in the sink and the used cereal bowls that crowded my countertop. Anything within my reach was fair game, and all of it ended up shattered on my tile floor.

The living room fared no better. Pictures of my teammates, awards that I'd won, paintings and decorations. I flung them each against the wall with more force than I knew myself capable of. I overturned the coffee table, the armchair, the lamps. Within minutes, the room was in shambles. Utterly destroyed. The storm and I raged through my apartment like a tornado, wrecking everything in our path.

And then I saw it on the floor, still somehow intact: the framed picture of Lee, Emm, and me that Lee had given me for my birthday. I picked it up from the ruins, holding it with both hands, and stared at them. My blood boiled all the more ferociously. The sight of that girl next to my dead sister made my skin crawl. She probably still had no idea of what she'd done. Hell, Emm probably didn't even care.

With all the vitriol I had, I snapped the frame in half with my bare hands, pushing my thumbs through its center. The glass and plastic sprayed across the room in a hundred pieces. I couldn't bring myself to tear the picture itself in half, but I flung it down into my pile of destruction.

In the next instant, the eye of the storm arrived. All went calm. As the photo landed, I realized something was stuck to its back. A small scrap of lined paper, folded in half, barely as long as my pinkie. As I picked it up, I instantly recognized the handwriting.

Happy Birthday, TD! Thank you for always including me in your adventures with Emma, and thank you for always loving each other no matter what. When I get my One Day, I hope I will meet someone who makes me as happy as you make her. You two are my favorite.

Love you forever big bro,

Lee

I had totally forgotten that Lee had always loved sneaking notes into her gifts, especially photos. Even when she was young, she'd draw a smiley face or a tulip on the back of her class pictures before she gave them away. She called them "later surprises."

As quickly as the eye of the storm came, it vanished, and the storm picked up once again. Lee's secret message brought me to the floor, where I became part of the wreckage. I immediately tried to piece the frame back together, but the damage had already been done.

There was no coming back from a mess this big.

For the next several days, I barely left my bed, and when I did, it was only to crawl into Lee's escape corner, where my sisters' scent still clung to her pillow. Where my little sunflower's imagination had sprouted so freely.

I turned off my phone. The only time I got up was to dismiss Sal, my uncle or Ken. One of them knocked on my door every few hours. I wouldn't let them in; I'd just yell through the door, telling them I was fine, even though I clearly wasn't.

I couldn't escape the grief, the anger or the loneliness. I felt physically ill—my stomach and my limbs ached as if they were sapped of their strength. I hardly ate. At night, I lay in bed, staring at a blank spot on the wall and cried myself into such an exhaustion that I'd pass-out for few hours, only to wake up and relive the horror again. Only to open my eyes and find the void inside overwhelming my entire being.

Wednesday night, I was buried in the darkness of Lee's escape corner when I heard an unusual, soft knock at my door. Knowing it couldn't be my uncle, Sal, or Ken, I tried to think of who else it could be. But after a second or two, I decided that I didn't really care.

I buried myself into Lee's pillow, but the knocking didn't stop. A soft tapping, but a persistent one. Like a form of repetitive torture.

"Go away!" I yelled, but the knocking didn't let up. Giving in, I finally left the safety of Lee's alcove, kicking a path through the pile of destruction that was my living room floor.

I looked through the peephole: no one was there, but the knocking still continued. Wondering if I was going mad, I opened the door and looked down.

"Sammy?" I said, startled. Of all the people I'd ever met, Sammy was the last person I expected to see. Especially now.

"Gru," he said plainly before walking into my apartment without even waiting to be invited inside. "My dad's downstairs, so this needs to be quick," he declared.

"What are you doing here?" I asked as he shoved a pile of stuff off the couch to free up some room for a seat. I didn't realize until he sat down that he had Moon tucked under his arm. He propped Lee's baby blue teddy bear up next to him on the sofa, including him in our conversation. Sammy's legs weren't even long enough to reach the floor.

As if he were a sixty-year-old man instead of a ten-year-old kid, Sammy began without prompting. "You know, I was confused at first when you gave Moon to me, but then my mom found this under Lee's pillow. When she was…clearing out the room." His voice cracked a bit, but his expression remained focused and serious.

Sammy pulled a crumpled piece of lined paper from his pocket: Lee's will.

I turned my armchair upright and took a seat as Sammy began reading the will out loud—as if I'd never read it before.

"…And number two says you and your teammates need to make it into the NCAA Tournament. Number three says—"

"—I know what it says, kid," I said curtly, cutting him off sharply. I didn't even raise my head as I spoke.

Sammy folded the paper back up and carefully placed it on the end table. Neither of us said anything for a moment, as we both stared at the official legal document.

"Then why weren't you at your game tonight?" Sammy asked. "You guys won, by the way."

I forced my chin upward and looked straight into Sammy's eyes. But the truth was, I didn't have a good answer. Other than one thing: Fear. Afraid of the sympathy, afraid of the condolences. Afraid to face the world. Afraid I simply wasn't ready. Yet, oddly enough, I was just as afraid of not telling Sammy the truth. My lies had broken Lee's heart. Could I do the same to this kid?

"I was scared," I admitted flatly.

Sammy didn't reply at first, carefully considering what to say next. And then, he did something braver than I'd ever been able to do. He told me his truth.

"I know about being scared. When I had cancer, everything was scary. All of it. And some days I just wanted to give up. But do you know what kept me going?" He paused, expecting me to reply. But I was in no mood for guessing games.

"You did," Sammy continued. "You and your team. I watched all your games from my bed in the hospital. I was probably your biggest fan, even though I hadn't even met you. No matter how much better the other team was or how much time was left in the game, it didn't matter to Tim Dexter. You didn't give up."

He paused again, hoping for a response. But I had nothing.

Sammy shuffled himself off the sofa, kicking a swath of carpet clear for himself so he could pace back and forth. "So neither did I, and eventually I won. Just like you always did. I beat cancer because of you and you didn't even know it." He grabbed Lee's will from the end table. "Lee Rose, my best friend and your little sister, trusted us. If she wanted me to look after her teddy bear, then that's what I'm going to do. And it says it right here," he said, thrusting the will into my face, "that your sister asked you to do two things, and one of those was to go to the NCAA Tournament."

As I listened to Sammy, I started to feel excited about playing again. How many times had basketball been my escape, the one place where everything was fair? Even if he was only half my age, Sammy had just reminded me that the court was the one place where life actually made sense. How this ten-year-old boy had just wrestled the void from deep inside me and stomped on it made my head spin.

"Yeah, kid, maybe," I muttered.

"Do it for her, TD, and do it for all the other kids watching. Do it for all of the other 'Lees' in the world." Sammy finished his lecture with an almost eerie authority in his voice.

I looked up at Sammy again and realized this wasn't the same quiet little kid I'd met a few months ago. When we first met, he could hardly shake my hand, yet now he'd mustered up the courage to walk into my house and set me straight. Much like Emm had taught me how to be more outgoing and spontaneous, Lee had taught Sammy to be bold and strong. He'd taken matters into his own hands because he didn't have

Lee to hide behind anymore, yet he intrinsically understood how important her last requests truly were. Because he knew Lee wouldn't have let me hang my head and sulk. Because he knew she would've pushed me to inspire other kids like her and Sammy.

I reflexively smiled, stood up from my chair and held my hand out for a handshake, but Sammy—now practically standing ten-feet-tall—slapped my palm away. Instead, he wrapped himself around my hips and hugged me.

No wonder my sister liked this kid so much.

Thursday morning, I woke up from a deep sleep. The first real sleep I'd had in almost a week. I felt…reasonably-human and spent the day cleaning up my place, mentally preparing myself to deal with the world the following night. Sammy had been right: There was no better way of honoring my little angel than taking home a league championship in front of all the people who had loved and supported us through our darkest storm. The toughest tough-love I'd ever received had come from the mouth of a plant-loving, ten-year-old boy.

I arrived in the locker room Friday evening as ready as I could possibly be, but nothing felt normal about this game day. It was the first time I'd left my apartment since Lee had passed. Everything felt a little fuzzy, but despite my swirling insides, I told myself to remain focused.

My teammates all stopped what they were doing the instant I walked into the locker room, almost like no one was expecting to see me. I knew every single one of them would offer their condolences, but I really just wanted to concentrate on the game. I greeted each of my brothers individually before asking Ken to announce that the "sad" part of the evening had passed—and the "winning" part had begun. I knew the guys would respect that. Their unison cry of "LEE STRONG" told me I'd been right.

"Lee Strong forever," I thought to myself. There was no way we could lose tonight. No way my angel up above would let that happen.

As soon as we trotted onto the court, I was surrounded by a sea of *LeeStrong* baby blue T-shirts. It seemed like every single fan in the stands was wearing my sister's fight on their chest.

Since it was the last game of the regular season, the team took a lap around the court to greet our fans. I'd never seen our arena so electrified in my entire career, and the crowd roared as if the game had already started. With lights on us and the stage set, my nerves were higher than they'd ever been. Our entire season came down to this one game.

Ken led the pack as we ran our lap. "Give them a wave, TD," he shouted over his shoulder.

"What do you mean?" I asked, trying to stay as focused as I could.

"Just trust me. Wave at the crowd, man. Everyone's here to see *you*. You're like the talk of the town!" Ken grew more and more excited as the words flew from his mouth.

The second I lifted my hand into the air, the place erupted, somehow becoming louder than it already was. Ken tried to say something, but I couldn't hear him over the crowd's flood of support. My ears began to ring as five-thousand fans lifted me up with their cheers. With their love. The arena was standing-room-only; every single seat in the entire gym was taken.

Every seat but one.

With minutes to go before the opening tip, I shot a glance toward Lee's seat underneath our basket. And there, where my sister should've been, sat Moon, with Sammy and Nurse Jen in the two adjoining seats. I broke out from our huddle, just like I used to when I would kiss Lee before our games. I gave both Sammy and Nurse Jen a kiss, not saying anything, but with a smile on my face. When Sammy, in his *LeeStrong* T-shirt, held Moon up for a kiss as well, the arena again exploded in cheers.

I turned to run back to my team, but—before I'd taken three steps—Sammy yelled to me, "Hey Gru!" Which was more than enough to catch my attention and make me turn around. Cupping his hands around his mouth, he yelled, "Kick their ass!"

And I planned on doing just that. For him—but, more importantly—for her.

Once I joined my teammates, we lined up on the baseline for a moment of silence for my baby sister. Instantly, the uproarious crowd became utterly quiet, the deepest silent-observance I'd ever witnessed. I closed my eyes and embraced my brothers. This would be the first home game I would ever play without my little sister rooting for me and, regardless of tonight's outcome, it would also be my last.

With my eyes still shut, a hundred different memories of Lee flew through my head. But, mostly, I remembered how much she loved and was loved.

Which then reminded me of Emm.

My eyes burst open of their own accord and glanced in the direction of Emm's old spot. But she wasn't there. I shot another look to where she'd been sitting this year with Matt, but she wasn't there, either.

My stomach lurched from a wave of conflicting emotions. Suddenly, I wished I was back in my apartment all alone. I shouldn't have come here tonight: I wasn't ready.

A buzz came from the crowd. It started so softly that I initially couldn't make out what they were singing, but it steadily grew louder and louder: "Lee Strong. Lee Strong. Lee Strong." And by some blessing, they continued to chant right up until the opening tip. Which gave me the strength to be Lee Strong, too.

The game was frantic. Both teams traded blows back and forth for much of the first half, until we finally reached halftime with a tied game. As excited and thrilled as I was to be out there, I wasn't quite myself and I knew it. The guys knew it too; they'd covered me without a single complaint or jeer.

Coach was furious. Once we were back in the locker room, he let us have it with a fierceness I'd almost never seen. But he was right. This game wasn't just the season finale, it was everything we'd been working for all year. For the seniors on the team like Ken and me, tonight would be our legacy-defining moment. All that Lee had ever wanted for me.

The second half was little better. Our opponents didn't give us an inch, but there was no way they wanted this win more than we did. In the last minutes of the game, the crowd made sure our rivals knew whose arena they were in. Their wild cheers gave us the extra push we needed to bring it home, with Ken landing his signature bank-shot off the backboard, scoring the final basket of the regular season.

"LEE STRONG!" he shouted as the final buzzer sounded. He threw the game ball into the crowd just as they rushed onto the court in a full-on celebratory stampede.

The madness that ensued was like nothing I'd ever witnessed before. Confetti fell from the ceiling, and two of the guys drenched our coach in a Gatorade shower. For the first time since Lee had passed, I smiled widely. Coach issued a blanket-statement from the locker room, asking the press not to interview me, but now I tapped one of the reporters on the arm and asked to make a quick statement. She readily agreed, and her camera-person focused on me. I delivered my final public message on my home floor:

"Over the past few days, I've received the most incredible display of support. Support that I didn't even think was humanly-possible. I thank my team, my coaches and all the fans, but I also need to give a shout-out to one fan in particular: To my late sister Lee's best friend, Sammy Woods. I wouldn't have made it here tonight without you. Sammy, you are—and always will be—Lee Strong."

It was another hour before our locker room celebration finally began to wind down. I wasn't my usual self, of course, but hanging out with my brothers after a career win like this bolstered my spirits in a way I don't think anything else could have. Not only had we solidified our school's first-ever NCAA Tournament berth, but more importantly, we'd just fulfilled one of Lee's last requests.

In the hallway, I was surprised to find Uncle Bill waiting for me. "Well done," he said. He didn't need to say any more for me to know he was proud of me. We walked quietly to the exit, until he finally said, "Small surprise for you." With that, he opened the door—and Sal, Dr. Mallory, Nurse Jen, Sammy and Moon were all waiting for me.

"Well, isn't it just my lucky day," I said, genuinely happy to see them all.

Dr. Mallory spoke up. "I thought it was about time I came to see you play. Nice game, TD."

Before I could reply, Sal pulled me in for his traditional double kiss. "*Ti amo*, Sal," I replied.

"I love you, too, and congratulations on the World Cup!" answered Sal. At which I couldn't help but laugh. Everyone else did, too.

Our group hung out for a little while as no one was in a hurry to leave. As much as I'd needed my self-imposed exile, I now needed this company even more. It was hard not having Lee with us, but it still felt right.

As we talked and talked, my eyes wandered to the sky above, to where my angel must surely be. The night sky was clear and starry. I stared upward for a good long while, letting a sort of peace wash over me. When I finally broke out of my trance, I glanced around at our group. No one had noticed my zoning-out; everyone was still chatting away. Everyone except Sammy. He, too, was enthralled by the stars shimmering above. As I looked at him, I could feel how much he missed Lee.

It broke my heart to think how much Sammy must have truly loved his Lee Rose. For all I knew, he could have been waiting for the perfect moment to tell Lee how much she meant to him. Only now, the moment he'd been waiting for was gone. Now, all Sammy could do was honor her request by taking care of her fuzzy blue friend. All Sammy could do was look into the night sky and perhaps find a glimmer of light by which to remember Lee.

When at last Sammy noticed I was watching him, he pointed his finger to the clear, star-filled sky. In a voice so soft I could barely hear him, he simply said, "Look." But he didn't have to say anything more for me to understand.

The storm had finally passed. What remained in its wake was the beautiful glow of a full moon.

Chapter 29

I'm So Happy at You

*G*od gives you what you can handle." I actually heard that from more than one person in the aftermath of Lee's death. To be honest, I'd never given that particular adage much thought; I'd never really needed to. My life had had its fair share of ugly moments, but I'd always found my way through them—and the main reason was Lee. I couldn't give up when times grew tough, and when it came down to it, I was all she had. Even through the darkest of storms, when I could no longer fight for myself, I had always fought for my baby sister. Was it really true that God was up there, conducting some kind of wicked crucible as to my threshold for pain? *Really?*

The morning of Lee's funeral, as I showered, I thought about that piece of advice more and more. If anyone ever told me that again, I'd emphatically reply that they were, in fact, wrong. God gives you what he *thinks* you can handle, the rest is up to you to figure out.

Yet surviving any of this without Lee was beyond me. Though I'd never fully realized it, I had dreams for my baby sister. Dreams far, far bigger than her illness. I dreamed of her One Day, but also of her going to college. Of her writing career. Of meeting the man who would love her, marry her and forever treat her like the miracle she truly was. Every time I fought, I was fighting for all those dreams. Yet those dreams had all been extinguished in just one cruel week. All that re-placed those dreams were now nightmares—real nightmares in the real world.

The only suit I owned was the suit I'd worn to the sym-phony. The moment I pulled it from my closet, it brought back memories from six-thousand miles away—of Emm in her red dress, of her being moved to tears by Vivaldi. Memories that made me cringe. I didn't want to think of her at all. Not to-day, maybe not ever. I didn't want to remember Lee's broken heart, nor did I want to admit that even now, a little piece of me still needed Emm. But since I had nothing else even remotely appropriate for the service, the suit—and its memo-ries—were my only real choice.

Lee's funeral was being held at one of the area's largest churches. I honestly couldn't fathom the number of people who'd said they'd be there, so I tried my best to stay in the moment as I drove across town. I didn't want to think of the crowd, of the stream of condolences that would do nothing to bring my sister back to me.

I arrived at the church around half-past eight, which was an hour before we were set to begin. My uncle and Sal had arrived even earlier. When Uncle Bill saw me walking down the long aisle, he threw his arm around me and held me closer than I could ever remember. "Together, TD," he said. "We'll get through today. Together."

Lee lay peacefully at the foot of the altar in the small-est casket I'd ever seen. Not ready to approach her, I took a seat in one of the still-empty pews to collect myself. The altar was beautifully decorated, overflowing with flowers, as if Lee's lush garden was somehow springing through the floorboards of the church itself. A meadow of color, bringing a tinge of warmth into this nightmare.

I sat staring at the flowers for an extended while, mostly because I didn't know what else to do. It seemed impossible that we were here, that this beautiful Saturday morning was the day I'd say goodbye to my precious sister forever.

At last, Sal came up to me. "*Carissimo TD*," he began gently. "This day is too sad, I know. But it's time for you to have *un momento privato* with Lee. Before the others arrive. Come, I will walk you." He reached forward and grabbed my hand, guiding me into the aisle and toward my baby sister.

I took a deep breath before looking down. Seeing her without monitors and IVs was oddly disturbing. For all their horror, those machines meant she was still alive; without their constant humming and rhythmic beeping, Lee was now stiller than ever.

Peacefully at rest in her most-prized outfit, the baby blue, sunflower dress we'd bought for her in Marseille. Around her head, covering most of the shaved part of her scalp, was the matching sunflower headband Emm had surprised her with on my birthday. Lee's tiny arms lay across her chest, and between her interlaced fingers was a single blue tulip, the only true baby blue tulip I'd ever seen—a flower of such soft blue that, together with her outfit, Lee looked as if she was part of the meadow behind her. My little sunflower, now eternally belonging to the most sorrowful garden ever planted.

As I gazed at Lee, I didn't pray. I didn't say much. All I could do was dream of hearing one final, precious giggle from my Little One. A possibility gone forever. The worst nightmare of them all.

I tore myself away as the guests began to arrive, knowing that if I didn't force myself to go now, I'd never be able to leave Lee's side. I took my designated seat but as the mourners entered, I couldn't turn around: I couldn't bear seeing all the sad faces behind me. Because no one could feel emptier or more filled with grief than I.

Mostly to distract myself, I pulled my notecards from my pocket and quietly began practicing my remarks. But as the church filled up, the sanctuary grew louder and louder—to the point where I couldn't hear myself rehearsing.

Frustration shot through me. I didn't want to speak anymore. I couldn't. I just wanted my sister back. I closed my eyes, hoping for the nightmare to be over, only to open them again and be anguished anew—my little sunflower, not sprouting with happiness, but forever withering in the darkness of her coffin.

The church, itself, massive as it was, began to close in on me. I bolted up and scrambled out of my pew, planning to slip out through the side door before the service began. But just as I pulled the door open, I stopped short.

Out of the corner of my eye, I saw her.

Emma Rey Finley entered the church, clinging to Matt tightly with one arm as if he were holding her up. Her free arm was in a sling, and she appeared to be limping slightly. Part of me couldn't believe she had the nerve to show up, part of me was flushed with relief and part of me was alarmed by her obvious injuries—all of which were thoughts and emotions I could scarcely process.

I did my best not to stare as they took their seats in the middle of the church. Emm gave Matt a kiss on the cheek and began making her way to the foot of the altar. Seeing her was too much to handle, yet I couldn't look away. I slumped down a bit and used the crowd around me as a shield, doing my best to hide from her gaze.

Without Matt's arm on which to lean, Emm's limp became more pronounced. When she reached Lee's small casket, Emm lifted her heavy black veil, revealing not only her face, but her sorrow. She hovered over Lee for a few moments, looking as though she were trying to heal my sister's broken body with her voice. Against my own will, I took a few cautious steps toward the casket, but was only able to make out a few of the words Emm softly purred to Lee. Yet her words were unmistakable, even from afar. Emm left our little angel with her favorite phrase: "I'm so happy at you."

Emm unfastened something from her wrist, then placed it into the casket beside my baby sister. As Emm turned to limp back down the aisle, I ducked again, hoping she hadn't seen me.

The funeral director announced we were starting, so I joined Uncle Bill, Sal, Ken and his parents in the front pew. Nurse Jen, Sammy and Dr. Mallory sat in the row behind us. The director began; none of her words made any sense as they reached my ears. All I could think about was the last time I'd seen my little miracle awake. Our last conversation wasn't filled with love or adoration, but disappointment. Disappointment that I—not Emm—had been the one who walked into Room 188 that day. A disappointment that had cost Lee her life.

Sal and Ken both spoke beautifully as they honored my sister's memory. Ken was even able to make a joke or two, which only he could've gotten away with. Tiny cracks of sunshine that the altar's meadow desperately needed.

The next thing I knew, the funeral director called me to the podium. Sal patted me on the back as I stood up and slowly made my way toward the altar. I didn't want to speak, but I had to. Prior to shuffling up the stairs, I went by my sister's side one last time. I stood beside her casket and took a long, deep breath before looking down at her again. I couldn't take it. I began to weep as I traced the outline of her dress with my finger. But it wasn't until I saw what Emm had placed in her casket that my emotions took complete hold of me.

Emm's turquoise bracelet, hugging Lee's little wrist. It matched her raiment beautifully.

The room spun. Whatever control I had evaporated instantly. Tears flowed so freely that I could hardly see, yet the whole church was still expecting me to speak.

I stumbled up the steps. Reaching into my suit pocket I pulled out my notecards, but my hands were shaking so violently and my eyes were so full of tears that I couldn't even read my own handwriting. I stood there and cried, collapsing not just from the weight of my own grief, but from the sadness of every guest in the crowd. An uncomfortable silence drowned the church.

Reaching for my notecards, I tucked them into my pocket, intending to give up; to simply walk away from the podium. But just as I started to turn, I realized Sal was behind me. He wrapped his arms around me and gave me a long hug. He slid my notecards from my pocket, laid them on the podium and nodded his head. He kept one arm wrapped tightly around me until I could face the idea of saying my final goodbye.

As I uttered my first stuttering, choking words, Emma Rey Finley met my gaze. She locked onto my eyes and we stared at one another—even though we were several dozen feet apart. Even though there were hundreds of others in the sanctuary. Without speaking, without moving her lips, Lee's superhero delivered the message that saved me: "Tell them how amazing she was."

And so I did.

After the funeral, we invited a few people to my uncle's house for a more intimate remembrance. I hadn't been there since Lee passed, but being back was made easier by being surrounded by the people I loved.

"How are you holding up?" Nurse Jen calmly asked me as I sat down on the sofa beside her.

"I'm okay," I replied. "Glad today is almost over, honestly."

"I can only imagine," she answered. "You did a really incredible job up there today, once you got going. I was going to join you on the podium, but Sal said it was his duty."

I couldn't help but smile. "I don't know what I would've done without you these past few weeks. Sammy, too—if it wasn't for him, I probably wouldn't have played last night."

Nurse Jen blushed. "As soon as he saw you weren't at Wednesday's game, Sammy insisted that his dad bring him over." She let out a small laugh. "He had to promise to drive him right after dinner. It was the only way my husband could get him to eat."

"That's one hell of a kid you have there," I said, smiling. "He made all the difference. Thank you for everything."

Nurse Jen turned serious, "No, thank *you*. It's people like you and Lee that make all those long hours' worth it, and Sammy is lucky to have you in his life." She paused, looking over at her son, who was at the buffet table.

While still looking at Sammy, she continued, "He loved her more than you and I will ever know, TD. Having someone to share his botany with—there's truly been a change in him these last few months. And watching you play last night was the happiest I've seen him since Lee passed." She paused, sighing deeply, "They had such an innocent love."

"Sometimes that's the best kind of love there is," I replied.

Nurse Jen changed the course of our conversation, asking about Lee as a young child, but I began to distance myself. Being in this house alone was difficult enough. I couldn't relive my memories just yet.

"TD," she began firmly, after I'd dodged a few questions, "you should hang onto those memories. Don't let them fade." Her voice turned softer. "If you don't want to tell me, that's fine, but talking is a big part of remembering. That's how we honor the people we love and keep them close to us."

I couldn't disagree, but before I could respond, Sammy came running up to us with a small notebook in his hand.

"What's that sweetie?" Nurse Jen asked.

"I don't know," he answered as he climbed onto his mother's lap. "TD's uncle told me to give it to him."

But I knew exactly what it was: My little miracle's handwritten words.

I carefully took Lee's journal in my hands. Nurse Jen was right. I couldn't let Lee's memory fade. Not today, not ever.

For the first time in my life, I opened Lee's precious

journal. I gave Nurse Jen a knowing glance before skipping through to the end, finding her last completed story, and began reading it aloud. The names and places were changed but there was no denying that "Morning Glory" was the tale of Lee and her *life-passions* friend. A story about nurturing their flowers, cherishing their moon and intertwining their small worlds into one expansive garden.

Later that evening, everyone said their heartfelt goodbyes. I decided to stick around my uncle's for a little while longer, eventually finding my way into the hall by Lee's bedroom. Out of habit, I cracked the door open so I wouldn't wake my sister if she was asleep.

I lay down on Lee's bed, wrapped her *Frozen* blanket around my shoulders and continued reading from her journal. Her writing was fluid, sophisticated far beyond her years. The stories made me both smile and cry. So much of her brightness, so much promise, so much drive, all preserved on the pages. So much potential that Lee would never be able to realize.

The door slowly opened. I sat up, expecting to see Uncle Bill, but that's not who I found standing in the doorway.

It was Emma Rey Finley.

"Hey," she began softly. But I couldn't respond, at least not yet. "I'm so sorry, TD," she continued.

As a surge of complicated emotions rushed through me, all I was able to say was, "Yeah."

She took a seat at the end of Lee's bed, with neither of us knowing what to say. After a few moments, Emm removed an envelope from the sling around her arm. "You should know… This came yesterday."

I really didn't care what was in that envelope, but I took it from Emm's outstretched hand. I glanced at the address: "Lee Dexter, head writer at The Nest."

I unfolded the paper within. The words jumped from the page, stinging both my eyes and my heart. "Congratulations," the letter began, "We are pleased to inform you that your story, 'Morning Glory' will appear in our next issue."

I looked up at Emm in shock. She broke into tears. Racking sobs. "She did it…She's an author now," she muttered between gasping breaths.

Before I even knew what I was doing, I put my arms around her and began crying right along with her. Emm and I held each other for what seemed like hours, grasping each other tightly. I could feel all of her pain. I could feel how hurt she was from not having said goodbye to our little girl. I could feel how much it killed her that Lee's dream had come true, yet my little miracle would never know it. Emm would never get to tell her prodigy how proud she was.

When we finally regained control, I managed to ask the one question I still needed an answer to. "She needed you, Emm. What happened?"

As her tears ran dry, Emm began, "We *were* on the road when we talked, honestly we were. But we got up so early that morning…and were both so exhausted. Matt suggested we stop for a couple hours of sleep, but I told him to keep going. I *made* him keep going. I didn't want to lose any time, so we switched off…one of us driving, the other napping in the back. And that was okay for a couple of hours, but when it was my turn…" Emm paused, fighting back heavier tears, "I was fighting to stay awake, to keep my eyes open. But, TD, you know that's something I struggle with. Our car veered into the median and we flipped onto the other side of the highway."

"Jesus, Emm," I whispered, too stunned to say anything further.

"I was so scared…and as we were waiting for help to arrive, the only thing I could think about was you and Lee. I wasn't there when you needed me most. Nothing else seemed important."

"And was Matt okay?" I asked. I didn't love the dude, that much was true, but I hoped he wasn't hurt.

"A broken collarbone and a concussion, that's all. Thank God. But me, I was in the hospital for two days. And the car was totaled. By the time we were able to figure out a way to come, Lee was…"

But she couldn't finish. Emm started rocking back and forth, as if the pain in her heart was pulsing into her stomach, her limbs. "We called you a million times. I made Matt call from the ER…and we kept trying to reach you all week. My phone was wrecked, and your number is the only one I know by heart."

My mind thought of the long list of entries in my call log—so many of them had been from the same number. Dozens really. Not a reporter, I now realized, but calls from Matt's phone.

"Jesus, no. Oh no." I covered my eyes with my hands, feeling my face turn white from the shock. "Emm, I was waiting for you. I doubted you. I even hated you a little. I…I… should've known better."

"Tim Dexter, I'm so sorry." She repeated the words over and over, reciting her own prayer of contrition. I wrapped my arms around her again.

"Emm, you're the best thing that ever happened to our little girl. All she wanted was to be like you. I don't know what we would've done without you these last few years. You have nothing to be sorry for. Nothing at all."

"But I wasn't there," she said, straining to get the words out. "I wasn't there," she repeated, as if my words had given no comfort.

I thought back to the night Lee passed. "But you were there, Emm—even if I didn't realize it. Just before Lee…left us…"

"What?" she asked as I paused to steady my voice.

"Sammy started to sing. Your lullaby, Emm…our song."

We sang the lines together until at last Emm's beautiful smile emerged and I almost burst. A sorrowful smile, but gorgeous all the same.

The moon's light suddenly shone in through the open curtains. The moon had finally seen us.

"Lee was so happy at you. She always was—and she always will be. *Forever.*"

"That's amazing," was all Emm could say, her eyes still

glistening with tears. "It's astonishing that Sammy knew our song, Did Lee tell him about it?"

"She did—but how he ever remembered it, I have no idea. I think maybe it came from somewhere deep inside. I think he knew, somehow, that Lee needed that lullaby."

"Poor little kid," Emm said sympathetically. "I'm glad he at least got the chance to say everything he needed to."

"I don't know about that," I explained. "Mostly he just sat with her. I got the sense he needed to say something, but couldn't. I don't think he ever got the chance to tell her how much he loved her."

Emm hung her head. "That's awful," she cried. "Too much." She wiped her eyes again. "TD, promise me something. Promise me we'll always be open with each other. No secrets. I know things have changed, but promise me that much."

At Emm's words, something inside me shifted. Even through the grief and pain, something changed. Something urgent, honest. My heart began pounding, just like it had during our last night on the pier. I opened my mouth, but someone had once again stolen my voice.

I took a deep breath to calm myself, then took another to find both my courage and my words. Now was the moment.

"Hey, Emm?" I asked.

"Yes, TD?" she asked as she turned herself fully toward me expectantly.

While envisioning Emm on the first day of college—the moment when I'd first seen her resplendence through my dorm's triangle window—I smiled just before I said my first line. "Can I tell you something?"

And then all of a sudden, I told her everything. Starting from the moment we'd met.

Chapter 30

MoonFlower

"Are you sure this is a good idea?" Sammy asked as he swung open the car door. "It's pouring."

"Just get in, kid, before I change my mind about taking you with me," I replied, half-shouting. Partly because I was in no mood to argue, but mostly because the rain was pounding loudly against the roof of my car.

"Okay, sir." Sammy shook the rain from his raincoat before closing the door.

"Sammy!" I cried, almost growing upset. "How many times have I told you not to call me 'sir'?"

"My bad," he replied quickly. "Gru." He broke into a strangely mature, knowing smile.

I sighed. This kid was insufferable.

Every Sunday for the last two months, I'd gone to Lee's grave to replace the blue tulips on her headstone. Nurse Jen and I had kept in touch, emailing every week or so, and I'd offered to take Sammy with me today. I thought it would be something good for us to do together: Lee would've liked knowing that I was still looking out for her friend.

"How has it been? Like…seeing her grave and everything?" Sammy asked timidly. Today would be his first visit to the cemetery, and this was the first time I'd seen him since the day of the funeral.

"Okay," I said plainly, although my last eight weeks had been anything but that. Without my little sister, I was lost. We'd made it to the NCAA Tournament like she'd asked, only to be eliminated in the first round. My basketball career had come to a screeching, unceremonious halt. Without Lee, without basketball, I had way too much time on my hands, coupled with absolutely zero focus.

Yet some days, none of that felt like the worst part. Some days, the absolute worst part was that I'd lost my buddy, too. On the same day I'd buried Lee, I'd also lost Emm.

The moment I finished my confession in Lee's bedroom, I knew Emm—*my* Emm, my shooting star—was gone. I knew it with every fiber in me. Her words had been kind enough, but it was what she *didn't* say that told me I'd lost her. It was in her body language, in the answer so clearly written all over her face. Her truth, the real answer, was that she didn't love me the same way I loved her. I had crossed that ineffable, critical line: Past the point of no return.

"I've just always seen you as more of a friend," she'd said tenderly turning herself away, almost as if my confession had penetrated her last redoubt of denial, as if she'd finally realized that everyone had been right about us all along. As if she only now understood there hadn't been anything extraordinary about our unique bond, that maybe nothing between us had ever been truly magical. That I was just a boy in love with a girl who didn't love him back.

And that was the moment when my cracked, glass heart sunk deep into the void inside of me and shattered—a painful shot exploding in my chest. In that moment, I couldn't hide the damage, the ache, the fall. My Emm was gone—completely, irrevocably…forever.

I'd desperately wanted to hit rewind and take back my words. But after seeing the look on Emm's face—when she saw the look on *my* face—we both knew it wasn't possible. And now that the one person who'd always kept us together was gone, there would be no going back to the way things were. Even if, in that exact moment, that's what both of us wanted. Even if it had been Lee's final wish.

For the first few weeks, Emm checked in on me every couple of days, but it wasn't the same. I was this new creature. This guy she could never love; this guy she was obligated to take care of because of our history. When I went back to school, the few times I saw her on campus, I didn't get that rush of happy inside, and when she smiled at me, it always seemed more forced than genuine. When she smiled at me, I had to force myself to smile back.

Breaking through the growing silence in the car, Sammy announced, "We have to make a stop before we get there." It sounded more like a demand than a request.

"Where?" I asked.

"A grocery store. Any supermarket would work." He looked out the window, panning the area as best he could through the downpour for possible stores.

"I'm stopping at the gardening place, kid. There's a supermarket next door." It didn't even occur to me to ask why a ten-year-old needed to go grocery shopping.

"That'll do. I have money," he answered. "And I don't need you to go in with me."

A few minutes later, we pulled into a local shopping plaza. Sammy and I bolted for the supermarket's door, trying to stay dry, which was impossible in this rain.

"Come meet me next door when you're done," I instructed, probably sounding a bit angry although I honestly didn't mean to. "The florist in there knows me—if you can't find me, ask her."

Sammy nodded. "I'll be done before you are." And with that, he shot into the supermarket with surprising speed.

In the garden center, I made my way to the floral department. They always had multiple buckets of the usual carnation/baby's breath/fern, pre-made bouquets for sale, but the florist put together a special order for me every week—the lightest blue tulips, as close to baby blue as tulips could get.

The line wasn't too long today, thankfully. I only had to wait a minute or two before I reached the counter. "Ah, Mr. Dexter. Always a pleasure. Is it Sunday already?" The florist asked as I pulled my wallet from my pocket.

"Yes, it is, Mrs. Shaw." I forced a little smile; she was always very kind to me.

"Just the usual today, or can I get you anything else?" she began. "We have a Mother's Day special—a delightful mix of sunflowers and roses."

"No, just the usual tulips, please," I said. She nodded, then turned around to open the refrigerator door.

"Tulips have quite the history, you know," she said as she handed me my sister's beloved flowers.

I had little interest in a horticultural lesson but, not wanting to be impolite, I humored her. "Oh yeah, why's that?"

Without further prompting, she gushed, "Well, these pretty little things ruled an entire country at one point—in the Netherlands. People bought and sold them until the tulips themselves became a form of currency. But it was all done behind closed doors." She paused, picking a stray petal from the counter. "People poured their money, their lives into tulips… even mortgaging their own homes just to buy one single bulb. The craze spread throughout the whole country until the market finally got so big it collapsed. In one day, the bubble burst."

"All that for some flowers?" I said, trying my best to sound like I'd been following her narrative the whole time.

"Yes, isn't that interesting?" she replied. "But there's a lesson to be learned, too."

I smiled at her obvious excitement. "What's that?"

"That it's better to appreciate all flowers for their natural beauty rather than to stake your entire future upon just one tulip bulb. The Dutch turned what was a beautiful flower into something idealized, something it never should've be-

come. Until one day, the illusion disappeared. Poof! Gone."
I thought she was finished, but then she took a breath and
added, "There are all kinds of flowers out there, and that's
what the tulip mania craze taught these people."

My mouth fell open so quickly that I had to turn away to
close my jaw. Tulip mania. Lee and Sammy's tulip mania.

I don't know what I said to Mrs. Shaw in reply, but it
must've been something weird because she hastily handed me
my change and smiled awkwardly at me.

As I stepped away from the counter, still a little bit stunned,
I heard a familiar voice say, "Fancy seeing you here." I spun
around: there was Emm.

"I'd just picked up my order when I saw you come in,"
she explained.

"Every Sunday," I replied. "Rain or shine." Then I looked
at Emm's own tightly-wrapped bouquet, suddenly wondering
why she was here. "Is your mother in town?" I asked.

Emm smiled. "No. I wanted to visit Lee today, too. I didn't
mean to intrude, honestly. I thought you came in the mornings."

"I usually do," I replied, both touched by her respecting
my "space" and angry at needing that from her. "But I have
Lee's friend Sammy with me today." Emm looked around,
puzzled. "He's next door buying something," I clarified. "He
hasn't been to visit her yet."

"Yeah, it's the first time for us, too, actually," she said.
But Emm also appeared to be alone, so I had no idea who
"us" meant. But before I could ask, the tiny "yip" of a puppy
barked through the air. A dog popped out of the nearest aisle,
scampering playfully: Matt appeared behind it, holding the
end of its leash.

"So that's where you disappeared to," Emm said, turning
to Matt and scooping up the puppy in her hands. A teacup
pug, probably not more than two-months-old.

"TD! What a pleasure," Matt said as he reached his palm
out for a handshake.

"Nice to see you," I said unenthusiastically. Matt was the

last dude I wanted to see today. Somehow his haircut looked even weirder.

Emm began introducing me to her pug. "And, TD, this is—"

"—Crow," I said, cutting her off. The teacup pug I was supposed to buy her for graduation.

"That's right." Emm smiled as she said it, but at the same time the gleam in her eyes flickered out.

I played with the pug for a few minutes to mask my disappointment. Fortunately, I was saved by Sammy who ran up to me with a brown paper bag under his arm.

"I told you I'd be done before you," Sammy said almost triumphantly.

"Well, what...should we do? Do you want your space? Or should we all go together?" Emm asked.

Truthfully, I wanted to be by myself. But I had Sammy with me anyhow, so that wasn't possible. I thought it would be easier for him if there was a group of us, so I answered. "Let's just meet up there."

Once we were back in the car, I asked Sammy, "Did you get what you needed, kid?" I didn't want to have to stop again.

"We're good," he replied before his face turned serious. "I'm glad you bumped into your friends. Maybe it'll...make things easier for you," he said, as if I was the kid and he was the adult. Even though he had no idea about the tragedy that was now me and Emma Rey Finley.

Sammy and I didn't say much else for the first few minutes. I didn't know what to say to a ten-year-old boy who'd just lost his best friend. I debated whether to bring up my tulip mania conversation with Mrs. Shaw, but I decided it wasn't worth it. Today was already going to be tough enough.

"It's not okay, you know," Sammy finally piped up, now sounding like a little kid again.

"What's not?"

"Everyone keeps telling me it'll be okay. But it's not. They're lying. Even my mom." He pounded his fist against the armrest in frustration.

"They're not lying to you, Sammy. It just takes time…a lot of time," I replied, not without sympathy but not knowing if that was the right thing to say, either. I was about his age when I'd lost my mother, and that's what everyone had told me. The advice had proved true enough, but healing took a long, long time. A longer amount of time than my eleven-year-old self could've possibly imagined.

"And it's not fair either," he continued. "Without Lee Rose, everything just seems so…so…"

"Boring," I finished for him.

"Boring. Exactly." He twisted around in his seat and faced me. "Nothing seems like it's as fun as it used to be. Not even botany."

"I know how you feel. It's the same for me." I reached over and put my hand on his shoulder before asking, "How's Moon?"

"He's good." Sammy smiled a bit. "I think he misses her, too."

"That's something we all have in common. We all miss her." I answered.

"I saw Lee's story in that magazine," Sammy said slowly, then carefully asked, "Do you really think it was about me?"

"Of course it was, Sammy," I answered truthfully.

Sammy pounded the armrest again, trying not to cry.

Sensing an opportunity to ease his pain, I added, "She really loved you, kid. And you're right, none of this is fair. But she'll always be a published writer; no one can ever take that from her."

I found Sammy surprisingly easy to talk to. Maybe it was because he knew Lee so well, or maybe it was because he was a fighter, just like her. Either way, hurting alongside him felt a little bit easier than hurting alone. So, we hurt together.

Despite the pouring rain, the cemetery seemed quiet and still. In fact, the rain made everything much eerier, especially since a fog had settled on the hillside graveyard.

"I can hardly see anything," said Sammy, squinting into the blanket of fog as we entered the gates.

"Don't worry, I know the way. Just follow me." I took his hand as we huddled under my inadequate umbrella. The rain had let up somewhat, but not by much.

"Are we almost there?" Sammy asked after we'd been walking for a minute.

"Almost, bud—" I cut myself off. I'd almost forgotten that I didn't have my buddy anymore.

We followed the muddy path for a few more yards. "We're here," I said as we reached Lee's grave. Sammy let go of my hand and huddled behind me as if he were afraid of the headstone.

I gave Sammy a minute to adjust. "Come on, kid, let's go read her epitaph. Together," I said gently, remembering how Sal had escorted me to Lee's casket. No wonder the poor kid was scared.

I scooted him toward Lee's headstone. The fog was dense, but the words were still visible.

Sammy began to read aloud slowly. "Lee Rose Dexter." But then he stopped, as if the words in his mouth didn't match his thoughts. He looked up and held my gaze, with the absence of his voice only growing louder and louder between us. Sammy's eyes reflected the very pages of Lee's journal—and in his gentle expression, I saw a pure love for my sister; the entire story of their *life-passions* relationship.

Only once he was sure I understood did Sammy turn his eyes back to the gravestone. He started reading again, this time even more slowly. "Lee Rose Dexter. Published Author."

After a long pause, Sammy again looked up at me, his eyes glistening with both joy and sadness. "She would've have loved that," he whispered.

"Thanks, kid." I looked down at him with a sad smile.

"We have to remember her together, just like my mom told me. It's just you and me now," Sammy said, trying to be brave. "Lee was your sunflower, but she was my rose."

I gently cradled Sammy with my arm "We'll remember her together, I promise." I paused for a moment, trying to think of something to make all this a little easier on him. "But you know Lee thought roses were cliché, right, kiddo?" I chided.

Sammy grinned. "I know, that's why I teased her. That's why I called her 'Lee Rose.' Because there was nothing "cliché" about her."

I grinned to myself. Puppy love. Maybe the best kind.

The rain grew heavy again, suddenly pouring down like sheets. "Come on, let's take cover," I said. "We can still see her grave from under that tree."

"*Quercus agrifolia*," Sammy muttered more to himself than to me as we took shelter. "Common name, California live oak."

"Whatever, kid, I call it 'dry.' We'll stay here till this burst eases up, okay?"

Sammy looked up at the sprawling branches of our tree, and so did I. The branches stretched out like the protecting arms of God, apologetically shielding us from the deluge.

"Gosh, can you believe this?" Emm's voice startled me. As I'd been gazing up, she and Matt had joined us in our safe haven. The rushing of the rain covered the sound of their approach.

"Where's Crow?" I asked.

"In the car. She doesn't do too well with rain," Matt answered.

The four of us slouched against the oak tree, waiting. Matt and Emm chatted quietly while Sammy and I were transfixed by the graveyard's eeriness.

Even after a good ten minutes, the rain showed no sign of slowing down. Matt finally said, "Emma, we should just go… This weather is nuts."

"No, Matt, we can't just leave," Emm replied forcefully.

"But it could be hours before the weather lets up," Matt grumbled.

A bolt of lightning flashed across the sky. We all gasped as we heard the thunder boom through the graveyard.

"Why don't we all run out and quickly put our flowers down?" Emm suggested as she unwrapped her bouquet, revealing her flowers for the first time. White flowers unlike any I'd ever seen before.

"Okay. As long as we're quick," Matt agreed.

We all darted toward Lee's grave in the pouring rain. But as the rain soaked through my clothes, I realized I didn't mind it at all. I handed my umbrella to Sammy and accepted the storm for what it was.

Emm's bare wrist jumped out at me as she and I reached down and placed our bouquets on Lee's grave. Only then did a realization crash through me. All these years I'd put Emm on a pedestal—a pedestal she could never possibly live up to—when, in truth, it was Lee who had kept me going. It wasn't Emm who brought out the best in me. It was Lee. And while my adventures with Emm had been fun, the *real* fun was in sharing those stories with my little miracle. The real fun was in making my little sister smile. Emm was the one who pushed me out of my shell, but at the end of the day, I only ever left that shell for Lee. And without Lee to keep me going, there really could be no Emm.

Despite the fog that surrounded us, I felt as if I could see clearly for the first time in four years, as if the rain had washed away my illusions, leaving nothing but reality in its wake. The girl before me was no longer Emma Rey Finley, but simply just Emm. Not a superhero or a shooting star. The girl before me was just exactly that: a girl.

There I was, standing in the rain, in a trance, with Sammy, Emm and Matt staring at me from the shelter of the oak tree.

"Come on, let's go," Matt said emphatically as I broke out of my daze.

"Just another minute," Emm pleaded, but Matt urged her again.

"Emma…I'm already soaking wet. Let's go home."

Emm and Matt turned, expecting Sammy and me to leave with them. But I didn't want to go. I wanted to stay with my sister.

"I think we're going to stay a little while longer," I announced, looking down at Sammy. He nodded his head in agreement.

"But, it's pouring. What are you, crazy?" Emm asked.

"I know, but I don't really mind it. I'm going to stay a while."

"Emma. Let's go!" Matt yelled as he began walking down the muddy path toward the gate.

"Tim Dexter, I'll…stay with you as long as you want," Emm offered.

"Just go with him, Emm. We'll be fine," I shot back with more bite than I'd intended.

"But what if I don't want to go with him?" Emm asked, hanging her head. "What if all I want to do is visit the duck park with you and Lee? With ice cream and taster spoons after?"

I paused to look into her big, beautiful brown eyes, feeling as though I'd never see them again, but I could hardly see their gleam through the rain and fog.

"I'm afraid that can't happen, Emm," I answered, wishing I could lock onto her eyes through the gloom.

"But why?" she pleaded, tearing up.

"Because Lee's gone, Emm, and you…you have him now." I pointed into the distance where Matt—a faint shadow in the fog—was approaching his car.

"But that's never stopped us before…" Emm begged, her words becoming quieter as they fell from her mouth. Almost like she had no confidence in her own voice; in what she'd just said.

The fog grew thicker, rolling in and blanketing us even more deeply. So thick that now I almost couldn't see Emm at all. Nothing but her silhouette.

"Goodbye, Emma," I choked out, emphasizing the last syllable, and turning away from her before I finished speaking.

She didn't reply, not for a long, long moment. Then I heard her cry, "Goodbye, buddy."

I turned around, but she'd disappeared. Whether she'd been engulfed in the fog or she'd returned to Matt, I'd never know. I didn't want to.

Sammy and I stood over my sister's grave together in the rain. He'd abandoned the umbrella, as well. Joining me in the storm.

I stared at the white flowers on Lee's grave. They were a beautiful true white, with a slight yellow tinge in the center. A gorgeous bouquet that reminded me of happier times. "I wonder what kind of flowers those are?" I whispered aloud without meaning to.

"*Ipomoea alba*," answered Sammy.

"What?" I was surprised he'd even heard me.

"A bouquet of *ipomoea albas*," he repeated matter-of-factly.

"Oh," I said, unsure of how to respond. "Good to know, thanks."

But Sammy continued, suddenly sounding more like a professor than a fifth-grader. "A truly fascinating species. One of the few night-blooming flowers. And as long as they have something tall to cling to, they continue to grow and thrive. Lee told me that's why she and Emma loved them so much."

"Nice, kid," I muttered.

Sensing my confusion, he went on. "I didn't get it at first either, until Lee told me about Emma not liking sunflowers."

Suddenly interested, I asked, "Yeah, I know that, kid. But what does that have to do with *ipomoea albas*?"

"Because of their common name," Sammy replied, as if the answer was obvious.

"Kid…" I began flatly, starting to lose my patience.

"*Ipomoea alba*. Their common name is 'moonflower'."

I stared down in disbelief. I didn't know what to say, so I didn't say anything.

Sammy reached up and grabbed my hand firmly, as if he'd sensed my shock. The moonflowers on Lee's resting place were all the more beautiful now that the rainwater filled their petals.

Sammy let go of my hand and began peeling the now-soaked paper bag open, revealing a small bottle of maple syrup. He leaned down and placed it beside the bouquet of moonflowers.

"What's that for?" I asked.

"For Lee's chocolate chip banana pancakes. I thought that she might need some to share with the other angels in heaven."

That was the last of my strength. The last bit of whatever had been holding me together inside snapped violently, completely. With no fight left, I fell to my knees, into the muddy grass, and wept. With Sammy's little arms around me as if he were trying to protect me from the storm. From the nightmare.

She was gone. My Emm was gone. They were both gone. My tears became the rain as I watered the garden that was now my sister.

My shooting star and my sunflower, both taken by the storm, lost forever. Leaving me with only the moon above and the moonflowers below.

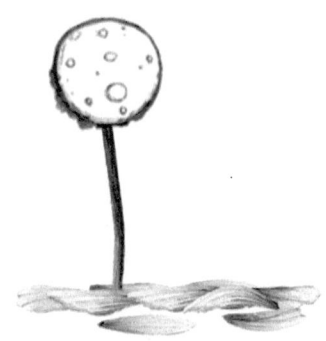

Author Information

To contact me, visit my schedule of upcoming personal appearances or for more information about *MoonFlower*, please visit my website and subscribe to my blog.

jdwritesbooks.com

You can also find me on:

Twitter: JD_Slajchert
Instagram: JD_Slajchert
Facebook: JD Slajchert

Please do not hesitate to reach out or just say hello on social media. I would love to get to know all of my readers and personally hear from each of you.

Cheers.

Acknowledgments

‿➤‿

I owe a huge "thank you" to the following people for their amazing roles in the creation of my first book: To my wonderful editor, Erika DeSimone, without you none of this would have been possible. To J. Bengtsson, your guidance and encouragement could not have come at a better time. To Gregory Moore, for showing me my first moonflower. To Jerry March, for providing my novel with a dash of my father. To Chris Varonos for never once turning down a ten-hour meeting at Crave Café. To Angie Alaya, who did a wonderful job designing the cover for *MoonFlower*. To my one-of-a-kind professor, Mashey Bernstein, for showing me how important one sentence really can be.

ABOUT THE AUTHOR

JD Slajchert wrote MoonFlower during his final two years as a student-athlete at the University of California, Santa Barbara. When tragedy struck and he lost his best friend Luc to Sickle Cell Disease, he felt the need to preserve Luc's spirit and honor his memory by penning this story. After writing the first draft by hand, JD moved off campus in order to complete *MoonFlower* before his college years came to a close. In January 2019, JD became the Director of Relationship Development for The LucStrong Foundation and a National Ambassador for The American Red Cross.

About the Doctor

Dr. Kris M. Mahadeo is an Associate Professor and currently serves as the Section Chief and Medical Director for Stem Cell Transplantation and Cellular Therapy at University of Texas at MD Anderson Cancer Center in Houston. His clinical research is focused on reducing toxicities associated with stem cell transplantation for cancer and non-malignant genetic diseases such as Sickle Cell Disease. He previously worked at Children's Hospital Los Angeles where he was part of the healthcare team that cared for Luc Bodden.

Luc's Photo Album

Matt Kemp and Luc Bodden during his bone marrow transplant at CHLA in 2013.

Kevin Durant, Kyrsha Wildasin and Luc Bodden during the NBA Playoffs in 2015.

Steph Curry and Luc Bodden during the NBA Playoffs in 2015.

Shane Bodden, Stacy Bodden,
Matt Bodden, Tarren Bodden,
Luc Bodden and Matt Kemp at
a San Diego Padres
game in 2016.

Shane Bodden, Luc Bodden
and Matt Kemp at a San
Diego Padres game in 2016.

Matt Kemp and Luc Bodden at
a San Diego Padres game
in 2016.

Luc Bodden at a San Diego
Padres game in 2016.

JD Slajchert, Shane Bodden
and Luc Bodden eating pizza
at Woodstocks in
Santa Barbara, CA 2016.

Luc eating a cupcake at his
8th birthday party.

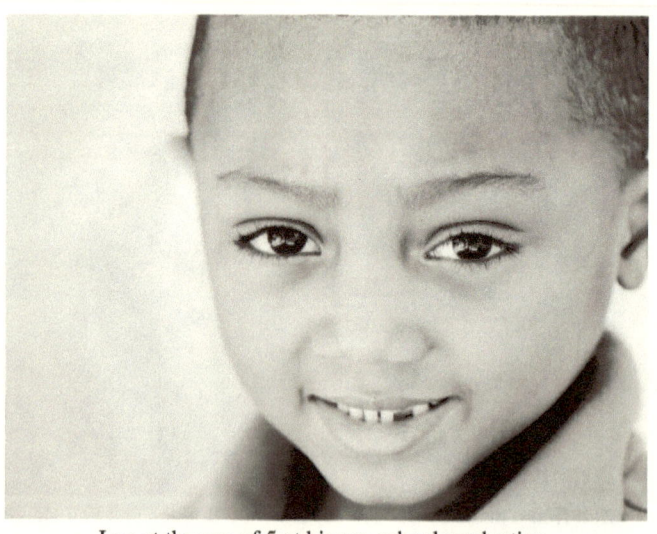

Luc at the age of 5 at his pre-school graduation.

JD Slajchert and Luc Bodden
at JD's high school
basketball game in 2013.

JD Slajchert and Luc Bodden
at a UCLA football game
in 2014.

Thank You
For Your Support

All Profits from this purchase we're donated to:

THE
LUCSTRONG
FOUNDATION
SUPPORTING FAMILIES WITH SICKLE CELL DISEASE